Robert Graham

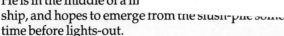

was born just before t
hill for Elvis. He belongs
He is in the middle of a lit
ship, and hopes to emerge from the slush-pile some
time before lights-out.

His fiction has been collected in a skip in a cellar.
He is married to a lovely woman, and they have but
one bundle of joy.

Keith Baty

was born in Carlisle, Cumbria, in 1958. He is the
eldest son of Vernon and Gladys Baty, original hosts
of Border TV's ground-breaking quiz show, *Mr &
Mrs*.

He began his working life, with brother Gort, in
Shadrack & Duxbury's Funeral Parlour. Guitar star-
dom beckoned and Keith was soon to be found tread-
ing the boards as the whammy pedal used by
ex-Shadow, Keith 'Jet' Harris. Age notwithstanding,
he continues to ply his trade on the international theatre and cabaret circuit. At time of writing he is touring, 'Oo-er, Missus! Where's the Tripe?', his one-man
tribute to Kenneth Williams. Keith is married, with
one wife (Hello, Doris!), and collects Aurora 'Glow-
in-the Dark' Movie Monsters. He is looking for a
'Hunchback of Notre Dame' (on the sprue).

ELVIS – the Novel

ROBERT GRAHAM – KEITH BATY

First Published in Great Britain in 1997 by
The Do-Not Press
PO Box 4215
London SE23 2QD

A Paperback Original

ISBN 1 899344 19 5

British Library Cataloguing in Publication Data. A catalogue record for
this book is available from the British Library.

Printed and bound in Great Britain by The Guernsey Press Co Ltd.

Prologue

Elvis Aaron Presley, future King of Rock 'n' Roll and the cheese-burger, made his first public appearance sometime after lunch on January 8th 1935 in a two-room wooden shack on the Old Saltillo Road, East Tupelo, Mississippi.

It is a date that has acquired enormous significance for popular music fans the world over, yet the true events of that historic day are not widely known, having been effectively suppressed by the Presley publicity machine in a process that started almost as soon as Elvis had taken his first faltering steps towards immortality.

Among the many stories that have developed concerning the entrance of the King are those which seek to explain his coming in divine terms, befitting his later world stature. Thus, we have tales of the East Tupelo electricity supplies mysteriously cutting out at the instant of Elvis's birth; or of how the Presley shack was bathed in an eerie, luminescent glow that afternoon.

The plain truth is that Elvis came into the world in a perfectly ordinary manner, the first of male triplets born to farmworker Vernon 'Snakehips' Presley, and his wife, Gladys Love Presley (née Smith), a sewing machine operator; it was only directly after the birth that the strange, fateful events which would mould Elvis's life began to take place.

At around 2pm on that day, Vernon, the prospective father, was taking his habitual post-lunch snooze in an old rocking chair on the back porch of the house as Gladys, inside, struggled with the pains of childbirth.

An ancient electric fan played a fitful breeze across his red, leathery face, lean and mean-looking even in repose, and a half empty bottle of whiskey lay cradled in his arm when, suddenly, he was startled awake by the screams of a new-born child. He lurched forward in his chair and the whiskey bottle tumbled to the floor. Later, he was to recall feeling as if he were going to die from the shock of being awakened before his sleep-cycle had run its full five-hour span, but at the time, he just responded to the crisis of the moment.

'It must be here somewhere,' he thought, shuffling round the porch on his hands and knees, peering amongst the piles of empty beer-crates that he stored there. 'How far kin a bottle roll, anyways?'

Scarcely minutes later, as a still-puzzled Vernon settled back in his chair, the cries of his first son were joined by others.

Twins!

Then some different ones again.

Triplets!

Then a loud thump was heard and one set of cries faded to noth-ingness.

Twins!

'Hmmm...' thought Vernon as he drifted back to sleep, 'maybe the durned bottle rolled clean off the porch and down the road!'

For Gladys inside the house, joy and sorrow commingled as first she saw Elvis Aaron born, a healthy boy, followed by Jessie Garon, also healthy, and finally Norbert Faron, a bit weedy but okay. Then she saw the midwife drop Norbert Faron as she tripped over the elec-tric cable which led from the shack's sole power-point across the floor to Vernon's fan out on the porch. Norbert Faron landed heavily on Jessie's crib before tumbling out and onto the floor. The metal rock-ers of the crib jarred heavily back onto the fan cable, severing it and sending a powerful jolt through Jessie and short-circuiting the whole left side of Old Saltillo Road (the cutting-off of supplies; the lumines-cent glow around the Presley home...).

Before the midwife could move, Jessie was burned black as a tar-baby. In later years Gladys would constantly remind the young, impressionable Elvis of the 'little black brother' he never knew, per-haps accounting, at least partly, for Elvis's unnaturally strong empa-thy with negroes and, subsequently, black music.[1]

Nobby Faron, for his part, was miraculously unhurt, but Gladys, always and forever after connecting him with Jessie Garon's death, took steps immediately to farm him out to distant and childless Presley relatives in New Orleans. There he was to remain in obscu-rity for many years until making a dramatic re-entrance into the life of the successful adult Elvis, and carving his own name on the pillar of rock history.

And thus began the bond between mother and son that was to last and strengthen through all of Elvis's fame and exists today, in his retirement; psychologists have tried, but never succeeded in explain-ing why Gladys, from that day onwards, devoted herself to Elvis in such a frighteningly claustrophobic way, but whatever the reason, there can be little doubt that this intense relationship contributed much to making Elvis into the highly idiosyncratic individual he turned out to be.

It was a fitting beginning, then, this strange nativity, for the strange events that were to follow in the growth and development of Elvis Aaron Presley, singer, movie star and, most of all, weirdo.

[1] *Elvis & Black American Consciousness* by Christo Bigglesworth (Scathing Books, 1977).

Chapter 1

The Story Begins

In the Deep South of the United States there is a tradition that extends to this day, of deep-rooted and universally held religious values and nowhere were these values more fanatically adhered to than in the family home of the young Elvis.

Every Sunday would see the playing out of a strange ritual beginning with Vernon picking himself up from the bedroom floor. Pulling the broom bristles from his backside he would look up at Gladys, saying, 'Jeez, you din have to heat me so hard with that brush dahlin'. Ah wuz jus' get nup.'

Then, having put on his best (and only) two-piece suit, Vernon would pick up his son and the three Presleys, with little Elvis in his sailor suit hanging from his father's arm screaming, 'You mean sonofabitch,' in echo of Gladys's favourite words of affection, and would head down the road to join the congregation of the revivalist First Assembly of God Church.

From the start Elvis expressed a desire to join the junior choir.

He developed a love for gospel music that was to stay with him throughout his life and would inspire some of his most painfully turgid recordings, and a love of fancy costumes that would take him in some different directions altogether.

When he was five years old Elvis started school. He attended the East Tupelo Consolidated School where he was, by all accounts, a quiet but averagely capable student. He joined in with sports but it was his love for music which shone through and he loved to perform whenever he could. Mrs Merle Barnett, a school attendant-helper, recalls an early example of the young Elvis's desire to entertain:

'Yes, it was in 1944 when Elvis was nine years old. He'd just got his first gittar from his ma. She'd paid six dollars for it, which was a lot then, 'specially with ole Snakehips not earning his full crust, but that's another story, I ain't vindictive, landsakes. Anyways he brings this gittar to school and is showing it to the other kids and they're purty impressed never having seen one before. Elvis is singing the one song he knows to them out there in the playground – it was "Oh Susannah" I remember. Anyway, they're so keen to listen and he's so keen to play that when they're supposed to come in the building they won't so I remember, I went down to bring them in and I tries to take Elvis's guitar from him and you know he started to cry. He just couldn't bear to be parted from that gittar and when I saw those tears I couldn't bear to take it so I asked all the children just to come in then I turned to walk away and next thing he hits me with his gittar. Just hits me, sayin' "No-one's gon' take ma gittar, ma ma bought it." I thought then and ah still do, that he's real weird is Elvis, all humble on top, but real strange below. He sure socked me good. I was in hospital for two days and I still get these mental aberrations. Ah say... look out... them there's Martians landed on your head!!!'[1]

After this initial setback in fortunes, Elvis, his guitar repaired, set about broadening his musical horizons, picking up firstly on the style of country singer Jimmie Rodgers, with a little help from his Uncle Vester. (Years later Presley was to perform Rodgers' 'Waiting For A Train' as part of his audition for Sam Phillips' Sun label.) Following this the nine-and-a-half-year-old Elvis happened by the newly opened Radio WELO, Tupelo, and asked to be allowed to sing on the air. Accompanied by local Country Star, 'Mississippi Slim' Ausborn, who was his first real musical inspiration, the young Presley performed the 1930s Red Foley number 'Old Shep' to the throbbing Tupelo populace. Letters began arriving at W.E.L.O. None mentioned Elvis.

'Old Shep' was Elvis's choice again when, the same year, 1944, he was picked by Mr Cole, his school Principal, to represent East Tupelo at the Mississippi Alabama Fair and Dairy Show. The Presley rendering made standing on a chair so he could reach the microphone won him second prize and five dollars. (The winner, incidentally, was a Louisiana boy, seven-year-old Jerry Lee Lewis, who received ten dollars for his version of 'Dirty Sam' McGee's 'I Set My Dog On Fire' which the judge 'Deaf Bill' Winkler thought to be titled 'I Put Logs On The Fire' and described as 'a homely good old-fashioned toon'.)

For the next four years Elvis continued to plod steadily on through school giving the occasional musical performance in church or at school or sometimes at home for his mother. He built up a mixed repertoire. Slim Ausborn taught him some old country blues numbers; Uncle Vester showed him some slick picking hoedown tunes; and Elvis himself began to work out some of the material he heard on the radio, from Bing Crosby numbers to songs from the shows which his mother especially liked (her favourites were from the musical, State Fair).

Then, in 1948, when Elvis was thirteen, the Presley family moved suddenly to Memphis, Tennessee. Vernon, ill at the prospect of find-

[1] *Elvis – I Sharpened His Pencils* by Merle Barnett (Terrible Incoherent Books, 1975).

ing a job, thought the family might be able to acquire rent-free accommodation superior to what they had in Tupelo. There were also suggestions that Vernon had to move in order to avoid the possibility of Gladys finding out about his gambling debts, the paternity suit that had been slapped on him by the father of the girl in the saloon, and the photographs of him dressed up as Greta Garbo that had been taken at a local Ku Klux Klan barbecue.

In a rare interview some years later Elvis said:

'Man, we was poor when we was in Tupelo. I mean, broke. So we just left, Dad packed all our belongings into boxes and put them in the trunk of his 1939 Plymouth then he put on a false beard and spectacles, to keep the flies off-a his face, he said, and we headed for Memphis. Things had to he better.'

While the Presleys, now residing at 572 Poplar Avenue, Memphis, looked for work, Elvis began at the LC Humes High School.

In September 1949 the Presleys moved to a better apartment at 185 Winchester Street, Memphis, part of a federally funded housing project, and began attending the local church. This played a big part in Elvis's continuing musical education for it was here that he could listen to the popular Blackwood Brothers Quartet, and the Stamps Quartet, close-harmony gospel groups whose influence can be strongly heard in Presley's recordings with the Jordanaires. Elvis assimilated the style very quickly and would mime the songs and arrangements at home with his stuffed toys. With Big Teddy Presley on bass, Rag-Tag Dog Pyjama-Case and Little Teddy Presley on tenor and Elvis singing lead, Presley was able to acquire valuable experience of hearing things that weren't there.

Gladys Presley at this time had managed to pick up a little sewing and laundry work which helped to keep the family economics buoyant. Vernon, meanwhile, was having trouble with his legs – they wouldn't move from his old rocking chair. Times were still hard for the family so Elvis, to help out, got a job as an usher at the Memphian Theatre in Memphis in the evenings for $13 a week. He was also at this time (late 1950) courting his first regular girlfriend, Dixie Locke. When Elvis finished work at around 10pm he'd hightail it over to Sal's Diner to meet Dixie for an hour. Dixie recalls:

'Sometimes we'd just sit an' drink coffee. Elvis'd tell me how much he wanted to help his family so they wouldn't be poor no more, or how he'd like to sink a machete into someone's head to see if it was true that blood in the brain is blue. Other times we'd go for a walk under the moon and Elvis'd talk about what it must be like to travel to the moon and look down on the earth, or what it must feel like to be a tree with a woodpecker pecking at you. He was so romantic. He dreamed of being an Arab prince or a one-armed helicopter pilot who becomes an Olympic swimmer, or a reclusive millionaire who sold jam jars of his own do-doos to his fans. Okay so he was a bit weird and he was a little shy but he was basically a good kid and he wouldn't touch my breasts even though I scrunched em in his face once. He just stood there and said, real quiet again and again, "Get thee to a nunnery, get thee to a nunnery." Such a sweet kid.'[2]

It was also at this time that Elvis started to develop an individuality in his style of dress and hair. Influenced by the classic noir films he saw whilst working at the cinema he, in turn, went through phases of wearing a black Homburg and long overcoat like Bogart, then a white boiler suit and small baker's hat like Cagney in *White Heat* and finally his favourite, a white suit and a fez like Sydney Greenstreet in *Casablanca*, even having his head shaved and wearing a padded vest to make him look 200lbs. Presley must have cut a strange figure walking around Memphis saying 'Is that pianist LOUIS Jordan, Rick?' in a mock-Moroccan accent, and adding 'As Time Goes By' to his burgeoning repertoire for a while.

After the 'noir' phase had rubbed off Elvis began to be influenced by the new generation of rebel figures appearing in films, such as Brando, whose appearance in *The Wild One* (sailor-type cap and leather jacket) Elvis would try to emulate in his second movie *Driving A Sportscar Down To A Beach In Hawaii* almost ten years later, with no success at all.

Eventually Presley settled on an image for himself as a James Dean-style figure (though Dean was yet to make it in films). He would go down to Lansky's, a black store in downtown Memphis, and buy pink and black clothes – a long pink jacket and black drainpipe trousers with white pedal-pushers constituted the second Presley uniform. He also grew his hair long, an outlandish act for a boy of barely sixteen in those days. It was a long process from the bald Greenstreet look to the greased-up rocker quiff he eventually had and, on the way from one to the other, a bizarre incident occurred. Dixie Locke tells the story:

'Yes I didn't like the Greenstreet look too much and I was always saying to Elvis that I wished he'd grow his hair again. Eventually he did but, while it was still very short, I remember them re-showing *The Jolson Story* with Larry Parks down at the Memphian. Well, Elvis was really turned on by the Jolson look and, after seeing the film for seven nights, he just wanted to be Jolson. There was a school concert the following week and Elvis, being known as a singer, was asked to do a song. Night of the concert he walks on stage with his guitar, blacked up to the eyeballs. Everyone had thought he'd do "Old Shep" *again* – well, he ALWAYS did – but this was a revelation, Humes was an all-white school and they didn't like negroes, not even pretend ones. So Elvis is on stage having snuck out of his dressing room, and is singing, "California Here I Come" and his guitar-playing is bad because he's wear-

[2] *Elvis and the Hamlet Complex* by Dixie Locke (The Arden Presley, 1963).

ing them white gloves. People begin booing and whistling so Elvis stops, rips off his shirt to reveal his white body and screams "I ain't as black as I'm painted. Get thee to a NUNNERY." Then he runs off out the school home to his ma. Weird, huh?'

The symbolic significance of the story is fundamental to an understanding of the Presley mentality. Presley was called the first singer successfully to fuse the sounds of black bluesmen and white country singers into the hybrid that became known as Rock 'n' Roll. He saw in Jolson what he was to become, someone who took the black sound (in Jolson's case the songs and styles of Mississippi riverboat negroes) and whitened it, giving it universal acceptability in the WASP America of the Twentieth Century. To achieve this synthesis successfully Elvis thought that he would have to appear black if he was to be successful. Hence his blacking-up. A psychologically simple role-play, and an early indication of how Presley used and needed alternative identities to project to the world so as to hide his true self from view. In truth, Elvis was shy. And a klutz!

In his Dean-like persona Elvis began to hang around the black areas of Memphis listening to the negro music that was played on street corners. He befriended a group of young black musicians who were later to become anonymously famous for their contribution to the development of the Stax black soul sound of the early 1960s. Together they'd pick out numbers by Rufus Thomas or Ike Turner, local musicians who were achieving a degree of national success through their recordings on Sam Phillips' small independent Sun Records, based at 706, Union Avenue, Memphis.

Elvis was also strongly, if accidentally, influenced by classical music to which he was introduced at this time by Giuseppe Giuseppe, owner of the local classical music store. At the Memphis Showhouse a bill was up advertising *Ride of the Valkyries*. Elvis asked Vernon what it was and Vernon told him it was a Russian version of *Custer of the West*. When Elvis got in, he was treated, not to a film, but to a live Wagner concert. Presley was inclined to leave but reluctant to lose his two dollars admission fee, so stayed and was totally overwhelmed and thrilled by the sounds he heard. (There is an Elvis bootleg in circulation from 1971 which has Elvis playing comb and tissue paper along with a Berlin Philharmonic recording of highlights from Wagner which testifies to the lasting influence of the music on him.)

As well as this, country music was widening its appeal across the nation mainly due to the recordings of another influence, Hank Williams, recently dead at the age of twenty-nine. All in all Presley was culturally very receptive to what was happening around him at this time but as 1953 drew on and Elvis approached leaving High School his thoughts inevitably turned to more serious matters – where to get a full-time job, and what to do with the rest of his life. It is likely that he saw himself settling down to a regular routine of wife, children, home, job, just like 99 per cent of his peers but, as everyone acknowledged, positively or negatively, Elvis Presley was different from the run-of-the-mill.

Fate had plans for him. Big plans!

Chapter 2

King Rocket

After High School, Elvis had to find work.

His mother and father were managing by a fine margin and Elvis needed to earn a decent wage to pay for his lifestyle.

What Elvis wanted was a car, preferably a Cadillac, a fully bought home for himself, his Mom and his Dad, money for the movies on weekends, money for hamburgers and money for his record collection.

So, in the summer of that year, Elvis applied for and got the archetypal American post of dog-catcher. His employers were the city council and he worked with Lamar Pike, a fat boy from the year above Elvis at Humes who had been dog-catching for ten months by the time Elvis began.

Together the two of them drove around Memphis in a '49 Ford pick-up with a dog-cage attached to the back. To begin with Lamar did all the driving since he had seniority over Elvis, but by the end of the second week Elvis had established himself as permanent driver. It was 'dullsville' to sit in the passenger seat and Lamar didn't mind *too* much, since it was good for his stature locally to be seen around with the Sideburn Kid.

On a typical day, the pair would cruise around the back streets in the poorer areas of Memphis' suburbs, prowling for stray mutts. When a target was spotted, Elvis would gently pull the Ford into the kerb and kill the engine. Then he and Lamar would softly step out of the cab, collect their dog-nets – strong hessian nets on a three-and-a-half-foot wooden hoop attached to a five-foot pole – and creep down, say, an alley towards their unsuspecting prey. More often than not the pooch would become aware of them at the penultimate moment and hightail it down the alley. A Keystone chase would ensue with Elvis hurdling trash-cans, often not quite successfully enough – this would bring out irate housewives shouting and throwing stones in his wake – and Lamar waddling a brief couple of hundred yards before collapsing, hands clutched to belly, against the nearest wall.

Lunchtimes, the boys would eat in the truck: filled rolls prepared by their respective mothers and milk bought from the nearest convenient grocery store.

If there was a favoured one accessible, Elvis would spend half an hour rifling through record racks in a music store. Thus a Monday lunchtime would find him in Kernohan's Country Music Store poring over Jimmie Rodgers album sleeves or snatching a listen to the latest Hank Williams number, courtesy of the cute little girl who worked for 'Cash' Kernohan. Wednesdays you might find him across town at MF Daley's, the R&B store. Here Elvis could buy BB King, Howlin' Wolf, Fats Domino and Harmonica Frank records. Then, on a Saturday, he might revisit both and he'd call in on Giuseppe Giuseppe to check out the Mario Lanza catalogue.

Elvis's sideburns, DA and bizarre outfits were his most distinctive aspects at this time, and these attributes still brought him the trouble they had when he was in high school. In high school, kids were of course crueller and more vicious in their attacks on this weirdo, but in the larger world of work in Memphis there were still many who would jeer and taunt the embryo Memphis Flash.

One example of this was the day Elvis and Lamar's supervisor at the dog compound sent Elvis to Feldman's, the meal merchants who supplied the compound. The supervisor, Howard Howerd, and Lamar arranged the hoax between them. Elvis was sent down to Feldman's with an order while Lamar was ostensibly cleaning out some kennels in the absence of one of the regular gofers.

At Feldman's, Elvis got out of the truck and walked into the front office. Behind the counter stood Irving Feldman himself, a plump man in his forties who was given to lugubriousness. Elvis walked forward in his mild-mannered way and announced his errand politely.

'Uh, 'scuse me, suh? Mr Howerd asked me to git a long weight offa you – he said you would know the kind he means, suh.'

Turning like a patient grizzly, Irving Feldman replied sonorously, A long wait, huh?'

Elvis paused to take in this non-committal response before mumbling his explanation.

'Tha's right – ah Mr Howerd, he said he needs one to counterbalance a new dog-trap he wants to make. He said you'd have one which mebbe we could lend, suh.'

Irving Feldman took his hands out of his pockets and leaned his elbows onto the counter. He nodded his head twice in slow motion.

'Uh huh,' he said. 'We-ell, son, I guess you'd better come uner the counter there and I'll show you where we keep it. C'mon,' he continued, lifting a flap off the mahogany counter, 'it's right out here.'

In one of the small storehouses by the main warehouse out back, Irving indicated a stack of full mealbags on which Elvis could wait.

Two hours later, Elvis's belly told him it was lunchtime and there was still no sight of his weight. He dandered up to the front office to see what the hold-up was.

'Uh – Mr Feldman?'

'Yes, son. What kin I get you?' replied Irving, poker-faced.

'It's just that I – ah – I bin waiting for the weight. You know, the long weight? And it's getting on for lunchtime now, so I thought I'd just ask if you'd found it yet.'

'Goldarnit, son, I forgot to get word down to you. Storehouse boys say we loaned the weight out last Toosday. Gee, I knew there was something on my mind to do this morning. I hope I ain't been keepin' you from chores you gotta do at the dog pound.'

Elvis shuffled wearily, waved a doghouse expression across his face and then settled for looking puzzled.

'Oh no, suh. They's just doin' some cleanin' up this mornin'. I'm sorry for your trouble, Mr Feldman.'

'Tain't no trouble at all, son.'

As the door closed on the Sideburn Kid, Irving Feldman erupted into volcanic barks of cigar-blemished laughter.

Apart from music, two pastimes preoccupied the eighteen-year-old Elvis Presley: going to the movies and combing his hair. On the whole, though, he tended to comb his hair more often than go to the movies.

Elvis would comb his hair with military precision and with the regularity of sunrise and set. Up in the morning, wash the face, clean the teeth, comb the hair. The combing of the hair was a delicate art. To begin with, one had to apply the Brylcreem and massage it across the surface of the skull to get a uniform coating on all the hair. Then there was the smooth, slick, steady sweep backwards on each side, providing a horizontal to the vertical of the sideburn. Next up was the cow's lick/kiss-curl, a delicate structure that required some swift and nifty sculpturing with the comb. Once finished, the remaining, final touch was the application of some zit cream to the Presley complexion. This done, the Memphis Flash was ready to face the day.

A work of art like Elvis's quiff had, of necessity, to have maintenance and repairs done throughout the day. To this end, Elvis could be seen reconstituting the DA before and after his meetings with anyone and everyone. Presley, reputedly the only male with sideburns in the whole of the South, would stop off at store windows, walls with reflective tiles, rear-view mirrors and puddles on Main Street to work on his hair. The kid had no shame.

Veronica Placid, a high school senior with Elvis, testifies to this: 'When it came to his hair, Elvis Presley just had *no shame*. Why, he would wear it everywhere. Weren't none of the kids at Humes had a haircut like that one. Do you know? Elvis Presley went to a *beauty parlour* to have his hair cut. Can you imagine? Once I even saw him check his DA in his girl's *compact*! Now at that time these were just *outrageous* things to do, but, do you know? today every high school football-player in Memphis carries his own compact! I guess Elvis Presley was just ahead of his time.'[1]

Apart from his hair, and music – and, maybe, fighting zits – Elvis's other passion was of course the movies. All through his late childhood and early teens, Elvis would go to the movies on a weekend, if he could afford it. He was a particular fan of Saturday morning B-movie serials and was able to develop this interest when he began his part-time work as an usher at the Memphian Theatre.

Elvis's favourite serials were the old ones from the '30s and '40s, which, fortunately for him, turned up pretty frequently. He was a fan of the *Flash Gordon* movies and therefore, of course, of *Buck Rogers* as well. Equally good were *Batman, Captain Marvel,* and *Daredevils of the Red Circle.*

Most boys of the '30s, '40s and early '50s would naturally identify with the heroic star, a space explorer or super athlete or super-hero, but Elvis, perversely, identified most with the mad doctors and dia-bolical villains. Given the chance, he would rather have been a char-acter somewhere between Ming the Merciless and Dr Zarkhov. This wasn't an ambition that the other Memphis kids in his circle could understand or appreciate, so on the whole, Elvis kept pretty quiet about it.

The one serial hero that Elvis could acknowledge – since this one *was* a hero – was the *King of the Rocket Men.* This gentleman had a leather jacket with rockets strapped to the back, a set of controls hand-ily attached to his chest, a ridiculous coned steel helmet and a predilection for blasting off from the canopied rear of a truck. He was admittedly a selfless, do-gooding hero like Flash or Buck, but in com-pensation he looked weird and acted even weirder. Anyone who ever saw him fasten on his rockets, set the controls and – best of all – take off, will bear witness to this. And if he was a trifle enigmatic, the great-est enigma was the serial's title: where were his subjects? There wasn't another rocket man in sight.

Elvis became thoroughly obsessed with *King of the Rocket Men.* More than almost anything else he wanted to fly out of the back of a canopied truck. Sure, it would blow his DA to hell, but he could fix that up after he landed.

The obsession grew and finally Elvis talked his Momma into mak-ing him a rocket jacket and harness. The jacket used was an old leather jerkin Vernon had worn to work over a good many years. Gladys fash-ioned a rocket harness out of old belts and two squares of plywood. Elvis painted the control panel on the front square (UP↑ DOWN↓) and

---

[1] *Elvis Back When He Was Just Plain Elvis Presley*, by Veronica Placid (Irregular Titles, 1968).

attached two cardboard tubes to the back square. The tubes had cones added, were painted silver and the outfit was all but complete. All that was needed was an old motorcycle helmet with a cardboard cone stuck on top, the whole also painted silver, and Elvis Presley, King of the Rocket Men In Memphis, was ready for action.

At first the KOTRMIM confined his activities to his bedroom, taking off from the doorway, landing right across there on the bed, but soon the desire to show his salt to the public at large drew him to attempt flight at night in dark alleyways.

Innocent passers-by would sometimes catch sight of a speeding leather-clad figure with an eccentric taste in headgear, bent at the waist, arms held horizontally behind him. The bemused bystander might detect a swift arm-movement at the end of, say, twenty yards, as the King of the Rocket Men in Memphis set the controls to UP↑. One of two things would then occur. Either the eccentric sprinter would carry on sprinting eccentrically or he would, since the best position for take-off was head-down, collide with something – another pedestrian, a garbage can, a stationary car or, if he were very unlucky, a brick wall.

Elvis enjoyed his ushering job immensely. When he was on duty week nights, he could get to see a great many of his favourite movies. His preference was for war movies, westerns and Dean Martin/Jerry Lewis comedy vehicles. Anything with John Wayne or Audie Murphy in was tops, just the neatest. A full-scale shoot-out would pump so much adrenaline through Elvis's system, he would practically fall out of his seat. Wayne's hard-bitten, tough persona was really something to aspire to, and after *Red River* or *Rio Grande*, Elvis would come out of the Memphian Theatre spittin' bullets and primed to blow somebody's head off with his index finger.

During what was to become a traumatic week for Elvis and a memorable one for Memphis – folks there still talk about it today – Elvis saw Wayne in *Fort Apache* Wednesday night and Audie Murphy in *The Kid From Texas* Friday night.

The thrills were too much for the fifteen-year-old future Memphis Flash; on Friday night he was so excited after the movie that he had to don his Rocket Man outfit and go on patrol. After a – surprise! – flightless perusal of the alleyways, Elvis returned home late, over-tired and over-excited.

The KOTRMIM changed back into his alter ego's pyjamas and spent a restless night, wound up with the excitement of being, or rather becoming, a hero.

Next morning, Saturday, he was due at the Memphian at 9.30 to usher and keep an eye on the kids at the Memphis Junior Movie Club. Most of the regular audience here were in the six to twelve age group, but there were a few others nearer to or around Elvis's age.

At 8.30 Gladys made Elvis his breakfast: coffee, scrambled eggs and grits. Forking the eggs into his mouth, it occurred to Elvis in a blinding flash that they were starting another re-run of *King of the Rocket Men* that morning. Still over-wrought from the night before, Elvis's tired mind seized on the notion of going to work in costume. Why not? Hell, it'd be a buzz.

His Mom had gone out to visit her cousin and buy in some groceries; there was nothing to stop him. He ran to his bedroom and gathered together his Rocket Man outfit. His impulse had been to put it on and 'fly' straight down to the Memphian Theatre. It suddenly seemed to him, however, that it would be more correct to take his costume down in a suitcase, hide it in the toilets and make a quick change when his hero was on screen.

The other serials and cartoons were shown and Elvis was standing at the back of the theatre, flashlight in hand, leaning on the wall. He was a little apprehensive now at the prospect of what he was about to do. Before the idea that he would appear ridiculous took hold inside himself, he kicked it out and marched towards the toilets.

Cellos, violas, bassa and violins winnowed and sawed: *King of the Rocket Men* was on. Now!

In the toilets, Elvis ripped off his ushering jacket and thrust himself into his leather jerkin. With a rip the zip was torn up tight to the neck. Arms flashing, he strapped his rocket harness on, being careful not to trip the thrust lever accidentally. Lastly, he carefully inserted his quiff into the coned helmet.

The KOTRMIM turned to the toilet mirror and studied his appearance. He checked his shoulders back a little and tilted his chin upwards. Then, subconsciously aping Ming the Merciless's minions, he banged his fist forcefully against his chest, striking instead his plywood control panel. For a few moments anyone coming into the men's toilets would have been presented with a very strange sight: the KOTRMIM hopping around the room wincing, grunting, groaning and shaking his right hand around for all he was worth.

But in no time at all the KOTRMIM was streaking down a side aisle in take-off position. Twenty yards down the aisle and a hand went to the control panel to make the famous UP↑ adjustment just in time for the corner before the screen; The King hung a hard left, reached both arms firmly behind himself again and tore across beneath the front of the screen just as his celluloid counterpart blasted-off from the back of a canopied truck.

Kids had begun to notice the Memphis Rocket Man by now and everyone in the cinema was aware of his presence as he leaned into another left-hand turn and accelerated, coned helmet at 90° to his legs now, up the centre aisle. A roar of shock and laughter swept across the young audience.

Meanwhile, inside the Rocket Man suit, the King, breaking sweat and breathing hard, suddenly felt his legs buckle under too much forward momentum. He tried but could not stop his legs going, going...

Gone.

The KOTRMIM nose-dived onto the floor and splayed across a few yards of carpet on his control panel. What stopped him sliding along further yards of carpet were the nether regions of Luther Bostock, the manager of the Memphian Theatre.

'Kin you all git up from offa ma feet whoever you are,' said Luther, in a wearily patient tone.

'Yessuh; scuse me,' replied the King. 'Muh rocket has failed to ignite, suh.'

Chapter 3

Rising In The South

One day late in the summer of 1953, Elvis and Lamar were on their way back from a suburban dog-catch when something on Union Avenue caught Elvis's eye: a sign proclaiming that you could make your own record for $4.

Elvis tugged the wheel towards the nearest sidewalk and jerked the pick-up to a halt.

'He-ell's be-ells!' said Lamar. It was an expression he had recently latched onto and would use at any and every occasion. 'Where's the goddam fire, Elvis?'

'You jus' cool the seata your pants there for a moment, Lamar. I won't be long.'

'Where you goin', Elvis?' asked Lamar, twitching and wobbling.

'Never you mind, son.'

The driver's door banged shut and Elvis skipped across the road towards the Memphis Recording Service.

'He-ell's be-ells!' Lamar repeated.

Inside the small building was a tiny office with a tall, large lady dwarfing her desk and typewriter. She looked up and took in Elvis.

'My oh my, honey,' she practically sang, 'what *have* you got on your head?'

Elvis shuffled, took his hands out of his pockets and folded his arms with embarrassment.

'Hit mohairum,' he seemed to reply.

'Y'all gon' haveta speak up, honey. I cain't make out a word you sayin'.'

'It's muh *hair*, ma'am,' Elvis declared, as clearly as he could.

'Well, well. So it is. Where'd you get hair like that, child?' said the big woman.

'Umm, I guess I always had it, ma'am.'

Elvis's hackles had risen slightly at being called 'child'.

'You sure are a singular sight, son. I'll give you that,' she said, standing now and walking around the denim-clad kid. 'A sing-u-lar sight.'

Elvis shifted around the linoleum some more.

'I come about the record, ma'am.'

The big woman, who wore a peroxide Dorothy Malone cut, settled her ample rump on the edge of her desk.

'Which record might that he now – what the hell kinda axle grease you got on your haid, honey?'

'It's just a little hair-oil, ma'am,' he replied, flushing.

The woman exhaled a whistle through her tangerine-painted lips. 'I'd call that haircut u-*nique*.'

'Amm-ah. About the record, ma'am?'

She stood up abruptly.

'You know, you're s'posed to buy the records from a record store. We make 'em; they sell 'em. That's the way it works, honey.'

This was a whole bunch harder than it ought to have been.

'I wanna *make* a record, ma'am,' he almost snapped.

'Okay!' She laughed. 'We been barking up the wrong tree, I guess.'

'Guess so, ma'am.'

'What record you wanna make, son?'

Elvis hadn't worked this one out. He thought quickly now, suddenly recalling that it would soon be his Momma's birthday. For that occasion, the best thing he could think of was a hymn.

'Wanna record a hymn, ma'am.'

'Very nice. Y'know, you get to make *two* songs for the $4.'

'Well… I gotta think of another one yet, ma'am.'

'That's alright, son. You cain't make the record right now anyhow. Sam ain't in at the moment and he does the recordin' here.'

The large woman booked Elvis into the studio for lunchtime the following Thursday. As he was on his way out she called after him.

'Hey, Sideburns. What do they call you?'

'Um – Elvis Persil, mum.'

'You gotta speak more clearly, son; I cain't make you out 't all.'

'*Elvis Presley*, ma'am.'

'Well, Elvis Presley, my name's Fay Vest and I'll see you Thursday. That sure is a singular hairstyle. Em-*hemm*.'

Thursday lunchtime, Lamar left Elvis off at the Memphis Recording Service and drove down to Sal's Diner for meatloaf roll, french fries, malted milk and apple pie à la mode.

Inside the studio, Elvis, toting his guitar, met one Sam Phillips, the owner of the MRS and of Sun Records. Phillips was in the business of recording black, and white, musicians from all across the South. What came to be known as rhythm 'n' blues was recorded there; artists like BB King, Howlin' Wolf and Bobby Bland all passed through Sam Phillips' hands. Sam Phillips was a purist, devoted to the finest in blues and country music. The Memphis Recording Service was a commercial sideline, designed to subsidise Phillips' struggling record label.

Right now what he had before him was a kid in a pink jacket, black pants piped with pink and what just had to be a Martian hairstyle. The kid kept his chin tucked into his neck and would knock his guitar neck against or into something every time he made a jumpy move.

Sam Phillips sat him down on an empty beer crate and went to fiddle with his recording equipment. He said nothing, just proceeded about his business like the craftsman he was. Elvis, apprehensive and generally out of his depth, sat as still as he was able to, only twice knocking over a microphone stand.

When Phillips had completed setting up to his own satisfaction, he came over to Presley and spoke to him for what was really the first time.

'Alright, son, what you gonna do with your record?' he growled.

'Uh, I wanna sing a little and play muh git-tar, suh.'

'Is that a fact? And just what do you want to sing and play on your git-tar?'

'Ah well, I'd kinda decided on doin' "Just A Little Talk With Jesus" – you know? The hymn? If'n that'd be okay, suh.'

As he talked Elvis picked and fidgeted out chords on his guitar.

'A fine notion, son. Who's it for?'

'Am – it'sa gon' be muh Momma's birthday shortly and I wanna do it – uh – for her, suh.'

'That's right noble, son,' said Phillips adjusting the vocal and guitar microphones. 'Now all you gotta do when I get back behind that desk is go through the hymn oncet for me. It won't be a take – 's just to get the levels. Okay? Ain't nothing to it: just take it real easy.'

All too soon, Elvis saw the man appear behind the window and, presently, nod. Edgily, Elvis broached the song with his voice and guitar. The first lines registered on the VU meters:

'I once was lost in sinnnnn

But Jesus took me innnnn…'

Sam Phillips was more than a little surprised. The kid with the funny haircut was singing like he wanted a part in *La Traviata*. He sounded like a goddam opera singer!

Elvis leaned into the notes as if he were obsessed with not missing either end of them:

'We-ulLL

He ba-athed ma heart in lo-ovve

And he wrote ma name a-bovvve…'

Phillips didn't like opera much in the first place, but this was really the pits. The kid sounded like somebody'd just nailed his foot to the floor. Wasn't Phillips' concern, though. The kid had paid his $4 upfront and was entitled to make whatever kind of caterwauling he wanted to. He could blow his nose to the tune of 'Froggy Went A-Courting' if he so wished. $4 to the good was $4 more than nothing at all.

The kid had finished singing.

Sam Phillips had an irresistible urge, which he acted upon.

'Hey listen, Elmer,' said Phillips, coming into the room again, 'do you *want* to sound like a oprey singer or *what*?'

Elvis flushed beetroot.

'Ah – suh – ummah veal beef on Oreole Landau.'

What the hell is he saying?

'You're gon' haveta repeat that for me, Elmer.'

'Pardon me, suh; tha's El-vis.'

'Pardon *me*, Elvis. You gone haveta be more distinct. I cain't make you out 't all,' said Phillips, lighting a cigarette.

'You cain't make out muh singin', suh?'

'No, Elvis. I cain't make out a durn'd word you *sayin*',' Phillips replied with growing impatience.

'Oh I'm-a sorry, sir,' said Elvis, fairly distinctly. 'What was it that you couldn't make out, suh?'

Sam Phillips broke into a tobacco-tinged chuckle.

'Damned if I know, Elvis,' he laughed. 'I couldn't make out a word you were sayin'.'

Elvis laughed too, not entirely uneasily.

'I think I asked you if you *wanted* to sound like a oprey singer. Do you recall?'

'Yessir. I said, I'm a real big fan of Mario Lanza.'

Phillips cracked up in another laugh riot.

'Hey you know, he's really something, Mr Phillips,' Elvis exclaimed defensively, jumping to the conclusion that this recording engineer didn't dig his hero.

'Hell, Elmer, I ain't laughing at Mario Lanza. I's laughing at your damn mumblin'.'

In a short while, Sam Phillips and Elvis Presley had two sides down on record. For the second side Elvis drawled his way through 'Volare'.

Standing with Phillips at the mixing desk, Elvis listened to the playback. He couldn't help smiling to himself. His Momma sure would like it.

Phillips handed over the record at the end of the playback and studied the kid's haircut again.

'You think they gone let you into La Scala under a haircut like that, Elton?' he teased.

Elvis curled a smile across his teeth. He knew when he was being japed. He just didn't know what the hell Phillips meant.

'I'm sorry?'

'La Scala. It's a oprey house. You get oprey singers there just like you get Hank Snow or Ernest Tubb on at the Oprey House in Nashville. I hope your Mom likes the record. So long, son.

'Thank you, sir. Ah – g'bye.'

In fact, Elvis Presley had developed a taste for Mario Lanza at Giuseppe Giuseppe's record store. Giuseppe was a Sicilian who'd wound up in Nashville on the lam from the Cosa Nostra in Chicago. In the Windy City for a brief spell in 1929, Giuseppe Giuseppe had been Al Capone's personal violinist. It's a little known fact, but Al Capone liked nothing better after a piece of wholesale carnage than to relax with his feet up while listening to recordings of Verdi or Rossini.

In 1929 Giuseppe Giuseppe – real name Giuseppe Lambretta – had been earning a meagre crust playing airs and arias on his fiddle in Topo Overti's, a cult restaurant just under the El near Marshall Fields department store. There one day (February 14, 1929 actually) Capone and a few of his boys came in for a quick tagliatelle after a job they'd pulled in an uptown garage.

Slobbering over his pasta, Capone noted Giuseppe's playing and found it infinitely more soothing than listening to scratchy recordings on his gramophone. He offered Giuseppe treble his current wage and had a colleague of his, a guy called Jack 'Joke' McGullet, sort out with Senor Overti the finer points of transferring Giuseppe's employment.

For a few months all went well. Capone went about his business, came home or went back to the office and had Giuseppe play to him while he relaxed and put his feet up.

Then things went terribly wrong for Giuseppe. The Sicilian fiddler was gay, a fruit, homosexual, a four-dollar bill, bent, not right or – as they used to say in the Chicago of the '20s – a pokin' soft lad.

One day Giuseppe made an ill-considered pass at Louis Macheti, a newly-hired, good-looking hood, twenty years of age. Louis, who was all mouth and not too big on the top storey, mentioned it to Luigi Castraticelli, the respected violin-case manufacturer for Capone's mob. Castraticelli was a notorious gossip and had once even spoken to Elliot Ness unwittingly before a big job, so it wasn't long before the tale reached Al Capone's ears.

When he wasn't being a- or im- moral, Al Capone was a very moralistic man. He thoroughly disapproved of homosexuality and, after careful debate with those who had his ear, decided that the best course of action in the circumstances was to take Giuseppe shopping for a pair of pink concrete slippers.

Louis Macheti may have been stupid enough to mouth off about Giuseppe's ill-fated pass and get the latter in Dutch with Capone, but he was neither vindictive nor callous. When he saw the way things were heading, he got word for Giuseppe Lambretta in time for the Fiddling Fruit to pack a violin case and scram.

Giuseppe, being more than a little on the cautious side of careful, decided that his best bet was to keep on the move as much as possible. He went first to Los Angeles where he managed to get some temporary work with the studio orchestra working on *Broadway Melody*. Three months was all the time he had in Hollywood before, fearful of a sinister-looking Italian key grip, he cut out faster than four bars of the William Tell overture.

1930 found Giuseppe painting the Golden Gate Bridge in San Francisco; steady, if slow, work. Everything was fine until one evening in autumn when he was eating in a trattoria near Broadway: the usual fear of an Italian face, a broad-shouldered suit and a black fedora sent him off and running. He rushed back to his lodging in a mid-town rooming house to pack and flee once more.

However, a letter awaited him which was to change his life – and that of Elvis Presley too.

'Mama mia!' he exclaimed. (He was a terribly run-of-the-mill Italian.)

'Memphis?' he puzzled.

He looked at the envelope's postmark.

'Ten-essy?' he puzzled again.

Then the news began to sink in.

'O sole *mio*!'

Giuseppe's aunt in Memphis, Tennessee, had died and left him her music store. 'Pasqualli's Music Store – Finest For Instruments & Sheet Music. (Advice on Pasta Recipes Also Available)' is how the enclosed business card read.

By the time Elvis Presley was a member of the record-buying public, Giuseppe Giuseppe's, as the one-time fiddler called his store – Giuseppe had dropped the name Lambretta during his brief spell in Hollywood – had become as much a record retailer as an instrument supplier.

Naturally, Giuseppe was a great admirer of the Sideburn Kid, and when Elvis started to come in for the odd Gospel record the old Italian took a (mainly) paternal interest in him. Giuseppe gently guided the young Presley towards other forms of music and what most caught the future Memphis Flash's imagination was the work of Mario Lanza, whom Elvis had previously taken to be a brand of sherry.

He adored 'More Than You Know' and 'Why Was I Born?' and would play them over and over again.

In 1951 Elvis had even undergone the ignominy of being taunted for a week after members of his class at Humes had seen him emerge from a Saturday-night screening of *The Great Caruso*. To have been seen going to a movie about a 'goddam oprey singer' was bad enough, but to get caught around the side of the Memphian Theatre singing an aria from *The Barber Of Seville* was just the grossest embarrassment.

Of course Gladys did like 'Just A Little Talk With Jesus' very much. She was 'real proud' that her son could and had made 'a recud'. Vernon thought that it was just a 'durn'd wasta money'.

There was no stopping Elvis now. He would sing Mario Lanza hits all over town; he didn't care who was listening. And when he got bored with Lanza – which took some considerable time – he would croon a Dean Martin hit as indistinctly as possible. What with his own habit of mumbling into his chest and this predilection for aping Martin, people would assume on first acquaintance that Elvis was a secret drinker.

Dog-catching with Lamar continued to occupy his days, but increasingly Elvis, who was, funnily enough, no fool, felt that he would have to take up something with more prospects in it. For the moment dog-catching gave Elvis enough readies to pay in at home, go to the movies and buy a few records most weeks. This in itself was alright for the time being, but Elvis wanted much more for himself and his parents: their own home with a sizeable yard, a Cadillac, a TV set, a trip to New York to see Mario sing at Carnegie Hall, a pink suit, a burger to beat all burgers and a little dog to sing Verdi at on the porch.

He could never hope to make enough to pay for all this at the dog-pound.

So what could he do? The answer was obvious – to Elvis at least. There was good money in chicken farming.

In the autumn of 1953, Elvis took night classes in Chicken Farming. He learned about heating, lighting, feeding and the economics of the business. He was informed that a man going into chicken farming in a big way was likely to turn over at least $10,000 in an unexceptional year.

'Momma, I'm gone be the Chicken King of Tennessee. Yessirree!'

'We'll see, honey.'

Who knows, the future King of Rock 'n' Roll might never have become such. In the winter of 1953, Elvis certainly looked set to go into chicken farming: his studies at night school were going well and he was brimful of enthusiasm for his subject.

However, in late November something went horribly wrong.

'Listen, boys,' said Johnston 'Porky' Prime, the class instructor, 'hit's done time you was out on a chicken farm seein' how the whole shebang works. So I've arranged for you to see the McGoofy farm out off Highway 40.'

The boys were quietly excited about this. They'd be able to go out, sniff some chicken-shit and dream of Cadillacs and TV sets.

'Porky' had them driven out towards Jackson in a Memphis school bus. There was singing and high spirits on the way out.

At McGoofy's farm, Dermot McGoofy himself showed them around the large, long hen-batteries. The chicken farming students behaved deferentially and asked interested questions. 'Porky' Prime was very pleased with them.

On the way home everybody sang some more. Everybody, that is, except Elvis Presley.

The one-time King of the Rocket Men In Memphis, future King of Rock 'n' Roll and would-be Chicken King of Tennessee was breaking out in unpleasant pink blotches and itching like a hound with fleas.

When Gladys got him to a doctor, it was discovered that Elvis was incurably allergic to chicken feathers.

No house.

No Cadillac.

No TV set.

No Carnegie Hall.

No pink suit.

No superlative burger.

No porch pooch.

"S jus' too bad, honey,' said Gladys.

'Chickens stink to hell anyway,' said Vernon.

Elvis went to his room to be alone. He sulked. He punched his mattress a good deal. He stood up and kicked the wall and said:

'Poke a *pig*!'

When he'd said it, he was quite taken with it and wondered vaguely where it had come from.

He said it again.

'Poke a *pig*!'

It sure had a good ring to it.

'Poke a *pig*!'

He chuckled and roared with laughter.

'Poke a *pig*!'

More laughter.

Elvis came running down the stairs laughing uproariously.

'What y'all laughing at honey?' asked Gladys.

'Aw tain't nothin', Momma. Say, I'm real frisky. I'm just gone go for a little walk, Momma. Okay? I'll see you later,' he said, giving her a peck on the forehead.

Elvis went for a reflective stroll around the KOTRMIM's former stomping ground. He reminisced pleasantly about the good ol' Rocket King days and, still perky after discovering his new expletive, decided that chicken farming hadn't really been his thing at all.

He returned home, hungry, after his parents had gone to bed. Matter of fact, Elvis was *very* hungry. Presently he was cooking up a quarter-pound burger and toasting a sesame roll. But then calamity struck: there was neither relish nor ketchup in the house.

'Poke a *pig*! Momma,' he grunted to himself. 'Whyncha get some more relish today. Shee-*it*!'

Looking around the kitchen for something damp to put over his burger meat, Elvis struck on the idea of melting some cheese over it.

'Hot dog!' he cried, grilling a slice of cheese on top of the burger.

When it was sufficiently melted, Elvis placed the top half of his toasted roll over the cheese and bit in deeply. It was *delicious!* It was good enough for John Wayne to eat over a camp fire out on the plains.

Let's face it: it was peachy keen.

Thus had Elvis made his first major contribution to twentieth century civilisation: the invention of the cheeseburger!

Later that week, after a Martin/Lewis comedy at the Memphian, Elvis asked Sal at Sal's Diner to make him a cheeseburger. Sal of course thought the idea crazy, but a couple of kids watching also ordered cheeseburgers apiece.

Soon the cheeseburger idea was copied by every burger joint in Memphis. Kids couldn't get enough of them. The craze spread quickly, through the Southern states and, in time, through the whole of the United States.

It didn't occur to the Sideburn Kid until years later that he threw away a fortune one night in 1953 at Sal's Diner. But years after *that*, he would more than make up for his naïve blunder...

Chapter 4

Dummy Run

Increasingly, Elvis spent time playing his guitar and singing, and more and more he was singing country music or Gospel music, the kinds of music with which he had grown up. This didn't arrest his fixation with Mario Lanza and Dean Martin; it simply grew back up alongside these obsessions.

In January 1954 it occurred to Elvis that he ought to make another record at the Memphis Recording Service. That Mr Phillips was a pretty straight guy and $4 wasn't much to spend for a bunch of fun.

Elvis spoke to his mother about it.

'Momma, I'm gone go make another recud with Mr Phillips, I guess.'

'That's nice.'

'I don't think I'm gon' do a opra one this time out though,' he mumbled.'

'That's nice.'

'I got me an idea for a recud, Momma.'

'That's nice.'

Elvis was totally bound up in his idea.

'I'm gone make a *surprise* for you this time, Momma.'

'That's nice, Elvis.'

'Ah hope you like it, Momma.'

'That's real nice, Elvis.'

A few nights later, after a movie with his girl, Rita Mae Watermelon, a quiet girl who lived up to her unfortunate surname, Elvis broached the subject in Sal's Diner.

'Listen, Rita Mae. I'm gone make another recud down at Mr Phillips' place, you know?'

Rita like the idea. She stopped slurping on the straw in her malted milk and slapped the table between them.

'Say, that's neato, El!' she exploded.

'Uh, hush a little, honey,' Elvis mumbled.

'Sorry, El,' said Rita Mae at a little more subdued decibel level. 'What're you gonna sing?'

'Uh, it's a surprise, Rita Mae,' Elvis mumbled.

Rita Mae stamped her stilettos on the floor in excitement and knocked the remains of her malted milk all over the table.

'Aww gee, I'm sorry, El. I'm real clumsy.'

Elvis fetched a dishcloth off Sal and mopped up.

Subdued for the moment, Rita Mae asked Elvis if it was 'a surprise for lil ol' me?'

'Iza Sue pies Formosa.'

'Gee, El, sometimes you're real hard to make out. *What* did you say?'

'Itsa surprise fer muh Momma,' Elvis reiterated.

'Huh!' was all that Rita Mae had to say to that.

As a point of interest, Rita Mae ended up in New York working as a model and she too had her place in history: she was the mould for the prototype of Playtex's first Double-D-cup-cross-your-heart bra in 1956.[1]

Elvis had it in mind to do something by Richard Rodgers from *State Fair*, his Momma's all-time favourite movie, but things didn't turn out quite like that when he returned to the Union Avenue studio.

Fay Vest was filing her nails when Elvis rolled in, guitar in hand, one Thursday lunchtime.

'Well lawdy lawdy! If it ain't the most singular haircut in town. Sam's waiting for you, honey.'

'Howdy, ma'am. I hope I'm not too late?'

'No, son. What you gonna sing this time out? Whyncha try "On The Street Where You Live"? Gosh a me, that Mario Lanza sure is *something*.'

Sam Phillips came in at that point.

'Hiya there, Elton. How's she goin'? Good, good. In ya come, and get your stuff put down.'

Elvis followed Sam into the studio, taking great care not to knock any microphone stands over. Inside, everything was ready to do a take. Phillips suggested that Elvis play and sing a little to loosen up and then he would set the levels.

Elvis strummed a few sloppy chords and shifted into Red Foley's 'Old Shep'.

The door between studio and office was open and this maudlin dirge drifted through.

'Lord God, Sam,' Fay exclaimed. 'What is that shit he's spouting out there? I'm gone *puke* if'n he keeps that whining up.'

When Sam set in to adjusting the levels, Elvis was running through the number he primarily wanted to record: the title song from *State*

[1] *The Anita Ekberg Bumper Brassiere Book* by Anita Ekberg (with Lucinda Hanfle), (Bazooka Publications, 1969).

Fair. Phillips kept his tongue between his teeth.

The song had been recorded second time through and Elvis was preparing to record 'Old Shep', a song he had known and loved for many years, when Sam Phillips interrupted the kid's strumming.

'Listen son, you gotta purty good voice there. Whyncha try your hand at some other material 'n' see how it goes?'

'Well I don' know, sir. What should I try?'

'You all know anything by Hank Williams?'

'Ummah Moo But Hanover, suh.'

'*What?*'

'"Move It On Over", suh. That's by Hank Williams, isn't it?'

'Uh, yeah. I thought you said something about "Hanover".'

'What?'

'Never mind. You wanna try that one then?'

'Which one?'

'"Move It On Over".'

'Okay. You better tell me when to start, suh,' said Elvis to his collar bones.

'About now.'

When the Sideburn Kid had finished, Sam Phillips said how he liked that much better than what Elvis had been trying before. Did he know any Jimmie Rodgers stuff?

'Uh, what did he do, suh?'

'Ah, "Roll Along Kentucky Moon"?'

Elvis's face was blank.

'"Mule Skinner Blues"?'

Elvis's face remained blank.

'"Waitin' For A Train"?'

'"S that go like this?' Elvis enquired, playing a few bars of the song in question.

He played the song all through.

Sam Phillips didn't show how much he liked it. Instead, he simply asked the boy what he wanted to do for the other song on this record.

'I'm gone stick with "Old Shep", suh. If you don' mind?'

'Okay. Let's slap it down then.'

Later, Sam quietly asked Fay to get a phone number for the boy; he had something in mind.

In the meantime, however, back at home, Gladys was very pleased with the record.

'That's real nice, Elvis,' she said.

It was about this time – summer 1954 – that Elvis discovered something else which was to give him almost as much pleasure as Mario Lanza, Dean Martin, movies, singin 'n' pickin' or cheeseburgers: what to do with a girl.

Or, as Elvis came to put it, 'humpin".

It's a well-recorded fact that sex wasn't invented until 1963, so in his humping, as in his cheeseburgers, his singing and, later, his moving, Elvis Presley was a pioneer.

Humping was a mighty strange business in 1954. First of all it was real hard to believe that you'd be able to find a girl other than a hooer in Memphis who'd let you do it.

In previous years, Elvis had only ever been able to persuade dates as far as a little (medium) heavy petting. Every so often a girl would let you take out her bazooms and once in a while, if you got real hot, she'd let you slobber over 'em. But mostly that was as far as it went.

Elvis knew – from bike shed gossip and books and magazines – that there was a whole lot more'n that to it, and he was hot to trot.

Rita Mae was beginning to concede the odd inch here and there during the spring. (Elvis's sap was up and he was more than usually persuasive.) One time he'd even been able to venture a hand down south of the border with only token resistance offered, but then something awful happened.

Elvis got a nose-bleed.

It wasn't a little itty-bitty nose-bleed either. It bled and bled. All over his lime shirt and Rita Mae's Double-D-cup bra; all over his yellow trousers and Rita Mae's polka-dot skirt. It was a real stubborn bleed too. It just wouldn't stop.

'Aww,' cried Elvis, 'POKE A PIG!!'

"What'd you say, Elvis Presley?"

'I said, *POKE A PIG*!!! Rita Mae.'

'Well just you cut out that kinda language around here. I don' wanna hear no alley talk when I'm out on a date. I 'spect to be treated with a little more respect.'

No reply.

'You hear what I'm sayin', Elvis Presley??'

'I hear you, Rita Mae. Ain't nobody this side-a Jackson *cain't* hear you. But my nose is bleedin' all over muh poke'n' clothes.'

Shriek!

SLAP!!

BANG!!

The door was closed and Rita Mae was gone.

Shortly after that evening, Rita Mae surrendered to Elvis's rubberised appendage. Once they got started there was no stopping them.

Elvis really liked to hump.

He humped in the dark at the Memphian Theatre; he humped in the cornfields out to the east of town; he humped in the back of a car when he could get the loan of one; he humped against walls on dark streets and he even humped under the table in a secluded corner at

Sal's Diner one night when business was slack and Sal was dozing over the *Memphis Chronicle*.

Humping was okay with Elvis Presley.

Rita Mae liked it pretty good too.[2]

Not long after Elvis's *State Fair* session at Sun, a phone message was relayed to him. He was to ring or call in at the studio. Elvis phoned Sun and Fay gave him Sam's message: ring somebody called Scotty Moore on 634 5789.

Sam Phillips had mentioned Elvis to Scotty Moore when Moore came in to record with his western swing band, Cecil Mumsford and the Cornfed Cowpunchers. Phillips' suggestion had been that perhaps Moore could lure Presley away from his unfortunate and potentially disastrous musical inclinations. The boy really had a distinctive voice and if he could be pointed more at contemporary music – well, there was no knowing what he might do.

'What'm I s'posed to say to this cat, M's Vest?' asked Elvis when given the news.

'Jus tell'm who you are. Sam said Scotty'd be expecting you to call.'

'Well, uh, who is he?'

'You know *Sam*. He owns Sun Records and he recorded you a coupla times, honey.'

Elvis chuckled.

'Who's this Scotty whatsit, M's Vest?'

'He's a git-tar player in a band, honey.'

'Which band? I mighta hearda them.'

'Cecil Mumsford and his Cornfed Cowpunchers.'

'Shee-ugar. If I'd a heard a them, I sure wouldn't forget about it.'

'Guess not, honey. You ring Scotty anyhow. 'kay?'

[2] *Elvis's Pelvis (And What It Got Up To)* by Fritz Klutz (Invective Dan Kamikaze Press, 1982).

Chapter 5

Elvis, Scotty & Bill

Elvis had arranged to meet Scotty one Friday evening at the guitarist's home in town. It hadn't been easy fitting in a mutually convenient date for this historic meeting. The Cornfed Cowpunchers were getting a lot of dates around Tennessee and even over in Louisiana and of course at that time Elvis had a pretty tight humping schedule.

When Scotty Moore opened his front door on Seltzer Street what he beheld stopped him dead for an instant. There was this kid with an every-which-way-greasy-kid haircut who was toting a guitar and not only wearing an outrageous combination of pink, black and maroon, but also, seemingly, a smattering of green eye-shadow under his fair eyebrows. The kid just had to be a fairy.

'Uh – hi,' said Scotty Moore. 'C'mon in. I'm Scotty. You must be Elvis Presley, huh?'

'Da rye. Pastor Mitchum.'

'I'm sorry?'

'I said that's right. Pleased to meet you,' said Elvis, very distinctly.

'Right. Good, good. Ah – sit down.'

Elvis sat down. He rested his guitar against a table with great delicacy and would-be precision.

'Get you a Coke? There's some cold in the icebox?' asked Scotty.

'Uhah thanks, man,' replied Elvis, fidgeting.

Scotty Moore was a neat dapper guy recently out of the army, with the quiet air of discipline and understated assurance that you often find in soldiers.

When they'd had their Cokes and chatted about Memphis and music – who they knew in common, what recording artists they admired – the two began to play together. Having heard from Sam that Elvis knew 'Move It On Over' and 'Waiting For A Train', Scotty suggested they begin with those songs.

While Scotty picked around the tune, Elvis strummed rhythmically and sang with increasing confidence. He would first of all reach the notes and proceed with caution 'til he felt his phrasing was falling in place. When he was satisfied with these facets of his performance, the Sideburn Kid would begin to goof around with his inflections, warbling and booming, underplaying and going just enough over the top.

Scotty noted this, but kept it to himself.

The pair moved on over 'I Love You Because' and then more country material and were having an enjoyable time. Scotty used the concentration he had over and above what he used on the guitar to take in details about this strange kid with the every-which-way haircut.

The kid was an outrageous dresser. His jacket was way too big for him and his trousers had piping down the sides. And, yes, he *was* wearing eye-shadow. What a durn'd weird! He was born to be a performer, Scotty thought.

Look at him move!

The greasy kid's whole body was snaking around behind his guitar body as he bashed the strings and hollered.

The kid acts like a coloured!

In your own front room it was kind of embarrassing, but a fellow could see how it'd be real exciting on a bandstand. The boy had something.

The two country musicians broke for a coffee and then Scotty excused himself to make a phone call.

Coffee and cookies out of the way, Elvis and Scotty were messing around without much direction when the doorbell rang. What Elvis saw next was this beefy dude hauling a double bass over the threshold of the room.

'Howdy, kid. Whaddaya know whaddaya say?' the double bass guy asked Elvis.

'Umma haw.'

Scotty got the beefy character a Coke.

'Jesus H Christ, boy, that's some outfit you got there.'

'Umma humma.

'You ever think about goin' in the circus?!'

The beefy character laughed.

Elvis smiled uneasily.

'Say! Are you wearin' make-up?'

Elvis's uneasy smile turned to truculence.

'What if I am, man?'

'Nothing. Nothing at all. I ain't never seen a *man* wear make-up before.'

'Well you seen one now. And I *am* a man. And if you give me any lip, man, I'll bust your face for you. Understand?'

'Yessir. I understand. I guess we'd better change the subject, huh?'

Scotty returned with the Coke and an armful of records he was returning to his friend.

'Say, I'm sorry, guys: I didn't introduce you all. Elvis, this here is

Bill Black, who lives right up the street here and plays this here piece of deadweight. Bill, this here's Elvis Presley, a friend of Mr Phillips down at Sun.'

Elvis and Bill Black shook hands stiffly and in a little while the three of them were making an assault on a few more unsuspecting country standards.

When the boys who would go on to catalyse the biggest entertainment industry of all time had packed up for the evening, Bill made a conciliatory remark about the quality of Elvis's singing. He said Elvis had really fuelled up those old country numbers.

'Yeah. They's okay, but I'm not sure yet.'

'How d'you mean?' Scotty asked.

'Well Scotty, it's like this. I want to be a better singer than Mario Lanza and I'm not sure this is the right material.'

Bill Black whistled.

'Y'know something, Elvis?' he said. 'You're a *weird*.'

Scotty Moore had occasion to meet Sam Phillips during the following week and the recording man was keen to hear how Scotty had hit it off with the Sideburn Kid.

'It was real interesting; the kid can really sing and he can really move. Plus he's weird lookin'.'

'Yessir, he ain't average, that's for sure. Lookyhere: why don't you and Elmer come in here when the studio's not booked and rehearse together? See what you can get him to come up with, huh?' Phillips suggested.

'Uh – that's *Elvis* you mean, Mr Phillips?'

'Sure. *Elvis*. What'd I say?'

'Elmer.'

'Hell, Elvis, Elmer – you know who I mean. The kid with sideburns.'

So began a period of intensive rehearsal. Bill Black got roped in too and the three of them developed a pleasantly jokey relationship, so jokey in fact that Elvis was even able to have his own way and get to sing the odd Mario Lanza hit, and, if Scotty and Bill were feeling *extra* magnanimous, now and again they would let him sing some Dean Martin.

Sam Phillips would look in on them every fortnight or so to see how things were coming along and began to encourage them to do songs from the coloured charts. Elvis went for this quicker than his partners, since he had been listening to blues and what became known as R&B for a few years now.

They rehearsed Fats Domino's 'Going To The River', Jimmy Reed's 'Baby What You Want Me To Do' amongst others and one time Sam played them a demo just done in his studio by a black singer called Arthur Crudup.

One Crudup song particularly caught Elvis's imagination: 'That's All Right Mama'. Elvis, Scotty and Bill kicked that around the studio in rehearsal for a few weeks until they got it the way that seemed to fit. Then they asked Sam Phillips to take a listen.

He did.

What he heard was this:

A sonorous slapped bass, a trebley semi-acoustic sounding guitar embellishment and this vigorous, muscular voice that was almost but not quite over the top. The Memphis Flash attacked the song punching and flailing with his body, belting and ducking melodramatically with his vocal cords.

The trio were anxious to hear what Sam Phillips would make of their interpretation.

"S good, boys,' he said. 'Play me some more.'

So the boys played him some more of the songs which they'd been working on, songs which would go to make up a hefty part of Elvis's Sun collection.

Sam liked the material a great deal; more than he would say at the time. Elvis, Scotty and Bill had worked hard to get a sound and now, after a few months, they had one that was exciting and fresh and youthful.

'Okay, boys,' said Sam after a few more songs. 'It's time to make a little record, I guess.'

July 6, 1954, Elvis, Scotty and Bill went into the Sun studio and recorded what would become their first hit record. The trio were light-hearted and Elvis was in exuberant form so after only a handful of run-throughs Sam recorded them on 'That's All Right Mama'.

It is as good to listen to today as it was on the first playback on Union Avenue. The difference lies in the fact that no one had ever heard music like that then. The buzz in the studio was overwhelming.

Next thing, they cut a bluegrass tune called 'Blue Moon Of Kentucky' and Elvis, having loosened up his musical muscle on the Crudup song, flexed high, wide and strong on this one. His performance verged on the comical.

When the great deed was done Elvis was higher than a kite on adrenaline. He punched the air repeatedly and swiftly, leapt off the ground to slap the ceiling and bellowed out, 'POKE A PIG, MAAN!'

Everyone present roared with laughter.

Even Sam Phillips was effusive.

'What we got here, boys, is *history*! You guys know what you done? Right here we gotta country 'n' western rhythm 'n' blues record. 'Tain't never been done before.'

It's often been reported that Sam Phillips wanted a white man who could sing like a black man. Now he believed he had one.

He had a little bit more than he had dreamt of besides.

'I don' know though,' said Elvis. 'I still think oprey's the thing of the future.

The following Saturday night saw the first airing of the record.

Destry Gumby, the Saturday night jock on Memphis station KRUD, played 'That's All Right Mama' as a favour to Sam. His show was a popular one and as soon as he played the Elvis record, KRUD's switchboards jammed with kids asking for it to be replayed. Gumby played both sides of the record all evening. Eventually he got tired listening to it and called the Presley home to fetch the boy in for an interview.

'It's a good recud okay,' says Destry today,[1] 'but I got durn'd tired a hearing it that night. I figured even doing an interview with some spotty kid'd be better'n playing those goddam songs again.'

Elvis was at the movies with Rita Mae. He was too wound up to listen to the Gumby show. Gladys, when she had the call from Destry Gumby, sent Roxy Mayhew, their neighbour's girl, down to the Memphian Theatre to get Elvis to hightail it over to KRUD.

Arrived at the Memphian, Roxy couldn't see Rita Mae and Elvis anywhere. She asked an usher if she knew where they were sitting

'I think you'll find them round the back, honey,' he replied 'but I'd holler before you spring on them. Know what I mean?'

Roxy Mayhew was an innocent girl, even by the standards of 1954. Fortunately for her naïveté, Elvis was just readjusting his trousers and Rita Mae powdering her nose when Roxy came upon them.

Destry Gumby did a swift and standard interview and when it was over Elvis, always the left-fielder, asked,

'Uh, scuse me, Mr Grundy –'

'– that's *Gumby*, son.'

'I'm sorry. Mr Gumby. Are you the Wolfman?'

'Who's the Wolfman?'

'Lon Chaney Jr,' said Gumby's lugubrious engineer.

Gumby chuckled, then looked at Elvis again. 'You're a weird, son.'

In the months that followed Elvis's records were local hits across increasing areas of the South, promoted by Elvis, Scotty and Bill touring long and hard in a big Chevvy. They signed with a manager, Rob Robb, a one-time country singer who got them gigs in country venues across the Southern states. Rob Robb's notion was that Elvis was a country singer and he tried to get Elvis to play down the fast part of his

[1] In the video cassette, *David Frost Talks To Some People Who Knew Elvis, But Didn't Have The Commercial Sense To Cash In With A Book* (Dogs Home Video, 1980).

act. This led to arguments with Sam Phillips who believed that the 'black' aspects of Elvis's act were what made it exceptional.

Elvis himself however still wanted to insert arias from *Carmen* and *The Flying Dutchman*.

Elvis's mother thought he wasn't getting enough sleep.

Rita Mae began to think that Elvis must be humpin' somewhere else.

Sal made more and more money on cheeseburgers.

Vernon still thought it a durn'd tragedy that Elvis wasn't going into chicken farming.

Fay Vest no longer thought Elvis's such a sing-u-lar hair-style: every boy in Memphis seemed to be attempting an every-which-way-greasy-kid cut.

And somewhere a real living Flying Dutchman was looming in the distant shadows.

Chapter 6

Dyke-Plugger Parker – the Untold Story

Piet van Nott was a Dutch American who had worked his way up from the bottom in the Ringo Brothers' Circus, a three-ring operation working out of Fort Worth, Texas in the '40s and '50s.

Piet served his apprenticeship in the School of Hard Knocks when he arrived in the United States, working first of all as a newspaper boy on the streets of Manhattan. Being very fat, he was mocked and bullied by street gangs who would kick his ass, steal his papers, push him over (not an easy task) and jeer at him, calling him unpleasant names such as Pigface, Blob, Porko, Piglet, Deadweight, Pogknocker, even sometimes Fatso.

Young Piet felt very strongly the need to do something about this and one day he spotted the very thing: an ad in the *Tribune* he was hawking for an institution going under the name of School of Hard Knocks.

'Being kicked around?' asked the ad. 'We will teach you to kick back!' The price seemed very reasonable and he knew exactly where Washington Street was.

He would investigate.

At the School of Hard Knocks, young Piet learned how to give smart-ass responses to smart-asses; how to trip people up and run away before they could get up again; how to cheat at patience; how to con your way into a government soup kitchen; how to rabbit punch a wild steer; how to beat yourself at chess hanging upside down from ankle-chains; how to lie convincingly about your age and get half fares on the subway; how to keep a deadpan expression when somebody stamps on your toes; how to come across like Humphrey Bogart when you feel like Fatty Arbuckle; how to sell a sow's ear as a silk purse; how to avoid getting in Dutch with a Sicilian; and a few dozen other little goodies guaranteed to prevent a young boy remaining a fool all his life.

Within six months Piet van Nott graduated with honours and the school in the back of a cinnamon warehouse on Washington Street presented him with a cute little diploma:

School of Hard Knocks

This is to certify thet Piet van Nott has graduated from the
School of Hard Knocks, with Honours, in the year of our lord 1935.
The graduate is now qualified to take shit from nobody and to
pull a fast one wherever and whenever he feels the inclination.

Signed

(Chancellor.)

John W Huckster

Irving S Devians.   (Vice-Chancellor.)

Upon graduating, Piet thought it a good idea to adopt a name
which better suited his new status as a wily youth. After much consideration, Piet decided that he would adopt the guise of an ex-sol-
dier. He became Colonel Tom Parker. School of Hard Knocks or no, it
never occurred to him that they weren't making colonels as young as
him anymore – if they ever did.

With his new name and his new trade, the young Dutchman
decided to follow the trail of the great American pioneers and go
West. There, he firmly believed, his future awaited him.

Arrived in Richmond, Virginia, Parker fell in with one Theobald
Blodgett, a Depression equivalent of the Old West's patent medicine
man. Together the fake Colonel and the loquacious quack toured
south and west selling their dubious wares to unsophisticated farmers, production line workers and housewives.

In Birmingham, Alabama, the dastardly duo had a close shave
when they fell afoul of an angry mob of disaffected housewives.
Blodgett and Parker had sold a job lot of headache powder as a male
aphrodisiac. The women of the west side of Birmingham didn't take
kindly to this when one of them discovered the truth.

The furious females pelted Blodgett and Parker's rickety truck
with eggs, tomatoes and flour.

Mrs Martha McNorton, now a grandmother and living in an old
people's home in Birmingham, was there at the time.

'I remember that time right well. Them two hucksters got caught but
good. It was a woman on the west side at that time that found 'em out. Her
name was Enid Achaude. She was mighty keen to get her husband Abner
going, so she put in a mite too much of this here powder that Blodgett was
sellin'. Matterafact, she put in a heap too much, 'cause she knocked Abner
clean out with it and hadda get 'im to hospital durn'd quick. Well, a course the
doctors found out what it was. Enid, she was outta that hospital like she'd

seen a skunk. It weren't no more'n an hour after that before she'd gathered up a buncha ladies what'd bought Blodgett's concoction. I was one o' them fools. Well, we caught Blodgett and his assistant – who was a shifty fat crittur – as they was hawkin' some more a this headache powder. I tell you, we *nailed* them two so's they'd *stay* nailed. Wasn't one bit a their clothes or that truck but that it was fair plastered with rotten vegetables, eggs, flour – you name it.

'And I do believe that if we'd caught them properly we'd a ripped that pair to shreds. But they just about got their truck going in time. They sure looked a sight, son. They sure did. That truck looked like a amateur omelette on wheels. Hah! Sure did. By the way, honey, are you all doin' anything tonight?'[1]

In 1939, Colonel Tom began work with the Ringo Brothers Circus.

He had known some good times and some bad after his time with Theobald Blodgett. It was just after one of the bad periods that he became gofer for Roger Ringo, the circus proprietor at the time. Roger Ringo was an old-fashioned showman in the Barnum tradition. He had heaps of flair and an abundance of style, but absolutely no luck at all. Roger Ringo's ideas were – or so his friends said – ahead of their time.

He it was who introduced the then extraordinary notion of the Elephant Flea Circus. The act was simple, just an ordinary flea circus but with the novel addition of elephants. Circus veterans all agreed that the Elephant Flea Circus was in the vanguard of the circus art, but audience reaction was mixed, to say the least.

Some audiences found the idea of having to conceptualise the activities of fleas wearing; all they had to go on was the commentary of the ringmaster, Roger Ringo himself. Sure, they could see what the elephants were doing, but that was only half the act and not the essential half at that.

For other audiences, the part of the act when Ringo bawled out, 'Ohmigosh, ladies and gennelmen, Ermintrude (an elephant) has just sat on Franklin (a flea). Jest a minute. Get *up!* Get up, Ermie baby! Up! Up! That's it. Is he…? I… ah… Ohhhh noooo! Ladies and gennelmen, Franklin has not survived this ordeal. What a tragedy, what a cat-*tast*-rophe*eee*! You have no *idea*! Franklin and I go back a long way, folks' etc, was a little *de trop*.

Starting at the bottom – shovelling elephant shit – Colonel Tom soon worked his way up to the exalted position of right-hand man to Roger Ringo. The Dutchman came to be responsible for making poor ideas like the Elephant Flea Circus sellable. Ringo insisted on putting on the acts that he liked and executing his own madcap ideas. (The

[1] Quoted in *Feminism in The South* by Ernie P Skyhook (Sacred Cow, 1978).

Elephant Flea Circus was the essence of good sense compared to Ringo's all-time personal favourite, Camelia and Her Foxtrotting Zebras.) But Colonel Tom did the spieling and PR work in each town that the circus rolled into.

Parker it was who rode through Main Street, Middle America, on an African elephant bellowing the good news about the Ringo Brothers Circus:

'Ladeezngennelmen! Roll up! Roll up! Tonight at six and eight for only one of three nights here in Hicksville, theee RRRINGO BRRROTHERS CIRCUS!!

'Unbelievable!!

'In-credible!!

'You will *not* believe your EYES and EARS!

'SEE fire-eaters blast TWENTY FOOT licks of FLAME from their mouths!!

'*SEE*!! Hortense, the world's only EL-E-PHANT CANNONBALL shoot A-CROSS the RRRING!!

'Stand back in AM-MAZE-MENT as you witness Nicky Dixon, the only bearded seven-year-old in the history of theee WORRLLD!!

'*SEE*!! The world's only EL-E-PHANT FUH-LEE CIRCUS!!

'HEAR the sound of Major Salt's MIXED BRASS BAND!!!

'Roll up! Roll up!

'Yes, ladeezngennelmen! Tonight at six and eight, two shows only tonight and for only two nights more! THEEE... RRRINGO BRRROTHERS SURRRCUSSSS! Get your tickets here and now ladeezngennelmen. Roll up! Roll up! Only a dollar fifty a head, children 75 cents! Buy 'em here! Buy 'em now! Roll up! ROLLL UPPP!!'

Colonel Parker soon decided that there was no business like show business and took to the circus showman's life like a duck to orange sauce. His training at the School of Hark Knocks and his apprenticeship with Theobald Blodgett certainly helped, but the Ringo Brothers Circus was largely responsible for turning Parker into the man he became: Colonel Tom, world-famous manager of Elvis Presley; the man who turned a fast, stylish, subversive Rock 'n' Roller into the biggest money-spinner in the history of entertainment.

Roger Ringo, today an ageing weatherman on TV Channel 9, St Louis, Missouri, reminisces:

'Yup. *Sure* I remember Parker. He was a good ol' boy. Matter a fact I admire ol' Tom more'n any man I heard of – 'cept maybe Huey P Long. Now *there* was a man. He gave the peopla Loosiana roads 'n' hospitals. He champeened the underdog. "Ev'ry man a king"! That's what he said, y'know. What? No, I'm talkin' about Governor Long. Who're you talkin' 'bout? Oh yeah, Tom Parker. Hell, he was a good ol' boy. I had the strokes-a-genius; he sold 'em to the public. *There* was a man could a sold the Lincoln Memorial to

Congress. Yup. There was a man coulda sold the Liberty Bell to the people a Philadelphia. What? Right. What was I sayin'? Parker? A sonuvabitch! Perfidious Parker's what I've always called him. And still do. You tell 'em I said so, son. You tell 'em Roger Ringo said so. Taught the bastard ever'thing he ever knew. Then he up an' leaves muh circus for a goddam hillbilly singer from Tennessee. A Tennessee boy! 'f I'd a got muh hands on Colonel Tom Parker in 1956, I'd a kicked his fat ass around the Southern states. Yes I would.'[2]

(Shortly after making this celebrated interview, Roger Ringo was mysteriously sacked by Channel 9, St Louis.)

At the circus, Parker learnt some valuable lessons.

During his months at the School of Hard Knocks, his tutors had taught him a great many things, but the point that Irving S Devious made most often and most emphatically at the Washington Street warehouse was the school motto:

'NEVER GIVE A SUCKER AN EVEN BREAK.'

In the time he spent on the road with Blodgett, Parker had it brought home to him strongly time and again that the world was simply jam-packed with suckers. There wasn't just one in every crowd: 90 per cent of the goddam universe consisted of Grade I, Class A suckers.

The training was completed at the circus. The rules which evolved were straightforward:

1. People have money which they want to spend.
2. If you don't take that money off 'em, some other bastard will.
3. In order to get that money, you have to sell your product.
4. To sell your product, you have to tell people about it.
5. Tell it BIG and LOUD.
6. Keep telling it BIG and LOUD until somebody buys it.
7. Move on and repeat the process.

---

[2] From the *Playboy* interview, 'I Was The One Who Taught Colonel Tom Parker All He Knows About Being A Conman.'

Chapter 7

Sex, Style, Subversion

In Memphis, Tennessee, in July of 1954, Elvis Presley still listened to opera, still liked Dean Martin, but found little time for either. His manager, Rob Robb, proved very successful at booking engagements for the young singer and his new band. Elvis, Scotty and Bill were soon playing all across Tennessee, Louisiana, Mississippi, Missouri and even into Texas. So Elvis was left with two of his then abiding passions to indulge: cheeseburgers and humpin'.

An Elvis Presley gig was an event. Elvis's sexually dangerous demeanour, his sultry pouting and suggestive movements sent girls wild and made boys feel dull or threatened or both. The over-the-top vocals sliced by Scotty's guitar tensions and backed by Bill's percussive bass slapping constituted sensual, animal music in themselves, but Elvis's vibrating rubber legs, pumping pelvis and flailing arms set on top of the music made for a spine-trembling experience. The origins of Presley's stage movements are surprising though.

One night at an early small-time gig in Memphis, Elvis was doing his then-normal stage routine. He had always felt the need to move with his music, but up to this point Elvis's movements on stage had been limited to the backward snap of his left leg and the odd finger-pop or two; the kid was a little inhibited.

On the night in question, however, all this changed.

Just before going on stage, Elvis had been having a beer and a chat with Scotty in the seedy back room in which the band had to change.

The audience was pretty much a bar-room crowd – men wearing their best Levi jackets, women smartly dressed in flaring, brightly coloured frocks plumped out with petticoats.

The band came onto the rickety little dais that served as a stage and tuned up while the jukebox played soft, slow country music. Elvis, Scotty and Bill looked about ready, then the record finished and the bar-tender switched off the jukebox.

'Manna Melvin Pretzel,' said the singer.

'What'd he say?' said Laverne McAlistair to her date.

'Durn'd if I know,' replied Morton Slab moodily.

'That there is Elvis Presley,' said Joe Doughface, a friend of

Morton's who was playing gooseberry that night. 'I guess he must have said, "My name's Elvis Presley." I dunno.'

'He sure talks funny,' Laverne said.

By now the band were strolling through 'I Forgot To Remember To Forget' at a steady pace. Elvis was swaying gently around the microphone stand as he crooned.

The number finished. There was sporadic applause.

Elvis announced 'Blue Moon Of Kentucky' ('Blancmange Can O' Turkey') and the pace quickened up sharply. The Sideburn Kid had just reached the line 'The stars were shinin' bright' for the first time when his pelvis catapulted forward, bouncing his guitar off his groin.

'Did you see that, Morton?' asked Laverne.

'Whut?' said Morton, swigging on his Budweiser.

Elvis hit the words 'Blue moon' again and once more his hips lunged forward into his guitar.

'There he goes again. Ohh *Morton*! Ain't you gonna do something? It's plain disgustin'.'

'*Whut's* plain disgustin'?'

'Morton Slab, you're not lookin'. That singer – whatever he's called – he's makin' lah-censhus movements with his – his… body.'

'What's that?'

'Lah-censhus movements. He's makin' them, Morton. With his *body*. Ain't you gonna *do* something?' trilled Laverne.

'Ah might do something, Laverne, if ah knew what the poke you was talkin' about. What in hell's name is lah-censhus mean, Laverne?'

Laverne apart, every other female in the room was riveted to the spot, eyes fixed on the greasy kid's gyrating groin. It sure was raunchy.

On the little dais, the greasy kid was quickly settling an immediate quandary. Something itching up his pants had catapulted his pelvis; an ant or a cockroach creeping around his backside. He must've picked it up in the unhygienic-looking changing room. After the first pelvic lunge he had felt real bad. What would his Momma say if she saw him getting on like that? He believed he had better go off at the end of the song and get rid of whatever was causing the irritation.

However, when his groin snapped at the microphone-stand a second time, Elvis caught a glimpse of a couple of girls sitting together at a table. Since he had discovered humpin' quite recently, he recognised that look on their faces.

History was made.

Elvis reached round with his right hand and gave his buttocks a forceful slap. The ant was dead now. Elvis came to the words 'Blue moon' again and whipped his crotch around before thrusting it right in the line of view of the two girls mooning at him from their table.

What do Mommas know anyhow?

During the summer that Senator Joe McCarthy's star began to sink, Elvis Presley's was definitely in the ascendant. The Senator went beyond the pale in attacking the army for 'coddling' Communists and blew it; the Memphis Flash went beyond the boundaries of '50s good taste and ensured his atomic-powered rise to the top.

That summer Elvis Presley and the Blue Moon Boys (Scotty and Bill) wreaked havoc in dance halls, country music clubs and at open-air dates.

Rock 'n' Roll as the adolescent art form we know was established right then and right there in two- and three-bit bookings across the South.

Twenty years later, Malcolm McLaren, manager of that quintessential Rock 'n' Roll band the Sex Pistols, summed up Rock 'n' Roll in three words:

Sex

Style

and Subversion.

To be exciting to a young audience – which is the first principle of Rock 'n' Roll – a performer or a group of performers needs to supply these three rare abstractions.

Elvis Presley was the first of his kind. John Lennon and others since Elvis have accepted that he was the first Rock 'n' Roller, which he was for a great many reasons. However, more than anything else, Elvis was the first Rock 'n' Roller because he was the first to market that magic formula of Sex, Style and Subversion.

SEX: Elvis had a sensual face given to animal, ecstatic contortions in performance; he had a wild, unkempt iconoclastic hairstyle, completely at odds with the predominant look of young men in the '50s, and, most of all, on stage, he moved like an uncaged panther looking for a mate. He wasn't dubbed the Memphis Flash for nothing.

STYLE: again, the every-which-way-greasy-kid-with-SHOCK! sideburns look and those tacky, brightly-coloured clothes which appeared to be several sizes too big for the boy? Land sakes, Wilma! He dresses like a goldarned negro pimp!!

SUBVERSION: most of the time he's on stage, this boy shows all the signs of wanting to hump. His guitar, the microphone-stand or even the damn' floor; anything will suffice until he can get off the stage and find himself a woman.

This is 1956. Eisenhower and Nixon are in the White House. Anyone to the left of Attila the Hun is out of work in Hollywood, courtesy Senator McCarthy, and the average high school couple make Clark Kent and Lois Lane look like moral degenerates from the Beat Generation.

Was Elvis Presley subversive? Was Rasputin horny??

Chapter 8

Going Dutch

About this time – after Elvis began making and selling records at a rapid pace and before Colonel Tom Parker came into his life – Giuseppe Giuseppe, the man who turned Elvis on to Caruso, had two more significant influences on the Memphis Rocket Man.

One day, in Giuseppe's record store, the ageing Italian fruit played a record of some Paganini violin pieces for the now locally famous kid with the funny clothes and sideburns.

'Hey, Dennis. What you think from that?' Giuseppe asked when the record was over.

"S okay, Mr Giuseppe,' Elvis replied. 'That Paga-whatsit cat plays some purty fast licks.'

'No, no, no, Dennis!'

Giuseppe called Elvis Dennis. Nobody has been able to find out why.

'No, no, no, no, NO! Issa not Paganini onna da recud. Issa justa guy playing Paganini's music. Paganini he'sa deada longtime.'

'Oh, scuse me, suh; I din know that.'

"S okay, Dennis. You notta to know. You nottan authority on classical music yet. Maybe someday, but notta yet. Now, Paganini, he quite a guy. He breaka all his strings but one and keepa playing.'

'He what, Mr Giuseppe?' asked a puzzled Elvis.

'He play like a hurricane and he snappa da strings one by one but keep on playing. Mama mia, but that getta da audiences going, Dennis! They go pineapples, Dennis!'

'Uh, pardon me, suh. What you say?'

'They go pineapples, Dennis,' Giuseppe repeated.

'Scuse me, suh, but that's *bananas*, I think.'

'Okay. They go bananas, Dennis. But they have a wonderful time anyway.'

Interestingly, Filbert Grossman, in his laboriously detailed and highly imaginative book on Elvis,[1] makes a comparison between the

---

[1] *Elvis – The Way It Might Have Been or Let's Piss On A Hillbilly* (Scurrilous Press, 1981).

way Elvis in the early days would begin a show by striking a note on the guitar so forcefully that he would break a couple of strings. Little did Grossman realise that Elvis had been directly inspired by the great Italian virtuoso.

Not very long after Giuseppe introduced Elvis to the idea of string-smashing, the little old Italian and the embryonic King of Rock 'n' Roll had a final, and sad, meeting.

In the shop one quiet Thursday afternoon, Elvis was listening to a new recording of *The Flying Dutchman* which Giuseppe had recommended and then put on the turntable.

''S purty damn good, Mr Giuseppe.'

'Eesa toppa notcha, Dennis. Eesathe *best*!'

The little Italian sat listening to the music and mooning at Elvis. He sure was a handsome hunka meat.

Presently, Elvis became aware of Giuseppe's trance-like attentiveness.

'Hey, Mr Giuseppe. Whatsamatter? You okay?' the young man enquired concernedly.

'Eh? Oh, I'ma sorry, Dennis. Issa justa thinkin'.'

'What about, Mr Giuseppe?'

'Well, Dennis. Now that yousa performing person, I think itsa good idea you make the mosta your appearance. Whadda you think?'

'Sure, Mr Giuseppe. I do muh best,' was Elvis's faintly absent reply.

'I thinka you could make a littla morea yourself.'

'How's that, Mr Giuseppe?'

'I think you looka plenty good if you change your hair colour by some dye,' suggested Al Capone's one-time fiddler.

'What colour?' asked Elvis, intrigued by the notion.

'Black like night, Dennis, black like coal, like oil, like diamonds!!'

'Uh, are diamonds black, Mr Giuseppe?'

'Eh? No, no, they's notta black, come to think of it. I just getta carried out! Anyway. You gotta make your hair black. It makea you a even bigger star. You be bigger than Mario Lanza, Dennis!'

Elvis liked this notion a great deal.

So it was that Elvis came to dye his hair.

Giuseppe did it for him then and there, in the back room at Giuseppe's Record Store, Memphis, Tennessee. (Giuseppe kept black hair dye for his own use.)

When it was over, Giuseppe Giuseppe could contain himself no longer. He drank in the beauty of his own creation adoringly.

'Santa Vittoria! Dennis eesha toppa notcha. Eesha glorious. Dennis you so beautiful I could cry! Mama mama mama! Dennis, oh Dennis, yousa beautiful!!'

And with that Giuseppe embraced the seated Elvis by the shoulders and planted a slobbery kiss on his cheek. Elvis sprang to his feet, losing Giuseppe like a soaked dog shaking off water.

'You cut that out, Mr Giuseppe,' cried Elvis. 'What are you, weird? You don't kiss men in this country, man. This here's America. You ain't in Italy anymore, man. Quit it!'

The newly raven-haired Memphis Flash cut across the room and banged the door in his wake.

Giuseppe slapped his forehead with his palm and moaned. 'Madonna!' he groaned. 'Why was I borned?'

It happened one night in Lubbock, Texas, that the Ringo Brothers Circus and Elvis Presley and The Blue Moon Boys were in town at the same time.

The Elvis show was being promoted by local radio station WANG and they had erected a stage at the drive-in movie park on the east of town. There were four other acts playing that night: Conrad Bimbo, a country balladeer; the Cement Block Boys, who were a barbershop quintet; Paddy Bland and the Deep Tones – a nondescript middle-of-the-road act; and 'Buddy' Holly and the Band (later to be Buddy Holly and the Crickets).

Buddy Holly and the Crickets!!
Elvis, Scotty and Bill!!!
On the same bill in 1955!!!!

What did they say to each other? Did they swap notes as founding fathers of the new music? Did they admire one another's acts? Was the air that night too rich to breathe?

It went like this:

The three acts who failed by a wide berth to go on to make a contribution to posterity did their turns and then the funny little guy with the ball of wool on top of his head and the wimpo spectacles played a fast, tinny but soulful set with his gormless-looking band.

While Buddy Holly played, Elvis sat in his dressing room (behind the popcorn, Coke and candy booth) feeding his face with Hershey bars. At the end of Holly's set Elvis was joined by Scotty and Bill who were enthusing over the bespectacled one and his band.

'Y'know, Elvis, you shoulda seen those boys go. They was real good,' said Scotty.

'They looked like shit,' said Bill, 'but they played sweet as a Georgia peach.'

Elvis pushed a last wedge of chocolate into his mouth, chucked away the wrapper and rose to his feet. Reaching for his big acoustic, he dismissed all talk of Buddy Holly simply by ignoring it.

'Okay, guys. Anything you wanna change in the set? No? Alright, let's get out there.'

So much for history's great moments.

Moments later, the Lubbock singer who unfortunately failed to exist for the show's star, stood in awe as the Memphis Flash came spinning out onto the stage just after Scotty and Bill had begun playing 'Mystery Train'.

This greased-up Rock 'n' Roll animal in a bright green jacket way too big for him, red trousers the same and pink shirt and socks seemed to have set all his limbs into perpetual motion. His legs spun and curled, his arms whipped and flailed and his guitar jumped and bumped off his gyrating torso. There was a wall of screaming as little girls wet their pants, bigger girls bit their lips and high school boys looked at the figure on stage, back at their own drab outfits and were suffused with inadequacy.

Scotty and Bill seemed to be holding the riff for an eternity; Elvis had catapulted to the mic stand and beyond already and now he had just retraced his slippery footsteps, missing the mic a second time. They knew what they were doing, he knew what he was doing: THWAK!!! Just like that, Scotty and Bill broke the riff precisely as Elvis hit the mic stand like a demonic lover and howled 'Train I ri-ide...'

The noise of the crowd as Elvis unleashed his voice was enough to whiplash the spinal cord – even that of a hard-bitten circus huckster like Colonel Tom Parker.

The Colonel had been passing on his way to town. The circus was all set up and ready to go for the first show the following night. Seeing the 2,000-odd crowd he stopped to get a closer look at the object of their attention.

What he smelt when he got closer was money. Not just money, but Money, *Money*, MONEY! This kid was driving these teenagers berserk.

There were an awful lot of teenagers in the modern world.

The Colonel decided to do a little market research.

'Scuse me, son. Who is that boy onstage?'

'That, sir,' said the kid he'd button-holed, 'is Elvis Presley. Ain't you heard of him, sir?'

The Colonel moved on and struck again, this time an eighteen-year-old girl.

'Scuse me, sweetheart. What d'you call that stuff they're playin' up there?'

NNNNNNUHHHRRRRRGGGGHHAAAAAAAAHHHHH!!'

Bemused and sprayed with spit, the Colonel moved on and repeated his question to a calmer-looking girl.

"S just peachy KEEN, mister,' she told him.

What Parker himself thought it was was a Godawful noise, but noise or no, it was definitely something big.

When Elvis had stirred up all the hysteria he was going to and the show was over, when he had knocked back a bottle of home-made lemonade that his Momma always sent out with him when he was working and when he had given himself a cursory mopping with a pink towel, the nascent star was accompanied to his car, a recently acquired Cadillac Fleetwood.

When he got to the Caddy, Elvis's face fell. The once-pink motor was covered in lipstick graffiti. 'I love Elvis, Signed Laetitia XXX' 'Elvis 4 Bernice' 'That's Alright (Elvis)' 'We Love You Because You're Elvis' and 'Elvis Is Keen!'[2] were typical of the brightly coloured scrawl that covered Elvis's first Cadillac.

Elvis practically wept.

'Poke a *pig*! I mean poke A PIG! D'you guys see that? Look at m'goddam car. They've ruined m' pokin' car! I'll kill the mothers! Shee-it! Is nothin' sacred to these people?'

'I kill the mothers, boss. Okay?' said Donald 'Montana' Cleaver, Elvis's one-time school pal and current bodyguard, a psycho highly regarded in Memphis. In Memphian circles, when the talk turned to psychopathic maniacs, Montana Cleaver's was the first name on everybody's lips. It was common knowledge at Humes High school that Montana used to beat his mother up when he got a bad school report and that he bred mice for bazooka practice targets in his back-yard. Everybody in Memphis knew Montana and everybody kept well clear of him.

A voice alien to the Presley camp intervened:

"T won't take much to get that fixed, son. Where you playin' next?'

Elvis glanced at the fat man with the big cigar and registered the owner of the new voice. He looked pretty prosperous and sounded very self-assured.

'Gonad Forward,' said Elvis meekly. This seemed like a formida-ble fat man.

'Fort Worth, huh?' replied Parker. 'I know a place in Fort Worth'll put that right for you in an afternoon.' Then he patted Elvis's shoulder in mock apology. 'Oh say! I di'n't interduce m'self. Parker is my name. Tom Parker. Folks call me Colonel Tom – from muh war days.'

The quaint thought occurred to Elvis that he hated the smell of cig-ars.

'Yep,' the fat man continued unprompted, 'fact of the matter is I'm a Dutch person. I come from Holland when I was a little bitty boy –'

---

[2] Interestingly, this became a popular saying amongst Elvis fans in those early days. The following year, 1956, Elvis had a cover story done on him by *Time* magazine. The writer, Horace Hearingaid, mistook the chant of 'Elvis Is Keen' he heard at a big gig for 'Elvis Is King'. The circulation of *Time* being what it is, Elvis as the King has become an accepted notion.

'Uh huh. I – '

'Matterafact – I don' tell ever'body this but I'm related to Queen Julianna – on her mother's side – and I'm sixteenth in line to the Dutch throne. Parker is onea the ristocratic names in Holland, y'see – '

'I – '

'But I run away from home. Guess I'm justa restless kinda fella. I got itchy feet, son. I like to keep movin'. You prob'ly a good deal like that yourself if muh guess is right, huh?'

'I don't know, sir, I – '

'Guess so. Yup. Guess so. Anyhow, I got business in Fort Worth tomorrow in any case, so why don't you all follow me over there in the morning'?'

'Well I – '

'Good, good. Here, have a cigar, son,' the fat man continued, poking a solid six-inch Havana at the Memphis Flash. 'Whyn't we go have us a little talk and get to know each other some? I seen your act, son, and, speakin' as a veteran of two decades in show business, I gotta tell you that you gotta lot of potential, but it needs developin' and marketin', son. Developin' and marketin' is the secret of where your success is gonna lie. I only got but two words to say to you, son, those two words right there: developin' and marketin'. Now let's find us a quiet spot for our little teet a teet. You know that expression, son? It's French for talkin' turkey. Mighty expressive expression.'

And turkey was exactly what Parker was about to make of Presley; gutted, stuffed, trussed and trimmed turkey, neatly laminated in a sanitised polythene bag.

Chapter 9

Big Time

By November of 1955, Colonel Tom, having quit the employ of Roger Ringo, had exchanged contracts with the Sideburn Kid as manager (Rob Robb had been foolish enough to sign no contract with Presley and the singer was easily persuaded to go with Parker, who promised to make him 'the biggest star in heaven'); had toured Elvis throughout the South; put Elvis on big radio shows like the *Louisiana Hayride*; signed Elvis to the biggest and best agency in the American entertainment industry, and, most importantly, persuaded BRA (Big Records of America), the country's most successful record label at the time, to buy Elvis's contract from Sam Phillips for $25,000 and a copy of Clarence S Doeful's definitive *Encyclopedia Of The Blues*.[1]

Elvis was happier than a pervert in a Roman baths. Big Records of America was the label that his heroes had all been with. Mario Lanza had done his best work on BRA. Soundtrack albums of the Dean Martin/Jerry Lewis movies came out on BRA, since Big Records was a wholly-owned subsidiary of the Gargantuan Corporation, owners of Gargantuan Studios on the corner of Sunset and Gower in Hollywood.

When Elvis signed with Big, he was a mighty proud man.

'I'm mighty proud to be with Big, suh,' he said to Ron Schnozzle, Vice-President in charge of A&R at Big and the man who was given the responsibility of developing Elvis's burgeoning career.

'That's mighty "Big" of you to say so, Elvis,' Schnozzle replied, digging the Colonel in the ribs and guffawing.

'Poke a pig,' Elvis thought dismally. 'What a goofball.'

If Ron Schnozzle was a goofball he at least worked for a record company with wide distribution. Wide as in complete.

Elvis went into BRA studios in New York over Christmas 1955. He

---

[1] This seemed odd to the vice-presidents of BRA, but at $8 a copy it meant they were getting the hottest new talent in popular music for a pittance – so who were they to grumble?

recorded with Scotty, Bill, The Jordanaires (on backing vocals) and the odd session musician to fill out the sound.

The first fruit of this came out in March 1956 and through exposure on nationwide television and a Parker-arranged press-blitz, 'Heartbreak Hotel' went to number one on the Country, R&B and Pop charts by April.

Ron Schnozzle says today that he was surprised at Elvis's studio *modus operandi*:

'Yes, Elvis didn't work at all like, say, Dean Martin or Perry Como. He would come into our New York studio with his band and then he'd begin some games to loosen up. His original band – Scotty and Bill – were used to his idiosyncrasies, but I guess the Jordanaires found it all a little strange at first. Frequently, Elvis would begin with a game of hide and seek. Scotty and Bill knew the ropes here: Elvis was never supposed to be found by whoever was seeking him. The new guys didn't realise this of course, and there were a lot of bad vibes when one of The Jordanaires found Elvis hiding – not very convincingly – under the studio piano.

'Sometimes, if the hide and seek went well, Elvis would instigate a game of piggy in the middle, with the understanding that neither he nor his bodyguard, Montana Cleaver, were to be piggy. It went without saying that Elvis should not be piggy; it was only common sense not to make Cleaver piggy – the guy was practically *rabid*.

'So when they were all loosened up, giggling and roaring with laughter mostly, Elvis would go off to a quiet corner and warm up his voice singing some operatic pieces. Yeah, I know it's kind of weird: the King of Rock 'n' Roll singing opera. But it's absolutely true. I remember that if the Colonel was there, he would be rather irritable if Elvis sang anything from *The Flying Dutchman*. I once heard the Colonel say to one of his aides that Elvis was being deliberately provocative. Maybe he was at that.

'Well, when his voice was good and ready, Elvis would go for a take. He was very, very meticulous and would do take after take until he was satisfied to the finest degree. He never tired of going over and over a song.

'You know the way Elvis moved on stage then? Well he moved pretty much like that when he recorded. It was quite a sight. There'd be all these singers and musicians working studiously, many of them from sheet music, all of them getting on with the job quietly. And then, there in the middle of the studio was this guy in the throes of an epileptic fit practically. Not many people ever saw Elvis at work in the '50s, but I can assure you it was really something.'[2]

Elvis's TV appearances in 1956 are by now justifiably legendary. To uncage on nationwide TV the sex beast that Elvis was purported

---

[2] From *Elvis – My Part in His Exploitation* by Ron Schnozzle (Schlep, Schmuck & Schlemiel, 1976)

to be caused a severe shock to the nervous system of 1950's America.

His best appearance was the first, when the new star guested on the Ed Sullivan Show, singing 'Heartbreak Hotel' and 'That's Alright (Mama)'.

Sullivan introduced Elvis in characteristic style:

'Now ladies and gentlemen, it is my great pleasure to introduce to you a new star who needs no introduction – where's my next cue – ah – Elvis Presley, the number one singer in the land.'

Sullivan broke a large cue card over a studio manager's head when the camera left him.

Elvis gave the nationwide audience his stage show verbatim and the director, a man of rare taste for his time and place, allowed mostly full-length shots of this whirling Rock 'n' Roll dervish.

In every American home with a TV set it was as if a Martian had landed on the living-room floor.

Picture it:

A serpent of subversion twisting around like a drug-crazed negro right before your hearthrug and your children.

Goddam nigger dancin'!

They shouldn't allow this on our TV screens!

Somebody oughta put that dee-generate in gaol!

In fact, Elvis did cause some severe outcry from the guardians of the nation's morality. The *Denver Dispatch* recorded a statement by Mrs Dolores Lillycrap made at the annual convention of the American Christian Decency Congress (ACDC) which was held in the Colorado state capital in April of 1956.

'This vile begreased hoodlum,' said Mrs Lillycrap, 'represents a regressive threat to our national conscience. This so-called singer cavorts before our nation's young people, exhibiting all the lascivious movements of a cheap burlesque dancer. This obscene Southern delinquent is doing his very worst to subvert America's adolescents with his base, immoral displays of wanton sensuality. Elvis Presley is little more than white trash, ladies and gentlemen, and something must be done before his disgusting attempts to arouse the libidos of our little girls begin to prevail.

'Elvis Presley, ladies and gentlemen, is un-American and *im*moral. If we want America to continue to be the great nation it has become over the last two centuries, then we must purge ourselves of this infection.'[3]

---

[3] Mrs Lillycrap later worked her speech up into a bestselling pamphlet: 'Rock's Demeaning Role: Why This Contagion Must Be Expunged' (Alfred E. Goebbels & Son Ltd, 1957).

One person determined to present this 'infection' in as moral a light as was possible when sandwiched between vapid celebrity chat and moronic adverts for irrelevant products was Steve Allen, presenter of the networked *Tonight Show*.

In his book, *Ten Minutes With Elvis On A Fifty Minute Show*, Allen tells of how he set about defusing this threat to the nation's virtue: 'Elvis's onstage movements back then seem pretty tame nowadays, but in 1956, before we had explicit sex scenes in movies, the way Elvis got on was strictly taboo.

'I thought long and hard about how I could best alleviate this problem. In the end the plan of action I adopted proved to be fairly satisfactory.

'I put Elvis in a bag.'

This was a drastic step, but not quite as extreme as it sounds. The bag was tied at Elvis's neck so that the millions of viewers watching were at least able to see Elvis's ecstatic facial contortions as he ripped through 'Hound Dog'.

Interestingly, here we have another example of Elvis's pioneering influence on the generation of artists that followed him. Although there is no record of John Lennon crediting Elvis with it, surely it is self-evident that the Lennon-Ono bagism of 1969/'70 was directly as a result of Lennon reading about Elvis's 1956 appearance on the *Tonight Show*.

As may well be imagined, Elvis didn't take instantly to the idea of being put under wraps for the telecast.

When Colonel Tom passed on Allen's idea to Elvis during afternoon rehearsals on the day of the show, the young singer exploded.

'A bag?? You gon' put me in a bag??!! Colonel, you gotta 'nother think comin'. I ain't goin' in bag. Are you *kiddin*'? You gon' stick me, Elvis Presley, the number one singer in three charts right now, into a pokin' bag on a network TV show?? You gotta be outta your *skull*, Colonel. Whynchaget back in a tent 'n' play with your pokin' elephants again??'

This rather atypical outburst – Elvis had, if anything, too much respect for the Colonel – shows the extent of Elvis's feeling about being curbed in any way. This was the man, after all, who moved on stage like an eel wired up to the Hoover Dam generators; he couldn't stand for this kind of tampering.

The odd thing is that he did.

The *Tonight Show* went out as Steve Allen had planned it. Viewers across the fifty states were intrigued by the idea of the hottest singer in popular music appearing bagged on their screens. Newspaper writers were derisive about what they saw as a cheap publicity stunt on the part of Elvis's management.

But Elvis went through with this undiluted farce.

Why? For the money, for the solid gold Cadillac that success brought him?[4]

What persuaded him to comply with the wishes of Parker and Steve Allen?

The simple answer is that we don't know.

Appearing on national television in a bag is the height of good sense when set beside some of the other dopy ideas Parker persuaded Presley to go along with later in his career.

One suggestion which has been floated is that Parker used to hypnotise his protégé.

Not much credence has been attached to this notion. The length and breadth of the issue, though, is that there just isn't any other explanation for the King Of Rock's practically masochistic subservience to his manager throughout most of his career.

Elvis's success in the US was repeated all around the world.

Rock 'n' Roll had arrived and, through a combination of hard work talent and media manipulation, the mantle of combined Rock 'n' Roll prophet and king fell upon Elvis's Tennessee shoulders. The global village was under way and somebody at this time had to be crowned king of the new music form. Posterity seldom makes mistakes and she cast her laurel at Elvis Presley, the most exciting and, by virtue of his white skin, palatable performer in 1956 Rock 'n' Roll.

Offers came in from all over the world for Elvis to go out and tour. Elvis wasn't averse to the idea, but the Colonel had little enthusiasm for any talk of leaving the North American continent.

The Colonel had other plans for his property.

In the autumn of that year, while Elvis, Scotty and Bill were hard at work touring across the whole bottom of the United States, an offer came to Tom Parker on the phone.

The secretary of Hal B Wallis, one of the biggest Hollywood producers of all time, was ringing Parker to enquire as to whether or not Elvis would be interested in a starring part in a picture soon to be made about the rock phenomenon.

When the Colonel passed the news on to Elvis, the singer practically perforated the Colonel's right ear drum, so loud was his ecstatic response.

'A movie?!!' he cried from a hotel room in Phoenix, Arizona. 'Do I wanna be in a movie?? Poke a PIG, Colonel, is General Motors in Detroit?'

---

[4] This specially commissioned Cadillac was so weighed down by 22ct gold fittings that it at first burned eight gallons to the mile. Later, its weight blew out the engine, leaving it virtually immovable.

'I'm gone sign you up for this picture, m' boy,' said the wily old dog, 'and when they see how good you are, they'll want you for a heap more pictures. Now you just sit on that one for a spell, son, huh?'

The movie when released was so rapidly a box-office smash that it was difficult to credit.

Jailhouse Rock was, for Hollywood in 1957, a laudably authentic version of the Rock 'n' Roll lifestyle in its infancy, made in black and white and on a budget that would have stretched Jesus Christ at the feeding of the five thousand. Despite the meanness of the studio outlay, the film still managed to garner some favourable critical response and of all Elvis's movies it is arguably the most watchable today.

Essentially, Elvis played the part of the angry, streetwise punk that many watching him in concert in 1956 took him to be. This was Elvis's image brought to life and it was only now and again in the plot that Elvis the polite boy who loved his Momma crept into view. Mostly, Elvis cut a convincing figure as a hard-nosed, embittered ex-con whose sensitivity has all but been dulled in prison. Vince Everett, the Elvis part, is a graceless know-nothing who can rock. Not only did the movie yield two of Presley's best post-'56 recordings – 'Jailhouse Rock' and 'Baby I Don't Care' –but it also contained the choice moment of Elvis's reply to a bluestocking who wants to know what he thinks about atonality in modern jazz:

'Lady, I don't know what the hell you talkin' 'bout.'

Chapter 10

Memphis Again

B
y this time, Sun Records had produced other hit-makers besides Elvis. Jerry Lee Lewis and Carl Perkins were perhaps the most notable, but also in there knocking out chart records were Roy Orbison, Charlie Rich and Johnny Cash. Billy Lee Riley, a downhome boy by upbringing and member of the lunatic fringe by inclination, was seen by many as the next Elvis.

With the Sun studios being in Memphis and Elvis still resident in the city, it was inevitable that he should know some of these performers. Several he had known when he was coming up himself and others, like Carl Perkins and Billy Lee Riley, he would know by sight or have heard of.

When production of *Jailhouse Rock* ended, Elvis returned to Memphis, pleased to get away from the rarefied atmosphere of the Hollywood Hills. In the movie capital of the world, Elvis had felt like what he was: a hick from the sticks. His whole experience of Los Angeles had been embodied for Elvis in one little incident at a party in Bel Air.

Introduced to a glamorous B-movie star walking away from her third divorce, Elvis was the soul of Southern gentility.

'I'm a piecea meatman,' he mumbled. (I'm pleased to meet you, ma'am.)

'How nice,' came the reply. 'That's just what I was thinking.'

Although the point of this remark escaped Elvis at the time, it was explained to him later. Elvis was justifiably incensed, and for years afterwards he would cite this tale as the epitome of Hollywood's attitude towards him.

Back in Memphis in 1957, resting up, Elvis paid a social call on his old patron, Sam Phillips. The resulting chat ranged over Hollywood; Elvis's new album; Graceland, the old mansion he had bought and was in the process of having renovated; Vernon and Gladys; Sun, and quite a lot more besides.

Elvis remarked on the recent Jerry Lee smash, 'Whole Lotta Shakin'':

'That boy went and did what I done all over, Mr Phillips. Ain't that something? Two records from Sun topping all three charts. I reckon this here's the centre of the universe, Mr Phillips.'

At this point, Elvis and Jerry Lee had yet to meet.

'When I come to Sun, Elvis was already giant,' writes Lewis in his autobiography.[1]

But Elvis, having been knocked sideways by 'Whole Lotta Shakin'', was anxious to meet the man responsible. He said as much to Sam Phillips on the occasion of this reunion.

Phillips explained that Lewis was back in Ferriday, Louisiana, at the moment, but promised to fix up something shortly.

'Maybe you boys could get together an' pick a spell.'

'For sure, Mr Phillips. It'd be a real pleasure. For sure.'

No more than two weeks later, Sam Phillips had indeed fixed something up. He had rung around a few people and now, right here in the studio, were sitting four of Sun's finest sons.

Elvis seemed reluctant to speak much at first, but Jerry Lee showed few signs of reticence.

'Hey, Elvis, I bet you all get through some chicken out there on the road, hey? What y'say? Hey?'

'I'm ah haw...' Elvis shuffled.

'Me, I get more ass than I can stash. You wanna know why?'

Silence.

'Well, I'll tell you why, Elvis. I git more chicken than I can use 'cause the Killer knows how to rock. Y'know what I mean? When the Killer rocks a girls she *stays* rocked!'

Elvis wasn't about to start discussing his sex life with a complete stranger, but he found this piano-pumper an engaging fellow.

'Yessir,' said the Killer, 'I seen some women and I ain't done yet. Good news travels fast. When them women get a taste a that good stuff I give 'em, the word gets around. I loved a lotta women and I'm gone love me a bunch more.'

Elvis stood bemused before this human dynamo.

In a little while they got down to playing a bit together, taking turns to hammer out gospel music on the studio piano. Johnny Cash and Carl Perkins, future touring partners, were there too and joined in with the Killer and the King.

Presently Lewis pounded into 'Whole Lotta Shakin'' and Elvis took up the mantle in the second verse, with Perkins picking reedily in the background.

'Oooh-ee!!!' hollered Jerry Lee as he bashed down the last chords. Everybody laughed.

[1] *The Killer Never Stops Rockin', You Mothers!* (Harvard Univ. Press, 1979).

'I wanna tell ya, Jerry,' said Elvis; 'this here's the most fun I had since I discovered the cheeseburger.'

Next, the Quintessential Quartet lurched into a shaky rendition of Chuck Berry's 'Rock 'n' Roll Music' in which everyone took a verse. In quick succession followed 'Blue Suede Shoes', 'Great Balls Of Fire', 'Shake Rattle & Roll', 'Blue Moon Of Kentucky', 'Hound Dog', and 'Tutti Frutti'. After that, Elvis, who was on piano now, took the tempo down by moving into 'Just A Little Walk With Jesus'.

With the topic of Jesus in the air, these four Bible-Belt products quite naturally began to discuss God and religion when they had finished the hymn.

'I know I'll always believe in the Lord, spite of all the boozing 'n' whoring,' explained Jerry Lee.

'Hallelujah, brother.'

'Amen.'

'Amen.'

'Fact is,' continued the Killer, 'I's gone' be a preacher 'n' everything, but it didn't work out right. Truth is, friends, I'm a weak man. I like to drink some an' I like a sweet woman better'n I like m'self. Can't say more than that. I tell you, boys, if God made anything better'n a woman, he kept it for Himself. 'S why I ain't a preacher, friends. It's sad, but it's true.'

There was a respectful pause.

'I tell you, Jerry,' said Elvis, 'a man does what he has to do in life. Maybe you just wasn't cut out for preachin'.'

'The hell I wasn't! 'F I'd a been a preacher I'd a hollered outta that pulpit so fine I'd a raised 'em outta the back pews!'

Everybody laughed.

Then this unique little gathering sang some more hymns which have since appeared on record, though, incidentally, the rockers they sang have never surfaced.

While all of this was going on, Sam Phillips was running the tapes and smoking a cigarette with Fay Vest. It wasn't the big deal that it would seem twenty years later, that was for sure.

When the musicians were tired of playing, talk turned to what the others were going to do when they got as big as Elvis. They all wanted a horse ranch and a Cadillac of one kind or another. Carl Perkins wanted a rare Gibson guitar and contentment; Johnny Cash wanted to travel the world's railways; and everyone knew what Jerry Lee wanted, so there was no point in going into that one.

Then a little tension developed.

'Tell you right here, Elvis,' Jerry Lee contended, 'I'm overtakin' you around the world right now, 'n' I ain't right started yet. I'm gonna be so big you gone look like Tom Thumb.'

Elvis rose to the bait.

'You watch your ass, Lewis. You ain't had but one little itty bitty bit of a hit.'

'Little itty bitty hit? I'm the only one but you that topped all three charts and I ain't but starting out. Ol' Jerry Lee is here now boy 'n' I'm durn'd sure here to stay.'

'You fulla shit, Jerry Lee,' said Elvis, laughing.

'Listen, bub, Jerry Lee's the Killer *and* Jerry Lee's the King! You mark that well, Elvis Presley.'

'Shit, you little peckerwood; *I'm* the King!'

Just then Carl Perkins chipped in his contribution.

'I'm the man behind Johnny Cash,' he said.

'And I'm gone to get me a drink,' said Cash.

In five minutes the studio was empty but for Sam and Fay.

Phillips gave his assistant a lugubrious glare and spoke dolefully:

'I just wanna be the first to say that rock stars were always a pain in the ass.'

Sam Phillips was a man out of his time.

Back in Hollywood in 1958, Elvis was being touted for the lead in *I Was A Teenage Werewolf*. This inspired piece of casting would have given the Hillbilly Cat his most apposite role, but things being what they are in Hollywood, this was just one more project that didn't go according to plan.

Elvis's agent in Hollywood, Mitchell de Graft, recalls this frustrating year in his memoirs.[2]

'In 1958 it was hoped, of course, to follow up Elvis's extraordinarily successful cinematic debut with a suitable vehicle. On the face of it, this doesn't seem like a very difficult task. With the benefit of hindsight, one can see that footage of Elvis clipping his toenails would have been a box-office sensation in that year.

'I guess 1958 was just a jinxed time for Elvis.

'First of all there was the attempt to cast Elvis in *I Was A Teenage Werewolf*. Personally, I was relieved when this didn't work out. I felt very strongly – and still believe to this day – that this was entirely the wrong vehicle for Elvis.

'When that fell through, the film version of *Sons and Lovers* was being mooted and negotiations for Elvis to play Paul Morel went to a fairly advanced stage before falling through. In the event, *Sons and Lovers* wasn't made until the following year with Dean Stockwell in the part. It's one of the tragedies of the history of cinema that Elvis didn't play Paul Morel.

'There was some talk of Elvis doing a picture with the working title of *Skinny Dipping Off The Seychelles*. This to me sounded like a sound

[2] *Elvis And The B Movie – His Part In Its Downfall* (Cashcow Ltd, 1967).

business proposition. In the movie, Elvis was to play a former farm-hand raised in poverty in Nebraska, who, after a series of dead-end jobs as merchant sailor, pilot, circus clown, taxidermist, female wrestler, bouncer and brain surgeon, ends up diving for pearls with a score of Asian beauties off the coast of the Seychelles. The plot had a lovely hook: the girls discover Elvis dyes his hair and, deciding that he is no more manly than themselves, establish a feminist colony which, in the picture's distinctive denouement, stages a coup and turns the Seychelles into the world's first independent feminist state. Elvis, meanwhile, learns his lesson, lets his hair grow out and lives happily ever after as an eccentric pearl-diver.

'This was a revolutionary movie in 1958. I loved it, Colonel Parker loved it and it didn't matter a damn what Elvis thought anyway. The only reason it never got made was that the Colonel asked too much money for Elvis and the project was blown out.'

All this time, Elvis was kicking his heels in a rented mansion in the Hollywood Hills, He wasn't particularly knocked out with any of the film projects which he heard about. (Fortunately he never heard about *Skinny Dipping Off The Seychelles*, or he would have had a portent of things to come.) Scotty and Bill were back in Memphis working with another band until they heard the Colonel's call. So it was that Elvis fell into a deep depression. Sure, there was no shortage of starlets to hump, but there was no Rock 'n' Roll in Los Angeles. There wasn't much Rock 'n' Roll anywhere in the world in 1958, but what there was of it was concentrated in places other than LA. Elvis began to pine for home, southern cooking and his music.

He was bored rigid.

When no firm project had materialised by July, Elvis returned to Memphis for the second time in as many months – this despite Parker's protests. The singer was broiled in frustration and coiled with tension.

His first night back, Elvis got in touch with Scotty and Bill and the Blue Moon Boys met up at Sal's Diner. Over cheeseburgers and chocolate shakes, Elvis told the boys about the tedious time he had been having under the shadow of the Hollywood sign. They listened sympathetically and tried to ease Elvis's troubled mind.

'Fuck 'em all,' said Bill. 'I guess Hollywood's always been like that. There ain't no soul up there. 'S all just money. No more, no less. Forget about it.'

Scotty Moore suggested they go back to his house and strum a spell. They piled into Elvis's Fleetwood and cruised down to Seltzer Street.

So it was that four years after the original Elvis, Scotty and Bill session in this front room, the band reformed and began again. They roared into the old material with verve and desire. Elvis's heart, which had been buried in Hollywood, soared as he howled 'Milk Cow Blues', 'Good Rockin' Tonight', 'Tryin' To Get To You' and 'My Baby Left Me'.

The air was thick with joy.

When they broke up to get some sleep that night, they agreed to meet again the following afternoon to do some more strummin'.

Next afternoon, Scotty suggested playing Elvis a pile of records he'd been listening to during the year and the three of them drank coffee and listened to the phonograph for a couple of hours. In the late afternoon they began to work out the songs that appealed to them most. By the time the trio was ready for bed they had rehearsed a set of songs that excited them more than somewhat.

After the torpor of Hollywood this exhilaration made it difficult for Elvis to sleep, but he finally managed to doze off.

By the time Elvis was awake and functioning the next day, Scotty had already made an arrangement with Sam Phillips to go into the Union Street studio and record that night.

The resulting, adrenaline-charged session yielded ten finished tracks. On the night of July 15, Elvis, Scotty and Bill, with Phillips at the mixing panel, cut the traditional 'Blue Ridge Mountain Blues''; Hank Williams' 'Hey Good Lookin'' and 'Why Don't You Love Me'; Buddy Holly's 'Rave On'; Fats Domino's 1957 hit 'I'm Walkin'''; Eddie Cochran's definitive teenage anthem, 'Summertime Blues'; 'Johnny B Goode', Chuck Berry's paean to a Rock 'n' Roller not unlike Elvis himself; Lieber and Stoller's 'Kansas City'; a new, slow version of 'Don't Be Cruel' and Little Richard's 'Good Golly Miss Molly'.

Afterwards, Elvis was moved to make an exuberant offer to mate with a porker.

In succeeding days Elvis was in touch with the Colonel, discussing the feasibility of releasing as soon as possible the fruits of this most recent Sun session.

The Colonel was as diplomatic as he could be, but when pushed he revealed that his plan was for Elvis only to release soundtracks from his movies in future. This was sound business sense, the Colonel argued, because the movies would sell the soundtracks and *vice versa*.

'Shit, Colonel,' Elvis cried, 'this here is the best music we ever made, sir. I want to get this stuff out right away. I been sittin' on m'ass up there in Hollywood half the year doin' sweet FA. I'm 'bout fit to be tied, Colonel. I ain't gone wait much longer for another movie. I want to get some singin' an' playin' done. An' I want this buncha songs out on an album *now*. Do you hear what I'm sayin', Colonel? Do you hear what I'm sayin'?'

Parker made some conciliatory remarks and flannelled. He had no intention of putting this album out now or in the foreseeable future.

If he could just get the deals closed in time, Elvis would be starring in a picture just going into production which, in Parker's opinion, suited him down to the ground. And the soundtrack album would have an even larger than usual market since there had already been a best-selling Broadway musical of the project. Yes, Elvis Presley in *South Pacific* would keep the Colonel in Havanas for the rest of the decade anyway.

Elvis's last Sun session never would have seen the light of day had it not been for the course of events which made a new career departure a necessity in the winter of 1958.

Elvis's role in the Rodgers and Hammerstein vehicle never came off, of course, and a subsequent attempt to cast him in a remake of the 1940s Saturday morning serial *Captain Marvel* (an ideal part for the former Memphis Rocket Man) also failed to get off the ground.

Meanwhile as 1958 ground to a conclusion, an increasingly irritable and anxious Hillbilly Cat slept by day in Memphis and prowled by night, partying and staging full-scale re-creations of some of his favourite historical events.

It was at this time that Elvis fell in with the men who came to be known as the Memphis Mafia. Bored with inactivity, Elvis turned to the fastest set in Memphis, the Orifices and the Burkes, two families who had all the organised crime in the city tied up. The Orifice/Burke gang ran a numbers racket and dealt in protection. For laughs, they liked to pummel the Cadillacs of Memphis businessmen with a baseball bat.

The Orifices, (pronounced or-eh-fee-chay), were of Sicilian descent and a lot of bad habits had descended with them. A prominent Memphis grocer who had reneged on protection payment woke early one morning to find himself floundering in a sea of pasta – macaroni, to be precise. If his wife hadn't returned at dawn from a tryst with her lover and opened the bedroom door, thus allowing the pasta mass to slither out into the hall and down the stairs, her husband would certainly have drowned in there.

The Membranes were an Irish family and used to enjoy a good game of hurling on rollerskates down the sloping aisles of Memphis' main supermarket. Many a housewife used to return home from shopping with a fractured skull or a broken ankle.

This was the group of people that Elvis adopted as buddies during the depressing winter of 1958.

Bill Orifice, today serving a 99-year sentence for posting a pizza-bomb to the Inland Revenue Service in Washington, fondly remembers the early days of Elvis's association with the Memphis mafia:[3]

<hr>

[3] *Good Clean Fun With Elvis And The Memphis Mafia* (Faber & Faber, 1977).

'We used to re-enact great moments of history right out the back at Graceland.

'I guess the best one we ever did was when Elvis and us boys laid in the right clothes and a bunch a girls from Hollywood and did the Rape of the Sabine Women. The only problem was getting those Hollywood girls to offer some resistance! Hell, it was the best fun we had since we put on our "Sheik out the Harem" do. That's one little party I don't intend to go into.'

In the twelve months up to Christmas 1958, Elvis had failed to star in *I Was A Teenage Werewolf*, *Sons and Lovers*, *Skinny Dipping Off The Seychelles*, *South Pacific* and *Captain Marvel*. The one-time Memphis Flash had not made a single concert appearance since *Jailhouse Rock* began production back in August, 1957. Elvis's last album, *The Christmas Album*, had been recorded with its predecessor, *Rock'n'Roll*, in the spring of 1957: a long time ago. The songs which had been recorded at Sun in July, 1958, had yet to be released.

Elvis's career was at a complete standstill, Something had to be done quickly.

Presley's notion was that a full-scale tour of the record markets of the world was in order. No rock star had set off to play around the world before. The tour could be billed as the 'Elvis Presley World Tour, 1959'. They could do dates in North America, Western Europe and Australasia. It would be a landmark in the history of popular music. Elvis would appear before *millions*.

Parker's notion was something else altogether.

A world tour, Parker argued, would be so complex as to be impossible to arrange, and – even if it were feasible – the expense of staging the tour would be astronomical, far exceeding any possible profit. He did, however, have an idea of his own, one which would take Elvis to every major city in the US and guarantee an enormous amount of publicity.

Nothing like Colonel Tom's plan had ever been staged before. It would be an extraordinary, unique experience for the tens of thousands of people who managed to get tickets for it. And, the Colonel contended, his idea would be just as much a landmark – more! – as Elvis's idea of a world tour.

The scheme which the Colonel had cooked up was, like all the best conceptions – and some of the worst – simple.

Colonel Tom Parker presents:

THE ELVIS PRESLEY ROCK 'N' ROLL CIRCUS!!!

After releasing four 45s from the *Jailhouse Rock* soundtrack, BRA were anxious to have more Presley material available – speedily. With the circus tour almost entirely set up now, and no sign of a movie project to yield another soundtrack album, Parker conceded that it might not be a bad idea to release the 1958 Sun sessions.

BRA issued Elvis's version of 'Why Don't You Love Me' backed with the new, slow version of 'Don't Be Cruel' to herald the opening of the circus. The record went straight in at number one on all three charts, which pleased everybody in North America but Jerry Lee Lewis. (These two sides were picked up by performers in years to come. Both Elvis Costello's 1981 version of 'Why Don't You Love Me' and Billy Swann's 1974 cover of 'Don't Be Cruel' are note-for-note copies of the 1958 Elvis, Scotty and Bill arrangements. Strangely, none of the music press spotted these similarities.)

The album, 706, Union Avenue was launched with the Elvis Presley Rock'n'Roll Circus on March 15, 1959. 706, Union Avenue, named after Sun's address, would have been hailed as a triumph by the rock press, had there been one. Instead, it was greeted by the establishment press in mixed terms.

'ELVIS RETURNS TO STICKS AND CLICKS,' said the *Variety* headline.

'Mr Presley has not yet lost his talent for disturbing the peace. No doubt this record will appeal to fourteen-year-old girls by the thousand, but as a piece of popular music it has little to recommend it in *this* author's view,' wrote the *New York Times* critic.

'Elvis Presley would do well to get back in his tree. On the evidence of this offering, perhaps he already has,' quoth *Time* magazine.

'Ten rockin' little records in one package,' said *Billboard*.

Nothing written at the time of its release does justice to 706, Union Avenue. For a proper appreciation we have to go to the British weekly *New Musical Express* and Charles Shaar Murray's 1976 in-depth feature on the Presley *oeuvre*. Murray lists only five essential Elvis albums, the 1958 Sun effort amongst them. Of 706, Union Avenue he writes, 'It's easy to see with the benefit of hindsight why Elvis was able to produce one of Rock'n'Roll's definitive recordings in the summer of 1958, but it's not so easy to see how three lone musicians can make so full a sound doing what were practically live takes and a sound so different from the first Sun sessions. Me, I think Sam Phillips was a sorcerer.

'Whatever the explanations, 706, Union Avenue assaults the nervous system and makes the adrenaline flow like nothing so much as sex. 706, Union Avenue IS sex. Down there in Memphis, Elvis, Scotty and Bill tuned into – and channelled onto recording tape for posterity – the fundamental energy sources of life.

'Rock'n'Roll is the beat of life and Union Avenue is Rock'n'Roll like nothing before or since.'

Union Avenue entered the American album charts at number one and stayed there for nineteen weeks, a record never equalled, not even by The Beatles.

The Elvis Presley Rock 'n' Roll Circus opened in Philadelphia on March 15. The big top was sold out for its six-day engagement a month in advance.

Now, on the occasion of its debut, a crowd of 4,000 swirled around the tent and its satellite attractions. For the punters, most of them teenagers, there were hoopla stands, pinball arcades, coconut shies, dodgem arenas, shooting galleries, carousels, a ferris wheel, a variety of stomach-churning rides, a little zoo, a freak show and, more than anything else, souvenir stalls.

These souvenir stalls, controlled by the Colonel, sold every conceivable piece of tacky junk that could be embossed with 'ELVIS'. Elvis scarves, T-shirts, sweatshirts, cardigans, jeans, baseball bats, sneakers, mugs, post-cards, button-badges, sew-on patches, beermugs, wigs, jackets, jerkins, statuettes, toilet-seats, wallpaper, rugs, tooth-mugs, pens, pencils, rulers, erasers, notepads, writing-paper and envelopes, flower-pots, lamp-shades, teddy-bears ('Just wanna be your...'), fluffy stuffed dogs ('You ain't nothin' but a...'), pendants, knuckle-duster rings, ear-rings, posters, photographs (autographed by Bill Orifice and Wilf Burke), wristwatches, toothbrushes, combs, brushes, footballs, softballs, car-stickers, tissues and – best of all – toilet paper.

Colonel Tom was nothing if not the soul of bad taste.

Inside the big top, audiences had a plethora of circus acts to wade through before they got to see the man for whom they had shelled out their dollars.

The ringmaster was none other than the Colonel himself, resplendent in a suit tailored from white cotton with a primary-coloured polka-dot pattern, towering under the roof of the big top on 15-foot stilts. All his experience with the Ringo Brothers stood him in good stead, as he piled hyperbole on hyperbole and weaved his spiel over the witless punters.

'Now, ladeezngennelmen, pre-ZENT*ing* the worrld's foremost trraPPeezze art-teests; frrom HUNGARRREE... the Garr*ribald*eeee Twinsah!!!'

And later:

'Soft and delicate, gentle and *fine*, the ex*quisite* Pat-RISH-a PARA-MOUR and her PERRFORM-*ING* PIGEONZZZ!'

And later:

'Ladeezngennelmen, a BIG hand for the most *dangerous* act in this fabulous ELVIS PRESLEY ROCK 'N' ROLL CIRCUS!!! What you are about to see involves the arteests rrRISKing EVERY *major organ* in their bodies. From POLAND, ladeezngennelmen, the most thrilling, chilling, AWE-inspiring FIRE-EATING performers in the circus world!!! *Theee* BADASKI BROTHERS!!!"

By about this time a chant of 'ELVIS! ELVIS!! ELVIS!!!' would break out amongst the teenybopper contingent of the audience – in other words, *most* of the audience. But the farce would continue.

…the most SKILLLFUL *jugglers* – the LEMON FAMILY!!!'

'ELVIS!! ELVIS!! ELVIS!!!'

And later:

'…from IND-EE-AH, ladeezngennelmen – INDIRA KHAN!!! And so can her EL-E-PHANTS!!'

'ELVIS!! ELVIS!! ELVIS!! ELVIS!!'

And later still:

…time for some *comedy*, ladeezngennelmen – from ITALY, that *well-known* and well-LOVED family troupe of CLOWNS, the CAN-NETELLETELLONIS, featuring CO-CO!!!'

'ELVIS!! ELVIS!! ELVIS!! ELVIS!! ELVIS!! ELVIS!!!'

And finally:

'And NOW, ladeezngennelmen, the man you've all been WAIT-ING for, the HILLBILLY CAT, the MEMPHIS FLASH, the *KING* OF ROCK 'N' ROLL –'

'ELVIS!!!!!' interjected the crowd.

And there, suddenly, was the boy himself, framed centre ring in a pale spotlight, wearing a boxer's dressing gown and swinging with a microphone stand.

Then ZAP! another spot framed Scotty and Bill and DJ Fontana, the drummer, and the Jordanaires, and a brass section all packed neatly into a mini-orchestra box at the side of the ring. They laid into the familiar chord slide that opens 'Jailhouse Rock' and right on cue Elvis stormed into the song as the audience shrieked its approval. The song finished to cataclysmic applause.

Elvis disappeared from view. Then – gracious me! – he returned on a – no it can't be; yes, it bloody is – unicycle?

Nobody could believe it, but it really was happening: the King Of Rock 'n' Roll, in his first concert appearance in over two years, was rid-ing a unicycle around the centre ring as he crooned 'Heartbreak Hotel'.

The audience was dumb-struck. But there was worse to come.

The King went on to remove his gown, revealing a gold lurex leo-tard and took his unicycle up to the high-wire. Then, with the protec-tion of a thoroughly tested safety net, Elvis rode his unicycle slowly across the wire as he sang 'All Shook Up'.

The Elvis Presley Rock 'n' Roll Circus had been booked through sixteen US cities with average stopovers of three days. Blitzed by the critics after the Philadelphia opening, the show headed south and west. Elvis was confused and angry. He hadn't wanted to involve himself in the circus end of the tour, but had, of course, been persuaded into it.

Relief, for Elvis, came by the time they hit New Orleans, where it was agreed that Elvis and the band should simply do a straight concert performance. By then, however, it was too late. Bad news travels fast, and sales in the cities succeeding New Orleans were so low that the Colonel was forced to cancel the rest of the tour.

The Colonel kept a very low profile around Elvis at this time.

Elvis raced back to Graceland and vowed that if he ever saw another circus he would hire some artillery and blow it off the landscape.

'Poke a pig, man,' he said to Bill Orifice. 'How do I let myself in for these things?'

Enough said.

Chapter 11

Elvis Is Back (Co-Co Is Gone!)

The failure of the Parker-Presley Circus tour brought about the first major slump in the fortunes of the Elvis phenomenon and it was obvious to all concerned that immediate revival was necessary if Presley was to avoid becoming the Captain Scott of Rock 'n' Roll.[1]

The huge losses incurred as the carnival had worn an ever-wearier and ever-emptier path around the Southern States had had a particularly dispiriting effect on ol' Colonel Tom. Smitten by another attack of *avaricious walletus* (symptoms – swelling of hands directly proportionate to diminution of artistic sensibility) the old boy was faced with a dilemma his stetson-shadowed brain was ill-equipped to cope with: where to invest his last million dollars.

The obvious and sensible answer was for him and his gofers to wind up the publicity machine afresh, to get Elvis in the studios to make a *good* album, then to line up some real live appearances for Elvis and a basic band. No fire-eaters; no human cannonball; no little unicycle for Elvis to ride across a tight-rope on while singing 'All Shook Up'. A little faith and a big media blitz and it was more than likely that the fans could be retained and the Elvis ship could sail into calmer waters.

But perhaps the Rock 'n' Roll business is often characterised by the lack of common-sense shown by its main protagonists. What else could explain Parker's decision to forget Elvis and hit the trail to Vegas, wallet bulging, casinos beckoning, to 'chew thangs over'?

A gummier chewer there never was.

Meanwhile, the former Memphis Rocket Man was spending his time at Graceland with the Guys welcoming a steady stream of would-be buyers for one Big Top (slightly used) and a convoy of wheeled animal cages. It must have seemed to Elvis that a jinx was on him at this time since he soon discovered that, even as a tent salesman, he was a failure. The Presley lawns remained draped in white canvas.

---

[1] A frozen turkey.

Commenting on this phase in Presley's career, Dennis Chang Jr said,

'Elvis, he's depressed. He can't sell the tent. He needs money bad. He doesn't hear from Colonel Tom. We say to him, Elvis, we say, something gotta be done, an' then we kick Elvis's ass. Real hard. An' he wakes up.'[2]

It was a time for decisions to be made and Elvis, totally without precedent, showed an amazing willingness to make them *all on his own*. Unable to reach Parker, Elvis was doubtless hurt and feeling rejected after his first run-in with failure. it was probably this which prompted him to call up his old mentor at Sun, Sam Phillips. Sam's assistant, Fay Vest, recalls:

'Elvis rang Sam *up*, y'know, and told him the position about the circus *flopping*, y'know? And he said what should he *do*, y'know? So Sam set up a time when they could meet. I'm so tired now... y'know what I mean?'[3]

The meeting took place in the swimming pool of the Memphis Travel Lodge on March 18, 1960. The date is remembered by rockophiles not only for its significance to Presley's subsequent career revival, not only as the one and only time that Elvis managed to erase the looming shadows of Parker long enough to get his nose back on the trail of his musical roots, but also because absolutely nothing else happened in the then stagnant world of Rock 'n' Roll that day.

After three hours in the pool two things emerged – a twenty-five-yards certificate for Phillips and, just as important, the execution of plans for the *Elvis Is Back* album. Mort Nightman, life-guard:

'Yeah. They wuz in there ah – ah – three hours. Yeah... ah... one, two... yeah – three. Dat Sam Phillips, yeah... good strokes. Slow. Strong. Yeah. Good.'

Seen now as an Everest on the Rock 'n' Roll landscape, *Elvis Is Back* took the Hillbilly Cat back where it all came from. Originally planned for recording in the cramped conditions of 706 Union Avenue, the old Sun Studios, the unexpected sale of the tent to a New Orleans sailboat manufacturer meant that Phillips and Presley and some of his boys could buy gas to take one of the caravans left over from the circus down to Nashville and BRA's Studio Z.

With Scotty Moore, Floyd Kramer, Bob Moore, Murray Harman and The Jordanaires all sat in back of the circus caravan, Elvis was brimful of optimism the morning they drove north on Highway 40.

[2] *Karate Time With Elvis* by Dennis Chang Jr, with Johnny Carson (Bimbo Books, 1978).

[3] *Elvis, Me, Three Orang-Utangs & Seven Different Adhesives* by Fay Vest (Restless Urges, 1981).

Elvis Is Back was recorded over March 20/21, 1960. The title had a particular significance for Presley. It came from a saying of his mother's right back when he was just another schoolboy in pink shorts and powder-blue pedal-pushers. Every morning he would leave the house for Humes High, to return five minutes later to the strains of Gladys calling upstairs to the lethargic Vernon, 'Elvis is back, he's forgotten his sandwiches again.'

Elvis Is Back is a seminal album that has been chronicled in' practically every rock history tome. The album shifts through a wide spectrum of musical moods from the bluesy 'Like A Baby' through to the orgasmic 'Such A Night' which simmers with understated eroticism before pounding to a climax in the final verse. The fourteen tracks on the album are all classic Presley, but perhaps the two which were deleted when the album was re-issued in the late '70s deserve special mention. On 'Brand New Cadillac' and 'Rockin's Set The World On Fire' the regular Presley band is augmented by Jerry Lee Lewis on piano and Roy Orbison on guitar.

In Presley's version of 'Brand New Cadillac' the regular beat is syncopated by Lewis's left-hand piano boogie, giving it a muddy, jumpy power which gains energy as the song builds to a blinding climax of sax, piano and Orbison's and Moore's guitars fighting for supremacy, leaving Presley to lapse exhausted as the song fades out to his legendary sign-off:

'Beat your brains out boys, I've had it... Poke a pig...'

The other title, an Orbison original, is a potent rhythm song in the vein of Little Richard's 'The Girl Can't Help It'. The lyrics must have had particular personal significance for Elvis:

'The boy just stands there
Guitar in hand
Twitching to the beat of the
Bar-room band
Hands pull his hair out
Feet slap the floor
Gone, gone, gone
They want more, more, more
Got anything you desire,
'Cos my rockin's set the world on fire.'

Throughout *Elvis Is Back* the old urgency and energy are back, but one wonders how much of this daemonic power would have reached the ears of the world if Elvis could have known what Parker was up to in the Las Vegas Hilton. Even as 'Fever' dripped from the Presley lips, the wily ol' boy leaned across to film producer Hal Wallis, Southern Comfort in hand, and said, 'I'll have my boy ready for you in three weeks.'

The controversy surrounding the release of *Elvis Is Back* is widely stated but rarely discussed. The stories which abound about Parker returning from Vegas, a three-film deal in his mitts, to find 'his boy' had not only recorded an album, but had authorised the pressing, are confusingly varied. Some tell of how Parker, on finding a demo pressing of the album on his desk, called Presley and, on hearing the story, told him their partnership was over. Others say it was Elvis who made the call. Some tell of Parker taking all his clothes off and bouncing on his head around his office singing 'Memories Are Made Of This'. Obviously some stories are more reliable than others.

In the event, a compromise was reached between Elvis and the Colonel, born out of a mutual recognition that the two were inextricably bound to each other, not only legally, but in an indefinable emotional way.

The compromise, plainly stated, was this – Elvis would get the album released and Parker would see to the attendant publicity IF Parker got his movies. In retrospect, Presley's acquiescence seems foolish. He blew the one chance he made for himself to square up to the Colonel once and for all. Elvis didn't need to back down on the album release. The sheer weight of Parker's personality was too much for Elvis's zilch character. The boy was put back under wraps even as *Elvis Is Back*, to phenomenal reviews, hit Number One worldwide, without even the benefit of a TV appearance.

Tracks from the album which were played on network TV shows were run over old films of Presley in his Sun days. Ed Sullivan scooped with a Sam Phillips interview. Steve Allen had to make do with Fay Vest, the first of eighty-four appearances she made on his show.

The album had been top of the charts for four months and still nothing had been seen or heard of Presley. 'Is Elvis Dead?' rumours began to crowd the newspapers and TV news, a neat counterpoise to the wave of 'Is Bing Alive?' badges flooding the nation at this time.

Elvis wasn't dead, but, for almost three years, he might as well have been.

Chapter 12

B-Movies?

On August 1st 1960 the world premieres of *Driving A Sportscar Down To A Beach In Hawaii* took place in twelve US cities simultaneously. Very little advance publicity had been planted. From July 4th onwards small ads had appeared in trade papers announcing 'New Elvis Movie Soon', finally stating the date and theatre of presentation in the week of premiering.

Expectant fans, hot from the energy of *Elvis Is Back*, packed the cinemas coast-to-coast to catch a glimpse of their hero on screen. The verdict was unanimous.

'An enormous pile of crud' – *Time*.

'Oh Gawd. Tack-*ee*.' *Variety*.

'Nyaagh.' *Chicago Tribune*.

'Lousy, steaming horse-shit.' *Washington Post*.

'Not as good as it might have been.' *Elvis Fan Magazine*.

On the face of it, a negative response.

With the benefit of hindsight, can we perhaps be said to have judged it too harshly? Of course not! It's an atrocious movie. The plot involves one-armed helicopter pilot Mick Jefferson (Elvis) and his efforts to become accepted as an Olympic swimmer despite his physical disadvantage. For no apparent reason Mick (Elvis) has to leave his penthouse suite in Los Angeles and fly to Hawaii where he can buy a red sportscar which he drives down to the beach every day to strengthen his one good arm.

Elvis plays golf[1], drives, swims, dives, flies, and, it is implied, screws a lot of women in beach-houses, but he cannot have the only woman he really wants – Sheree (Nancy Sinatra), the wife of pioneering doctor Ernie (Bill Bixby) who, towards the end of the film, fits Elvis (Mick) with a new plastic arm indistinguishable from the one he loses in the tussle with a shark which he has in the opening scene of the epic.

Some scenes more than others stretch the audience's credulity. For instance, in one memorable set-piece Elvis is driving Sheree to the

---

[1] The film's publicists were subsequently sued by the Advertising Standards Authority of America for using the slogan 'You'll Give Your Approval For Limb Removal When Elvis Tees off Wide.'

beach in his Porsche. Two close-cut close-ups show Elvis's hand on the wheel followed by a shot of him with his hand down Sheree's blouse. In several other scenes Elvis is shown playing guitar and getting a real tuneful sound, chords and lead licks and all, simply by slapping the instrument against his thigh.

The songs, by Colonel Parker's newspaper boy, Ned Wombat, are less than memorable: 'Sittin' In The Sand (Lookin' For My Hand)', which follows the shark fight, is a forgettable ballad in the vein of 'Fever', but without the strong melody or the intelligent lyric. Other hits include 'Do The Frug As You Twist About With Your Hula Hoop Spinning Round Your Short-tops', 'I Got Sand (In My Eye)', 'Fell For You (Stood On A Jelly Fish)' and the single from the soundtrack, 'Sheree, Ernie, You're Both Wonderful People'.

For the movie's director Trevor Pillock, this was to be the end of the road. 'Myopic Trev' as he was popularly known seemed to have difficulty spotting what was on and what was off camera. Shots are badly lined up, cameras are in view – even old Trev himself appears in shot from time to time. Pillock's final work ranks right up there with *Attack Of The Killer Tomatoes*.

To be fair though, Pillock cannot be expected to carry the can for the whole fiasco. Parker, for instance, ever-conscious of the need to save money, insisted the film be shot on 8mm stock and blown up. It was Parker as well who forced a compromise out of Pillock: that the beach scenes be shot in the Nevada desert. This explains how Mick and Sheree can take those long walks to the beach and never get there. All good space for passion to grow.

The whole shebang cost only $16,000 to make and, in view of the profits, was the soundest business *ever* made (that's ever likely to be made in the whole history of the world) but at what sacrifice to Elvis's artistic credibility?

After the first week, box-office receipts plummeted to zero. The single from the album of the movie sold less than 70,000 and went only as far as 97 on the Hot 100 for one week, even as *Elvis Is Back* still reigned supreme at Number 1. The single from the album hit Number 14, mainly on the strength of the B-side, the alternative blues version of 'Blue Moon of Kentucky' recorded for Sun back in 1954.

The movie was an unqualified disaster. Elvis, in Graceland, followed world reaction on his giant TV, with increasing depression, resentment growing against Parker. The Colonel, for his part, saw only the mountain of greenbacks filling his basement and smiled.

For Elvis *Driving A Sportscar Down To A Beach In Hawaii* brought back traumatic memories of the circus tour, the big difference being that, this time, there was no Big Top to sell and put the disaster to an end.

The disaster this time was due to run and run. After its initial success and flop *Driving A Sportscar...* made enormous profits on the cult cinema circuit in the manner of *The Rocky Horror Picture Show*. Cinemasochists would cram out small theatres nightly to revel in the glorious kitsch. Dressed in their Elvis garb, one hand secured behind their back, they would sit and mouth all those dumbbell lines memorised from incessant exposure to the picture. It was an unreality inspired by the unreality of the movie itself and one which continued until the final print was withdrawn and destroyed in the enigmatic Presley Purge of the mid-'70s.

Elvis, naturally, was less than keen to participate in the follow-up to *Sportscar*, but Parker had acquired a written statement from him promising that he (Elvis) would turn over Graceland and all his record royalties from 1960 onwards to Parker if the three movies weren't completed. Colonel Tom hadn't graduated from the School of Hard Knocks for nothing.

It was a surly, half-hearted, mumbling Elvis who stumbled through *Little Girls Grow Up Fast And Grope Me*. The plot was worse than the previous movies: Elvis, a teacher in a convent school, is continually attacked by his classes before regaining the voice he lost at college and becoming a pop-star. The songs ('Take Your Little-girl Eyes (Off-a My Thighs)'; 'Don't Get Bored, Look At The Board'; 'Let Me Lick The Chalkdust From Your Nose' etc.) were dire, period.

The movie, another artistic catastrophe, still managed to amass huge profits at the box-office. Die-hard Elvis fans couldn't believe that *Sportscar* was anything more than a momentary lapse.

Throughout the nine months during which the two movies were made Presley's domestic life diverted in another of its series of bizarre directions. By day he was a plastic movie actor making bad plastic movies. By night he sought to escape from the superficiality of his daytime reality by making his own movies.

With some help from Ted Geppeto, one of the Guys and an ex-pro puppeteer, Elvis learned how to sculpt puppets using fibre glass and wood. He picked up the skills of lacing the bodies together and even made up clothes for his toys. Then, using bare continuity scripts, written by Elvis, he and his friends would put the puppets through their paces in a short series of movies that were, ironically, nothing more than microcosmic re-tellings of his own professional mishaps.

Some were almost completely autobiographical – *Roustabout* had a puppet Elvis as a Wall of Death rider who joins a carnival: no disguising the allusions to the circus tour. Others such as *Speedway*, about a racing driver in a red sportscar and *Blue Hawaii*, about a happy-go-lucky beach boy, also have obvious links with Presley's real – if it can be termed that – existence.

The puppets are immaculate, the songs less execrable than in the big movies, but there's something weird about the whole exercise. The films, not unearthed from Elvis's private files until 1975, reveal a concerted effort to achieve a perverse psychological balance by Presley. Much the same way as a drunk tries to put his hangover headache in order by having a few shots of whiskey.

The final film (there were seven altogether) is a four-minute display of the puppets burning. It was probably produced in March 1961 – precisely a year after *Elvis Is Back* was released – coming just as Elvis fulfilled his three-picture contract for Parker with *Lotsa Lady Lifeguards, Acapulco*.

However, before the last of this uplifting movie cycle was released to an undeserving public, Elvis had totally disappeared. He was not to be seen for nearly two years.

Chapter 13

Lost Weekend

The Lost Weekend was the title of an old Ray Milland movie about an alcoholic who begins to lose his memory.

Elvis's lost weekend, from March 1961 until beyond Christmas 1962, didn't involve Presley reaching for the bottle to escape. He took a more drastic measure by walking out of Gargantuan's studios in Los Angeles after final shooting on *Lotsa Lady Lifeguards, Acapulco* was completed.

Elvis took a limousine to the airport, booked onto a Boston flight under the name of Ernie Sullivan (the Bill Bixby part in *Sportscar*), and, pausing only to buy a few clothes and a copy of Jack Kerouac's *Desolation Angels*, hit the coast road to Cape Cod.

The first night he slept on the beach. The next day, looking dishevelled and depressed, he went into the Cape Cod barbershop for a close-cut that would make him unrecognisable as the King of Rock 'n' Roll.

Jennie Lee Marshall, daughter of the barber shop owner:

'I remember this guy coming in and me thinking there was something familiar about him. I was alone in the shop. I used to help my daddy out sometimes and he'd gone sea-fishing that day. Business was real slow then, just before the tourist season began but, anyway, this guy came in and says "Mmmmmmmm" and I said, "What did you say?" and he said, "Shortcrop haircut, miss," and I cut it and suddenly I realised this was Elvis Presley.

'I said, "Hey, you're Elvis Presley," and he said, "Don't tell no one, miss. Please don't tell no one, miss. " So I said, "You made some dumb-ass movies and turkey records lately," and he said, "I ain't gon' make no more though. Don't say nothin'".'

'I didn't. I was the only one who knew who he was and he stayed up here eighteen months and I got him a little job selling winkles and cleaning out boat-houses. All the time he was there we'd lie in bed and look at those newspaper headlines about him being in Frankfurt and all that stuff. They were happy times. The world wasn't so crazy then.

'But I always knew he'd go eventually.'[1]

Of all the revelations about Elvis that have come to light, Ms Marshall's must count as the most remarkable. Though strange, the idea of the King selling winkles is just about plausible – BUT ONLY IF HE WASN'T IN THE ARMY. And there are eighteen months worth of headlines which prove that he was.

The Official Elvis Biography, published in 1981 by Parker's publicists, states the following:

March 19, 1961 – Elvis conscripted to US Army.

Elvis Presley was passed A-1 at the pre-army medical and given two weeks' notice of departure for US Army base, Frankfurt, West Germany. At a special press conference Colonel Parker said that he was proud of the way his boy was facing up to his responsibilities. Adding that Presley was unable to be present as he was spending his last few days at home with his folks, Colonel Parker read a short statement from Elvis which simply said:

'Sorry I cannot be there. I trust the Colonel will inform you of how proud I am to be given this opportunity to serve my country. God Bless America.'

(This press conference was later made available as an EP by BRA, *The Colonel Reads Elvis's Press Statement On Going Into The Army*.)

The biography substantiates its report with back views of Elvis's new haircut and German photographs of Elvis in a tank 300 yards away or Elvis 'just out of shot' in an Army athletics meeting. Here are some of the newspaper headlines through to Christmas 1962:

ELVIS LEARNS TO SHOOT; PRIVATE PRESLEY ON PARADE; PRESLEY TRIES LONG JUMP (picture of apparently one-armed, long-haired Presley in enormous sand-pit with hulahoop around his short-tops).

All the evidence points to a gigantic fraud cooked up by Parker to dupe the world into believing that Presley was out of sight in a noble cause.

Jennie Lee Marshall:

'Hell, he simply couldn't believe what they said about him driving tanks and all that stuff. He'd sit back and laugh, especially when he saw that statement Parker read out for him. "God Bless America," Elvis repeated, and continued: "and poke the world."'

It seems incredible now that Parker managed to pull off this unlikely ruse. Elvis had in fact already been called up in 1959 but Parker had managed to get his boy exempted from regular service on the grounds of the good work he was doing for the population in general, a plea unanimously accepted by the Forces Appeals Comm-

[1] *Elvis' Secret and his Enormous Dangler* by Jennie Lee Marshall (Verging Publishing, 1980).

ission. The episode, not unnaturally, had been kept under wraps at the time to stop accusations of shirking exactly those duties that the Colonel was later to exalt in the press.

As Elvis winkled, washed and womanised, the Colonel and BRA were not sitting back. Parker managed to persuade BRA to put the William Morris Agency onto the case to keep Elvis's name in the media. Not that he was worried by the disappearance, but he knew that the army hoax would soon have run out of steam. One cunning ploy had given the Colonel two years' relaxation but there was always the chance that someone would discover that, amongst the thousands of men in the numerous US camps in Frankfurt there was no Elvis.

The boy would have to be found eventually but, for now, there was no need to panic. BRA continued to release albums despite the prolonged absence of the man behind them. *Elvis Is Back* stayed Top Ten for almost 15 months and Top 100 until 1965 – an incredible phenomenon. The Sun material was re-packaged into one album, *Sun of Elvis* (really), which went Top 20. Other tasteful BRA packages released during Elvis's disappearance were *The Best of Elvis's Movie Songs plus Three Other Great Hits*, which scraped into the Top 20, mainly on the strength of the other great hits; *First Person Elvis*, which was a group of songs with 'I' in their titles, and *Elvis Sings/Elvis On The Telephone*, a double set, the first record being a collection of almost all the dross not good (!) enough for the soundtrack albums ('I Beat My Bongos On The Beach", 'Pump Up My Arm Bands', 'Who Stole (My Board Rubber)' etc.), and the second a series of short discussions Elvis had on the phone with various luminaries, taken from Colonel Parker's personal tape catalogue.

Highlights include 'Elvis Gets Mad At His Grocer':

ELVIS: You din bring m'tomatoes today.

GROCER: Ah did, Elvis.

ELVIS: You did NOT. Get over here NOW with it.

GROCER: Ah cain't. M'wife just died.

ELVIS: You lyin' sonofabitch.

GROCER: She did.

ELVIS: Okay. G'bye.

GROCER: Ain't you got no feelings you – CLICK.

Or there was 'Elvis's Phone Busted':

ELVIS: Hello? (Brrrr) Hello? (Drring drring) Hello… it's Elvis. (Brrr) Dang! This pokin' phone's busted.

The album was packaged in a gilt-coloured sleeve containing pictures of 'Elvis In The Army' and sold for $10. It hit the record stores and nose-dived.

Elvis, whiling away his time in Cape Cod, took Jennie Lee up to the mountains for weekends and, like Kerouac in *Desolation Angels*, they'd just stare and think and dream. It was the happiest time of Elvis's whole life. But it would soon be over.

In November 1962 Cape Cod was caught up in a blizzard when two men in dark overcoats drove slowly into town. Booking into the only hotel open at that time of year, they asked where they could get a shave and trim. Pointed towards the Marshall barbershop three doors away the men sat in the chairs provided as Jennie Lee and her father – who was now aware of Elvis's true identity – set to work on their three-day beards. Old Marshall, nonchalantly friendly, asked them what brought them to the Cape in November. One of the men replied that he was looking for his brother, whom he went on to describe. Jennie Lee and her father's eyes met in a flicker of understanding. These men were detectives who were looking for Elvis.

When the men had returned to their hotel, Jennie Lee went and told Elvis of the incident. Taking the $8,000 he had had with him when he had arrived at the Cape, Elvis, in the Marshalls' pick-up truck, beat the trail for New York. Fighting through appalling conditions it took him almost twelve hours to reach Idlewild Airport. There he booked onto the first flight to London.

As Elvis landed at Heathrow on November 28th, 1962, Jennie Lee and her father watched despondently as the three men walked past the barbershop. The third man was the missing brother...

Chapter 14

The Holy Grail

London was fog-bound. Shortly after Elvis arrived, the airport was closed for two days. Presley looked around, probably wondering what he was doing there, then went up to the customs gate. Customs officer Charles Minns remembers the feeling he got when he opened Elvis's passport:

'Well, of course he was travelling under his real name; or at least his passport had his name in it. I looked at the passport, looked at him and told him he'd need a visa. Some woman back down the queue was whispering to her friend and, though he didn't look like the Elvis I'd seen on TV, I heard her mention his name. So I took him into the office at the back and looked after him.

'All through the visa business and the waiting, Elvis was awfully nervous. He didn't want anyone to know he was there and offered the two other blokes and me quite a large amount of money to keep quiet. Naturally we didn't take it, being British.'[1]

From Heathrow, Elvis took a cab into the heart of London. He walked around until he found a cheap hotel, left his small bag of clothes there and took off for a walk.

At this time Elvis's appearance was substantially different from the conventional image we have of him. He had a half beard, being in the habit of only shaving when he took a notion of it. His hair, even in these pre-Rolling Stones days, was long – over his collar – and fell into a straggling fringe at the front. It had returned to its natural blond colour and Elvis had given up grease. Effectively, he could have been any beatnik, and was able to walk around London unheeded.

Presley stayed in London until the fog had lifted and spent most of his time walking and thinking. Most of what we know about the early part of his stay in England is built up from conjecture, but we do know that he went to the Eros beat club on the evening of the 29th. Appearing that night were Beatcombers Inc and Stormy Weather and the Hurricanes. It was Elvis's first experience of what was to become

[1] *My Life Before I Met Elvis Once*, by Charles Minns (Dulldouanier Books 1976).

the second great phenomenon of Rock 'n' Roll – the British Beat Boom. But it wasn't to be the last.

What must Elvis have thought as he watched the two bands play? They were billed as 'rhythm 'n' blues but they must have seemed far-removed from the R&B Elvis had grown up with. No sweating, world-weary black men here, but all-white, all-clean city boys. Yet the songs were the same.

It must have been an irony that was painful to Elvis to see a new generation covering the old generation's material. *His* generation's material, which, in its time, had been a refinement of what they had heard when they were as raw and as hungry. A fly on the wall of Elvis Presley's hotel room could have told us whether the experience was a depressing or an invigorating one.

The British beat boom was to bring big revivals in the careers of first-generation rockers like Chuck Berry and Carl Perkins. Could it also pave the way for an Elvis resurgence?

The *Daily Mirror* carried the following headline on November 30th, 1962: ELVIS IN BRITAIN? GI POP STAR SEEN AT AIRPORT.

The exclusive story had been related to the *Mirror*'s newsroom by the lady in the customs queue spotted by Charles Minns. It was a pretty flimsy tale with no one offering any concrete evidence that Elvis really was in England, and it had been filled out by bottom-of-the-barrel 'Elvis a deserter?' text.

The story was enough however to make Elvis apprehensive. By noon he was on the first train he could find out of the first mainline station he came across. The train, he discovered, was bound for Liverpool. He'd heard something about that place when he was in high school. It had been a great port for emigrating to the Promised Land of America. It would be as good a place as any for him to go; perhaps it would be the gateway to opportunity for him too.

But when he came to be standing on the banks of the Mersey looking to the west, the dark lonely sea seemed to offer anything but opportunity. He felt tired and alone. Watching the rhythm of the sea, its unpleasant colour and polluted depths made him feel ill. His stomach heaved with the tide and he threw up the egg and tomato sandwich he had eaten on the train. Then, out of the blue, he felt a hand on his shoulder. At first he thought it was somebody who had recognised the Memphis Flash, but the grip felt reassuring and Elvis turned to face the clear blue eyes of a small thin man in his thirties.

'You okay, buddy?'

There was no mistaking the New England accent. Elvis gulped.

'Sure. Thanks. I don't go too well with these waves.'

'Hey, you American?'

'Yeah.'

'Yeah. Tennessee boy, huh?'

It was the beginning of Elvis's first conversation in days. The small man, it turned out, had just arrived from the States on a freighter. Elvis told his tale, but no names were exchanged so it sounded as if Elvis was just some guy on the run from a couple of detectives.

The sailor was headed for London and, within a few hours of their meeting, Elvis was all ready to go with him. They would hitch rides to save the rail fare; said the sailor, little realising that Elvis had upwards of $5,000 with him and was worth a thousand times that in his socks. Deciding against revealing who he was yet, Elvis went along with everything the sailor said.

It was difficult to pick up lifts in the middle of an English winter and particularly difficult for a wiry sailor and a long-haired beatnik.

They made it as far as Manchester, then had a two-hour wait by the roadside until they were picked up by the popular presenter of the TV show *Sunday Night At The London Palladium*, comedian Bruce Forsyth, who recalls:

'Well, alright. Yes, of course I didn't know it was Elvis. I'd only seen him on the telly. Alright. So, of course I just talked to them. About things. The sailor seemed to have a thing about American novels. Well, I don't know much about them, or about English novels come to that, but I babbled on anyway. Might as well, eh? If you keep talking, you never know, you might come up with something funny. And that's it really. Alright my love?'[2]

Elvis and the sailor arrived in London on November 30th. They stayed at a doss-house near Charing Cross station. During the days Elvis and the sailor would take in the sights, and in the evening they would go to counter-culture jazz clubs. Although Elvis and the sailor had become firm friends, Presley could not understand his companion's reaction to the music. The sailor would go frantically wild and gyrate furiously in the middle of usually small dance floors. Occasionally he would grab a girl and they would shake it down together in a frenetic free-form jive-dance. The sailor always tried to get Elvis up too but the singer never would until, one night, he heard a guy playing 'Volare' like Charlie Parker. Memories of his favourite Italian operas crowded his brain and suddenly he was up on the floor, left leg twitching, lip curling, hands slapping thighs. In the middle of this free crowd he looked weird but people generally took to his odd dancing.

When they were bedding-down that night, the sailor, through the darkness, whispered, 'You're Elvis Presley, ain't you?'

Elvis felt no hostility in the question.

'Yeah. I am.'

'Not in the army?'

[2] Bruce Forsyth in *The Rolling Stone Interviews* (Nowhere Press, 1971).

'No. How'd you know it was me?'

'The dancing, man. The King Of Western Bop – he dance like that. Nobody else. I suspected it first when we went in the record store and you turned all the Elvis album sleeves back to front. You get a nose for these sorta things.'

'You gon' tell anyone?'

'Go to sleep, man.

The final night they were in London, the sailor suggested they go somewhere different. He had a ship the following day and, despite Elvis's offers of a job or financial assistance, he would join it early the next morning.

The sailor wanted to see something of the new group music that was currently blossoming, so it was for this reason that the two men found themselves sitting in the Kingfisher Cellar just off Soho watching a rhythm 'n' blues band from Liverpool. As they drank beer and watched the band, Elvis felt a growing excitement clambering over his jaded musical spirit. He looked around. Most of the crowd were kids of maybe 17 or 18. All of them were totally immersed in the music pouring from the little AC30 amps and the battered drum-kit.

A sense of déjà-vu caught Presley and it took him a moment to realise that it wasn't him that was exciting these teenagers, nor was it likely to be unless he got off his ass and did something again. If he needed more of a kick than this, he got it when the leader of the group, a stocky short-sighted youth, made his final announcement:

'We're gonna finish now with a song that was a hit for an old hero of us all. Elvis went in the army and is dead over in Frankfurt... "Blue Suede Shoes".'

Walking from the club the sailor put his arm around Elvis's shoulder: 'Hey man, they was just joking. You ain't dead. You's just asleep.'

'No, they was right. Who was they?'

'Called The Beatles or somethin'. Man they sure had beat, I tell you. Now, how about another drink?'

The next morning came and the parting was brief if emotional.

'I never did know your name.'

'Well you know all us sailors, we called Jack. Jack Tar. Just remember Jack. Maybe I'll write a book about you someday.'

'What you mean? You a writer?'

'I had a couple books out. But this is life. Livin's life. Don't forget that, Elvis. See ya.'

And he was gone.

Presley, in that strange crossover mood between despair and determination, walked and thought and booked a flight back home.

But, before he left, he slipped into the offices of the *Mirror* on Fleet Street.

'I'm Elvis Presley. Look: here's my passport. I just wanna say I ain't in the army. You think this is maybe news?'

Chapter 15

Bringing It All Back Home

The headlines in the British newspaper the *Daily Mirror* on December 22nd 1962 blew the gaff sky-high with its announcement 'Presley – The GI Who Never Was'. Elvis had given a fairly superficial account of his life since the third film, but, by cross-referring events actual with events announced by the Parker publicity machine, the text made formidable and impressive copy. Presley also allowed himself to be photographed in the English winter and, though he still differed appreciably in looks from his publicity pictures there was no doubting the depth of the eyes and the curl of the lip as belonging to anyone other than Elvis Presley.

It was the run-down to Christmas, world-wide, and the newspapers, as ever, were looking for some human-interest story to give them the chance to play down the usual international incidents, skirmishes, disasters and so forth, and Elvis's revelations were the ideal peg for the hole. When the rest of the media got wind of events there was a mad rush to procure radio, TV and magazine interviews with the ex-Sideburn Kid, but Presley refused all, save an interview with BBC chat-show man John Freeman. Freeman, on his *Face to Face* programme, was famous, in part, for having pulled some painfully honest responses on the contemporary adolescent conditions re society, sex, drugs, the generation gap, etc. with English singer Adam Faith. Faith had proved an intelligent, honest respondent, bright and articulate. Elvis, as he sat under the lights awaiting the recording to begin, suddenly realised that here he was, for the first time, hiding behind no superficial image, faced with the prospect of making naked revelations about the myths behind the legend he had become.

With five seconds to go, Presley froze, then, strangely, regressed into another persona. A transcript of the interview, which was never shown, is exclusively reproduced below.

(MUSIC)

JOHN FREEMAN: Good evening, ladies and gentlemen. As you no doubt know, over the past few days there have been some startling revelations made in the national press by, and about, ex-King of Rock 'n' Roll, Elvis Presley. Tonight, I have here with me, Elvis himself.

Elvis, can I begin by asking you how you came to be in England?

ELVIS: Well, Frank and Bing were coming over. I thought I'd join them for a few rounds at St Andrews.

FREEMAN: I'm sorry – you came to play golf?

ELVIS: I did.

FREEMAN: Well, this wasn't in the papers. What about the Army? You were never in it?

ELVIS: No, Italians aren't liable to US conscription.

FREEMAN: Italians?

ELVIS: Yes sir.

FREEMAN: You're Italian?

ELVIS: Yes sir.

FREEMAN: Astonishing. And Elvis Presley? That's not an Italian name?

ELVIS: No it isn't.

FREEMAN: So how did you come to be called it?

ELVIS: Called what?

FREEMAN: Elvis Presley.

ELVIS: I'm not.

FREEMAN: Not what?

ELVIS: Not called Elvis Presley.

FREEMAN: Then what are you called?

ELVIS: I'll sing one of my hits you all know me,

at which point Elvis stood up and ran through 'Volare'. He thought he was Dean Martin! Freeman and the studio audience were astonished, even more so when he launched into 'Memories Are Made Of This' in straight Italian. Finally the show's producer, Dick Mellot, cried, 'Somebody carry this crazy out' and Elvis/Dean, babbling in perfect Italian, was escorted from the studio. As far as anyone knew he'd never received any instruction in a foreign language and, frankly, had trouble with American. It was a bizarre psychological phenomenon.

By this time the Colonel was back on the ball and had sent orders through to his London agents to get Elvis back to America immediately. On arrival at New York's Kennedy Airport, Elvis, still convinced he was Dean Martin, was escorted dazedly (the Dean identification extended to the symptomatic drink-numbed personality) to a waiting car, pausing briefly to call Jerry Lewis and tell him he never wanted to work with him again, before being whisked off to a private sanatorium near Boston.

For the next two months Elvis rested, 'dried out', played golf and so on while Parker appeased the world with tales of how his boy had been in the Army but had been discharged in a shocked condition on the death of his non-existent sister, Eloise. (The gullible world, as ever, believed the publicity machine but these, finally, are the facts.)

By the beginning of March 1963, Parker, after a series of consultations with Presley (now restored), had convinced him that the time had come for some more recordings. Studio time was booked at the Californian Disneyland Recording Studio but Presley had a new adamance and determination about him now. He didn't want to cut records in a place populated by Mickey Mouses and Donald Ducks, where all the session men were made of candy and the songs of candy floss. As he put it straight to the Colonel:

'No more of that goddamn film-type shit.' The Colonel, uncharacteristically uncertain of himself at this time, re-booked at BRA's studio in Nashville. Presley, meanwhile, had called Sam Phillips and asked him if he'd produce what was planned to be Elvis's first completely country album. Phillips felt he would be out of his depth, being more of a bluesman, and put Elvis in touch with Owen Bradley who had worked with Patsy Cline and Jim Reeves and was peerless in the respect he received from the country music community. Bradley was surprised but agreed to take on the challenge. Parker, on Presley's insistence, put Bradley in charge of finding musicians and material. Then, on May 26th and 27th, 1963, Elvis laid down another album that was to restore him to the peaks of his earlier successes – *Western Bop & Country Boogie*.

To be frank, some of Bradley's earlier work with big country names had brought accusations from some quarters that he had contributed considerably to the 'dilution' of country music into pop, and therefore rather transient, music. Jim Reeves, for instance, had made the crossover from being a straight, ethnic country star into an international showbiz singer. Inevitably, when an artist begins to outgrow that first cult following of hard-core fans, and sees his market expand, the 'Sell-out' cries reverberate endlessly. Bradley could hardly be criticised for his work with Presley, however, of a sell-out. There are none of his less acceptable commercial devices evident on *Western Bop & Country Boogie* – none of the too-clean dobro work or angelic choral backing vocalists, or syrupy strings. A tougher sound was achieved by using only a basic fiddle/guitars/bass/drums country combo. This was necessary, for Elvis didn't want to clean up his sound: the appalling film soundtracks were antiseptic to the point of nausea. Rather than smoothing the dirt out, Elvis and the band, under Bradley's guidance, shovelled it in, and with considerable success. Elvis, fresh from his lay-off, felt tough and restored, and it showed in his voice.

The album, released in July 1963, contained some of Elvis's finest recordings ranging from a fast-paced 'Lonely Weekends', the old Charlie Rich number, to a bouncy mid-tempo 'Walking After Midnight' to a hauntingly beautiful re-recording of 'How's The World Treating You?' which Presley had first put on acetate back in

1956 shortly after his move from Sun to BRA. The thirteen tracks on the album covered a wide range of country sounds – the maudlin ballad, the boogie-woogie Joe Turner style, a little rockabilly, and it all came dressed in a plain red sleeve with only the album's title printed in small white letters at the top and, along the bottom, in lower-case typeface the words 'Elvis Presley sings thirteen country classics'.

Reviews for the album were excellent in general, though a few of the newer critics, aware of the blossoming folk-rock circuit, raised doubts as to whether or not the album was appropriate to the modern music scene or whether it was merely an old rocker being nostalgic. Sales, however, were poor. Disc-jockeys, still trying to live down the embarrassment of premiering 'new, unheard Elvis' singles like, 'Sheree, Ernie, You're Both Wonderful People' which went straight from the mailbox onto the turntable and into the dustbin, had written Elvis off as a musical force and, in the swinging teenage scene of early '60s America, he seemed as relevant to youth culture as the Great Caruso.

Parker was disturbed by the album's sales. By August 14th, 1963, one month after release, the album was still nowhere to be seen on the Pop Hot 100, though it had reached the lower twenties of the country charts. A single from the album, 'Waiting For A Train', made the Top 30 but Parker, in his infinite wisdom, flipped the single when sales began to drop off, hoping to squeeze more money from it. The B-side, 'Throw Down Your Satchels And Let's Do The Frug', from the teacher movie, did nothing to restore public faith in the new Elvis sound.

Again, something was needed. In late August Parker called Presley to his office in the Las Vegas Hilton to discuss publicity plans. Parker's 'Watergate' tapes, discovered in 1975, tell the story.

PARKER: Well, Elvis boy, nobody's buying th' album.

PRESLEY: No sir.

PARKER: Ah don't know wha', boy.

PRESLEY: 'Cos they think I'm a dumb shit has-been, sir.

PARKER: Yeah, so we gotta git you back out there, show em you ain't.

PRESLEY: But I am sir.

PARKER: You AIN'T! We gotta be positive. Now I think you should tour.

PRESLEY: Ah, poke a pig! Not another poking circus.

PARKER: We was just unlucky last time Elvis boy. We'll be okay this time.

PRESLEY: I AIN'T GONNA GO TOURING IN A POKING CIRCUS AGIN!

PARKER: YOU IS!

PRESLEY: AH AIN'T.

PARKER: Okay Elvis boy, Forgit the circus. But you gotta tour.

PRESLEY: Where?

PARKER: Ivrywha. All over tha' country.

PRESLEY: No circus.

PARKER: Jus' a coupla fire-eaters.

PRESLEY: NO POKING FIRE-EATERS!

PARKER: Elvis, boy, we needs a GIMMICK! Now, why not ride a unicycle across the stage in one of your numbers?

PRESLEY: Okay. On one condition.

PARKER: Yeah?

PRESLEY: That ah can park it IN YOUR DAMNED ASS!

The tour was booked, provisionally for ten dates, beginning in mid-October and ending November 16th, 1963. Venues proved difficult to find mainly because, as ever, Parker was hustling for more of everything – more money, better facilities for his boy, more seats – only this time promoters were unconvinced that Presley could pull enough of a crowd in whilst riding on the reputation of the circus tour and the terrible movies. Nobody was willing to take any risks. What finally corrected this was Parker's offer to put Elvis on for free, in Memphis, and invite possible clients to observe and hear the new-style Presley.

One of those rolling up to the Memphis Auditorium on October 12th, 1963, was promoter Barney Lovell, (now a millionaire baby product manufacturer); Lovell: 'We were sceptical. Elvis, to us, had joined Chuck Berry, Jerry Lee, L'il Richard, Carl Perkins and them in Nothingville. Those guys were legends but only in people's heads and in their old record collections. They just din' sell no more. They were nostalgia. So we were really goin' to the show for the free cars fat Parker had promised. About eight o'clock, we were all sat there, about fourteen promotion men and Parker and his staff and maybe 3,000 others all there for free. Man, things are so dull in Memphis, they'd a gone to see ma grandpa cut his toenails. Anyway, we were sat there and then he's on stage, Elvis –just him and a l'il country band. He begins with 'Mystery Train' then does a couple of his old Sun things, then begins on his new stuff and pretty soon we're all rivetted. He's hot and sweaty and the band's really cookin' and then about 35 minutes into the show – just after he does 'Move It On Over' – there's this yelp from the audience and this guy bounds on stage and I see Parker mouthin' "Oh no, who's this jerk?" Then we see it's ol' Jerry Lee himself and he turns to us and he says, "Man, this Elvis can GO! He's COOKIN'" and then he speaks to the piano man and the band and next things we know Elvis with Jerry on piano is doin' 'The End Of The Road', then 'Great Balls Of Fire', then Jerry stands up and says to everyone, "Elvis is the King. Ain't never seen no-one better than that," and there was no-one disagreein' with him that night. Man, ol' Jerry Lee, he's a crazy dude.'

The phenomenal success of the concert meant instant bookings though the promoters were inevitably shrewd enough to realise that, even if THEY knew Elvis was back that wouldn't be enough to convince the punters, so things were still cagey.

At some point between the concert and the beginning of the tour Elvis went to see Lewis in Nashville. Although friendly, the two men didn't socialise but it seems that Presley was there to ask Lewis to do the tour with him. Jerry Lee, recording at the time, was committed for the length of Presley's jaunt, but invited Elvis to sit in on a few numbers in the studio with him. Elvis, conscious of the legal tie-ups of his BRA contract, was keen to be reassured that all tape-machines were off, then he and Lewis, with the Memphis Beats, Jerry's back-up band, ran through a wide repertoire of Rock 'n' Roll and country classics.

The session became legendary, and stories radiated from the studio about how seasoned session men, normally mechanical and indifferent in their reaction to music put down, were leaping around ecstatically, thrilled by the generated tension of the Lewis/Presley synthesis. Rumours persisted that a tape did exist, after all, but these were denied by both protagonists until an interview Lewis gave in 1977 to Norma Brudda of the LA free paper, *Sunspot*:

There is a tape. I have a tape. Elvis has a copy. After recording we went back to my hotel and I brought it out and played it. Elvis wasn't happy with the legal thing if it got into the wrong hands. But we were both convinced it was the best thing either of us had ever done, before or since.

BRUDDA: And is it ever likely to be released?

(At this point, Brudda notes, Lewis leaned forward in his chair, stuck his finger sharply into the middle of her chest and said, sucking on his cigar) Mother, the goddam world don't DESERVE such class, no ma'am.

NEVER.

This was to be the last time Lewis and Presley would meet for five years, though Lewis recalls a curious phone-call while Presley was on the country tour.

'He rang me up and sounded good and said the tour was going great guns. Then I heard someone come into the room behind him and suddenly he began singing "Volare" and he said to me "I ain't makin' no more films with you NOT EVER or my name ain't Dean Martin an' yours ain't Jerry Lewis", then I heard a groan and someone go out and Elvis said, "That was the Colonel. Sorry about that, but I like to keep the old guy on his toes now and again – puts the do-doos up him." I never did understand Elvis completely, weird guy!'

Chapter 16

Ooh, Mah Soul!!!

The tour was a storming success, gathering momentum as it wound its way across Tennessee and Mississippi and into Texas. The word was out that Presley was back with a vengeance and from the initial half-full auditoriums numbers rose until everywhere was sold out and dates were extended until mid-December.

At some point someone decided that it would be a good idea to make a film of the new Elvis show and top director DA Pennebaker was drafted in to capture the trials and tribulations of the on-the-road events. The subsequent film, *Elvis On Tour*, is a thrilling and innovatory collage of interviews, over-views, comments from fans, from the band, from Elvis interspersed with exciting live footage of the concerts. To this point pop music films had been of the thin-plot-dressed-with-thin-songs approach geared to give maximum exposure to their stars, but never touching on anything substantial. The documentary approach of *Elvis On Tour* was influenced partly by '50s jazz-films which took a much rarer and more realistic perspective of its inspirational centre than Rock 'n' Roll had ever done, perhaps because jazz, like much minority music, doesn't need or acknowledge the unreal pretensions inherent in the mass-appeal pop industry. So, in many respects, *Elvis On Tour* is an unpolished work but it succeeds because of that. It stands with such films as Pennebaker's later effort *Don't Look Back* and, in a different way, *A Hard Day's Night* on a pedestal of vigour and honesty so much lacking in the majority of rock movies.

The film opened in early '64 as *Western Bop and Country Boogie* stood at number 16 in the Hot 100, its highest position. Despite sell-out concerts, ecstatic reviews, and now a brilliant film, Presley had still not completely recaptured his old market and, at this point, seemed unlikely to. The new sounds in music were making themselves heard more and more loudly and, although Presley had regained critical respect – most important of all – commercially he was caught at a crossover point. He had become, at twenty-eight, too old for teenagers, and yet he was too young to be there with Sinatra or Tony Bennett, who still sold regularly and well. He was in an image-limbo and we can only be grateful that, at this point, both he and the public had the sense and the wherewithal to recognise the worth of his music.

Elvis On Tour was a big success on the cinema circuit but country music was less yielding financially than the rock market, and it was in the rock market that the boom came. The British Beat Boom, spearheaded by The Beatles, Gerry and the Pacemakers, and the Animals, hit America in mid-'64.

Just before the British invasion it seemed as if the diabolic spectre of Rock 'n' Roll had been erased from the mainstream of American culture forever. After the first couple of years the threatening purveyors of the form had been replaced by more respectable and therefore infinitely less interesting carbon-copies. Bobby Rydell, Bobby Vee, Bobby Darin – the whole world was full of Bobbies, with the odd Fabian or some other Neapolitan neo-rocker, mouthing their latest pap on nationwide TV to a gawping audience of teenagers with no memories of hot sweaty boogie. Those poor kids!!!

As representative a representative of American culture as you might find at that time was the Dick Cavett chat show of July 22nd, 1964.

A couple of movie starlets – Debbie Reynolds and Ann-Margret are wheeled in with token intellectual, and a man with some previous experience of blonde starlets, playwright Arthur Miller. The only surprise is Rock 'n' Roller Little Richard Penniman but it may be that Troy Shondell is tied up that night. At the front of the show, to the left of your screen, Toothy Dick Cavett himself, the master of aural agony. And, looka-there, plumb in the middle of them all it's good old Elvis Presley, looking dumb and feeling dumber, Parker's got him here to sing a song and talk a little and earn $5,000.

They're talking, Debbie has a new TV show, she's telling us all about it. Ann-Margret's maybe going to be in one episode. What does Arthur think about writing TV comedy shows? He doesn't think he could do it 'cos he ain't funny. Elvis has made some funny films. Did he enjoy it? Not really, sir. The fire is way down tonight. The Dark Side of the Presley lies dormant. Little Richard isn't getting too much of a look-in. After all, he isn't funny. About the funniest thing he ever did was throw his jewellery from the San Francisco Golden Gate Bridge and he's not talking about it. Why is he here, we're thinking. He and Elvis have never met until now. Elvis is uneasy. Richard looks a crazy dude. Oh wow. He's talking to Elvis. Dick and Debbie and Arthur and Ann are rambling about Beverly Hills and Richard's mumbling. Elvis is sweating. What's he saying?

'This show's Dullsville, Arizona. Ah'm only here so ah can do something crazy.'

Oh boy, Elvis looks at Cavett. No one's heard Richard talking. Oh, he's talking again.

'Elvis man, what you doin' here? Ah lahked yer country album but those dumb movies... oh wow. Ah figure you must be a little screwy.'

Elvis grips the arms of his chair.

'Hey, Elvis. What about these fine-lookin' gals?'

Elvis freezes, looks at the monitor. Suddenly he's on it and looks panicky. Cavett's voice is asking him some dumb-ass question about private swimming pools. The mic above him is on. He knows because Little Richard is raving about a gumbo restaurant they can take the girls to after the show. Elvis starts to speak but the camera is already back on Arthur Miller. The time winds on. Richard is still speaking. Elvis is practically comatose by the time Cavett announces a legendary pairing on a legendary song and Elvis ambles after the scurrying Richard to the piano and grins falsely at the Little Richard band. Two verses and one piano break into 'Long Tall Sally' Richard screams to Elvis to take it and disappears off camera. Elvis's eyes are drawn to that monitor again and his singing is soulless.

Then Richard's face is full in frame and his big lips are wide open and he's saying to Debbie Reynolds, 'Ooh mah soul! Ah'm Little Richard and you be the best-lookin' gal I seen all afternoon. I don' mind that you white. We all got our cross.'

And the director quickly snaps another camera onto Elvis. Elvis has had it. He is shrugging. He is silent. 'Sing!' comes from behind the camera.

'Volare, wo-oh.'

It's a bad dream. It is happening. Oh my!

The only positive outcome of the Cavett show for Elvis was the meeting with Ann-Margret. She was, at that time, working her way up the ladder of artistic credibility, but still making relatively low budget movies with some singing and dancing. Candy floss.

After the show Elvis lay in his dressing room alone when there was a knock on the door.

'Poke a pig! Who is it?'

'Ann-Margret. Are you okay?'

'Yeah. C'min.'

The door swung open to reveal as much of Ann-Margret as could be revealed, with acknowledgments to the slimline, low-cut black dress she was wearing.

'I just wanted to come and say what an honour it is for me to meet you, Elvis. It's always been one of my ambitions to meet someone who commands such a high place in the development of popular music and I've seen all your films.'

Zzzzzz.

Elvis was asleep. One of his most positive character traits was his lack of interest in people recalling his achievements. He wanted only to be accepted as a person, not as a cultural image.

It was a bad start to a relationship but things progressed positively very quickly as Presley woke to the sizzling smell of big fat cheeseburgers.

After the feast, which Ann-Margret admitted she'd planned after reading *What Elvis Likes To Eat*,[1] Elvis started to open up a little. He admitted his embarrassment at Little Richard's behaviour but also admitted that if he'd had the nerve to do it himself he would have, but he was losing his rebellious streak. With some coaxing. Ann-Margret later recalled, Elvis ran right through his life-story, talking about his fears and fantasies and incidents like never before.

Elvis saw a lot of Ann-Margret over the next couple of months. In many ways it was Elvis's most normal relationship. They'd drive up to Lovers' Leap in Memphis and look down on the gleaming wrecks in the car-breakers' below. Other times they'd stay in at Graceland and Ann-Margret would cook cheeseburgers and watch Elvis shoot up a few TVs.

Presley, however, became increasingly preoccupied, as 1964 progressed, with the new movement in music that had knocked America wide open. By September The Beatles and Gerry and the Pacemakers had blown the charts into a new ocean and Elvis, already feeling himself to be slipping, realised yet again that a new impetus to his career was needed. He consulted Parker, albeit grudgingly after an impasse stemming from the time of the Cavett show which Presley held Parker responsible for. He was storing up a series of such grudges against the old Colonel – the circus tour; the films; the decline in record sales; the diminution of the Presley image, and yet the two men's positive achievements together would always outweigh the bad points and they still had this mutual hypnotic draw to each other.

This time, after a series of secret conversations at, alternately, Sal's Diner in downtown Memphis and the Colonel's suite in the Memphis International Hotel, the two men decided on a plan of action that, for once, was remarkably sound in its reasoning. What they had to do was rescue the waning legend from total destruction by the British Invaders. What better way to approach this than to go right out there, to the source of the problem, and play the pretenders at their own game?

Thus, it was decided, in early November, 1964, the Presley European Country Tour would begin. First stop, Hamburg.

---

[1] *What Elvis Likes To Eat*, by Dennis Chang Jr, with Johnny Carson.

Chapter 17

The European Country Tour

The dates for the Elvis tour of Europe took Parker and his men a couple of months to set up and it was late January, 1965, before the Presley entourage flew out to West Germany for the first stop on the twelve-date, six-country itinerary.

Elvis had just spent a very quiet festive season at Graceland after the amicable cessation of his affair with Ann-Margret. He had a surprise Top 20 singles placing with the EP of old recordings with a festive flavour – *Elvis Sings Four Old Christmas Songs Just In Time For The Festive Season*. This consisted of 'Santa Claus Is Back In Town', 'Santa Claus Is Coming To Town', 'Here Comes Santa Claus (Down Santa Claus Lane)' and the previously unreleased 1956 recording of the old Bats 'n' Bob hit, 'Santa Claus Is Too Fat (To Get Through The Central Heating Pipes)'.

The success of the EP is interesting, highlighting as it does the fact that to the public there were now three distinct Elvis Presleys. The first was the old Elvis of Sun, *Elvis Is Back* and *Jailhouse Rock* – mean, moody and magnificently raw. Then there was the turkey persona – the bimbo Elvis of sportscar movies, circus tours and 'Sheree, Ernie, You're Both Wonderful People'. It was the first Elvis, with tried and trusted material that scored the Christmas hit. The second Elvis was a bad memory. Then there was the third and, at that time, current Elvis, who wavered between the other two – capable of brilliant recordings but, sadly, often inconsistent and unpredictable in his behaviour and a mite suspicious in the eyes of a more aware and less fanatical public (hence the relatively poor sales of the country album).

By the time Elvis and his party flew out of America, the British stronghold on the US charts was well-established with The Beatles, Gerry and the Pacemakers and Herman's Hermits all having scored number one hits.

As the Presley plane – nicknamed 'Skyburger I' – dropped onto the runway at Hamburg airport, Elvis, not for the first time in his career, must have been wondering, 'Am ah gone fall on muh ass AGAIN??!?'

The notoriety of Hamburg seems to have increased over the years.

Perhaps initially known for the Reeperbahn, the infamous red-light area and twilight world of prostitutes, pimps and porky German business men, Hamburg came to the notice of '60s youngsters as the early stomping ground of The Beatles. Clubs such as the Kaiserkeller and the Top Ten and, most famous of all, the Star Club, had enjoyed great success in the wake of Merseybeat. Jerry Lee Lewis had recorded a live album at the Star Club and both Little Richard and Gene Vincent had appeared there. However, Elvis and the Colonel had wisely decided that the Presley phenomenon needed to transcend its Rock 'n' Roll legend and progress. These clubs would surely have branded Elvis as a self-revivalist. Besides, they were too small.

Presley's European standing had not (save in Britain) diminished at anything like the rate it had at home. Europe always seemed to take its lead in rock from the USA or Great Britain and as, to date, the States had offered no Presley successor, Elvis continued to knock up immediate number ones and bestselling albums. (An album by Dennis Chang Jr, *Fortune Cookie Elvis!*, which was half interview, half Chang playing some old Elvis numbers on the electric vibraphone, even went Top Ten, demonstrating the ludicrous fanaticism of continental Presley fans.)

Elvis, then, was booked in for two almost instantly sold-out dates at the Hamburg Opera House. A good proportion of the audiences were American servicemen, which inspired an incident recalled by 'Restless' Randy Trousers, Presley's drummer on the tour:

'It was just before the show on the second night and Elvis and the band were sitting in Elvis's dressing-room feeling very optimistic because the first night had gone so well. We were talking about the GIs there and Elvis was laughing about how the old Colonel had had to tell all those stupid lies about him being in the army when he wasn't. Suddenly the door opened and in came the Colonel, obviously bubbling with excitement. "I got us one cookin' idea here, y'all," he said in Dutch-Southern, "Why not make a movie in which Elvis is a soldier stationed in Germany and one day a buddy spots a gorgeous dame and bets Elvis he can't get to stay the night with her and he tries and gets nowhere and goes to puppet shows and thangs and generally shows himself to be a good guy, but she's not impressed. Then by some freak, he spends a night with her – BABYSITTING! All innocent! We could call it mebbe *GI Blues* 'cos Elvis really lahks her and is morose at having to dupe her. How about it?"

'And Elvis looked at the Colonel and said, 'cos he was on a real high just before the show, "Colonel, you's a real dumb shit sometimes, but that's the *dumbest* idea y'evah had".'

The two nights, January 25th and 26th, 1965, set a formidable precedent for the rest of the tour to live up to. The Hamburg shows were phenomenal successes, not just in terms of the box-office, though that was encouraging enough, but also in terms of artistry. The American tour had really sharpened the Presley show up and yet it still retained enough rough edges to allow a truly powerful and raunchy feel to permeate. The 'Presley charisma was full to the brim and the confidence Elvis displayed offset the dumbness of some of his stage announcements. (For instance, before singing 'Hound Dog' each night Elvis would sing the refrain from the *Paint Your Wagon* number, 'I talked to the trees, but they only barked at me... ho ho ho... and talking of barking, here's a song about a place I once stayed near London.' Nobody knew what he was talking about, but he persisted with this. Fortunately, inter-song chat was minimal.

If Elvis handled the gigs well, he was less successful in adapting to the cultural differences of some of the countries in which he found himself – often with quite humorous results. For instance, in Athens, the second city on the itinerary, Randy Trousers recalls the time when Elvis, walking through a market-place, stopped and pointed at an ample young girl playing a stringed instrument: 'Elvis said, "Look at that. Y'ever see anything like it?" and I said, "Yup, them's called bouzoukis," and Elvis said, "I know they is, but I'm talkin' about the little banjo she's strummin'".'

Greece was also to provide the inspiration for some of Elvis's later, little-known poetry-writing. In the early '70s, Presley built up a fair backlog of poetical works which he would read to his bored boys as they waited around before and between shows. It all sprang from a trip the Elvis party took to Lamia on a day off after the Greek concerts. It was whilst in Lamia that Elvis's bass player, 'Nervous' Fred Wilmester happened to mention that he once read something by some guy called Keats about this place. Elvis enquired further and discovered that Keats was an English poet much given to Romantic compositions. Elvis began thinking and suddenly announced to his boys, 'Hey, it's just like writing songs. Anybody could do it. Let's have a poetry competition.'

They did and, not surprisingly, Elvis won. As Randy Trousers said, 'We let Elvis win everything 'cos otherwise he got mad. I still remember his poem – we could write about anything we wanted though most of us couldn't think of nothing and we wasn't interested anyway, but Elvis's, it went,

"I'm here in Greece, the sun is out,
Colonel Parker's very stout.
We're on a tour, it's going well,
Pity about that cigar smell.
I've had good times, I've had bad,
Any more bad ones and I'll shoot his poking head off!"
Crazy shit!'

From Greece, the Presley tour wound northward up to Yugoslavia for two dates in Belgrade. The capital is a bleak place and resembles an American or British provincial city in size, but there is an atmosphere of restraint. In 1965 portraits of the beloved (and now late) President Tito hung everywhere. It was towards one of these portraits that Elvis addressed himself whilst on a stroll around the centre of the city. (He was, it should be noted, almost always unrecognised in much of Europe. If recognised, mostly he was dismissed with a passing, 'It can't be *him*, here.') Strolling into a café with Restless and Nervous, Elvis pointed at the picture of Tito and said, 'Hey, that's like Parker. Fat Boy Parker. Who is it?'

Restless, an educated man, replied, 'That's Tito.'

'Titto?' said Elvis, and laughed.

'What you say about our President?' came a Slavic voice from behind.

'I'm Elvis Presley, the meanest sonuvabitch ever walked this earth. Poke a pig, that guy's UGLY!'

Elvis was discharged in time for the first Belgrade date, his fingers healing well, according to press reports. So! Even a legend can be a dumbo klutz.

As if in sympathy with the country's hostility, Superburger I, on leaving Belgrade airport, developed engine trouble and was forced to make an immediate landing. Mumbling 'Glenn Miller, Buddy Holly, Jim Reeves, Patsy Cline, The Big Bopper', over and over again, Elvis was led from the plane and told that the trip to Venice could be just as conveniently made on a Yugoslavian airplane, but, as Elvis looked down the runways and saw a proliferation of turboprop relics of the Berlin Airlift, he instantly decided that the entourage would travel to Italy by train. Despite some gentle hints as to other alternatives from the Colonel, the Elvis party duly booked onto one of only two trains which ran daily to Venice via Trieste. On February 6th, the day before the Venice show, they boarded the train and were ready to go.

Yugoslavian trains were and remain appalling. Old, decrepit, invariably hours late, their most disconcerting features are the crowding of passengers up to three deep in corridors maybe eighty inches wide and the frequent stops for a guard to get out and check that the wheels are still secure. At top speed, a Yugoslavian train can threaten 40mph. Journeys to Italy can flash by in 18 hours. There are no refreshment facilities and reaching the toilet would be feasible for a Welsh prop forward.

The Presley gang took up their compartments and at least had seats. As the journey wore on, slow and increasingly terrifying like a Conrad novel, Parker's bladder filled to the brim. Eventually, he resolved to find the john. Save for Elvis, the others in the compartment were dozing. As the Colonel disappeared into a torrent of the Yugoslavian for 'Watch my feet you fat jerk' Presley dragged down one of his suitcases from the rack above. Opening it, he pulled out a variety of Yugoslavian head-veils and, without making a sound, draped them over the heads of his sleeping boys. He then sat down and donned one himself.

Six hours later, the boys were awakened by Elvis gurgling with laughter. Looking at each other with the surprise you register when you realise you're on a date with a virgin, they could hear ol' Parker's voice from the compartment next door shouting, 'Elvis, ah know you're here somewhere boy... poke, ah bin up an' down this train three times – takes an hour 'n' a half each time, an' all I find is ol' women an' peasants. POKE IT!'

If Venice went well (and it did!), Rome was a revelation. By the time of his show on February 8th, the whole feel of the Italy that the young Elvis had seen inside his head listening to Mario Lanza records had permeated his consciousness. Restless!

'Yeah, Elvis was really prancing around there in his stripy T-shirt saying things like, "This is the land of Dean Martin. I feel it. I feel it," and stuffing his face full of ice-cream,' recalls one aide.

The day after another really successful concert, Elvis was resting at his hotel when he suddenly started from his bed and said, 'I've gotten idea. I wanna meet the Pope.'

A shiver went through the boys. They were well used to Presley's whims and to him forgetting them almost immediately; it was just that, from time to time, he had to see an idea through. They hoped that this wasn't going to be one of those times. Alas.

'Uh, bonjourno. Yeah. 'S that the Vatican...? You speak English? Yeah! Ah'm Elvis Presley... yes, Elvis Presley... the singer... the King of Rock 'n' Roll. Yeah, that one. Lissen, I'd like to come by an see you... what? Why... hey, is this the Pope or what? Well, put him on... What? He don't receive. Hell, we'll see.'

As Elvis slammed the phone down, he barked an order to the newly arrived Dennis Chang Jr, sometime Presley aide and part-time photographer for the *New York Times*, now in Rome to cover the end of the tour:

'Hey, Slanty, send the Pope a pink Alfa Romeo... how the hell do I know where you get one a them? – jus' do it!'

Dennis Chang Jr:

'I look round and find a man who will spray Alfa Romeo pink good like new and I get him to take it round to Vatican when dry and two hours later he come to hotel an say car outside an Pope he don't drive.'

Presley, so used to having his own way, was furious at the return of the car. Curiously, his anger was not directed at the Pope himself, for he never believed that the top people wouldn't see him – it was just that underlings never made it clear that it was Elvis, *the* Elvis, who wanted an audience.

Chang Jr: 'Elvis megalomaniac? Does the sun rise in the east?'

After dark, brooding deliberations, Elvis rose and left the startled boys in the hotel. He got into the car and drove off.

On arriving at the gates of the Vatican, he demanded to see the Pope and was asked why. His quite outstanding reply was, 'I think we got a lot in common. We both got lotsa fans.'

Again he was refused admission and began to attract much attention by sporadically sounding the car-horn. Soon a crowd gathered and, recognising Elvis, one American tourist called out, 'What's up, Elvis buddy?'

'The Pope don't wanna see me. Uh. Me, Elvis Presley.'

The next minute, the gates of the Vatican opened and the figure of the Pope himself appeared beside Elvis.

'You wish to speak with me, Mr Presley?'

A red-faced Elvis, his gusto blown out by this, accompanied the Pope into the Vatican in the pink Alfa Romeo and the gates closed. Several hours later, Restless recalls, Elvis returned:

'He was a different man. He didn't say anything of what happened except that the car was to be auctioned and the proceeds to be used to help the poor and Elvis was to send $300,000 to the Pope's secretary. Parker near swallowed his cigar and tried to talk Elvis out of it, but the man was adamant. Several days later he rushed in excitedly saying, "I got it, I got it, I got it." We wondered what the fuss was about until he held it up. It was one of the Pope's old skullcaps. I tell you, Elvis was ding-dong. But he was never as childish about wanting anything after that.'

On February 9th and 10th, Elvis followed a week-long engagement by The Shadows at the Paris Olympia. The Shadows stayed on to see the first night Elvis did. Lead guitarist Hank B Marvin was so impressed by the new country style that not only did he advise his close friend Cliff Richard to go to Nashville to record some country material (which he indeed did, scoring a British number one with one of the songs, 'Wind Me Up, Let Me Go'), but he wrote Elvis a song, The Day I Met Marie', which gave Cliff another big hit. The Presley version, recorded at the sessions for the second country album, was unreleased until the 1977 compilation, *Elvis Is Gone*, came out. It seems a pity that the public had to wait so long to hear it, as it is distinctly superior to anything else recorded for that album.

The Paris concerts were taped for possible release, as were the final dates on the tour, Liverpool and London, but, as yet, though bootlegs are common, a technically sound version of these legendary concerts has never reached the masses.

England brought back many good memories of the time when he befriended that footloose sailor. Liverpool, in particular, was a momentous occasion for Elvis as he was now right on the point of the musical spearhead that was currently conquering the world's record charts. Any fears Elvis might have had as he stepped onto the stage at the Empire were dispelled immediately by the magnificent reception.

After the show he walked, incognito, around some of the haunts from his last visit and his band recall him returning, his eyes wet with tears, and not saying a word to anyone. For all his eccentricities, he still retained a romantic melancholy that only occasionally entered his recorded voice, but when it did it produced some of the most emotive singing in recording history.

The next day, to a chorus of ecstatic press reviews and a British top ten album, Elvis and the band returned to Nashville in Skyburger I. The Colonel followed a day later after completing his business in London.

For Elvis another zenith had been reached and the perpetual problem of a follow-up had to be faced.

Chapter 18

Country Turkey

Reports of Elvis's European success shifted many copies of celebrity rags in the States, but the music press were more suspicious, given his erratic track record, of how he would capitalise on this success. The pattern in the past had been for him to follow a success with a failure, but when he announced, at a press conference in New York shortly after his return to the US, that he was booked to re-enter the Nashville studios to make a follow-up country album, the future looked promising for once.

It was at this same press conference that Elvis almost inadvertently blew it in a big way. The Beatles, currently on their second American jaunt, had experienced violently unpleasant reactions to Lennon's contextually misquoted, 'We're bigger than God,' with copies of their records publicly burned by the Ku Klux Klan in the Bible Belt. After fending off questions about The Beatles and the British invasion, Elvis was asked about Lennon's remark. An enterprising Canadian reporter asked Presley if he thought he was bigger than God, to which he responded with a very definite 'No'. The Canuck then asked, 'And what do you think of Jesus?'

'Oh, I'm bigger than Jesus alright,' mumbled Elvis.

'What?'

Ears cocked at this revelation. Dreams of promotion flew up from every notebook.

'You're bigger than Jesus... ?'

'Mm? What you sayin'?' replied Elvis. 'Hell, I said, "I figure Jesus was right." Don't go tryin' to cover *me* in *that* horse shit. Now poke off!'

Disappointed reporters shuffled out of the conference. The King of Rock 'n' Roll had used words that would sell millions of newspapers – but they were all censored by the Obscene Publications Act from quoting Presley verbatim.

It was by now mid-1965. Presley entered BRA's Studio Z in Nashville on July 26th. Owen Bradley, producer of *Western Bop And Country Boogie*, was otherwise engaged, so another veteran producer, Mervyn Wang, was brought in. Wang had worked with Jimmie Rodgers back in the '30s and had engineered the early hits of Eddy

Arnold and Hank Snow in the late '40s. As the '50s wore on, Wang found it increasingly difficult to get work, as he had a reputation for coming up with a dated sound – this largely as a result of his refusal to work with electrically amplified instruments. Eventually he had been forced out of the music business completely and had used his meagre savings to set up a button-badge manufacturing business. The late '50s saw him marketing unauthorised badges with legends such as: 'I Love Elvis', 'Jerry Lee Lewis, The Pumping Piano Cat' and 'Johnny Cash, Country King'.

One day back in 1958, Colonel Parker, who had hired a private dick to track down the illegal badge-maker, called in person at the factory. It wasn't a social call; the porcine one had come for money. The factory, off Broadway in Nashville, was nothing but a small, prefabricated shed. Wang had built up enough business to employ three people and Parker's first sight, on entering the badge factory, was of this low-budget production line.

'How y'all doin' there?' he enquired, with his usual phoney geniality. The next second a chill went through his body as the three turned to face him: they were none other than the Fantoni Brothers or, to be precise, three of the Four Fantoni Brothers, who had been a popular country act in Tennessee several years previously. They were unique in their interpretation of country standards in that they often translated them into their native Italian. Parker, who in the early '50s had persuaded Roger Ringo to put on the odd musical evening in his tent, had got the Fantoni Brothers a $500 booking one Sunday night in a Ringo promotion. This was 1953.

The Four Fantonis went down well until they went into a Sicilian version of 'Just Out Of Reach Of My Empty Arms', at which a heckler exhorted, 'You wops get off and let some true Americans on.' Mario Fantoni's knife was between the guy's ears before you could say 'O Sole Mio' or 'Que Sera Sera' or even 'Shit, a knife in my forehead.'

Parker, who had $500 from Ringo for the brothers in his pocket, decided to beat a retreat at this point. The case reached court and was open-and-shut. Parker was not required to testify and Mario Fantoni went straight to the chair. The, Fat Dutchman had not laid eyes on the others since. Until now.

Bobby, the eldest Fantoni, spoke:

'Parker? Is Parker? Parker who run out with our five hundreda dollars. How is Parker?'

The Colonel saw the spectre of death come into the brothers' eyes and felt waterfalls of sweat cascade down the back of his silk shirt. The Fantonis, teeth gleaming, began to advance slowly on him.

At this point, the strains of 'Santa Lucia' rose from the back of the factory. The brothers suddenly stopped looking menacing and went down on their knees in prayer. Parker just had time to see Mervyn

Wang wink at him before he scurried out on his fat-boy legs.

Not usually eternally grateful for anything, Parker figured that he owed Wang one, so when the production seat for Presley's second country album came vacant, he called Wang up and offered him $500 – a sentimental figure – to produce the recording sessions. Wang, his badge business gone under, jumped at the offer.

So, on September 24th, 1965, Elvis Presley sat at a microphone in downtown Nashville and said, wryly, 'Okay. Ready when you are.'

'Yeah, Elvis,' Wang replied. 'Ah won't be but a minute. Where the hell's the mains switch for this goddam desk thing?'

'I don't understand it; the tape was rolling alright,' he said at the playback of the first song, which was a pretty good record of the bass drum's performance, though nothing else at all.

'You gotta use these buttons and knobs to set the levels, Mervyn,' Elvis explained patiently.

'Ain't that the durndest thang, boys,' said Wang. 'Back in the ol' days we jus switched on the damn tape recorder. What they gone think of next? I'll be damned.'

The recording of *Downhome Elvis* was completed in six days. Fourteen tracks, of which eleven made it onto the album, were recorded. The album was eventually released in mono, as explained by sound engineer Fred Mist:

'Hell, Wang was the producer, so I did what he told me to do, but when we listened to the rough mix, all we heard was one big mess. I don't think Wang knows what stereo is. He had Elvis's voice and all the instruments coming out of one speaker and just the drums coming out of the other. He kept saying, "The kids'll go for the *beat*. Lettem hear the drums." I can't think of the disaster we'd have had if the Colonel hadn't ordered me to mix everything down into mono. Even now it sounds like the band was playing underwater.'

Whereas *Western Bop And Country Boogie* had been comprised of contemporary versions of relatively modern standards, *Downhome Elvis* was, at Wang's suggestion, full of 'good ol' traditional' country material like 'Yellow Rose Of Texas', 'Old MacDonald' and 'On Top Of Old Smokey'. The band used was a group of experienced session men rather restricted by having to use acoustic instruments backed up by one big drumkit to 'get that beat that the kids love'.

The album might have worked in the hands of a more gifted producer – or even of a *gifted* producer – and some of it was passable, but, after selling well on initial release, Presley's inconsistency was confirmed in the critical public eye. He was plunged, once again, into a slough of despair, but by now he was too listless and lethargic to care. *Downhome Elvis* was the final straw that blew the camel's brains out. For now, at least!

Chapter 19

Screwy

It was now ten years since 'Heartbreak Hotel' topped the Pop, Country and Rock 'n' Roll charts in the US. Elvis had finished his first decade as a rock singer, something nobody thought any rock performer could do. Rock 'n' Roll *was* here to stay.

The seeds that Elvis, Buddy Holly, Fats Domino, the Everly Brothers, Carl Perkins, Little Richard, Chuck Berry, Bo Diddley, Eddie Cochran, Johnny Burnette and Jerry Lee Lewis had sown had taken root not only in the US, but in England, and Rock 'n' Roll's second wave came from there.

The Beatles had soaked up the styles of these original Rock 'n' Rollers and re-animated a tired and bland form which had been plasticised in America by the big wheels of the industry. In their wake came the Stones, the Animals, the Who, the Kinks, Them, the Pretty Things, the Yardbirds and the other British bands who had studied the recorded output of the Rock 'n' Roll greats and came up with their synthesis of the styles of the great.

Some, like The Stones, The Animals and The Yardbirds, dug deeper for their influences and mined the urban blues vein, coming up with music suffused with the influence of such bluesmen as Muddy Walters, Howlin' Wolf and BB King, some of whom had been supported and recorded by Sam Phillips in the Union Avenue studio before the advent of the Sideburn Kid.

The British wave in turn inspired a reactivation of Rock 'n' Roll at grass roots in the US when artists such as Bob Dylan, The Byrds, The Grateful Dead, Sir Douglas Quintet, Jefferson Airplane, The Velvet Underground and The Doors picked up on the verve, drive and imagination that was coming out of the United Kingdom.

Rock 'n' Roll was alive and well and living in Liverpool, Manchester, London, Belfast, Newcastle-upon-Tyne, New York, Los Angeles, San Francisco and San Antonio. But Elvis Presley, the man who had practically given birth to the ethos, had strayed far and wide from his baby, doing everything but what he was best at – rocking.

In 1965 The Beatles had made a futile attempt to persuade Elvis that the sessions leading to *Downhome Elvis* were uninspired and pointless. As we have seen, Elvis stuck to his guns and released the turkey.

When he saw what the critics had to say about it, he took to his bedroom suite at Graceland and began to eat, sulk and lead an increasingly strange lifestyle.

It didn't escape Elvis that what he was doing was less than contemporary and that he had fallen out of vogue. He didn't fail to appreciate the freshness of the British wave – or at least what he heard of it. At the back of his mind was a nagging sense that he had not been true to himself. But over and above this twinge of guilt was the forceful conviction that he could do as he pleased with his life. And something in him was pleased to be self-destructive,

The first strange occurrence at Graceland was when the King ordered the windows of his palace painted black from the inside. He felt threatened by the outside world and, depressed by his inactivity, he began to surround himself with dark and sombre objects and trappings. He took to dressing in black and travelling the corridors of Graceland in a motorised wheelchair. On particularly morose days, Elvis would don a black Balaclava to complete his outfit. He would sometimes ride a black horse in the afternoon. He kept a black cat which he would fondle and stroke before an open fire in the drawing room. Those Burkes and Orifices to whom Elvis was closest now lived in at Graceland, and Elvis disseminated his black obsession amongst them. Bill Orifice and Wilf Burke were informed one morning in April 1966 that all of the Memphis Mafia now in Elvis's employ would be expected to dress in black.

'This upset a lot of the boys,' recalls Bill. 'Not all of us felt that we looked good in black. My brother Luther, for instance, was a great believer in a chalk-stripe suit, or failing that, a pin-stripe at least. This was now strictly out. We even had to wear black socks and some of the guys were stung about not being able to wear yellow ones anymore. Me, I could take it, but Sarnie Burke had a thing about yellow socks.'

Some of the mafia thought it best to inform the Colonel that Elvis was out of sorts. The devious Dutchman was on the West Coast embroiled in negotiations to return Elvis to Hollywood. The fat man had an obsession about Elvis and films. The very best way for Elvis to function as a performer, he argued, was to do a movie and issue a soundtrack album. The returns on the two were mutually stimulating.

The Colonel acknowledged Bill Orifice's message to the effect that Elvis was going doolally, but was too busy in Los Angeles to return to attend to it. However, he resolved to get Elvis working again as soon as possible; that would halt the progress of Elvis's eccentricity.

During this period, Elvis's sleepwalking, a habit he had had as a child, returned to plague him, and, because of Elvis's perverse sleeping schedule, everyone else at Graceland suffered. When his black fit had descended upon him, Elvis had taken the unusual step of reversing the order of his days. He would sleep in the daytime and function – in his peculiar way – at night. The guys, he insisted, were to accompany him in this left-field behaviour.

Well, at first the guys did as they were told and so there was the odd situation where Elvis, the Orifices and the Burkes lived by night and slept by day while the rest of the household kept more regular hours. The guys were fond of order and good health though and soon made up their minds to stop breaking nature's hours. Once they did stop, it was a week before Elvis even noticed that he was the *only* person in Graceland who wasn't asleep during the night.

To begin with this irked, him more than somewhat, and he told the guys as much in so many words, but soon he began to savour his nocturnal solitude and would read aloud to himself or play solo croquet on the upstairs landing.

Now that everyone but Elvis was asleep during the night what the King did at night wasn't of much concern, as long as he didn't make too much noise. No, the only hassle that Elvis's inversion of the day created was the disturbance his frequent sleepwalking would cause in the daytime.

There you'd be, dicing carrots in the kitchen, playing checkers in the den, reading the paper in the drawing room or re-enacting the St Valentine's Day Massacre with blanks in the garage and Elvis would glide around the corner in his black silk pyjamas muttering to himself, '*Skinny Dipping In The Seychelles*? Poke a pig! *Lotsa Lady Lifeguards, Acapulco*. Ennnn. *Little Girls Grow Up Fast and Grope Me*. Ummnn... no, no... errrggghhh... ssspplluugghhagerrgerrgurrghh...'

The aggravation that Elvis's daytime somnambulance caused is perhaps best described in her book by Elvis's cheeseburger chef, Wilma Mae Armpit. In her excellent account[1] of Elvis's preferences in burgers, Miss Armpit does, every now and then, uncover a little gem of Elvis trivia. When she mentions his sleepwalking, she writes:

'The hell of it was that no matter what he was doing, unless he looked set to injure himself, you just dare not wake him up. Many's the time I had just grated a pound of cheese onto a dinner plate and Elvis would loom up, grab the plate and pour the gratings over his head.

'The worst I ever saw was the time Elvis poured a freshly made pot of coffee over Montana Cleaver's lap. Montana was hired as Elvis's bodyguard and he was not a nice man. (Folks called him "Psycho" behind his back. I guess he was.) He leapt to his feet holding his hand over his mouth and sprinted out of the room. Thing was, you see,

[1] *Grated Not Melted – Elvis, Me And The Cheeseburger* by Wilma Mae Armpit (Dislexic Press, 1979).

there'd be hell to pay if Elvis got woken up for no good cause. Once he was out of hearing range of the boss, Montana screamed and hollered and ranted. That man was fit to be put down for rabies for a week after that. I guess most people enjoyed that little incident more than any other connected with Elvis's sleepwalking.

'I know I did!'

It was during 1966 that Elvis first showed his fondness for the martial arts. A mild, academic interest in the eastern arts of defence grew into an obsession with karate and the philosophy behind it. The Hillbilly Cat liked to study books on karate, yoga and even Buddhism. He liked too to take a tumble on the Graceland gym mat with one of the guys or to flex and spin and breathe deeply and grunt. Most of all, however, he liked to dress up in his (black) karate outfit and flex, spin, breathe deeply and grunt before the gym's ten-foot-square mirror.

Practising karate from books wasn't enough of course; if any real progress were to be made something more was required. An ad was placed in the *Los Angeles Times*, appropriate candidates were interviewed but in the end it was Dennis Chang Jr, a longtime on-and-off Presley associate, who was appointed as Elvis's karate instructor.

Chang became an important part of the Presley household. His role extended far beyond that of a mere karate instructor. The nearest parallel with his function at Graceland is that of the fool in a Shakespearian royal court. Chang's job was to act the clown when Elvis was in low spirits (which was increasingly the case) and to prick Elvis's conscience when he wasn't giving of his best, or acting in his own best interests. Unfortunately Chang, being a first generation American of Shanghai parentage, knew nothing about Rock 'n' Roll and as much about Elvis's role in that form of music. It was difficult then for the little Chinaman to be much of a spur to Elvis's musical conscience, but he was good-natured and well-meaning and proved to be as solicitous a friend as Elvis was to have in the coming years.

In his book, already cited, Dennis Chang Jr speaks of Elvis's confusion during 1966, his black, despairing moods and of how karate practice was almost the only thing that could alleviate Elvis's psychological ills.

'When Elvis become depressed, all he want to do is nothing. Lots of nothing. He get very, very *down*. He not want to sing, he not want to play guitar or piano. Elvis just want to eat cheeseburgers or sit in his room watching the fire.

'The only thing that cheers Elvis up is a little karate practice. So I get him into habit of practising karate every night when he get up (just before I go to bed). We practice one hour and Elvis very content for short time.

'Karate only thing that takes Elvis out of himself. Oh! I forget!

Karate and *Batman* TV series! *Batman* cheers Elvis up very much.
Nothing else, though.'[2]

One other pastime which Elvis made repeated attempts at enjoying – but to little avail – was spending money, lots of it. This was a regular hobby and no matter how much Vernon or Dennis Chang
reminded Elvis of how little pleasure spending gave him, the
Memphis Flash kept right on doing it, in larger and larger amounts.

Notable purchases in 1966, for example, were grizzly bearskin
overcoats for all the guys – not much use in a Tennessee summer; an
18 carat gold-thread suit, for Elvis himself, which was so stiff that it
was impossible to sit down in it; an ice hockey stadium in which to
play hockey with the guys; two Sherman tanks for games of stock-car
racing out the back; a Lockheed Lightning for annoying neighbouring
farmers; a Ford pick-up like the one he had driven at the dog pound
for each of the guys; and an authentic, highly detailed copy of Adam
West's Batman outfit.

This last purchase turned out to be more trouble than anyone
could have reasonably expected. First of all, Elvis took to wearing
the outfit while watching episodes of the TV series. Harmless
enough you might think and indeed it was – unless somebody interrupted his viewing. In this event Elvis would scream out that the
person was to 'Shut the poke up' and throw a Batarang at him or her,
More often than not the Batarang missed, but if it hit, the person on
the receiving end frequently needed hospital treatment: stitches or a
plaster cast.

The threat of the Batarang was not the worst problem to do with
Elvis's Batman fetish. It was unpleasant certainly if Elvis hurt members of his camp but if he damaged himself or risked his life then
everybody's status was threatened. Damaging himself was exactly
what he was likely to do as he began aping Batman stunts from his TV
screen or – worse – from the comic books themselves.

Abseiling in full costume down the east wing of Graceland from a
Batrope made everybody connected with Elvis nauseous with apprehension. Sooner or later disaster was bound to strike.

That was when Elvis tried to swing on a Batrope from his bedroom
window to the garage roof. The outward swing looked promising
enough. Elvis dived off, feet thrusting towards the hoped-for rooftop,
arms tensed on the rope. It looked very good for a successful landing.

Below, Vernon, the house and garden staff and the Guys held their
breath, prayed, crossed their fingers or covered their eyes.

Sure enough Elvis the Batman's feet touched down on the flat,
gravelled roof as he reached the farthest point of his radius. Sadly his

---

[2] *Karate Time With Elvis*, by Dennis Chang Jr, with Johnny Carson (Bimbo
Books, 1978).

feet had no more than touched the gravel before the momentum of his forward swing hauled him helplessly backward. His legs flailing desperately, Elvis slammed back against the wall beneath his bedroom window. A massive grunt (like this: OOOOFFFFFF!!!!!) was knocked out of Elvis's chest by the wall before he fell, unconscious, to the ground eight feet below.

An ambulance was summoned and Elvis was shortly laid out in a private ward, suffering from concussion, two sprained ankles and a contused thumb.

When he was able to think and speak clearly again, he gave Vernon precise instructions:

'Daddy? I want you to burn muh Batman costume. I'm done fightin' crime. I'm gon' stick to watchin' the TV show. I guess Adam West has stunt men to do them kinda things fur him. I ain't gon' do 'em no more, I tell you that.'

Soon after the Batman incident, the Colonel returned from his Hollywood negotiations and informed Elvis that he expected him to sign another three-picture deal with the Gargantuan Corporation. Elvis's response was a flat 'No'. He didn't even want to hear the plots of the scripts Colonel Tom had brought down from L.A. Elvis simply didn't want to do a movie. The King made it plain to the Colonel, in fact, that Elvis Presley would not be doing anything whatsoever until it suited him again.

'Aw now, come on, m'boy,' whined the Colonel. 'Y'all can't just turn down these movies out of hand. These movies are *quality*, son, and movies that you'll *enjoy* to act in too. I promise you, Elvis. These here movies'll be a laugh a minute for you. 'Twon't be nothing like it was in '58. There won't be no hangin' around. No hangin' around at all. Matter 'a' fact the production of this first one here, *Not Quite All There Is To Do With Girls After A Cocktail*, is ready to begin just as soon as you move up to Los Angeles.'

'I'm *not* doing any more films, Colonel.'

'What're you gonna do, then?'

'I'm gonna do nothing at all 'till I decide what I'm gonna do next.'

'Nothing at all?'

'Nothing at all.'

'What about your family? What about your staff? This house? You gonna keep that all goin' by doin' nothin'?'

'Colonel, you know I can afford to live like this for the resta my life even if I never lift another finger, so will you just *leave* it? I told you my answer. That's it, that's all.'

The Colonel lit a troubled cigar.

'Well son, I have to tell you, you're making a mistake.'

Tom Parker wasn't a man to keep on hacking at an obstacle in his path. Best way was to find a way round this. Best way round it was probably to leave Elvis for a couple of months and see if he'd changed his tune by then. If not, then something more drastic would have to be done.

Meanwhile, if Elvis had no plans to work, his back catalogue would have to work for him. The Colonel got onto the phone and spoke with Ron Schnozzle at BRA. If there were to be no more sound-tracks this year, there would have to be some different kinds of record. The first fruit of this conversation between two men of such discretion and good taste was *Elvis Presents a Showcase of His Golden Records Vol 1*, released in July 1966. This assiduously compiled hotchpotch of hits and fillers came in a charming sleeve which featured on the front a still of Elvis in *Lotsa Lady Lifeguards, Acapulco* (Elvis in Hawaiian shirt and Bermuda shorts reclining against a canary-yellow surfboard held vertical by eight bikini-clad beauties in pancake make-up) and Parker's sleeve notes above Elvis's signature on the back.

A sample paragraph gives the general idea:

'These songs are my own choice of the recordings I have made which have given me most pleasure – although not all of them are my best-known hits. You may not think "Take Your Little Girl Eyes (Off-a My Thighs)"[3] or "It's Your Hand on The Joystick That's Sending Me Above My Operation Ceiling"[4] belong to the list of my best-sellers. They don't – you're absolutely right. But they *are* among my favourite records. Honestly.'

Elvis Presents A Showcase of His Golden Records Vol 1 was a number one album, and so, inevitably, BRA followed it up in September of 1966 with *Elvis's Golden Records Vol 2 and Some Hits from His Movies*. This classic of its kind had the balance tipped in favour of movie hits with the score giving Proper Records 5, Movie Hits 6. Naturally, this selection includes the inimitable 'I'm Sitting In The Sand Looking For My Hand'.

When *Vol 2* went gold it seemed only fitting that Ron Schnozzle and his cohorts should squeeze out another compilation, *Some More Hits From The Movies and Elvis Recorded Talking In His Sleep At Graceland* before issuing *Elvis Wishes You All A Merry Christmas*, a best-selling album of Christmas carols recorded in Nashville by Charlie Rich. Nobody except for Elvis and Sam Phillips spotted that it was somebody other than Elvis wishing us all a merry Christmas. (Scotty Moore would without doubt have detected the fake recordings, but he had by now given up collecting or even listening to anything Elvis put out.)

Sam Phillips rang Elvis to inform him of the scandal.

[3] From, of course, *Little Girls Grow Up Fast And Grope Me*.
[4] An out-take from the *Driving A Sportscar Down To A Beach In Hawaii* Sessions.

Yeah, I know it ain't me. Y'think I wouldn't know about it? If I'd a recorded the 23rd Psalm I'd a remembered it, Mr Phillips.'

'Listen, Elvis,' Sam drawled, 'You gone sue them assholes at BRA, aren't you.

'Naw, I ain't, Mr Phillips.'

'That ain't you on the record. That's a crime, Elvis.'

'Who cares?'

Chapter 20

Another Place

The summer of 1966 was less than invigorating for Elvis. He would stomp about the house menacingly and pull ugly faces at himself in the mirror. Anyone irritating the King risked a cheeseburger in the face.

Elvis Presley was not a happy man.

One day however there came a phone call which at least offered the opportunity for him to interrupt the tedium of his daily vacuity. The caller was Brian Epstein who was phoning from CBS's studio in Nashville. The Beatles, he informed Elvis, were over to make a radical departure in their career: they were in the process of making an album which fused together the styles of the early rockers they had admired, Elvis included, and the country material which John Lennon and Paul McCartney had very recently begun to dig. Between writing the new material they were jamming country and Rock 'n' Roll standards in the studio. They were having 'rather a good time, actually'. Would Elvis care to join them for a day or so?

When Elvis received the message from Bill Orifice, who acted as a sort of telephone receptionist at Graceland, he didn't need too much persuading to fly across to Nashville.

He announced the decision to his father:

'Hell, I'm gone go, Daddy. I don't think these English boys know too much 'bout country music, or Rock 'n' Roll for that matter, but it might be fun to help 'em along a little.' The night, four years earlier, when he had witnessed the early Beatles in Soho, London, had sunk without trace in Presley's mind.

When Elvis's extensive black limousine drew up in the executive car park at the CBS studios the King stepped out of the back royally. The King was wearing a black shirt open at the collar and a cream suit with black pin-stripe, narrowly double-breasted and eight-buttoned. He looked like an Italian nightclub owner. He looked around airily – a reflex action rather than an attempt to spot something – and walked towards the highly-polished smoked glass double doors of the studio foyer.

Suddenly:

BONK!!

A plastic soccer ball descended from the sky and biffed the Memphis Flash right on his quiff. He staggered slightly and wheeled around.

'Poke a PIG!!!!' He thumped the limo's roof with the base of his fist causing a metallic reverberation THUNNKK!!

'Where in hell did that come from? I'm sure gon' *kill* somebody.

Two Beatles appeared from around the side of the studio.

'Hey mister! Can we have our ball back please?' said John.

Elvis stared in semi-shock.

'I tell you, son,' he shouted at the one who had spoken, 'I'm 'bout likely to give you balls in a paper bag to take home to feed to your goldfish. Now get outta muh sight 'fore I kick your scrawny asses. I got work to do in there.'

Lennon's hackles rose. He didn't much like the idea that his hero hadn't recognised him. What was the matter with Elvis? Did he really take himself so seriously?

'Hey, wait up,' Lennon called. 'I recognise you mister. I've seen your films. We all listen to your records back in England.'

Suitable pause while Elvis's ego is soothed. A man likes to be treated with due respect. 'You're Fabian, aren't you? Can I have your autograph for me auntie, please?'

Elvis fixed this English kid with a look that was designed to knock over a rhinoceros at twenty yards and stomped through the smoked-glass doors.

John Lennon kicked his special world cup souvenir football at Ringo who was unable to stop it for sniggering. The pair giggled like geese.

Orville Orifice, Elvis's chauffeur, stared at the two amateur soccer players in surprise. Recognition dawned on his face like a steam-roller coming over a hill at half-speed.

'Say! You guys are The *Beatles*!' he exclaimed.

'No,' said Ringo, 'we're out of Herman's Hermits. We're over on tour with The Beatles.'

'Aw, come off it man. You're The Beatles. Hey, y'know: I *love* all your records. That one – um – "Token To Ride"? It's – real neat, I wanna tell you.'

Lennon, standing on one leg, was tapping the ball off his right foot repeatedly. Ringo was feigning modest embarrassment.

'Aw shucks,' he said.

'Hey,' said Orville, 'I don't know which ones you are but I'd sure appreciate your autograph for muh girl?'

The two Beatles had by now turned back towards the area from which they and their ball had emerged.

'Sorry,' said John, retreating. 'We never sign autographs on Sundays.'

They disappeared from sight.

Orville sat back in the sumptuous driver's seat. 'Doggone!' he said, lighting a cigarette. 'Doggone!' He slapped the dash with a grunt of approving dismay. Then a thought occurred to him.

It was Wednesday today.

Inside the studio Elvis was greeted by a super-polite Brian Epstein, who proved to be the soul of courtesy, taking Elvis's jacket and asking if he would like a cup of tea. Having declined, Elvis was introduced to two Beatles, Paul McCartney and George Harrison.

'God, it's great you could come!' oohed McCartney as he shook Elvis's hand.

'I'm sure I've seen your face somewhere,' said Harrison when he was introduced.

This helped to break the ice.

Chitchat about touring, the fans, making movies ensued. Elvis asked The Beatles about their hits worldwide, which countries were the most fun to tour in, what their biggest buzz had been in the United States. George asked Elvis if it was true, as fan magazines had rumoured, that he had invented the cheeseburger.

'Sure is. Right over there in Memphis, in ah – oh, I guess about 1954 or '55. I can't remember rightly just now, but I'm the one that came up with them little mothers. Yup. Wish to hell I'd a patented em though.'

'We've been eating a *lot* of cheeseburgers over here,' said Paul. 'And thick shakes. We love your thick shakes. I like chocolate especially.'

'Oh,' said Elvis.

There was an awkward hiatus. McCartney and Harrison exchanged looks.

'Where's John?' Epstein enquired.

'Think he went for a walk,' said Paul.

'No, he went out for a bit of footie with Ringo,' said George.

'Footie' went over Elvis's head. He sat down at the studio piano and tickled a few chords.

'So – ah – what you all planning here? I'm not sure I caught your drift on the phone. You making an album of country and Rock 'n' Roll standards – is that it?'

'No; actually Elvis, we're gonna have a go at writing our own stuff in that vein, y'know. 'Cos like when we were at school we useta listen to all that sort of rock thingy,' McCartney said. 'Carl Perkins, Gene Vincent, Little Richard, Chuck Berry and, like, yourself, y'know? Well we sort of decided that we've kind a gone as far as we can along our present path y'know with our last LP which I don't know if you know y'know ah *Revolver*? An' we thought we'd like to get back to basics y'know.'

'I hear you,' said Elvis, nodding sagely.

'Well like when we was doin' our last tour over here we met a bloke in San Antonio who as well as really digging our stuff has had hits of his own – maybe you know him like, em, Doug Sahm?'

Elvis shook his head: 'Uh uh.'

'Well anyway he took us out in Texas and showed us a good time in these bars like and we saw a lotta good bands y'know and he bought us a whole buncha records to take back with us sort of. Um… there was a Hank Williams sort of greatest hits thingy – am – Jimmy Rodgers – Roy Acuff, Loretta Lynn, Hank Snow. Y'know all that sort of thing. So I guess we're gonna make an LP of songs somewhere between the two. Y'know like maybe a sort of country – rock thingy.'

Elvis took all this in paternalistic bearing.

'Yeah, I see what you're getting at.'

By now Brian Epstein had dug up John and Ringo. Dewy with sweat after their kick about, they bounced into the studio laughing.

'Hey John, where've you been?' said Paul.

'Wotcher Fabian,' said Lennon, winking at Elvis.

Elvis's face dropped as he realised his error.

"What the – you little pecker wood!' cried Elvis, breaking into laughter. 'I oughta break your ass for that.'

'Well you oughta know a Beatle when you see one,' replied John.

They both laughed good-naturedly.

'So – ah – how far into this here project are you now?' asked Elvis presently.

'Well we've got seven songs actually written,' said John, 'and half a dozen bits and pieces which need knocking together and we've just this morning recorded basic tracks for three of the seven songs.'

'Y'all put your vocals on last, right?'

'Yeah, that's right.'

'Well – ah – d'you mind if I – ah – watch you workin' for a spell?'

'Well I – I think we'd all be inhibited trying to record while our first-ever hero was watching. But it'd be good if we could maybe do something together. What d'you think Elvis?' asked John.

Elvis drummed a few more piano chords out.

'It'd be nice, but I'm not working right now. I'm – ah – takin' a little time off.'

'This would be fun,' said Paul, 'but if you don't wanna do it, like, that's cool, y'know.'

'Yeah. We had Slim Whitman on the phone this morning. He's *achin'* t'do it,' said Ringo.

Everybody laughed.

'Come on Elvis,' said John. 'How often does a soddin' genius get the chance to work with other geniuses?'

'Well… what y'got?'

What The Beatles had for Elvis was the roughs of their new material and together the five musicians messed around for two days with songs and bits of songs until there were a dozen numbers either recorded or well enough rehearsed to record. By the end of the second day The Beatles had seven tracks for their album in the can. They were pleased with what they had done and Elvis was quite impressed at the speed with which they worked; these were guys after his own heart.

The seven finished pieces didn't all find their way onto The Beatles' highly influential 1966 album *Another Place*,[1] so it's worth listing the material that Elvis had a sneak preview of back then. There was the bluesy rocker, 'Matthew Street'; the country ballad title track; '(The Train's On Time, I've Arrived, But You're Not On) The Platform' – a Lennon rocker in the Gene Vincent tradition; some Berryesque Rock 'n' Roll in 'Austin A30'; a plaintive McCartney love song – 'Too Little Time' – which featured George Harrison's very first attempt on steel guitar; the token Ringo vocal number, 'Me Money's Run Out', which has of course since come to be known as the 'Phone Kiosk Song'; and Lennon's problematic tackling of the Hank Williams ballad style in 'I'm Quite Lazy'.

Elvis had insisted that The Beatles do a selection of their songs on their own before the five of them made a stab at recording together. The truth of the matter was that he felt highly insecure about working with these English boys who had been conquering the world whilst his own career had fallen into some confusion. Sure, he was proud of his first country album, but the second one had definitely been a mistake. And now here were these young turks coming onto his patch and writing successfully not only in the genre he had just been dabbling in, but also coming up with the best new Rock 'n' Roll songs written since the late '50s. It was frightening; there was no getting around that.

On the other hand, threatened as he might be, there was no way he could leave this studio without recording with these guys. He could look like a fool – or worse, a nut – if he walked out on The Beatles now, and he respected them too much not to have them respect him.

So it was that during the course of the second day in the CBS studio that Elvis steeled himself to take on these young pretenders and show them the stuff a *real* rocker could strut.

When they had all listened to the playback of The Beatles' seven finished songs and the last strains of harmonica and steel guitar in 'I'm

---

[1] *Another Place* was acknowledged by Gram Parsons as one of the catalysts for The Byrds' *Sweetheart Of The Rodeo* from which came modern American country rock.

Quite Lazy' were echoing around the studio, Elvis cast down his gauntlet.

'Uh, listen, guys. I wanna record with y'all tomorrow, okay? Y'know that sort of Little Richard-style y'all were practising yesterday' – he was referring to the now notorious 'I'm Gone' - 'I wanna try that one time if 't'd be alright.'

The Beatles exchanged pleased looks.

'Well, Elvis,' said John, 'I hope you won't take this too hard, but we had kinda ear-marked that one for Perry Como.'

On the third day:

Cracking snare drum-roll   !!!!!!!!!!!!

Bass guitar and bass-drum thuds   !!!!

Two brief chopped guitar chords   !!

Two slammed piano chords   !!

Paul's index finger up the keyboard   !

Then we get, somewhere in the region of 'Lucille' / 'Good Golly Miss Molly' (quite a region):

'The word is out honey
It's spreading all over town
Yeaaahhhhhhhbhh!!!!
The word is out little girl
It's spreading all over town
Everybody I've been talking to
Says that you've been putting me down
                              (down down)
You better find another fellow to walk on
    'Cause I'm gone.'

The first attempt wasn't to everybody's satisfaction, so, since they were aiming for a live take, Elvis Presley and his new backing group, The Beatles, went into 'I'm Gone' a second time. At the end of that, all were satisfied.

'Ever thought of doing this for a living, Elvis?' said George.

Flushed with success, the Quintessential Quintet naturally wanted to do a second number. 'Deck Chair' and 'Father's Pigeons', which of course later turned up on *Another Place*, were offered but Elvis complained of not being able to relate to the subject matter. In the end they did a song which should have been obvious from the start, a slightly melodramatic piece of Lieber/Stoller-style rock called 'For A Laugh'.

On this Elvis really broke out the show-stopping vocal inflecting that had made his name in 1956. The Memphis Flash took his tone from the title and sang in the rather jokey style that had invigorated 'Blue Moon Of Kentucky' and 'I Don't Care If The Sun Don't Shine' way back when. Elvis's delivery of the punch-line,

'Ain't gonna follow no beaten path
When I do something it'll be for a laugh
For a laugh
Oh yeah
For a laugh',

is one of the most purely joyous moments in the history of Rock 'n' Roll records.

There seemed to be nothing to do after this but go and have a drink somewhere. Paul suggested a little bar on Broadway down in Nashville: Shooter's, where there was a dingy little resident band playing hillbilly Rock 'n' Roll every night.

Elvis balked at the prospect.

'Uh I can't go into no bar-room. I'm like to get ripped to shreds if I go out amongst people.'

'God, Elvis,' said Lennon, 'we've been going into this place regularly since we came to town. And we *are* quite well known. Nobody gives a bugger. And the ones that do recognise you only stare a bit or at the worst ask for an autograph.'

'Aw, I don't know…'

'C'mon, Elvis; live a little.'

'You sure?'

'Is the Pope Catholic?' said John Lennon.

In Shooter's, with two Beatles bodyguards, the moptops and Elvis drank beer and shouted in one another's ears whilst the band ripped through 'Poppa Let Me Borrow The Car', 'Honey Hush', 'That'll Be The Day' and the like. They laughed a good deal and swapped reminiscences and The Beatles encouraged Elvis to do something himself – record, tour – anything to get him out of the rut that it was obvious he was in. Elvis made only non-committal responses. Everybody got very drunk and the party overflowed into Elvis's hotel suite. When the night came to an exhausted end in the wee wee hours, the five of them agreed to have breakfast together late the next morning before Elvis flew back to Memphis.

When Paul McCartney rang Elvis's hotel at eleven the morning after, he was informed that Mr Presley had checked out.

Clearly Elvis had gone home early.

In succeeding weeks, Epstein spent a good deal of time on the phone with Parker and in October 1966 the Elvis/Beatles single was issued by EMI in co-operation with BRA. 'I'm Gone' /' For A Laugh' would have been a number one hit around the world had it featured nothing more than the five of them doing animal impressions. As it was, the record was in fact a hot piece of Rock 'n' Roll, the heights of which The Beatles were not to re-attain until they recorded 'Lady

Madonna' during the sessions for their 1969 valedictory album *That's it – We Quit*. Elvis, as we shall see, was to wait some time himself before he too could function at this level of artistry again.

'I'm Gone' went straight in at number one on the American and the British charts – something never achieved before. Not even John Lennon's eccentric statement in Newsweek could halt the record's irresistible rise. In one of Lennon's little idiosyncratic fits, the thinking person's Beatle had claimed in all seriousness that 'I'm Gone' and 'For A Laugh' were *not* Elvis/Beatles recordings.

No. The hottest single in the history of the music business was a fake recorded in London by Jerry Lee Lewis and the Merseybeats.

'Ask anyone at EMI,' said Lennon. 'They'll tell you.'[2]

---

[2] Incidentally, this little joke of John's led indirectly to the break-up of The Beatles. Paul McCartney thought Lennon's joke thoroughly irresponsible, contending that it could have affected the success of 'I'm Gone'. A bitter argument ensued, as a result of which McCartney vowed never to work with or speak to Lennon again. It remains one of rock's best-kept secrets that Lennon and McCartney never spoke to each other between 1966 and 1974. They exchanged messages via George or Ringo. Had they been on speaking terms, not only might the break-up of The Beatles have been avoided, but so too might their 1967 movie disaster *On The Bus, Jack*. This film involved John, Paul, George and Ringo catching a number 36 bus in Kennington, finding that the conductor was Kenneth Williams and ending up in a laundrette in Florence. Lennon, suspicious from the start, hated the rough print and told George to tell Paul that he wanted the movie destroyed. George forgot to pass on the message and the movie bombed at the box-office.

Chapter 21

Nostalgia

Inside Graceland, sheltered from view by trees and a civilised distance from the main road in Whitehaven, Elvis brooded through the late summer and autumn of 1966. Living by night and sleeping by day, he returned to the pattern of life he had established before The Beatles had interrupted his sojourn in the doldrums. Depressed and at odds with himself, the King attempted to alleviate his despondency in bacchanalian excess.

On one of his more excessive nights, Elvis would breakfast and then go for a walk in the grounds of Graceland, where he would throw hand grenades into neighbouring gardens in a desperate attempt to rid himself of his boredom. Returned from his exercise in destructiveness, the waning King of Rock would escape to his bedroom suite and order three girls to be brought up from Memphis.

When the ladies arrived, they would find Elvis sitting in a leather-bound armchair, wearing a lapis-lazuli blue velvet suit. Bill Orifice would make the introductions and arrange seats close to Elvis for his guests. Perhaps Elvis would talk to the girls a little: ask them their names, whereabouts in Memphis they lived, what kind of music they liked or what they thought of Spiro Agnew's tailor.

Then, without rising from his seat, Elvis would ask the girls to remove their clothes. As a matter of course, the girls summoned by Bill would do so until Elvis would stop them from taking off their panties. This would always be a surprise to the girls, for none of them ever visited more than once, and all of them expected to accommodate Elvis. They would try not to register surprise, however. Their efforts in this respect would have to be doubled at the next move. Elvis would point to some cans of shaving foam on a table by the hearthside and request that the girls coat each other with this (Gillette Lemon & Lime Foam was almost always used), being careful not to put any foam on their hair, their faces or their panties. When this was complete, Elvis would open the beautifully bound copy of Kahlil Gibran's *The Prophet* on his lap and begin to read to the assembled shaving-creamed beauties. If any girl so much as moved Elvis would abruptly stop reading and insist on repairing any cracks in her shaving-foam skin.

When Elvis had read 'til his heart was content, he would carefully close *The Prophet* and rise from his seat. Walking over to the mantel-piece he would place the book there and warm his hands at the fire. Then he would ask the girls to stand up before producing a plastic kitchen spatula and beginning to super-delicately scrape off all the shaving foam from each of the three bodies.

Twenty minutes later – it would take that long – Elvis would lie down on the bed with the three girls and ask them to close their eyes. When everyone was comfortable Elvis would begin to fantasise aloud a situation where the four of them were sitting in a convertible at a drive-in movie. Usually the girls would be quick to pick up on the spiel and the four of them would converse as if in the convertible.

ELVIS: Sure is a dull movie, girls.

GIRL ONE: Uh huh, sure is.

ELVIS: D'you see *The Searchers*? Now there *was* one helluva good movie.

GIRL THREE: Yeah, I saw that. Isn't that the one where Kirk Douglas and Burt Lancaster are out to get each other?

ELVIS: *What*? You crazy? 'S got the Dook in it.

GIRL ONE: Who?

ELVIS: The *Dook*. John Wayne. He's muh favourite actor.

GIRL TWO: You're thinkin' of *I Walk Alone*.

ELVIS: I ain't seen that one. What'd he play in there?

GIRL TWO: Who?

ELVIS: The *Dook*!

GIRL TWO: He wasn't in *I Walk Alone*. It was Kirk Douglas and Burt Lancaster. The movie *she* was talking about.

ELVIS: I don't like Lancaster. He looks like he's asleep.

GIRL THREE: Oh I *love* him. He's real cuddly.

ELVIS: I don't like Kirk Douglas neither.

GIRL ONE: Why ever not? His dimple is just *gonesville*.

ELVIS: Naw. He's a Armenian. Y'should never trust an Armenian. Anyone'll tell you that.

GIRL THREE: Hey, come off it. He's American as apple pie.

ELVIS: No he *ain't*! He come over here from Armenia. I read it in a magazine.

GIRL THREE: Y'can't believe everything you read in magazines and papers. They tell some o' the most awful whoppers in newspapers.

GIRL TWO: Well he sure don't *talk* like a Armenian.

GIRL ONE: Why? What's a Armenian talk like?

GIRL TWO: Why, he talks like an American.

ELVIS: A Armenian talks like an American??

GIRL TWO: Noooo! Kirk *Douglas* talks like an American.

ELVIS: Aw hell, I'm sicka this argument. Let's get some coke and popcorn. Who's gone go?

GIRL ONE: I'll go, I'll go!

ELVIS: Well here, take some money, an' can y'bring me a large nut Hershey bar, huh?

It was during this reclusive period of Elvis's life that the star was buttonholed one night in early 1967 by a freelance journalist at the gates of Graceland. Elvis, stalking the grounds with thin polythene bags full of natural yoghurt which he used for chucking at unsuspecting porcupines (the entertainment lay in the dicey business of whether or not the bag burst on the porcupine's spines), was stopped in his tracks as he passed close to the gates.

'Excuse me? Mr Presley?' came the stage-whispered cry.

'UuuhuHHH!!' cried an alarmed Elvis jumping in the air.

'Oh, I'm sorry: I didn't mean to startle you,' the voice apologised.

'Goddam, son,' said Elvis, 'don't ever come up on a man from behind like that. I'm carrying a .44 magnum. A man gets caught from the rear like that is very likely to spin around an' blow the head off whoever is dumb enough to come up on him from behind. You understand all of that?'

'Oh, yessir, I do,' said the voice, still whispering.

'This here revolver's bout likely to leave you more hole than head if'n I's to use it on you. A Colt .44 Magnum'll blow clean through a engine block.'

'I'm sorry I was so thoughtless, Mr Presley.'

'Well now, get away from m'gates.'

'I just wanted to ask you Mr Presley. Do you – ah – have any plans to make more records or movies?'

'What's your name, son?'

'Uh, Bradford Dork, sir.'

'What do *you* know about records or movies? Huh?' sneered Elvis.

'Well – I – ah – that is –'

'Whyncha just go away now, son, 'fore I lose muh temper.'

'Just one thing, Mr Presley', said Bradford Dork from his side of the gates.

'Better be quick,' Elvis threatened.

'Have you got any statement for the – ah – press, sir?'

Elvis thought about this for a moment, toying with his revolver as he did so. In a moment, Elvis raised his arms into a V at right angles to his torso, squatted slightly as he took aim, and blew a ten-inch diameter branch off a nearby pine. Then he turned to Bradford Dork and mumbled something.

What it sounded like to Dork was this: 'I'm gon' nuke the gooks!'

What Elvis *actually* said was: 'I'm gon' cook the goose!'

(This was prompted by Elvis's recent experiments with poultry and pork, which led to the burger breakthroughs of 1974.)

Dork sold his story to the *Washington Post* and news of Elvis's bellicose intentions was syndicated around the world within the week. Colonel Tom tried to issue a disclaimer, to little effect and finally Elvis had to issue a statement saying that he had never made this outrageous claim – which of course he hadn't. By then though the damage was done. People in just about any town south of the Mason-Dixon Line were demanding the destruction of Hanoi.

BRA were on the ball quickly and, realising that no publicity is bad publicity, slammed out a hastily compiled and shoddily packaged compilation of Elvis's Rock 'n' Roll work from the '50s. *Elvis Rockin'* went gold in March, 1967.

Elvis's culinary experiments in 1966 coincided with a renewed interest in religion. Elvis's research into spiritual writings sprang from a natural interest in religion that had been with him his whole life long. Vernon and Gladys had sung hymns with Elvis when he had been a boy and had encouraged him to be Christian and attend church. Always lurking at the back of Elvis's nature was the fundamentalist Christianity of his upbringing, despite the temptations of the star's life and the vicissitudes of his personality. Now, however, his interest extended into Eastern religions and Kahlil Gibran was only part of his readings. Lobsang Rampa, Buddhist scriptures, the Koran and writings on the occult all engrossed Elvis at one stage or another.

It was during a faddist spate of religious reading in 1967 that Elvis became caught up in an unlikely sequence of events which were to lead him across half a continent and alter his life radically.

One warm evening in May, Elvis was out cruising the streets of Memphis in his latest model Cadillac Fleetwood. Driving himself, with three of the guys along for the ride, Elvis was coasting quietly through areas he had haunted as a boy.

There was Humes High School. And a fond reminiscence of the days he spent there would follow. The guys would feign interest, but the pretence was difficult to maintain: they had heard all of these memoirs many times before.

There was the Memphian Theatre.

'Any you guys remember Rita Mae?'

'Rita Mae who?'

'Rita Mae Watermelon. Jeez, she was a little goer, for sure.'

There was the dog pound.

'Anyone ever see Lamar Pike these days?'

'Hell, no. He left town years ago.'

Giuseppe Giuseppe's.

'Still goin' strong, huh. I must git along in there someday soon an' check out the opra stuff. It's a long time since I had a Mario Lanza record on the phonograph. He was a good ol' boy, Mr Giuseppe. Useta show me some real fine stuff.'

'He's a freakin' soft lad, boss.'

'You shut your face, Frank. Ain't no need to say that. Ain't no business of ours what he is. He's a kind man.'

There was Sal's Diner.

'Great man, Sal. I gave him my cheeseburger recipe, y'know. Ain't many people knows I invented the cheeseburger. But I did. Yep. Elvis Presley invented the cheeseburger. Someday I'm gone get me some credit for that.'

The car glided on, passing along suburban streets bordered with poplars or wild cherry trees, copper beech or young elms. The guys broke out some cigars and they smoked one apiece, enjoying the soft light and calm of a Southern summer's evening.

'Hey boys, what say we get us some food? I got a mind for a heapa stefados at Ron Scrupulous's place,' said Elvis as he picked up the car phone to ring for a reservation. 'Awww, poke a *pig*, man. This phone's dead again. Whyncha just get a new phone installed, Bill? This one's not worth repairing again.'

'Boss, stop quick! There's a call-box,' cried Orville.

Elvis got out and entered the booth. Before he could drop his loose change in the receptacle, the phone rang. Without thinking Elvis picked up the receiver.

'Hi,' said a loping feminine voice. 'Is that Shades Club?'

'Aw no, ma'am,' said a disconcerted Elvis.

'Is that Las Vegas 853 4662?'

'Ah no, ma'am. This here is a Memphis phone booth, ma'am.'

'Are you putting me on? Look if you're messing me around, man. … This is just *too* much. I was *promised* a reply by the end of last week and you guys have just left me out in the cold. I wish you people would show a little more courtesy and consideration. I have to eat like everyone else and to eat I have to work. Now have I got the job or *what*?'

'What job?'

'Ohh! Gawwwd!! The go-go dancer job you auditioned me for last week in San Francisco.'

'Ummm I – ah – I didn't audition you for no go-go job, ma'am. This here's Memphis. I'm standing in a phone booth waitin' to make a call out. Your call came in before I could get going properly.'

'For chrissakes! Who are you, you *stiff*?'

'Muh name's Elvis Presley, ma'am.'

Laughter guffawed across the telephone wires.

'Yeah and I'm Benjamin Franklin.'

'Who?'

'Forget it. Who are you really?'

'It's like I said, ma'am. I'm Elvis Presley.'

'Oh yeah? Well if you're Elvis, sing me something to prove it.'

'What you wanna hear, ma'am?'

'Aw hell, lemme see. Shit, what was it he useta sing?'

'You're awful good for a fella's ego, miss.'

'Hey, wait a minute; it's coming. Elvis sang "Blue Suede Shoes", right?'

'Well ah listen…' And the real Elvis really sang 'Blue Suede Shoes' along the phone lines. But not very well; after all, he was rusty.

He did just a verse and a chorus.

'Shit, man, you don't sound much like Elvis to me.'

'Well, I gotta tell you I *am*, ma'am, and one thing's for certain: I got things I could be doin' besides trying to persuade you who I am.'

'Groovy! Hey, if you're Elvis why don't you come buy me a drink.'

'Yeah, I'd like that okay. I's just gone out for a bite to eat with the guys. Where are you and I'll come by and pick you up?'

'Right now I'm in Oakland but I can meet you in San Francisco if it makes things any easier.

'San Francisco!! You're in San Fran*cisco*!! I thought I *told* you: I'm in Memphis, Tennessee.'

Elvis sounded fit to blow a valve.

This didn't faze his phone-pal one iota.

'Well gee, if you're really Elvis I guess you just gotta leap into your private plane to get over here in a flash,' she teased.

'You're a bare-faced one, I'll give y'that,' said Elvis, in admiration.

'It's cool. If you wanna fly over, it'll be fine. I don't mind if you really *are* Elvis Presley. It's no problem. Really.'

Elvis chuckled with surprise at the nerve of this girl.

'What's your name honey?' he enquired.

'I'm Joanna Wade. Look, you hop on your plane and I'll meet you – ah – well, when'll you be here?'

'I guess I'll be there in time for lunch tomorrow.'

'Okay. I'll meet you in the Howard Johnson's on Fisherman's Wharf. How'll I know you?'

Elvis paused. Then he laughed.

'I guess I'll try m'best to look like Elvis Presley,' he said. 'How'll I know you?'

'I got black, black hair that's long an' wavy and I'll be smokin' a pipe most likely. Don't worry about it, man. If what y'say is true, I guess I'll know you.'

'Okay. I'll see you tomorrow.'

'Right. About one. Byeeee.'

Chapter 22

Head Case

Arented limousine picked up Elvis with Bill and Orville Orifice at San Francisco airport, whisked them up and down the city's inclines and drew up outside Howard Johnson's on the Wharf at 12.45 the following afternoon.

Walled into his limousine luxury by reflective windows, Elvis sat and twiddled his thumbs apprehensively. He seriously wished that he had not made this impulsive, foolhardy trip. This woman was going to turn out to be a pig in pink lipstick, he just knew it. Her assertiveness and the golden confidence of her sun-tinged voice had set off chains of chemical reaction within him. But there was no sense with this, no sense at all. He was making a fool of himself and no mistake.

One of the guys lit a cigarette.

'Put that out,' said Elvis. 'It's buggin' me.'

He reached over and depressed the electric window rocker switch momentarily. A crack of unfiltered sky appeared in the sombre environment of the limousine. There was the sound of cable-car bells and seagulls. Elvis lowered the window some more and inhaled the light sea breeze.

He looked at his diamond-studded gold Rolex.

1.02.

Tensed like a bow-string, he sprang from the car, checked the guys when they went to follow him and strode into Howard Johnson's.

Elvis was dressed in a red Harrington, cream canvas jeans and a navy-blue tennis shirt. He wore dark glasses.

Inside he looked around for the girl with the black hair but couldn't see much through his dark glasses – which he certainly wasn't going to take off. The hell with it, he thought, making for a table; let her find him.

He hadn't been sitting more than a couple of minutes when a woman appeared, a beautifully curved, calm-faced, poised woman.

'You're Elvis Presley,' she said and sat down.

Elvis was a bit taken aback. When he had recovered his composure, he replied, 'Yes, I am. I tried m'best to tell you that on the phone.'

'Right, right. So what's happening?' she drawled in the coolest of intonations.

Elvis looked around him, perturbed.

'Is something happenin', ma'am?'

'Y'all *is* a suthen gen'l'ma-an, ain't you,' she teased.

'What are you, then?' asked Elvis.

'I'm a poet, man,' she replied.

'A poet, huh. Don't think I ever met a poet, ma'am. What d'you write about?'

'Well, a lot of things really. Circumstance. Coincidence. I try to get behind my problems, work through and get clear. My poetry is an exorcism. I'm also trying to find out what's happening. Why it's happening and what it means to me. That's a pretty *explicit* answer, I guess. Could I have a lemon tea?'

Later they walked through the leathercraft, art and jewellery stalls around the Wharf. The girl was eighteen years old. She couldn't 'relate' to her parents. She wished they'd 'get off my case'. She felt that the 'generation gap' was 'just mind-boggling'. The problem was that her father was in a 'low credibility situation' and her mother was 'an ongoing plastic drudge'. Did Elvis dig? All she really wanted to do was to dance.

'To dance is to live. When I dance I free my psyche of all the white middle-class plastic shit.'

Frankly, Elvis didn't know what she was on about half the time, but her dogmatic manner and self-possession were totally absorbing to him. She was the first woman in an age, it seemed, that he actually wanted to hump. The terrible thing was, nothing he would normally say in such a circumstance seemed very appropriate for this left-fielder. What put the icing on the cake of her attractiveness was her failure to ask Elvis anything at all – not one thing – about his life as a Star. No dumb questions. She made him feel dumb.

'Let's get outa here,' she said presently. 'The ocean is cool but I can't stand to be around all these tourist traps. It really brings me down.'

Elvis led her to his waiting limousine and the guys. Bill and Orville, after being introduced, tactfully sat in the front leaving Elvis and his new acquaintance alone in the smoked-glass limbo. Joanna suggested that they go to the place where she was staying.

'I don't have a place a my own anymore, y'see. I was counting on this dancing job in Vegas that I told you about. So I'm staying with this guy up Haight/Ashbury, like. You can come in, though. It's cool.'

When he was with this girl, it seemed that the cat had got his tongue. All he could do was sit and stare and respond.

'Everything's happening in San Francisco, right now. I guess it's the hub of the universe,' she went on. 'Of course the reason is astrological but there's been a growth of energy here for a few years now.

I've grown with it. I mean, I have a consciousness now which I didn't have at all when I left home. I understand the basic structure of the universe now. Like I don't know *everything*, of course, but there is a basic structure which I now understand through just *being* here.'

'I been lookin' for meanin' too, Joanna. I been readin' about God an the Spirit but I can't say I can pin it down like that.'

'It's not *everything*. It's just the basic structure. Like the seasons and birth, growth, maturity, decay and death. I guess we're like that. Everything is like that. That's the arc of the universe. A project, a relationship, a *day* – they all describe an arc of growth and zenith and decline and death. Like the sun. All of this knowledge is here, right here in San Francisco.'

Joanna's enthusiasm for her subject matter was affecting.

'But why are you tryin' to go to Vegas?' Elvis asked. 'If everything's here in San Francisco, why leave it all?'

'It's obvious, man. Because of the arc of the universe. I've reached the bottom of the arc of my relationship with San Francisco. I gotta move on.'

When she had directed Orville to the place she was staying, Joanna invited all of them to come up. Rather than risk the boss's displeasure, Orville and Bill declined the offer.

Inside the apartment, Joanna talked to Elvis from a bedroom as she changed. Listening and replying, Elvis took in his surroundings. The room was filled with junkshop furniture. Run-down '30s and '40s stuff, most of it. The walls were a decayed cream – they had probably once been magnolia. He rifled through a pile of records carelessly. Jazz; he hated jazz. Many of the artists were a mystery to him and didn't look from the cover shots to be jazz musicians.

Joanna emerged in a long flowing cheesecloth dress which was embroidered haphazardly with tiny petalled flowers. She wore Jesus boots on her suntanned feet.

'Would you like some jasmine tea?' she asked and went about making it.

Try anything once, thought Elvis.

'This apartment belongs to a friend of mine,' she continued. 'He's a lapsed Catholic priest who's into Buddhism and sex. He's real funny. He says he wants to perfect the art of immobile sex. You'll see him tonight.'

'Why? What's happening tonight?'

'Well I'm goin' to a be-in at the Fillmore. You'd like to come, wouldn't you?'

'I – ah – what's a be-in?'

'It's an event. They had the first one in January in Golden Gate Park. It was the Human Be-in. This won't be quite that special but it should be a buzz. Andy Warhol's Plastic Inevitable are in town.'

'What's that?'

'The Exploding Plastic Inevitable? I don't know. It's got a rock band in called the Velvet Underground who're supposed to be really *mean* and it's a multi-media thing. Things at the Fillmore tend to be okay. You comin'?'

'Well, I'd like to, honey,' said Elvis, 'but I don' wanna be recognised.'

'Nobody'll know you. We'll mess up your hair a little and I'll lend you some clothes. Come on, man. Live dangerously.'

Elvis and Joanna walked into the Fillmore amongst a burgeoning crowd keen with anticipation. Elvis looked like any other hippy dude with his hair messed up and a blue Indian cotton kaftan on. The air was heady with incense and joss. People in fluorescent-painted bell-bottom jeans and love beads greeted one another as tapes of Ravi Shankar, The Grateful Dead, The Great Society, Jefferson Airplane, Dylan, The Beatles (not *Another Place*) and Donovan pumped through the PA. Tie-dyed T-shirts and lentil stews were on sale from peripheral stalls. Couples shared plastic cups of freshly squeezed orange juice and paper bags of dried fruit mix. A long-haired hippy with a badly woven thong headband distributed handbills which declared: 'LOVE IS HAPPENING.' In one corner a large, lumbering, scrap-metal kinetic sculpture sat ominously, breaking into motion only when somebody triggered its weights and counterbalances with a blow. LOVE was day-glo-ed on the wall in lime green. The music changed. Rather than the folk musicians of youth, strange bubbling, gurgling, rippling, sizzling electronic tones and cadences danced and rumbled through the PA now.

In two corners speedy stroboscopes began to flicker alarmingly for intermittent three-minute bursts. In the periods of more normal light, balloons and streamers jiggled or floated through the air. Elvis spotted boys and girls with multi-coloured paint all over their faces, even a girl in granny-glasses with eyes painted in the lenses. Light projections spread fluid, nauseating patterns across innocent walls. Now and again coloured lights blinked or flashed, police-patrol-car-like beacons spun eerily, flashing blue across the sea of absorbed, distracted faces. Dancers frugged and jerked, one girl removing her calico blouse and bouncing her rounded breasts frantically.

'Poke a pig!' Elvis whispered.

'Everybody's here,' Joanna explained. 'Kesey, Cassidy, McClure, Ferlinghetti, Ginsberg, Garcia, Kantner, Pigpen, Grace Slick. You picked a groovy time to come to town.'

'I didn't pick nothin', sweetheart,' Elvis laughed. 'You twisted my arm into coming. Who'd you say was here? I ain't ever heard a none a them.'

'They're all local figures. Writers, poets, musicians. This is a big night: New York comes to San Francisco.'

The Velvet Underground assembled and stumbled into a feet-up-and-relax version of 'Waiting For My Man'.

'God Almighty!' said Elvis. 'And I thought Dylan couldn't sing!'

The band played 'Venus in Furs'.

'Shee-it. Do we haveta wait this one out? I never heard a noise like this. Sounds like somebody swingin' a cat by the tail.'

'It's a real downer, I'll admit,' said Joanna. 'I thought they might be more – uh – positive, but, like, this is real demoralising stuff.'

The audience muttered and shuffled. Songs about addiction and masochism were beyond the experience or range of interest of your average San Francisco hippy.

'I mean, like, negative vibrations.'

After the 'event' there was a party in a warehouse off Market Street.

Elvis was introduced to Joanna's lapsed Catholic priest friend. Joanna neglected to mention who Elvis was, so when asked he said his name was Wilf.

'Well, Wilf, did you get off on the Velvets?' said the lapsed Catholic priest.

'Excuse me?'

'Did you get off on the band, man?'

'No, it's ah not really my kind of music.'

'Not your bag, huh?'

'No, not really.'

'Here: y'wanna toke?'

'No sir; I don' smoke.'

'That's cool.'

'I understand you useta be a priest?' said Elvis.

'Surely did. I fell off the straight an' narrow an' missed the Pearly Gates.'

'That's a tragedy.'

'No it ain't. I got wise to the universe. The microcosm is the macrocosm. When I go into me I go into God. I peeled the onion and set the record straight. Y'know where I'm comin' from?'

Elvis nodded uneasily and excused himself.

He went looking for Joanna, wading through people, bottles and crockery. Along the way he passed Orville and Bill in separate places, one staring blankly before him as saliva ran down his lower lip, the other having his wrist nuzzled by a pre-Raphaelite nymph wearing only jeans.

When finally he found Joanna, she was sitting in the lotus position before an uncurtained window. On closer inspection it was clear that she was studying the stars. He didn't disturb her. She was the prettiest little thing in the whole wide world. For a long time he just sat there and soaked up her presence. Then he put a gentle hand on her shoulder.

'Whyncha come back to Memphis with me, for a spell,' he said. 'This ain't my scene here, but I think you're real neat, honey.'

Joanna took him by the hand and led the Memphis Flash back to the lapsed Catholic priest's apartment. With no vestiges of San Francisco or Memphis close enough to come between them, they nestled close and Joanna proved herself to be a poet for Elvis. In the morning she sent him home, in the nicest possible way.

The night was such a night that the coals in Elvis's chest warmed him all the way to Memphis and for a week after his return there.

The King of Rock was so renewed by his brief contact with this teenage hippy that he got on the phone to Los Angeles and fulfilled a long-time ambition. Elvis arranged with the show's producers to make a guest appearance on the *Batman* TV series.

Elvis's episode was filmed quickly and went out in the fall of 1967. In it, our hero plays a villain specially invented for his appearance on the show. Elvis is a criminal genius who hypnotises unsuspecting audiences of debutantes with his rock music while his partner deftly relieves them of their jewellery. King Rocker, the Elvis part, was costumed in skin-tight pink leather. Per Centage, his partner, wore a pinstriped suit and carried an attaché case.

Elvis's characterisation of King Rocker on *Batman* merely confirmed the singer's growing reputation as an eccentric reclusive weirdo. Critics expressed shock and horror, while Elvis's die-hard fans watched in concerned silence.

BRA, never stuck for a commercial proposition issued *Elvis Rockin' Again*, a barrel-scraping of his '50s Rock 'n' Roll material, the week that the King Rocker episode of *Batman* went out.

Chapter 23

Come Back, Baby, Come Back

Elvis's appearance on *Batman* left the Colonel an unhappy man. He couldn't help feeling that 'his boy' was getting at him in this unusual television appearance. The *Batman* show apart, the good ol' Colonel was anyway far from being content. Elvis hadn't made a personal appearance since 1965 and there had been no recording done since the sessions with The Beatles which in any case had produced only one worldwide hit, and that a shared one. To compound this, any talk of a return to the movies prompted Elvis to run off and hide in the nearest wardrobe.

Yes, the Colonel was not satisfied with the productivity of his investment. It was true that money flowed in from Elvis's merchandising – Elvis Presley pliable dolls with sixteen costumes/accessory packs were currently very popular – and from the repackaging of old material. The latter, though, was finally beginning to wear thin. This prompted Ron Schnozzle and his boys at BRA to come up with the startlingly original idea that became *Elvis Demos*, a US Top 20 album. What the title of the record suggests, a collection of rough takes sung by Elvis, is scummy enough, but the reality is far worse. *Elvis Demos* is in fact a dozen songwriters' demos sent to Elvis for possible recording. In the event, all of these songs (including 'I Made These Bookshelves Myself', 'Keep Off The Grass (There's A Fine Involved)' and 'I Love You So Much (Since You Had Your Operation') were turned down by Elvis. But not by BRA. Critics by and large ignored the release, which was so crass that even the devout Elvis Presley Fan Club of Great Britain described it as 'not a first-rate Elvis record, though it is of interest'.

Then again, there was a fair amount of money to be made from the annual US tours the Colonel had been sending Elvis's solid gold Cadillac on since 1966. Sitting, predictably, in a tent, the car that had never been driven because of its immovable weight attracted hordes of Elvis's devotees in major cities. At $1 a viewing for adults and 98c for children, the income was not to be sniffed at.

'Elvis, son,' said the old buzzard on a visit to Graceland one day, 'if'n you don't get out and get seen, you ain't gon' have no more hits and you ain't gon' be able to call yourself King no more. They's a bunch of competition out there now. They got a band now called The Monkees is on TV an' they's selling records fast as they can press 'em up. I think it's time you did a TV programme all of your own.'

Elvis mulled this one over.

'Hmmm. What's the point a that, Colonel? I'm a singer. 'F I want to *do* something then I guess I might make a record.'

Seizing at this grand concession the Colonel secured the idea and tried for more:

'Sure you gon' make a record, m' boy. Sure y'are. But it's a different world now. When you was comin' up TV was mighty useful to plug your records. Now they ain't an act in the business can have his records *without* TV. The Monkees, The Beatles, The Beards – all a them there groups is all over the goddam TV networks. Yup. What you gotta do is make a record and a TV show at the same time.'

'Well...'

'Listen, m'boy. It's like the movies: the one sells the other.'

'Hey, Colonel,' Elvis exploded. 'You cut that out now. Y'all said y'wouldn't mention the movies t'me again. Y'know I can't stand the thought of a movie. Sometimes I think you just bring up the subject to *torment* me, I swear.'

'Whoa now, son. It just slipped m'mind. It won't happen again, I give you m'word of honour.'

'Sonovabitch, Colonel! What the hell's that worth?'

'Heh heh heh. That's awful funny, Elv. We gone haveta put you in a comedy show. Heh heh heh.'

'Yeah, yeah,' Elvis groaned. He'd been putting up with this for better than a decade now. 'What kinda TV show you got in mind, Colonel?'

'A *big* one, son. *Big.*'

'What kinda "big" show?'

'Big orchestra, big sets, big star guests. A wonderful *American* occasion.'

'Well, uh, I don't know, Colonel.'

'Wait'll you see more definite plans m'boy. You don't know what it's gon' entail yet. It'll be a stoo-pend-us occasion. It'll go right out at peak viewing time and the record will be a smash, Elvis. I can hardly wait.'

'Oh good,' Elvis muttered insubordinately. 'I'm mighty glad you like *your* idea.'

But the Colonel was out the door and on his way to his office where he could make a series of phone calls to network executives.

During the few days that followed this historic discussion, the Memphis Flash received a number of fervent phone calls from his manager.

'Listen, son. I gotta nidea here can't fail.'

'Colonel, I'm s'posed to be out back with the Guys now. We gone play with the caterpillar and the Sherman tank.'

'Listen, m'boy, listen. You gonna *love* this mother. Okay. We start with a helicopter shot of a big forest – like a National Park. The 'copter is shooting over the trees, it lifts up and there all of a sudden is Mount Rushmore. The orchestra which has been playin' this real strong march music, swings into "Dixie" and the camera zooms in on Abe Lincoln's head and there, on top of his skull, is Elvis Presley, the Greatest Entertainer in the history of showbiz, wearin' a buckskin suit – 'cause the pioneers were the greatest Americans – and singin' "Dixie" for all he's worth. Eh?! How 'bout that? Ain't it the most spectacular opening sequence that will ever be seen on the TV screens of the world? Godamighty, boy, I wanna kiss m'self for that idea. That really is some idea.'

'Uh, Colonel,' said Elvis from his end of the line, 'Mr Lincoln was the Chief Man on the Union side.'

'What the hell are you talkin' about, boy?'

'"Dixie" is the *confederate* anthem, Colonel, an' Lincoln was on the side of the Union...'

The next day, another phone call:

'Okay, son. Forget Mount Rushmore. It was a good idea there ain't no question, but it got let down by a few stray details.'

'Uhhhuh,' Elvis mumbled, waiting for the next humdinger.

'No, I got us a winner here. What's the most glamorous city in this great country of ours? You tell me. Eh? What's the most glamorous city in the US of A?'

'Aww, Colonel, how the hell do I know. It's different strokes for different folks.'

'Think, boy! Gimme an answer quick, off the toppa yer head.'

'Shit, Colonel, I got some girls upstairs that are waiting to hear some philosophical readin'. I can't keep 'em waiting while you give me a general knowledge quiz.'

'Go on! Tell me, m'boy,' the Colonel enthused.

Jeez, I don' know. New York, Nashville, LA? What the hell does it matter?'

'Wrong. You're WRONG, Elvis. It's Las *Vegas*.'

'Who says so?'

'*I* say so, boy. I say so with *authority*,' the old bastard insisted.

'Well, hell, Colonel, it ain't glamorous to me. That's for sure. I ain't interested in gamblin'. I got plenty a ways to spend m' money without that –'

' – Yeah, Las Vegas. So we put you in a big production show at the Flamingo or the Sands an' we sell it out for a month an' we film it for TV. There y'go: y'make a personal appearance, y'make money.

Y'make a TV show outa yer personal appearance; y'make even more money. It's a cinch, m'boy.'

'Wait a minute, Colonel. They don't do Rock 'n' Roll in Vegas.'

'I tell you, son, every great entertainer goes to Vegas. Dean Martin, Sammy Davis, Perry Como, Frank Sinatra -'

'I HATE the sound of his name. Don't you ever mention his name again. I ain't gon' go near no place where that Eye-talian shrimp been. *Never!*'

The Colonel was surprised by Elvis's vehemence.

'I'll call you back, m'boy,' he said.

Before very long:

'What about a chat show? You'd be good talkin' to celebrities, Elvis.'

'I don' want *no* celebrities on any show a mine. There ain't room for nobody 'cept me in there. 'kay?'

'Sure.'

The next day:

'Wait for it, son. You'll love it. You give a guided tour to Universal City and you do a different production number at each one of the show-pieces. Picture the scene. You could be standin' on the porch of the *Psycho* house hollerin' "Stuck On You". Don't you just *love* it?'

'It sucks, Colonel.'

Finally Elvis laid down his criteria for a good TV show:

'I ain't been seen properly for over two years an' I gotta re-stake m'claim, Colonel. Y'all think about how I got established. I got established singin' hard n' moving fast. So what I'm gone do is sing some Rock'n' Roll an' knock'em dead. Jus' like the old days. An' I wanna do it in front of an audience. An' lastly I want a mean, dirty-sounding Rock 'n' Roll band. Y'got all that? No Mount Rushmore, no big production, no Vegas, no Johnny Carson shit and no Universal Studios pantomime. Just raw, fast rock 'n' roll. Y'got that, Colonel? You fix that up and it'll make us both a pile a money. That's what you want, ain't it?'

'Oh come on Elv,' said the Colonel. 'You *know* I'm only interested in your artistic development.'

In the next fortnight, the Colonel made all the arrangements attendant on a major television special. NBC paid the winning price for the star, and the programme was to be made by Steve Binder with musical direction from William Goldenburg.

While all of this was being set up Elvis moped about his mansion, mulling over his recent trip to San Francisco and feeling the first pangs of nervousness at the prospect of his return to public performance.

Filling up with apprehension, the returning king considered costumes for his TV special. The Sydney Greenstreet outfit was one idea, but, perhaps not. He then thought of the clothes he had worn in the mid '50s, hefty, loose jackets and baggy peg-legged trousers. A possibility. One costume which underwent surprisingly serious consideration was a formal morning suit. This takes a little explaining.

During the '60s Elvis had developed a passion for the British Royal Family. He thought they were the zenith of taste and dignity and felt strongly that, as a King, he should disport himself in a like manner. Nobody close to Elvis is aware of when precisely this fixation began, but by 1967 Elvis would never allow himself to miss any television coverage of a Royal Event, however insignificant. The Queen Mother launching a ship, Prince Philip making a Royal Visit to Abu Dhabi, Princess Anne falling off a horse, Prince Charles going to Cambridge – even the attendance of Princess Margaret at a show or the marriage of Princess Alexandra: no event in the Royal Calendar was too insignificant to be of less than obsessive interest to Elvis Presley.

Pretty soon the household at Graceland was enjoying the ritual of afternoon tea, accompanied now by crumpets or muffins, now by cucumber sandwiches or scones. Tea services were flown in from the Royal Doulton factory in England. Soon even Bath Olivers had been discovered by Elvis's relentless fetish and the day Elvis found out about the hot water jug which is so much a part of the ritual of afternoon tea, he could be seen, after teatime, running around the garden going, 'Hoo-eee!! Hoo-eee!!!'

It was at the height of Elvis's Royal obsession that the city fathers in Memphis decided at last to honour their most celebrated son with a street name. The main artery coming out of Memphis and past Graceland was to be renamed Elvis Presley Boulevard.

On the day of the opening ceremony for Elvis Presley Boulevard, a small local scandal was caused when Elvis turned out in a morning suit – pin-striped trousers, penguin jacket – the works – and announced:

'We are mighty proud to have a road called for us. We declare this road officially open and humbly thank all of our friends hereabouts.'

In the end it was Vernon who persuaded Elvis that morning suits were unsuitable for a man trying to revive his image as a raw Rock 'n' Roller. Elvis capitulated – but not before he had been to Hollywood and recruited an English butler, one William Butler, real name William McConkey.

At least, Elvis *thought* he had been going to Hollywood to recruit an English butler. Butler/McConkey was in fact a hopelessly optimistic Orangeman from the Shankhill Road in Belfast who had come to Hollywood to become a Big Star. Only two things had obstructed his progress: first, he couldn't act to save his life and, second, he had a Belfast accent so thick you could cut it with a chainsaw. He had taken the name Butler to ease his passage towards a footprint outside Grauman's Chinese Theatre, but McConkey had never had the slightest ambition to become a *butler*.

It came about like this. William Butler, desperate for work, was in a temping agency one day looking for anything at all, when this mean-looking guy with a Southern accent came in looking for a butler. The agency weren't able to help him, but Butler scuttled out after the man, who was, of course, Bill Orifice.

'Hold on, mate!' cried Butler.

'What y'say, son?' said Orifice.

'Will ye hang on a sac, chief?'

'Whassa problem?'

'Ye lukkin' fer a butler? Ei'm a butler. Ei'm yer mawn. Ei've butled in the best steately homes in Inglan.'

'Slow down, son. Ah cain't amake out a durn word you sayin'.'

'Ei says, Ei'm a butler,' the Ulsterman insisted.

'C'mon over here then,' said Bill, leading him to a block-long limousine. Orifice opened the back door and Butler saw a plump bloke in a morning suit, with ill-matched Easy Rider shades.

'This here boy,' said Orifice, 'says he's a butler, boss. Tha's what y'all want, ain't it?'

'Howdy,' said Elvis. 'Wha's your name?'

'Butler. Wulliam Butler.'

'*Wull*iam?'

'No! Wulliam.'

'*Wull*iam?'

'No! *Wull*iam. Leike gude King Bully.'

'Who?'

'Gude King Bully. Wulliam of Ornge.'

'Uh huh,' said Elvis, still mystified. 'You worked as a butler before?'

'Dead reight, meate. Butler bei neame, Butler bei neature. Thut's whut Ei says. Ei worked in the steately homes of Inglan.'

'D'you ever work for the Royal Family?'

'Gawd blass 'em!' cried Butler springing to attention.

'What?' asked Elvis.

'Gawd seave arr greacious Queen!'

'Y'like the Royal Family?'

'Listen, meate. Yer talking to a Ollstermawn –'

' – A what?'

'A *Ollster*mawn.

'What's that?'

'A mawn from *Ollster*. Mei Gawd! D'yez speak Inglesh? A mawn from Norn Iron.'

'Where?'

'Norn Iron. D'ye naver hear tell a Norn Iron? Ei'm a Belfawst mawn.

'Oh! Belfast!'

'Reight! Nei yer talkin. Stickinn' out, chief!'

'So, you like the Queen?' said Elvis.

'D'ye nat know yer histry, boass? Didn't Gude King Bully bring over hus trupes ta dreive the Peapist Jeames out of Arland an make Arland seafe fer Pradestans? Whan it comes ta gratitude, some people huv a vary short mamory. *We* don't. We don't forgat a thing leike thut. Remamber 1690! Remamber the Boyne! No surrander! Gawd seave the Queen! Know whadda mean, squeire?'

'Well, I think I do. You's a good guy. Anybody likes the Royal Family is awright with me. Y'all wanna come work for me down in Memphis?'

'Where's thut? Ei naver hearduvet.'

"S down south. Y'can be m' butler.'

'Okeay. Whei nat? Dead on, boass.'

Elvis laughed good-naturedly.

'Ah'm gone call you Butler the Butler, son,' he told his new employee.

'Listen here, chief. Y'can call me Eamon De Valera if ye pay me reight!'

Butler the Butler soon settled in well and fast became Elvis's primary counsellor on many aspects of life. Diet, wardrobe, finance, career and even Elvis's emotional life were all advised upon by the harshly spoken Ulsterman.

Butler the Butler's advice was nothing if not consistent.

'Boass,' he would often say, 'ye've gotta teake the long view. Think hei this wull luke a hunnerd years from nei.'

To begin with, Elvis would touch his upper lip with finger and thumb and furrow his brow over this suggestion, but when the novelty of the distant perspective wore off Elvis grew impatient of Butler's all-purpose solution.

'A hundred years from now I'm gun' be dead, Butler the Butler[1] and they ain't nobody gone be puzzlin' over the problem of whether or not I should wear a trilby hat.'

One attribute of Butler's at which his employer never ceased to wonder was the great silence of the Ulsterman's movements.

'I swear Butler the Butler,' he would say, 'you're quieter'n a butterfly wearin' a silencer on his exhaust.'

'Until Ei open muh mouth,' said Butler.

The TV show which was made in 1968 turned out, as is now well known by Presley aficionados, to be a return to the early power which Elvis continually lapsed from throughout his career. Steve Binder, as much as Elvis, realised how crucial the show was for the singer's

---

[1] Elvis always called Butler the Butler Butler the Butler.

career. The producer pushed Elvis into the rawness Presley sought to revive from his early days and the result was a rough, powerful collection of performances which satisfied the star, the producer and millions of television viewers around the world. And as it turned out, Elvis plumped for skin-tight leathers rather than a morning suit. It seemed more in keeping with his return to Rock 'n' Roll. The album from the show is, of course, one of the acknowledged peaks of Elvis's recording career.

Satisfied Elvis might have been, but before it went out the Colonel was not at all sure about the format of the show.

'I ain't been in this business all these years to put you in the kinda show you coulda done when you was startin' out, son,' he remarked. 'I don't wanna see just *musicians*. The great American public deserves better'n just a bunch of hoary ol' *songs*. They want a show on a big scale, with dancers and exotic costumes. They wanna see great glittering sets that revolve and go up in the air. They wanna see the Greatest Entertainer of All Time in surroundings that befit his greatness. D'you hear me, Elvis Presley?'

Elvis took a breath and replied.

'Colonel, you ol' sack a wind, you're absolutely right. You just hit the nail right on the head. I could not agree with you more.

'I'm glad you see my pointa view, boy.'

'I do. But the great American public is not making this show. If the great American public got its choice it'd be watchin' *Ed The Talking Horse* all the time. The great American public don't know its ass from a hole in the ground. Okay?'

There was a silence before the Colonel spat into a tin waste-paper bin.

BDINNGG!!

During the rehearsals for the TV show in NBC's LA studios, Elvis went out back for a little fresh air one afternoon. Two of the Guys were with him. From the dark alley where Elvis stood you could see the sun-soaked street where cars, pedestrians and buses flowed in either direction. Tired from several hours' work Elvis leaned against a wall and watched the world go by.

'I tell you, guys, I feel like I'm in a Eddie Cochran song.'

'How's that, boss?' said Orville.

'Y'know. Summer in the city; watching the girls go by.'

'Uh huh.'

'Sure got some fine-lookin' girls on this street.'

'Uh huh.'

'Emm *hemm*!'

'What?'

'That one there.'

'Where?'

'C'mon.'

Moments later Elvis, flanked by Orville and Bill Orifice, had followed the girl in question into a health food restaurant and was ideally positioned for ogling at her.

'Boy is she beautiful!'

'Yes boss.'

'Sure is.'

The subject of their attention was a pretty, unadorned girl in her early-twenties, who was now eating bagels and cream cheese. Elvis took in her green eyes, her shining auburn hair and her firmly set breasts.

'Great bazooms, guys.'

And her firmly set breasts.

'I gotta talk to that girl. I gotta *talk* to that girl,' said the King.

'Should we get her, boss?'

'*No*. For God's sake, Bill, you wanna scare her right off? I'll go speak to her.'

And presently Elvis and his goons had arrived at the unsuspecting girl's table.

'Afternoon, ma'am,' said Presley. 'Mind if I join you?'

'Why?' said the girl, who lips were flecked with cream cheese.

'Ummma hummn…'

'Yes?'

'I – um – it's just that I'd – ah – like to talk to you.'

'I don't know you from Adam, buster. Why should I talk to you?'

'I'll introduce myself. M'name's Elvis Presley.'

'Okay,' said the girl. Her indifference didn't even seem to be studied. 'So why should I talk to you.'

'Because you're awful purty an' I'm fonda lookin' at you.'

There was a pause.

'Get rid of your goons,' she said.

When they were gone Elvis sat down and there was a silence between the pair which the girl broke.

'My name's Laura Clemens.'

'Howdy, ma'am.'

'You *are* Elvis Presley aren't you?' she asked.

'All m'life, ma am.'

'Well, well, well. I used to watch you on TV when I was a child.'

'You like my work?'

'I don't know. I haven't listened to any since the '50s.'

'Don't you like Rock 'n' Roll?'

'It's okay. Mostly I listen to classical or jazz.'

This didn't leave Elvis much to say. He just sat and ogled.

'Will you stop staring at me? It's not comfortable,' she said.

'Pardon me, ma am.'

'And stop calling me ma'am. I told you my name's Laura.'

'Pardon me, Laura.'

'Buy me another coffee.'

This proved to be an alarming experience for Presley, since the restaurant was self-service and he wasn't sure where to walk or who to ask for the coffee. Finally, however, he returned with two coffees.

'D'you wanna come visit with me at Graceland?' he asked, too hurriedly.

'Where's that?'

'It's m'home in Memphis. I thought ever'body knew that.'

Now there was a pause as she thought about this sudden offer.

'No.'

'Why not?'

'I don't know you.

'So come get to know me.'

'Uh uh. I'm going to Europe this week.'

Elvis looked upset.

'Why are you doin' that?'

He seemed to take it as a personal affront.

She laughed.

'I'm just travellin', that's all. I like to travel.'

'Well, come to Graceland when you get back.'

'I might. If you give me your address, I might drop you a line from Italy. Okay?'

Elvis gave her his full address.

'Now I gotta go,' she said.

'You gotta go?'

'That's what I said.'

She was on her feet and walking.

'Byeee,' she called.

'Hey, don't go, Laura.'

'I got an appointment.'

'But –'

'See you.'

'Come back –'

But she didn't.

This had never happened before. The girl was gone. And Elvis was standing unprotected in the middle of a large restaurant. Anybody could attack him. Somebody might kidnap him. He could be mobbed any minute.

And she had just walked off like that.

Weeks passed and Elvis still thought of Laura Clemens from time to time.

'I must be gettin' soft,' he thought.

But not so soft that he would go along with the Colonel's latest publicity master plan: to sing at Republican rallies and support the Presidential campaign of Richard M Nixon.

'You gotta be joking, Colonel,' said Presley. 'Lookit his face. I wouldn't buy a Cadillac off that guy, and I'm a man that likes to buy a Cadillac.'

Chapter 24

Hell

It was at this time – just after the TV special in 1968 – that one of the legendary names connected with Elvis first appeared.

Filled with energy after his TV success and edgy with frustration over Laura Clemens, Presley threw himself headlong into rigorous karate practice. Each day began with a two-hour work-out in the gym at the back of Graceland, but after a few weeks Elvis grew weary of strutting and flexing on his own while a handful of the Guys watched.

'What I need is *opponents*,' said the karate student.

'Yes, boss,' said the Guys.

So, the search for karate partners for Elvis was on. It was decided that what was needed were the finest exponents of the martial arts that money could buy. It went without saying that Elvis's partners would be black-belt fighters, but more than this was required: they would have to be expert instructors. And then even this wasn't enough...

'I don't want no one stupid enough to lick me on the mat,' said Presley. 'I want karate champeens that got the sense to *lose* to the man who's payin' 'em. That clear?'

Finding men who had devoted their lives to the mastering of this martial art and who were willing to let themselves be beaten by an inexpert, but millionaire, apprentice wasn't any easier than it sounds. Finally, however, the Guys, who had searched on the West Coast, back East and in the South, came up with four very disparate, some would say desperate, characters.

Delbert Nelson, Bonar Wyeth, James 'Jim' Toole and Abner McCluskey had nothing in common beyond their karate expertise and their severe greed. Neither were any of them of much interest. Despite this, these four men have become legends to millions of Elvis fans all around the world. There can't be a Presley fan anywhere who hasn't heard of the Million Dollar Quartet. Some, admittedly, have held the erroneous view that the Million Dollar Quartet was Elvis, Carl Perkins, Jerry Lee Lewis and Johnny Cash when they recorded together in the Sun studios[1].

---

[1] See Chapter 10 for the true story.

But as every hard-core Elvis Presley fan well knows, the Million Dollar Quartet were Delbert Nelson, Bonar Wyeth, James 'Jim' Toole and Abner McCluskey who between them were paid a Very Large Salary (though not as much as a million a year) to lose to Elvis on the karate mat.

A strange story, it's true, but the truth is almost always stranger than fiction.

The Colonel's spies amongst the Guys reported Elvis's high octane energy at this time and the old boy was soon feverishly making plans to put it to good use. Touring abroad was the obvious route to more Big Money, but the problem here is thought to have been a private one between the Colonel and the US immigration authorities. Another TV show wouldn't pay enough. A US Tour was also not sufficiently profitable. What else was there?

A phone call one day from Casper Moolah, the manager of the soon-to-be-opened International Hotel in Las Vegas provided the answer. Elvis and the Colonel could walk away with $1,000,000 between them at the end of a month's engagement. This in itself was fairly tempting, but the thought of the fringe benefits from Elvis merchandising in Las Vegas was what lured the Colonel on to make the deal. Before all was agreed, however, the old buzzard haggled for free accommodation for Presley's entourage and for himself, unlimited credit in the hotel's casino, a regular supply of his favourite Havana cigars, and a 10 per cent discount at Outsize Man draper's shop on the Strip.

All Presley had to do to earn these riches was to perform twice a night for the month of August, 1969.

'That's the deal, m'boy. Ain't it a *peach*?'

'What the poke do they know 'bout Rock 'n' Roll in Las Vegas? I might as well do a gig in a igloo. Eskimos know as much about Rock 'n' Roll as the kinda folk you get in a hotel in Vegas. Whyncha get us a tour through colleges, Colonel? Rock 'n' Roll is for youngsters.'

'I signed you for the montha August, son, so y'can't do anything but play the dates. You'll like it when you get there.'

'It'll be a cold day in Palm Springs 'fore I like singing to fat businessmen and their fat wives, you ol' *buzzard*.'

With which Elvis hung up very noisily.

'Poke a *PIG*!' he said to Orville.

'Yes, boss,' replied Orville.

But there was nothing to be done. The contracts were signed and he wanted to do live work again after the buzz he had had from working with a studio audience for the NBC special. He would just have to make the most of it.

In the succeeding weeks Elvis hired his band for Las Vegas and began to rehearse them down in his barn. The best and most obvious approach to the live show seemed to be featuring a cross-section of Elvis's career. They would start with early hits and work through to present-day material, including most probably some of the material which Elvis and his Vegas band were planning to record and put out before the opening night.

With the line-up from the barn – James Burton, Jerry Scheff, Ronnie Tutt, Glen D Hardin and John Wilkinson – Elvis went into the Stax studio in his home town and spent the best part of the month of June 1969 recording. Producer for the sessions was Booker T Jones, the man who had had so much to do with the Stax sound. The idea to do something in the soul vein was Elvis's. His mailman at Graceland had turned him onto artists such as Otis Redding, Sam and Dave and Solomon Burke. From there, Presley had explored the vein on his own, discovering much that turned him on. Now he wanted to attempt this style himself.

The track listing of the autumn 1969 album *Memphis* would suggest extraordinary work from Elvis. Looking down the list and noting the inclusion of 'That's How Strong My Love Is', which Otis Redding had recorded, Sam and Dave's 'Hold On I'm Coming', Solomon Burke's 'Down In the Valley' and Clarence Henry's 'Ain't Got No Home' would make one almost assume the record to be top-calibre Presley.

Well, it is and it isn't.

From the way in which Elvis had interpreted other songs established by different artists one could reasonably expect that some or most of the time he would be able to challenge the versions of these songs recorded by the undisputed greats of soul music. Strangely, it's only on 'That's How Strong My Love Is' that Elvis even equals the previously recorded versions of these songs. On 'Hold On I'm Coming' Presley sounds so uninterested that one doubts whether he could keep anyone waiting with his plea.

It seems fairly likely that Presley recognised his failure in this direction, for it was 'In The Ghetto' which was issued as the single, and this proved to be an enormous success for Elvis, his greatest since 'I'm Gone', the hit he had shared with The Beatles.

'In The Ghetto' was climbing the charts when Elvis, to the accompaniment of unprecedented razzmatazz, opened in Vegas. The Colonel had surpassed himself in publicising Elvis's return to the concert platform. The month's engagement had been the subject of news stories and features in much of the world's press throughout July. Parker had even bought space on US Mail franking. The message beside the time and place of postage read:

ELVIS IN VEGAS
August 1st-31st.

What the gold and diamond set beheld, with half of the entertainment press of the western world, was Elvis stretching him self to his limits. After all, how was he to know he could still cut it live? A lot had happened since 1966. There was all kinds of weirdness in rock music now. Just look at those Velvet Whatyamacallits he had witnessed in San Francisco back in '67. He might go out there and seem about as contemporary as Danny and the Juniors had when The Beatles first hit.

So it wasn't until he had catapulted through 'Blue Suede Shoes', 'Johnny B Goode' and 'All Shook Up' and won clamorous applause that the returning King felt relaxed enough to speak to his audience.

'Whoo!' he exclaimed breathlessly. 'I gotta tell y'all I ain't felt this good since the first time I humped Rita Mae Watermelon back home more years ago than I care to remember.'

There was uneasy laughter: did he say what I thought I heard?

'Guess some of you folk go back 'bout as far as I do. 'F that's so, I spose y'all might recall me singin' this next song on TV way back then. I's in a bag at the time.'

'Hound Dog' followed, of course, with appreciative laughter.

Later in the set Elvis spoke at greater length after a rendition of 'Rocky Road Blues' covered by him on *Memphis*.

'Weeell. I tell you it's been a long road.'

Applause.

'I come a long way, I guess you all have too.'

Applause.

'Not everything I did was the right thing to do but –'

Applause.

'– but –'

Applause.

'Hey, what the hell are y' clappin' for? Cut that out, now. I can't hear m'self think.'

Laughter and applause.

'Ah shucks. Who cares? What was I sayin'? Oh yeah: I made some mistakes. But a man can t be right all the time. I seen a lotta this country – ah – I seen a lotta women –'

Applause.

'Just stop that, now. What are you, crazy? I lost m'thread again, dammit. Anyway, I guess it's been a good career for a man, though I still wisht I'd been Batman.'

Uproarious laughter.

'That ain't no joke now. Y'can laugh if y'want, but that ain't no joke. Ain't none of you guys never wisht you was Batman? No? I guess you was brung up wrong. Ha ha ha. Better sing a song again I s'pose. Where are we? What'm I doin' here? Ha ha. Y'all didn't hear that last bit. Don't tell the Colonel. The ol' buzzard'd be mad. He's real pleased 'bout this engagement. Won't a been my choice –'

More laughter.

'Ha ha. That ain't no joke neither. 'F I'd m'druthers I'd never set foot in this town again. It's a goddam sewer –'

Laughter, and Elvis mutters to the wings, 'Boy, they're so dumb.'

The band are by now getting feisty, and the members of the orchestra, hired by the Colonel 'for that *big* sound, m'boy', were trying very hard to pretend to be somewhere else.

'Y'all all probably loved m'movies –'

Applause.

'– but they sucked, folks. However, I'm gonna do this next song for a laugh. Remember this?'

Everybody remembered 'Do The Frug As You Twist About With Your Hula-hoop Spinning Round Your Short-tops'. Who ever forgot a title like that?

Elvis's cynicism towards Las Vegas mellowed as the first week of his engagement went on. Performing live again gave him such a high that he wasn't particularly bothered, when it came down to it, what kind of audience was out there. The mellowing put Elvis in a more receptive frame of mind for the Colonel's suggestions. The Colonel happened to be very fond of Last Vegas. A gambling town was his kind of town. So the first deal that was clinched was a two months' return engagement at the International, one in each half of the year.

Heartened by Elvis's willingness, the Colonel went on to sign Elvis up for two more TV shows, this time with the PPP network, who outbid NBC and the other majors. These took some sorting out.

The first, produced in November 1969 and broadcast over the peak viewing Christmas period, was the kind of TV show the Colonel had had in mind for the NBC special. Big productions and big stars. The King of Rock 'n' Roll sang two carols with Bing Crosby and schlepped his way through 'Volare' with Dean Martin before an open hearth.

'I gotta admit you were m'main man when I was sixteen years old, Dean,' said Elvis across the hearth.

'Don't look down, boy: the ground's spinnin' round.'

'Ha ha. I guess you just naturally funny. Some people got the knack, huh.'

'What say we sing "Volare"? That's what I'm gettin' paid for, Elvis.'

Historic television.

The second show for PPP was, arguably, well conceived and, though the finished product can't be termed a glowing success, it certainly was entertaining.

Elvis and his Fans featured interviews with the most fanatic of Elvis fans, the most fanatic fans in the world. Elvis clones and hysterical women wearing Presley memorabilia sewed onto their clothes mixed with normal-looking followers who proved to be just as doolally as the ones who dressed up.

The pinnacle of the show's excess came not, as you might expect, when the real Elvis was watching film of twelve international Elvis impersonators (including Elvis Shintu, Giovanni Presley and Elvis Ravi Nehru) and muttering indiscernibly, but when the King was put face to face with Bruce McCrae, founder and President of the King Elvis Rules Forever Appreciation Society of Western Queensland, Australia.

During the course of this brief episode, Bruce repeats over and over again as he pumps Presley's hand, 'It's really you, it's really you...'

Finally, Elvis tries to lighten the situation by attempting some humour.

'I tell you, Bruce, y'all can be Elvis if y' want. The job's not all it's cracked up to be.'

Canned laughter was tacked on here before Bruce finally articulates.

'Is this gonna be on film? Cause the boys back on the sheep farm'll never believe this. I don't believe this. I really don't believe this.'

'Here I'll give y'lessons on how to be Elvis,' said Elvis and the scene ends with Elvis showing Bruce how to snap his right knee in the traditional manner.

'Okay. You see? It's real easy. Now you do it,' Elvis told the Australian.

'I don't believe it. I don't believe it.'

And the snippet ends with Elvis chortling good-naturedly.

Having talked Elvis into this fiasco, the Colonel didn't find it hard to persuade his boy to put his name to *The Elvis Presley Rock 'n' Roll Correspondence Course*, which didn't teach you much more about Rock 'n' Roll than the chords of Elvis's fifty hits. Though not a big hit in Europe, the correspondence course has continued to sell well in the US and in Japan, particularly in Japan, where the three-page guide to constructing a quiff was atrociously translated. Many Japanese kids ended up looking more like Sad Sack the cartoon strip character than Elvis Presley.

This masterpiece of good taste appeared on the market as Elvis returned to Las Vegas for the month of April 1970. Prototypes of the course material had not pleased Elvis and he was not enamoured with the prospect of more Vegas work when he could have been on the road properly. Depression loomed as he began the engagement.

By the end of the week the star had ceased to chat to his audience between numbers and, after a fortnight, it was clear to discerning onlookers that Presley was going through the paces very half-heartedly.

It was during this listless month that an offbeat meeting occurred between two of rock's giant figures. Bob Dylan, the man who in the '60s had at least as great an effect as The Beatles on the development of Rock 'n' Roll, turned up one night with a party to see the man who had started it all off perform. Afterwards, a meeting was arranged in Presley's dressing room.

'Well, well, well,' said Elvis, as Dylan was shepherded into the room.

'How are you,' they said simultaneously as they shook hands.

'Enjoyed the show, man,' said Dylan.

'Thank you. So what're you doin' at the moment?' Elvis asked, racking his brains to think of what the hell this young lad had done in the past.

'Ohh, just moochin' about, y'know.'

Elvis felt the need to be sociable.

'Hey I really dug that record of yours, y'know, "Mellow Yellow". Lovely song, I tell you.'

Bob Dylan was too surprised to put Elvis right.

'Well. Good meetin' you,' he said.

'Yeah. Thanks for stoppin' by now,' Elvis replied.

Shortly after Dylan's visit, Elvis entered a period of nervous anxiety which resulted in him becoming obsessed with sending postcards to the famed and the powerful. Movie stars and heads of state would receive plain postcards bearing the message, 'Help me I'm a prisoner of my manager. Elvis Presley.'

As might be expected, most of these never got further than the secretaries of the great men and women petitioned, but on the few occasions when a follow-up enquiry was made the Colonel or one of the Guys would placate the caller, assuring him or her that this was merely a manifestation of Elvis's bizarre sense of humour.

By coincidence, it was at this time that a postcard arrived from Greece for Elvis.

'Getting a lot of sun and meeting some good people. Often think of our strange encounter in Los Angeles. See you are a Las Vegas Megastar now. Sounds like bad news to me! Laura Clemens.'

This message from out of the blue upset Elvis considerably and audiences for the last three days of the April engagement were forced to suffer an entirely downbeat set with never a rocker in sight.

Nobody knows whether the omission of Elvis's up-tempo hits was noticed by these audiences. Certainly their response was no less rapturous.

'I'm in *hell*,' said Elvis during the last show in April. The audience laughed and applauded.

Chapter 25

The Death of Parker

As the shows came to an end so too did Presley's patience and it was a pent-up man who left the theatre after that final show and simply drove off into the night, for another lost weekend. This time he went to the Grand Canyon, alone in a dusty Cadillac with only a card postmarked 'Athens' for company. Ron and Ella Williams were other early-season visitors to the canyon and they recall, with great poignancy, how they came upon this huge car parked on the edge of the great natural abyss and saw the lone figure strumming a guitar and softly humming McCartney's 'For No One', his head inclined downwards into the darkness.

As always, however, Presley's sojourn into soulful melancholy and isolation came to an abrupt end. He never quite seemed to be able to shake his conscience off regarding his responsibilities and, as May 1969 dawned, it saw Elvis's automobile gliding softly once more up the drive at Graceland after a long drive from the West during which time Elvis saw and spoke to no one save the occasional amazed gas-station attendant. Parker, as usual, had a welcoming party out to greet 'the boy' and, as usual, nothing was said of Elvis's 'diversion' – they all assumed he'd turn up soon when he went missing and they were always right.

'Why Elvis, boy!'

Parker's greasy hand stretched outward to be met by a swift downward chop from Presley's fingers.

'Hot shit... owww... Hey, Elvis, boy. 'S good to see you. Have I got a hot one for you.'

'Mm gettin' sumthin' t'eat. Poke you an' your boys.'

'Now Elvis, listen a moment.'

Presley's play of rebelliousness had become as much an accepted part of the ritual of easing him into the next venture as had Parker's toothsome diplomacy and everyone had their reactions rehearsed off pat. After a period of mock interplay Parker produced his plan.

'Oh no. Ah ain' doin' it, no – o – o – sir. You ain' gon' git me on world network TV fur nuthin'. Ah don' mind the odd TV special, or

even a Vegas show – tho' ah ain' keen, f' sure – but NO way am ah doin'
a LIVE BROADCAST BEFORE 400 MILLION PEOPLE. Ah'd rather
slide ma little red rooster into a nest of snakes, NO SIR, ah mean
YESSIR… or somethin'…'

The telecast would be a farce and Elvis knew it. This time the plan
was to have twelve Elvises from the 'Elvis Presley – Inspired – My –
Plastic – Surgery' Buffalo Club of Wyoming singing along with the
real thing whilst 400 dancing girls whipped up their legs in a 'Gold
Diggers of '69' sequence that was to climax the show. The setting – in
Acapulco – involved the total rearrangement of four acres of land as
power cables, seating, camera scaffolding, stages, a helicopter landing pad, toilet facilities, a restaurant, and enough of everything else
to provide an underdeveloped country with 'instant Westernisation'
was moved in.

Rehearsals for the show began in mid-June '69. The songs were to
cover a wide range of Presley's repertoire as well as some numbers
Elvis liked but hadn't tackled before. It was during preparations that
Presley caught a Frank Sinatra *A Man And His Music* TV Special. Set
in a little studio with Sinatra's daughter Nancy guesting, it had taste,
intimacy, warmth and class – everything, Elvis knew, that would be
missing from *his* telecast.

He approached the rehearsals with a definite lack of enthusiasm.
Apart from anything else he was appalled by the way some of his hits
had been rearranged. As he was to say later:

'In the name of the Holy Lord, a HARP on "Hound Dog"! 'S like
givin' ole Satan a Purple Heart for his contribution to the war effort
or… or… somethin' of that sort.'

The climax of the show was to be a rendition of a newly-commis-
sioned song. 'I Love You All, Such A Lot', which contained the memorable lines,

'You, my friends, have given me everything,
Everything, everything, all of it,
And you, my friends, gave me
All I've got,
All of it, the whole lot, not just a bit,
And l love you all,
Such a lot',

to be delivered as the dancing girls plucked the petals from 200 dozen
roses and threw them into the lens of the overhead camera.

The rehearsals ground on and down and finally, with four days to
the telecast, Presley went into Parker's luxury portable office, boiling
over.

'Hey, Colonel. Ih's *had* it with this shit. Ih's blowing the gig. Them
plastic surgery guys. They may look like me, they may sing like me,

they may even sniff beaver like me BUT I got doubts they can throw up on cue when I do, "cos that's what's gonna happen if you make me go through with this.... this... BIZARRE FIASCO!'

'Now Elvis, boy... cool down. Have I ever made you do anything you din' wanna?'

'Yep.'

'Have I ever forced you into embarrassing situations for the sake of pulling in barrowfuls of loot?'

'Yep.'

'Have I ever exploited your gullible personality an' amazing talent fur my own ends?'

Yep.

'Sure ah have so ONE MORE TIME WON'T MAKE NO DIFFER-ENCE.'

'Why you goddam dyke-plugger...'

And once again a familiar train was back rolling down the line.

'... an' what's more – I ain't doin' that crummy final song – "I Love You All, Such A Lot". Man, that's one TURKEY.'

'Then what you GONNA do?'

A second of silence followed, a second in which Elvis saw a slinky Nancy Sinatra on her daddy's TV show, purring into the microphone.

'...my baby shot me down.'

Crowded in alongside this image was a clear picture of Laura Marshall saying her goodbye to him.

'Ah'm gon' do "Bang, Bang, My Baby Shot Me Down".'

'You ain't.'

'Then ah ain't doin' NUTHIN'.'

'Okay, but you gotta keep the rest of the plan.'

A point won can seem like a decisive triumph to a man on the defensive. Elvis had his little victory in having milked a concession out of the bull-headed Colonel and he was happy – for now at least.

As 135 million hands reached for their on-off TV switches Presley's mind began to reel at the sheer power that sat beneath him. Power, in itself, was not a new notion to him but, on this scale – it was a state unparalleled even within his extraordinary experience. Tomorrow – or was it today? – workers in offices would yawn in exasperation at the seemingly unending day, frustrated from a night of no sleep. Even as Elvis showered and dressed he was being cursed by bar and café and restaurant managers in those countries where it was early evening, as they regarded, helplessly, their empty establishments. Factories were being flooded with calls from suddenly 'sick' workers as the Acapulco sunset flickered into fluorescent life in seemingly infinite corners of innumerable living rooms the world over.

And all because Elvis Presley was to be on TV.

Yes, Elvis was aware of the position he held. And it made him wonder, just a little, why he should be throwing up into a little paper bag behind a wooden wall on a paradise island.

7.28pm, July 29th 1969 – two minutes early – Elvis walked out onto the nine-feet-high stage, the vomit rising again in his throat. As the 100,000-strong audience rose and applauded he could see Bimbo Wilton, the telecommunications co-ordinator waving at him and mouthing something excitedly. Presley could finally make out the words. They were:

'Get off that goddam stage you freakin' hillbilly – you're too early.'

Later, nursing his broken fingers, Wilton was to apologise for his rudeness.

7.31pm, July 29th 1969 – Elvis walked out again and, again, felt a deafening crack as the human earthquake erupted beneath him. As the 40-piece orchestra burst into life behind him he was straight into 'Such A Night' from *Elvis Is Back* and, for two hours straight, he spun, now wildly, now tenderly, through a repertoire composed of his greatest numbers and, in spite of the Colonel's advice, devoid of all the crappy beach movie numbers.

At 9.40 he stood before the microphone and spoke to the thronging millions:

'Ladies and gentlemen... you're a wonderful audience and I'm a wonderful guy and it's wonderful to be here – at the end – but, jokin' apart... huh huh... I'm only here tonight because of my very wonderful manager – Colonel Tom Parker. C'mon take a bow, Colonel.'

And Elvis turned to the right wing where Parker was stood designing the cover for the *Telecast* album on the back of a 'Cap'n Crunch' packet.

'Holy shit,' said Parker to Leroy Filke, one of his aides. 'Ah ain't goin' out there.'

'It's good publicity, sir, for you to be seen with your boy. It could shift us another 300,000 units of the album amongst old ladies in rocking-chairs worldwide,' said Filke, but, even before he had finished, Parker had his wide public image grin opened out and was strolling right onto that stage, arms outstretched to clasp his boy in joyous bonhomie.

As the Colonel hugged Elvis, ignoring the puke that rose gently up and out of Presley's throat, the Wyoming Plastic Presleys took the stage.

'And now,' said Elvis, 'as an extra special surprise, along with these boys here I got, for you all, the "Plastic Parkers". Big hand!'

To an amazed audience, from stage left came twelve die-cast Parker clones. As the band slid into the opening bars of 'Bang Bang', a huge canopy behind the stage lifted to reveal the dancing girls, resplendent in short black negligees.

'That ain't the costume ah ordered,' Parker growled at Presley, still smiling, 'an' those guys... you dun this to 'nnoy me.'

'That's right, Fat Boy. Now you listen, an' you listen good. Ah'm gonna shoot your ass off durin' this number. Got it?'

'Who... ?' yelled Parker then, as the orchestra hit Presley's intro note, he smiled and thought to himself, 'This boy sure does have some crazy fantasies.'

'Bang Bang' ran its first two verses then, as the orchestra hit the instrumental break the Plastic Parkers, who had been gyrating across the stage with an impressive uniformity, turned mock-melodramatically, as the Plastic Presleys brought out mock revolvers and mock-fired. At the same instant 400 million TV viewers saw the red explosion of flesh as the real Elvis stood, gun in hand, before the now prostrate body of the Colonel who was clutching the hole in his chest with visibly weakening resolve.

'PRESLEY KILLS MANAGER ON WORLD-WIDE TV.'

Endless variations on the theme ran through the world's newspaper presses, the following day. Elvis himself, said the *New York Times*: 'is undergoing psychiatric examination by top doctors. Presley insists he was *not* responsible for the fatal shot and his testimony is backed up by witnesses who say they saw a glint of metal in the audience as the shot was heard. Experts from the Acapulco Police Department are reviewing the film of the fatal last moments of Colonel Thomas Parker...'

The following day, the headline ran:

'PRESLEY'S GUN DID FIRE THE FATAL SHOT', with a quote from Elvis, now in a private nursing home in Acapulco:

'Ah din' know it was loaded. Ah din' do it.'

Controversy raged on the media outlets. Did Presley do it or didn't he? It seemed to make little difference that 400 million people had seen him with a gun in his hand and the Colonel lying before him. It seemed to make little difference that twenty-seven forensic experts had testified that it was Presley's gun that fired the shot. A great tidal wave of pro-Presley fever seemed to wash over everything with a sense of 'Even if Presley had committed homicide then he didn't mean to'. For a month the battle raged and Presley sat in his private room watched by National Guardsmen sent in by the President. Elvis was a Grade-A security risk. If he should disappear, be it into the hands of kidnappers out for ransom, or worse, into the hands of some of Parker's cronies, then the surge of national and international outrage could, it was anticipated quite seriously by sober experts, have brought about the fall of the Acapulco Police Department or even have led to the ultimate defeat of the

Government, so fantastically overwhelming was Presley fever. Then, after a month of debate...

NOTHING!

Suddenly the media fever seemed to die as abruptly as it had risen. There was no mention of what was happening in the newspapers or on TV, as if a thick fog had swirled around events in Acapulco, blotting them out of existence.

Meanwhile the telecast events were producing big business for the Elvis money-making machine. An album of the concert was a worldwide hit. No allusion was made to Parker or his death on the sleeve or label – a first, as he was usually credited with being 'Creative Consultant'. A re-run of the telecast, minus the final gruesome moments, attracted a bigger audience than the original broadcast in the United States and Britain.

The next thing anyone knew of the outcome of events in Acapulco was a front-page 'Exclusive' spread in the *Chicago Tribune* which showed a grainy but visibly authentic picture of Presley, ashen-faced and heavy-looking, arriving at Nashville airport, surrounded by his own security force and members of the Tennessee police department. The photo, taken by an amateur and sold to the highest bidder, was backed up with a thin story that made flimsy assumptions about Presley's current position. It was thought, ran the report, that Presley was either headed for Graceland, Nashville Penitentiary or a local bughouse.

In fact he headed for Ferriday, Louisiana, birthplace of Jerry Lee Lewis and home of Jerry Lee's preacher cousin, Jimmy Lee Swaggart. Elvis went to Jimmy Lee for advice and help but, due to his excessive TV commitments, Jimmy Lee could not spare the time Elvis obviously required so put him in touch with another local fire and brimstone stoker, Herbie Lee Delmont.

So it was that the Presley entourage arrived at a small chicken farm off the main route to Jackson and pulled up beside the neon sign proclaiming the legend,

'Link up with the Lord with Herbie Lee's help – and get cheap eggs too.'

Leaving his entourage outside to chuck chicken shit at each other Presley followed the beckoning finger of Herbie Lee Delmont into a small room, with darkened windows, luminous religious artefacts shining on the walls, and background music of Herbie Lee's first album, *Herbie Lee Hits The Ivories, Hallelujah!*

There then followed a preliminary discussion about Presley's overriding sense of guilt concerning Parker's death. Why, for instance, had he waited until 1969 to shoot him? Why couldn't he have done it in 1960 before the rot set in? Why did Elvis shoot him and not suspend him from a meat-hook by the left eyeball? As Herbie Lee threw these questions and more at Presley, Elvis twitched visibly thinking:

'Oh Jeez... why do Ih meet no one but CRAZIES?'

However, as things progressed, a good relationship grew between Herbie Lee and Elvis culminating in that now famous announcement on September 25th, 1969, by Herbie Lee Delmont:

'Elvis and I, we have done lots of talking. HALLELUJAH! Now ah want all you press boys to say "HALLELUJAH" after me jus' like that, okay? And, the sum result of our discussions is that we have decided that, following the accidental death of his manager, Colonel Parker, and the ruling made by the Acapulco Justice Department on the third of August, this year of our Lord 1969, that it was an accident, HAL-LELUJAH...'

('Hallelujah,' groaned the press boys.)

'...an ah want you to make it clear that that ruling is not connected with the Acapulco Police Force's new acquisition of a fleet of Cadillacs... HALLELUJAH... then.... what was ah sayin'? Oh yeah. The Lord has told me to direct Elvis Presley to purge his SOUL by makin' a religious album with me. HALLELUJAH!'

Cynical reporters, watching the dollar signs appearing in Herbie Lee's eyes as he completed his announcement, went back to their respective editors and duly produced their copy, boosting the conclusive news of Elvis's absolution to front page status, and hardly mentioning the part about the album.

However, in November, just in time for the Christmas market, *Repent (Elvis Sings For His Soul With Herbie Lee Delmont)* hit the racks. Backed by Herbie Lee's regular band, The God Squad, it was a very sombre Presley who purged himself on what was a surprisingly good album. The record-buying public, put off by Herbie Lee and the prospect of listening to songs like 'Oh God, I'm Sorry', 'Why Did the Lord Give Me Such A Good Aim?' and 'The Fat Man Fell Heavy Upon My Heart', responded less than overwhelmingly to the album but it charted and was accepted as a sincere response by Elvis to the terrible tragedy.

Presley returned to Graceland and the Parker publicity department, minus Parker, distributed photos of him weeping over Parker's grave. It wasn't until the '73 Presley Purge that Elvis's shopping list for July 29th, 1969 – 'Cheeseburger rolls, cheese, burgers, cream cakes, six bullets, toilet rolls, 24 scarves' – cast some doubt as to the reality of events on that fateful day and Elvis's sincerity thereafter, but, of course, all unpleasant memories were easily suppressed at the time.

There are many unconfirmed reports from around this time that some of Parker's friends were out to get Elvis, but as the attempts presumably came to nothing, Elvis's period of retreat to Graceland became less than noteworthy, news-wise.

The only thing that disturbed Elvis, and to which the press and fans alike were oblivious, was another brief message from Laura Clemens – this time a postcard from London which read:

'I pray for you. I know why you did it.

We must meet. Laura.'

And, once again, the Elusive Dream came together then dissolved before Presley's tear-filled gaze.

Chapter 26

I Spy

It took some time for media attention at Colonel Parker's 'accident' to cool off and while the heat was on Elvis lay low at Graceland. To begin with, Elvis was suffused with a sense of liberation and renewal. Now, he told himself, he would never again do anything that he didn't wish to; now he could do only those things which he really, really wanted to. No more circus shows, no more goofball movies, no more dubious albums, no more blue-rinse audiences. Now Elvis was completely his own man and life was his to make what he would of it. He was free as a bird.

What the hell was he gonna do?

The problem was eased by the necessity of keeping a low profile for six months or so. But then what was he gonna do? He didn't want to think about it. The Colonel had decided everything. What had he ever done on his own? The Sun recordings, *706 Union Avenue* and *Elvis Is Back*. He'd never fixed up a date, a tour, a TV appearance, a movie – he'd arranged next to nothing for himself. Sure, he didn't want to go on appearing before rich, fat couples in Vegas, the city he had come to think of as the asshole of the universe, but where else was there to go? The Colonel was the definitive manager, wasn't he, so surely he must have known Vegas for a good thing? If there'd been anything better for Elvis at this stage in his career, then the Colonel would have seen to it.

For a moment Elvis almost wished that he hadn't shot the old buzzard. Only for a moment.

The stranded King decided that the best thing he could do for the moment was nothing. If in doubt, defer. And while he was putting off the problem of what to do with himself publicly, he plumped for indulging himself privately.

The boys saw to it that Elvis had all the bevies of beauties he could handle and Bill Orifice laid in a bulk order of Gillette Lemon & Lime Shaving Foam. When he grew tired of Kahlil Gibran, Elvis would read from *The Shadow* comic-books to his small invited gatherings:

'Who *knows* what evil *lurks* in the minds of *men*? Hey, Cindy, keep your damn'd ass still! You're crackin' the foam.'

And, as he had often done in the past, Elvis took comfort in extravagance. The harder he tried not to think of what to do with his career, the more ludicrously he flung his money around.

In those early months of 1973, Elvis's shopping lists are ridiculous enough to feature in a comic novel. Vernon Presley passionately hated to see his son spend his money foolishly and in his memoir,[1] Vernon lists as among Elvis extravagances for spring, 1973, Yellowstone National Park, the Smithsonian Institute, sixteen Cadillac Fleetwoods, fourteen of which he gave away to girls who came up to Graceland to play, a two-ton caterpillar for pushing the Guys into the swimming pool, solid-gold denture mugs for Vernon and for Elvis's Grandma, a haemorrhoid-cream manufacturing business (odd one, that), proper 35mm studio prints of all Mario Lanza's movies, a full-scale model of the Eiffel Tower which he never got around to assembling in his backyard, and one gross Armalite rifles for pigeon shooting on the chicken-farm he bought, in a fit of nostalgia, during March. In addition, Elvis made an ill-fated bid for Honolulu, which Congress, after due consideration, turned down, declaring that the Hawaiian islands would have to go as a job lot or not at all. Elvis couldn't see this presenting any problem, but when he came down to breakfast one evening he found that Vernon had cut his American Express 'Gold Star' Card up into shreds, and left the pieces on a dinner-plate at Elvis's place setting. This resulted in a row so protracted that by the time it was resolved, Congress had informed Presley that the islands were no longer for sale. (No mention was made of it but Congress had made emergency plans to offer Hawaii to President Nixon if he would stand down from office. The President is believed to have held out for Alaska as well. In the end, as we now know, he would have been wiser to have taken Hawaii while the going was good.)

When he wasn't taking comfort in spending, Elvis, a creature of habit, sought solace in eating, and in 1973 a new passion appeared to join Elvis's cheeseburger addiction.

He discovered yoghurt.

First it was just any old fruit yoghurt – raspberry, strawberry, pineapple or banana. Then, as his addiction grew, Elvis sought out finer and purer forms of yoghurt, yoghurt which wasn't full of monosodium glutamate and made from real cream. Finally, when one of the Guys flew some back from Los Angeles, Elvis became a Finnish yoghurt junky. Especially *Maitosokeria* brand choklad yoghurt. Elvis couldn't get enough of it until one day it was explained to him – God knows who by – that *Maitosokeria* choklad yoghurt con-

---

[1] *My Son, Elvis, The Great Entertainer and Humanitarian, But, Above All, Golden Goose*, by Vernon Presley wlth Ricardo Elastoplast (Viking, 1978).

tained *aromivalmisteifa*; artificial flavours. That was the end of the yoghurt fad.

In early April, though, Elvis's progressive degeneration into total self-indulgence was halted by news from the outside world.

Perusing a copy of *Variety* one evening, Elvis came across an extraordinary news item:

PRESLEY PRETENDER?

In New Orleans this month, word has leaked out of one Nobby Faron Presley who, despite a lifetime in the Paris of the South, now claims to be the long-lost brother of King of Rock 'n' Roll Elvis Presley.

Nobby Faron, who undoubtedly looks like a less well-formed version of Elvis, claims that he and Elvis and Jesse Garon were triplets born to Gladys on the same night of 1935 in Tupelo, Miss.

Mr Presley, whose birth certificate is 'mislaid', says that he is 38 years old, the same age as the better-known Presley he now claims for his brother.

The pretender to the throne of Rock 'n' Roll has dared challenge the King on his own turf by recording a collection of early Rock 'n' Roll songs for which he is seeking a record deal.

'I'm mighty proud of my brother,' said Nobby Faron, 'and I hope he will accept it with dignity that he is *not* the most talented of our family. Folks around the world have much to look forward to when they get to hear my record. I do all the stuff that Elvis shoulda done when he was doing Rock 'n' Roll back in the '50s. I done some a Conway Twitty's best, and some a Pat Boone's and that peach by David Gates "Rockin' Baby Doll".

'I figure that history made a mistake in going with the Memphis sound. The sound of Oklahoma was more interesting by a country mile.'

As Nobby tells it, the brothers became separated at birth. Jesse Garon died soon after coming into this world while both Nobby and Elvis were born healthy. Unfortunately, says Nobby, somebody attending at the birth dropped him on his head, and, fearing that he might turn out mentally defective, the Presleys sent the bouncing baby down to the loopy branch of the family in New Orleans.

Nobby Faron Presley, who until this year had been working at the New Orleans abattoir, has a parting shot for his alleged brother: 'If Elvis had any blood feeling in him he'd see to it that my record gets out. Blood is thicker than water and Elvis can't allow the fact that this here is a finer recording than he *ever* did stand in the way of his family duty. Do you hear me Elvis Presley?'

The world of rock awaits the recording debut of Nobby Faron Presley with bated breath.

'Poke a pig!'
'Whassamatter, boss?' said Orville Orifice.
'Poke a PIG!'
'Hey, whasgone on, boss?'
'Jesus H Christ!'

Elvis closed the paper and flung it to the floor.

'That's the best I heard yet.'

Gradually his irritation changed to amusement. He laughed out loud.

'I tell you Orville, that boy sure has got a nerve.'

'*What* boy, boss?' Orville demanded.

Elvis gave him the paper to read, and nothing more was heard of Nobby Faron Presley until Orville mentioned it in passing to Vernon the next day. Elvis, a sceptic, had dismissed the story from his mind almost immediately.

Vernon, of course, was fully appraised of the True Facts in the strange case of Nobby Faron. He mulled this unlikely upshot over for an afternoon, wondering whether or not he needed to come clean with Elvis over the issue. Taking the easy way out, Vernon decided to keep schtoom and hope for the best.

About a fortnight later Bill Orifice knocked at the door of Elvis's bedroom suite and padded in to announce the arrival at the gates of some 'Loosiana hayseed claimin' to be your brother'.

Elvis was in a mood to be amused.

'Hell, bring the bozo on up here. Let me get a look at him.'

Presently, Nobby Faron was escorted into the King's chamber. Dressed in cowboy shirt, Levis and cowboy boots, he shuffled about nervously as he was introduced to Elvis.

'Howdy,' said Nobby Faron.

'How y'doin' boy,' said Elvis Aaron.

'Some grand mansion you got here, Elvis.'

'For sure.'

'I wanna tell you I 'ppreciate y'all seein' me, Elvis.'

'It's m'pleasure, boy. You're a star. I been readin' about you in the papers.'

'Zat so? Well, I gotta admit I had a little publicity.'

'Now don't be modest, son. You're a star,' Elvis snorted. Elvis studied Nobby's features carefully all the time they were breaking the ice. It must be so: Nobby was simply a gross, blond version of himself. Were Elvis not to dye his hair or watch his weight so carefully, he and Nobby would be distinguishable only by the differences in their clothes and their dental work.

'I bet you gotta upstairs toilet in a place like this.'

They both laughed at this dry Southern wit.

'Listen, son, I never heard nothing about you from Momma or m'father, but you sure as hell *look* the part.'

'Well I was raised by the McClutches, our mother's cousins, and they never told me nothin' bout you neither. It's kept very dark indeed. Then, back in November, the man I called Daddy, Raike McClutche, passed on – rest in peace – '

'– Amen.'

' – but before he died, he told me the truth about m'parents. I guess if you read the newspaper story you'all know all about that.'

'Guess so.'

'So here I am, brother.'

'Let's go eat a few cheeseburgers an' shoot the bull a spell, uh… ah…'

' – Nobby Faron.'

'Nobby Faron. Right.'

They did so, and Nobby Faron was persuaded to settle in right there at Graceland. Elvis bought Nobby's recordings off him and stored the master away in his wall-safe. Vernon was always very uncomfortable around Nobby and would frequently try to convince Elvis that Nobby should go.

'I tell you, Elvis, the boy's not right in the head. 'Tain't no fault of his own – he got dropped on his brains when he came out the womb. But I tell you that ain't a boy playin' with a full deck. Y'all gotta get rid of him before he has a brainstorm and hurts somebody.'

Elvis, however, continued to defend Nobby Faron, dismissing his brother's slavering fits on a full moon as an allergy.

It was during this period – the first half of 1973 – that Elvis grew bored with his image. He came to believe that he would need a whole new look, one appropriate to a man approaching that turning point, 40 years of age, when he made his next public appearance. For the moment, Elvis was still unsure of the nature of his next series of performances but he had decided that he wanted a whole new look. The same held true for his garb in private life. He had grown bored with the Napoleonic collared jackets he had taken to wearing after the television special.

For a couple of weeks Elvis experimented with the old Sydney-Greenstreet-cotton-tropical-suit-and-fez look, but nobody round Graceland seemed to think it was a very sound notion. That of course had never stopped Elvis wearing anything he wanted to in the past. What he couldn't stand was people calling out 'Ha ha sir, you *are* a rogue' or 'Where's the black bird, bub?' when he wore the outfit around Los Angeles.

The ideal look appeared before Elvis in a vision one night when he was attending a special late night viewing of *Diamonds Are Forever* at the Memphian Theatre. Presley had always been a devotee of '60s spy movies, Bond features especially. Flint, UNCLE and Matt Helm movies were, with the James Bond series, among the most requested at Elvis's late night special viewings. As much as he wanted to be King of the Rocket Men, John Wayne or Batman he had, since the early '60s, longed to be James Bond or more recently Napoleon Solo. As a fantasy it was a great buzz: Colonel Parker as Bernard Lee or Leo G Carroll to Elvis's licensed-to-kill spy at whose feet all the cheesecake in Hollywood threw themselves.

Well, the Colonel was no longer, but wouldn't a Savile Row gabardine suit with a long, narrow-lapelled jacket, slit twice at the back and crisply cut, slightly tapered trousers, be just the thing for a man of the world in his late thirties?

It would.

Elvis thought about augmenting the outfit by wearing striped shirts with white collars, but in the end decided upon, for the most part, pin-collared shirts. The ties, naturally, were sober colours woven from purest silk, Jaeger or Christian Dior.

The King got heavily into his act: he had a Roger Moore haircut during the summer of 1973, and forsook his by now mandatory sunglasses.

Elvis Presley, spy, reached a peak and a climax in June of that year when he took it into his head to seek employment with the CIA.

Edgar Hoover had been a hero of Presley's ever since he had seen James Stewart in *The FBI Story*, and for that reason alone he thought long and hard about offering his services to the Bureau. It would be terrific to meet Mr Hoover and to discuss what had made their country great. Truth, justice, the American Way – things like that.

But no, the FBI was too much like police work, which was fine but would Solo or Bond spy for the police? Hell, the police didn't spy, they tracked and trailed and hunted their men with logic and perseverance. Real spies had special miniaturised equipment: cigarette lighters that killed, pen-top two-way radios, collapsible one-man gyrocopters – you name it. Real spies worked in Belgrade, Moscow, Paris, London, Rio de Janeiro, Johannesburg. Real spies had dramatic man-hunts on the Statue of Liberty, the Eiffel Tower, the Taj Mahal, the Berlin Wall. Real spies were much more likely to work for the CIA.

Elvis phoned the Pentagon in Washington pronto.

BRINNNG! BRRINNG!!

'Good morning – Pentagon.'

'Hmmm mah, ma'am.'

'What can I do for you, sir?'

'Well, ma'am. This here is Elvis Presley speakin', an' I'd like to speak to the director of the CIA about a matter of grave national concern.'

'I'm sorry sir but the director's not available to speak on the phone at this time. Perhaps you'd care to speak to the Public Relations Office?'

'No ma'am. I wanna talk to the top dog. Just when will he be able to come to the phone?'

'As a matter of fact, sir, he *isn't* available to speak to you on the phone at any time. It's nothing personal, sir. He wouldn't speak to

President Nixon on a normal phone, either.'

'I wouldn't speak to Nixon on any phone, ma'am. What does that prove?'

'The director is not a man to whom the public has access, sir. Perhaps if you told me what the matter in hand is, I could connect you to somebody who can deal with it for you, sir.'

'I'm sorry, ma'am, but I intend to speak to the Director himself. I'm gonna come over there right away.'

Good as his word, next day Elvis, with Bill and Orville Orifice tagging along, landed at Washington airport and was at the Pentagon within the hour. He went through the same rigmarole with a pretty receptionist in the main foyer. This time, however, Presley's physical presence and the prestige attached to his name got him an interview with W Herbert Claw, a gentleman of unspecified office in the CIA.

A silent elevator ride to the fourth floor and a long walk with his grinning female guide led Elvis to Mr Claw's office, where the man himself gave Elvis a brusque, tight handshake.

'Mr Presley, it's an unexpected privilege for us to have an entertainer of your stature visit with us here at the Pentagon,' was Claw's welcome.

'It's good of you to see me, Mr Claw. Now I wonder, could you arrange for me to see the Director – I don't know just who the director is but I'd sure appreciate to chew the rag a spell with him.'

W Herbert Claw smiled. The effect was of a zipper being pulled across a bullet shell.

'Naturally, Mr Presley, a great American like yourself should talk directly to the director but I'm afraid it's not always possible. You'll have to make do with me, I'm afraid, but I'm sure I can help you out with your problem.'

Elvis shifted in the Scandinavian leather and tubular steel armchair he had been sunk into.

'I'm sorry, Mr Claw, I don' want you to feel that you ain't important enough for me. I'm sure you're a very important man. I'd like to see the Director though. I mean, hell, who *can* get to see the Director?'

'I can't answer that, Mr Presley. I don't know who the Director is, you see.'

Elvis took a moment to register this alarming statement.

'Shouldn't I be speaking to somebody who maybe does?'

Claw flashed another push-button smile.

'Ah, *nobody* knows who the director is, Mr Presley,' he replied. 'We hope he knows himself.'

W Herbert Claw launched into a staccato burst of laughter at his own small witticism.

Elvis Presley looked dumbfounded.

Silence.

'Now then, Mr Presley, what *is* your problem?'

Elvis paused before striking into his subject with as much fervour as he could muster.

'Well, I wanna tell you, Mr Claw. I love m'country. I believe in the American Way and the American Dream. I'm living proof of both. I's born in the Depression an' m'folks had no money, no home to call their own an' little hope a gettin' one. We couldn't afford *meat* in those days, and it was all m'Momma an' Daddy could do to get me shoes when I come to school age. Yet here I am today, rich and famous, Mr Claw. That could only happen in America. America was *made* great by the founding fathers as an alternative to the Old World. America holds up the flag for democracy and liberty and opportunity. As I've said, America has made me what I am today, Mr Claw, and I want to pay it back –'

'– Mr Presley, I –'

'Today the American Way is being threatened by punks on the street and Communists in the colleges. I believe it is the duty of every American to combat this threat. Let me work for the CIA undercover. I can use a gun and I know a commie when I see one. I want to clear the streets for our young people, I wanna make democracy safe in America, Mr Claw.'

Claw scratched his temple with a delicate forefinger and produced a Gucci cigarette case, which he held open for his guest.

'Uh, no thanks, suh. I don' use 'em.

Claw lit up, and pulled the draught of a strained man from his cigarette. This idiot was serious. What the hell, might as well play it down the line.

'Mr Presley, I'm moved as an American to hear your fine, decent words. What can I say in reply to your observations? It's the *darned truth*. There is a deceitful erosion of standards at work here today, but I must tell you that we at the agency are as aware of that as you yourself. As we *should* be. Our men are working against the slippery forces of evil night and day, Mr Presley, night and day.

'Now what makes it possible for an agency operative to be effective in this low-profile battle situation is one thing and one thing alone. Can you hazard a guess as to what that might be, Mr Presley?'

A pause for thought.

'Uh... American technology?'

'Well ah yes, Mr Presley, that of course too, but what I was thinking of, what the first principle of undercover intelligence work is –'

'Coded messages!' Elvis declared enthusiastically.

'Yes ah, yes indeed Mr Presley. That too is important. But I'm talking about *anonymity*. An-non-nymity. What makes it possible for our operatives to function *fluently* is their virtual invisibility. Do you see my point?'

A puzzled pause.

'Umma haw… no, suh.'

'You, Mr Presley, are hardly an invisible man, are you?'

Claw laughed a big American laugh.

Elvis joined him uncertainly.

'It's difficult for the most famous man on earth to pass unrecognised in the devious sub-world of espionage. Wouldn't you say so?'

'Ummma humma…'

'However, I can't help but be aware, Mr Presley, of the value of your offer to the Agency. So what I'm going to do is make you a *Code ZX* agent. You won't know what this means, but I'll explain. A ZX has no contact with headquarters at all. It's imperative that no one can connect a ZX with HQ. A ZX has no papers or equipment which would give any sign of his *special relationship* with the agency. What a ZX must do is gather information about government threats: watch for reds, subversives, degenerates and indeed any un-American activity and record and store his information. Since it's a *primary* imperative that a ZX works alone you must *not* attempt to relay your findings to me or to anyone at the Agency. Simply record what you see as you *spy* for us and some day, maybe *years* from now, one of our operatives will get close to you and execute a *Honeybee*. Again, you won't know what that is at the moment, Mr Presley, so I'll explain it to you. A Honeybee is the collecting of ZX information that occurs, *always*, in the field. When you are about to be Honeybeed, our operative will identify himself with the simple *password* "Pollen". Got that, Mr Presley? *Pollen.*'

'Pollen, suh.'

'Good, so what is your mission as a ZX, Mr Presley?'

'I gotta spy on punks an' commies and keep a record for when a Honeybee comes for the Pollen.'

'Just so. It may take *years*, but when the Honeybee comes, you will be ready with the Pollen, will you not?'

'I will, suh,' said Elvis, practically saluting from the depths of his Scandinavian seating arrangement.

'Excellent, Mr Presley, excellent,' said Claw pressing a button on his desk. 'Now, Miss Divan will accompany you to the foyer again and you must get out there and begin as a ZX agent. *Nobody* must know about your work, Mr Presley. You must swear this on your honour as an *American.*'

'I swear it, suh,' said Elvis. A tremor passed down his spine.

'Now get out there and give 'em hell, ZX. Truth, justice and the American Way, ZX,' said Claw, who knew a thing or two about comic-books and, evidently, about guys like Elvis, 'and remember –'

Pause for effect.

'Suh?'

'Mum's the word,' whispered Claw.

'Mum,' Elvis replied with some feeling.

Miss Divan breezed in behind her wall-to-wall smile and accompanied a grateful Elvis out of Claw's office.

W Herbert Claw exhaled a sigh and took another cigarette from his Gucci case.

'Sheesh. What a schmuck!' he muttered and settled down with the sports section of the *Post*. The White Sox were playing the Yankees; foregone conclusion, really.

Chapter 27

Night At The Opera

Elvis returned from Washington buzzing with the high of being a ZX. Obviously not just anybody could be a ZX. If ZXs were common he would have heard the term before in his studies of the espionage world.

Poke a pig! It was good to be a spy.

Then something happened which put a new complexion on life for Elvis.

On the night of his return to Graceland, he came across the news in the Memphis *Chronicle* that his old mentor in opera, Giuseppe Giuseppe, had died. The news took some moments to sink in, but when it did Elvis was considerably saddened. Giuseppe had given him a lot of time and a lot of care. Were it not for Giuseppe, Rossini, Verdi, Mozart, Wagner and, above all, Mario Lanza would have been unsavoured pleasures. Had it not been for Giuseppe Elvis would still be fair-haired. Who would have believed him as a dangerous rocker with fair hair? He wouldn't have convinced himself as Bond or Batman without his raven crowning glory.

Elvis mulled over the lonely life of the little old Italian fruit and felt for him strongly. In his musings, Presley reminisced over his own beginnings and the paths he had travelled since Sam Phillips first pushed him into doing some recording. But he kept coming back to Giuseppe and the thought of the old man made the former Hillbilly Cat melancholy. The mood stayed with him for days. Melancholy for Giuseppe turned into dissatisfaction with his own life. He must do something with his God-given talents. He wasn't born to be a ZX agent. Jesus, no. He was born to sing, and he *could* sing. He would make a record of which Giuseppe, rest in peace, would be durn'd proud.

Right there by the swimming pool at Graceland, as he toyed with his unicycle and was suffused with regret that he'd ever had anything to do with a circus, Elvis latched onto what he felt was the greatest idea of his life.

Picture the sleeve design: a grand, ornate, rococo set for, say, *Don Giovanni*, with Elvis in flowing purple and maroon robes of velvet and silk, crowning the centre of the stage, his arms extended towards the heavens. Above the photograph the title, in classic gothic typeface *A Night With Elvis At The Opera*. It wouldn't just be a magnificent tribute to the memory of Giuseppe Giuseppe or a joyous celebration of opera – it'd be a pokin' Work of Art!

Within the week, Elvis was holed up in New York's Waldorf Astoria hotel having discussions with BRA house producer Curtis Limp, a man who'd listened to opera. Once.

Two weeks later the album, including selections from the work of Verdi, Rossini and Mozart and some of Mario Lanza's biggest hits and recorded with the Friends of Italian Opera Orchestra and Choir at BRA's Madison Avenue studios, was finished. Difficulties, such as the Friends of Italian Opera's profound lack of confidence in Curtis Limp and Elvis's less than complete understanding of the ins and outs of opera singing, were overcome. Not satisfactorily, but they were at least circumvented.

Curtis Limp describes the sessions in his book about his brief working relationship with Elvis:[1]

'Elvis was great to work with, a wonderful entertainer, a dedicated professional and a great humanitarian. Elvis always had time for the little guy, you know? Anyone under five-six, El wouldn't cut him out. No way. Why, there was a little Genoan who couldn't have been more than five-one and Elvis used to say "Hi" to him. Yes, Elvis always had time for the little guy. Everybody in those sessions loved Elvis, and he loved everybody there. It was a deeply humbling experience.'

No one says much about the *Night At The Opera* sessions, but it's a dollar to a dime that they were less than harmonious. In any case, the resulting album was meaningless in rock terms and treated as such by the critics:

'Elvis is, not to put too fine a point on it, full of shit,' wrote Dave Marsh in *Rolling Stone* in a September, 1973, issue. (By the end of December though, *A Night With Elvis At The Opera*, was high on the *Rolling Stone* Records of The Year list, prompting Elvis to remark to John Lennon at a later date that *Rolling Stone* was full of shit.)

By opera criteria the record was a total turkey. Richard Arpeggio, the esteemed classical music critic of the *Chicago Tribune*, wrote that 'in his cadences, projection and inflection throughout the recording, Mr Presley shows himself to be, at best, not one with his material, at worst, antagonistic towards the fundamental form of the medium. With the exception of the understated nuances of the Friends of Italian Opera Orchestra, and particularly their, I suspect, first violin section, *A Night With Elvis At The Opera* is, I would venture, a turkey.'

One side effect of *A Night With Elvis At The Opera* was the odd phe-

[1] *Some Bullshit About Elvis* by Curtis Limp (Verging Books, 1979).

nomenon of the Presley Purge. When the true horrors of the record and its ramifications for Elvis's stature, already battered, as a rocker emerged, a wave of protest broke out amongst rock cognoscenti in the United States. On major university campuses and in front of the art galleries of great cities devotees of real Rock 'n' Roll burnt not only copies of *A Night With Elvis At The Opera*, but also the very worst of his back catalogue, as well as publicity stills from *Driving A Sportscar Down To A Beach In Hawaii* and *Lotsa Lady Lifeguards, Acapulco.*

Nothing daunted, Elvis decided to perform *A Night* before a live audience. Vegas seemed the easiest place so he had Butler the Butler, now acting as Presley's business manager, book him in at the International Hotel for the month of October.

Wasting no time Elvis hired the Mormon Tabernacle Choir from Salt Lake City, Utah, and the City of Las Vegas Surprise Symphony Orchestra[2] and re-booked his regular Vegas band. He intended to do a two-hour show split equally between opera and Rock 'n' Roll.

Intensive rehearsals began at one of Gargantuan Pictures' sound stages in Burbank and by the last week in September things were coming together to the satisfaction of Simon Spiel, the man Elvis had hired as musical director because he had so admired his work on the bio-pic, *The Mario Lanza Story*.

Not surprisingly, you could have written down everything Spiel knew about Rock 'n' Roll on the point of a hi-fi stylus. Little wonder then that the version of 'Mystery Train' they were preparing for an unsuspecting world had the main guitar riff transposed to the cello section.

A rock audience would have pilloried Elvis, the Tabernacle Choir and the Surprise Orchestra on opening night at the International. But the crowds that flocked to see Elvis when he appeared at the International were as remote from a rock audience as it is possible to be.

The show was a triumph as far as the Vegas blue-rinse and gold-fillings brigade were concerned. They loved it to death. One fan who travelled all the way from Blackpool in England, Rachel Gushing, attended the Elvis Opera Show at Vegas once a week for the month-long run. She wrote up her account of the experience for the long-running British fan magazine, *Elvis Monthly*:

'The first time I went, I couldn't believe it when I actually saw Elvis up there on the stage. It was like a dream come true. It *was* a dream come true. He was so tall and cuddly and handsome. He was wearing purple tights, like an Elizabethan, and a maroon silk doublet with a flowing crushed velvet cloak in a cherry shade. He looked so regal when he moved. I couldn't believe it. He started with the opera stuff.

[2] So called because who would expect an orchestra to exist in Vegas?

I don't know what it was he sang. I just stood there and screamed with the other women.

'Then suddenly it was the interval. The lights went up and I had to go to the Ladies'!

'In the second half he'd begin with a Rock 'n' Roll medley like only Elvis could. You know: "Blue Suede Shoes", "Jailhouse Rock" and "Hound Dog". Then he'd do "Suspicious Minds" and I'd crack up. I just couldn't get through that song without howling my heart out. After "Suspicious Minds" I don't know, as the security men always came for me before that song was over. It just broke me to pieces.

'What I saw of the show was great. Elvis was great. If I'd have had the money I'd have gone *every* night to that show. But I'd never be able to get through "Suspicious Minds", I suppose. But I'll always remember Elvis's dazzling personality and those twinkling eyes. He had a smile like I don't know what. Like Elvis Presley, really. He had a smile like Elvis Presley. Nobody else could *glow* like that.'[3]

A less effusive appraisal of the show was to come one night during the last week of the opera show's run, when two Los Angeles degenerates took it into their heads to travel over to Las Vegas and witness the spectacle that was at the heart of the latest Elvis Presley controversy.

[3] *A Night With Elvis At The Opera* by Rachel Gushing, *Elvis Monthly*, No. 226.

Chapter 28

Rock 'n' Roll

It was in the second week of October, 1973, that, for whatever reasons, John Lennon and Yoko Ono had separated. Lennon quickly moved to the West Coast and, with his new lover, Prudence Li Ho, rented a beach house at Santa Monica. Lennon's career had had its ups and downs since he and Elvis had met during the recording of *Another Place* back in 1966. After The Beatles' final offering *That's It – We Quit*, recorded in 1969, released in 1970, Lennon had taken his own road.

First there had been *Lennon In October*, his venture into the *avant-garde*. In classic *avant-garde* manner, John and Yoko had stood before the gates of their country estate between 9 and 10am each weekday throughout October 1969. There they recorded their conversations and the sounds of the place: passing traffic (cars, infrequent lorries and a good many tractors), birdsong and falling leaves. During these location sessions, the couple spoke of art, love, peace, politics and the fuel consumption of a Rolls Royce Silver Shadow. The more interesting passages of conversation are drowned out by the noise from the road. EMI pressed up an optimistic 100,000 copies of *Lennon In October*; most of these can still be found in record store sale-bins.

The next recording, though, was his most passionate work ever, the stark, extremely personal *Myself Mine*. Songs from that such as 'Mother', 'Remember' and 'Can't Stop Thinkin' About Me' have been justifiably acknowledged as post-Beatles classics. However, there followed the dreary, trite social commentary of *Whatever It Is, I Protest* in 1972, which was the nadir of Lennon's songwriting career, followed by *Confused* in 1973, an album which lived up to its title and showcased a Lennon almost as uninspired as the creator of *Whatever It Is, I Protest*.

With his art in the doldrums and his marriage to Yoko, the greatest love affair since Adam and Eve, apparently over, Lennon took to the bottle with a vengeance. Connecting up with Keith Moon, no stranger to the bottle himself, he set into an extensive bender that made him the laughing stock of the West Coast. And there has never been any shortage of laughing stocks around LA.

On a particularly drunken night with Moon, having earlier

dropped their pants collectively at a nightclub, the intemperate two-some were sitting around the hi-fi speakers at Lennon's beach house. In mid-conversation Moon passed into a stupor. Left on his own, for Prudence was a person of regular hours who seldom went out to play with the boys on their nightly wanderings, Lennon turned reflective and, lighting one of his untipped Gauloises, began to read a current copy of *Rolling Stone* which somebody had left lying around.

Flicking through the journal, he came upon a news story on Elvis's opera show.

'What the... ?' he gurgled.

He studied the story as best as he could in his dazed state. Lennon simply couldn't believe it. He knew the Elvis Vegas shows weren't exactly the last word in edgy Rock 'n' Roll, but fucking opera??? Either Elvis had gone doolally or else this was a put-on. Bugger it, he oughta go over and see for himself. The show was evidently on for the month. He could get tickets for one night in the last week, surely. If there were any problems, being an ex-Beatle couldn't hurt.

'Do y'wanna go see Elvis, Moony?' he asked the slouched, sleeping figure.

'Whaddaya mean, Elvis who?' he answered himself.

By the time Elvis appeared, Keith and John had imbibed anything and everything intoxicating that came their way. Lennon was wired up to the moon (excuse the pun), and the two of them had drawn attention to themselves before the houselights dimmed by flicking maraschino cherries at a couple sitting at an adjacent table. 'Lennon was particularly foul-mouthed,' insurance salesman Logan Squiffy told the *Time* magazine reporter who quoted him in *Time*'s now legendary piece on the events of that October night.[1] According to Squiffy, Lennon told his companion very audibly that the audience were a tasteless, tacky bunch of shits who just happened to be rich.' Lennon and his pal pointed, ogled and ridiculed individual members of the audience 'like a bunch of delinquent kids', said Squiffy.

Then the lights went down and, according to first-hand accounts, no more was heard from the Lennon table for a good quarter of an hour. It would be fair to assume that this unexpected silence was born out of shock.

The Elizabethan pimp's outfit!!
The Las Vegas Surprise Orchestra!!
The Mormon Tabernacle Choir!!
A Scat Version of 'The Ride Of The Valkyries'!!
Lennon just sat there, mouth agape, eyes riveted to the extraordi-

[1] 'The Night The Stars Went Down In Vegas' by Chester J Banjax, *Time* Magazine. Nov 3, 1973.

nary spectacle going on before them. This was the man who *invented* Rock 'n' Roll? *This* was his biggest hero when he was fifteen-years old?

In another mood, John Lennon would have wept for this desecration of the grail of Rock 'n' Roll. He passionately hated to see a man being so untrue to himself. Sure, Elvis had made turkey films and crummy albums, but to sit here and watch his former idol make a fool of himself before the very people against whom so much of Rock 'n' Roll had been a reaction made Lennon furious. What a soddin' farce!

Twenty minutes into the opera section of the show and signs of life on the Lennon table again became apparent. Logan Squiffy told Chester J Banjax of 'heated discussion' between the drunken rockers. This lasted a few minutes before the first bombshell hit:

'ELVIS!' Lennon bellowed.

On the stage, Presley, always aware of the possibility of an armed fruitcake in the audience, dropped onto one knee and sang on, praying for his life.

A shiver passed through the 2,000 capacity audience; those closest to the voice of unreason turned sedately to look, trying very hard not to seem overly inquisitive.

'YOU'RE A BLOODY TRAITOR!!'

Moon sniggered unpleasantly, but Lennon looked as profoundly upset as he sounded.

Security men began to trot discreetly towards the offending party, but then a gentleman in a paisley patterned velvet tuxedo, evidently in authority, held up a delaying hand: he had recognised the men at the noisy table and thought it best to leave them for the moment in the hope that they had shot their bolt now and would shut up.

Elvis the Valkyrie finished going 'BA BA BA BA BAA BAM BA BA BA BAAA BAM' to supportive applause – we love you Elvis: ignore this unpleasant drunk. Then, nonchalantly ambling across the stage to the wing that faced the area front which the rumpus was emanating, Elvis's famous smile curled around his cheek.

'We got an English fellow here tonight, folks. You probably heard him just now. I know I did. Well, all the Englishmen I ever met were the soul of politeness. Sounds like our friend here is a little too well oiled. Sure isn't the way you expect the English to behave, is it now,' said Elvis. 'Anyhow, I wanna thank you for your appreciation of these here operatic pieces. I always been a big opra fan. I'm sure pleased these pieces mean as much to you as they do to me. Amma aww...' (Pause) 'I can see that a lot of you folk here tonight probably go to the regular opra. Well... I wanna say I hope I'm not upsettin' any opra fans with my little interpretations of these here favourites. Y'see when I was a boy back in Tennessee I useta listen to a lot of opra records. Matter a fact the reason I recorded m'latest album – that's the opra one – was 'cause of a lil ol' Eye-talian guy in Memphis who ran a record store and got me listening to a bunch 'a' stuff I'd a never got round to hearin'. Umma humma – Mr Giuseppe he passed on this year... ' (Audible sigh of compassion from the audience) ' ...an' ...uh ... well – I guess I wanna dedicate this show to the memory of a great Eye-tal-ian American.'

Accumulative applause spread through the crowd.

'This next one is one that all fans of Rossini will know and—'

'What about ROCK 'N' ROLL, ELVIS?'

Keith Moon sniggered uncontrollably at his friend's latest out-burst. The audience palpably held its collective breath. Elvis again attempted to defuse the situation.

'Say, fella, y'all think we're deaf up here? You know it's bad man-ners to interrupt a guy when he's talkin'. There'll be plenty a Rock 'n' Roll in the second half of our show... if you're still on the top side of the table by then.'

The audience, loving this, applauded and howled with laughter.

Elvis finished off introducing his next piece and the Surprise Orchestra began the introduction. Before Elvis could join them, the sardonic tones of the drunken Englishman returned:

'You sold yer SOUL, Presley. You turned your BACK on what made you GREAT,' he screamed.

Elvis raised his hands in a gesture of humorous resignation, while three security beefs swarmed towards Lennon, who was by now on his feet. In whispers and mutters the word spread about the suddenly recognised star: Lennon, John Lennon, Beatles, ex-Beatle, John Lennon, John Lennon, Lennon – *shock! Horror!*

The security men spoke to the irate figure and one of their num-ber gripped him firmly by the elbow. According to Logan Squiffy in the *Time* account, Lennon shook himself free, 'stating firmly that he was "fucking going now anyway", then he turned back to the stage with a demented look and said in a quiet, level tone, "You're full of shit, Elvis." It was so hushed in there by now that Elvis heard this part-ing shot clearly. Elvis just stood right there on the stage looking con-fused and dismayed. I don't think he knew what to make of it all. I don't even know if he had recognised Lennon.'

Next, apparently, the bouncers grasped John Lennon by the elbows, which caused him to swing a roundhouse onto the heaviest one's chin. With that it was only a matter of thirty seconds before the heckler had been removed from the Showroom Internationale. Ten minutes later the former Beatle was sitting, rather dazed, in a police cell just off the Strip.

Looking out his little window at the neon glow, squirming in the arid heat coming off the desert, he spoke to himself in a highly lucid tone:

'This city is the arsehole of the universe.'

By eleven, Elvis was back in his hotel suite cooling off after a hot shower. Word had reached him during the interval of his show that the loud-mouthed heckler had been none other than who it was. His first reaction had been one of anger that a fellow performer had given him such a hard time: Lennon must know what it's like dealing with a heckler. Why would he put Elvis through this? The *mother*. Presley thought back seven years to 1966, when he had worked with The Beatles in Nashville. That had been one of the best weeks of his entire life and he and Lennon had got on so well, it had always seemed. Hell, tonight didn't mean anything – the guy was drunk.

Elvis asked Butler the Butler for a half-pound cheeseburger, but found that when it arrived he couldn't manage it. What was wrong with doing opra? He could do what he durn'd pleased.

Pent up, the King paced his quarters. Nobody was allowed near him.

He *was* doing Rock 'n' Roll. A solid hour of it. So what if he'd replaced Scotty Moore's original ecstatic guitar riff on 'Mystery Train' with a cello section? What if he had let Spiel talk him into doing a Glenn Miller-style arrangement of 'The Girl Of My Best Friend'? Who was to say exactly what Rock 'n' Roll was, anyway? That limey peckerwood had his nerve trying to tell the King what to do with his music. Elvis Aaron Presley had *invented* Rock 'n' Roll and he knew better'n anyone else what made for exciting music. Let Lennon cool out in jail. It'd do him good, the drunken bum.

By 11.30pm Elvis was entering the police station that held his antagonist. Keith Moon was arguing not very coherently with the desk sergeant.

'Wait a fuckin' minute. Ish Elvish. Hiya Elvish. What you doin' down here? You lost your dog?' said Moon.

They turned back to face the desk sergeant.

'Now look, Orifice,' Moon declared, 'that'sh a ex-Beatle in there. That'sh not a Byrd, or Door, or a – ah – a Jefferson Helicopter. S'not one of your lousy Crosby Spills Mash-ers. Oh no. 'Sh a Beatle.'

Giggles. Sniggers.

The sergeant breathed a heaving sigh and removed his spectacles.

'Ain't gon' tell you this but once again: I got no objections to bail for your drunk friend. What I can't do is release him on bail without the actual bail. You get some money and I'll let your friend out. On the other hand if y'wanna stand here wastin' m'time, I'm like to stick you in there with him. Okay? That penetrate?'

'I gotta cheque book, ossifer. Look,' said Moon slapping his cheque book down before the desk sergeant. 'I gotta cheque book – Will-i-ams and Gu-*lynn* – and' – SLAP – 'I gotta cheque card. See. My name: Keith Moon. Sh-me, Orifice.'

'Scuse me son,' said a deep oak voice in the background, 'M'name's Elvis Presley. How much bail y'all need for this here English boy?'

'Moon wheeled around again to take this in.

'Good *Lord*!' said Moon in an exaggerated upper-crust accent. '*Elvis* is here. I thought you were a hallucination earlier on.'

Elvis decided it was best to ignore this idiot; if he took much notice of him he was likely to lose his patience.

At lunchtime the following day, a call came through for Elvis. Informed that the caller was John Lennon, the Clown Prince of Opera decided to take it.

"S that Elvis?'

'Uh huh.'

'It's me and my big mouth here.'

'How y'doin'?'

'Well I don't feel as bad as I ought to, that's for sure. Look I'm sorry I ruined your show last night. It was appalling behaviour.'

'Ah – you're entitled to your opinions.'

'Yeah. But I shouldn't mouth them off in front of 2,000 people who haven't paid to see two jaded musicians compete for the Errol Flynn Excess prize. Anyway I just rang to say I'm sorry for the rumpus and uh – I'll send you round a cheque for the bail, y'know – ahm – thanks for that. It was kind of you.'

Elvis said nothing for a moment or so.

'You're sorry for the *disturbance* is what you're sayin', right?'

'Eh? What d'you mean?'

'You're sorry for how you said it, but not for what you said, huh.' Lennon chuckled self-consciously.

'Welllll – yeah. I s'pose that's about it. You see you were my all-time hero and I – ah – I just think you're wastin' your ability at the moment. Y'know, I'd like to see you rock, Elvis, 'cause I think you're basically a rocker, y'know. I mean, I am too. But – ah – that's just my opinion, for what it's worth.'

'Say, whyncha come on over here,' said Elvis. 'Let's talk, huh. Been a long time since Nashville, huh?'

'Okay. Why not? I'll be over in – well, how long will it take from–'

'– Where are you?'

'The Tropicana.'

'I'll send Butler the Butler over with a car.'

'Okay. See you in a bit then.'

John Lennon and Butler had a few moments of shared nostalgia on the way back. *The Goons* and Tony Hancock, *Desert Island Discs* and classic chip shops.

When Butler showed the Liverpool lad into the Royal Chamber, Elvis had coffee and cookies waiting for them.

'How you doin',' said Elvis, shaking his guest's hand. 'I got you some black coffee in. I figured you'd be ready for it. Huh?' He laughed exuberantly and Lennon joined him.

When they had got used to each other's company again and been through recent developments in one another's lives, Elvis turned to the subject uppermost in his mind.

'So what's with this Rock 'n' Roll kick, man? You limeys got a bigger thing 'bout our music than any of us singers back in the '50s ever had.'

'It's an obsession, Elvis. Y'know until there was Elvis and Little Richard and Chuck Berry on the radio over there, there was nothing. My life began the day I heard "Heartbreak Hotel". You know the old Chuck Berry line "It's gotta be Rock 'n' Roll music." Well that's the story of my life. You must have felt that too, no?'

'Yes I have, John. Now that I think about it, I often felt that.'

'So why are you foolin' round with this opera shit?'

'I like opra, you know? I always liked opra.'

'Yeah, but it's not *you* Elvis. You should be out there rockin' your life away!'

Elvis countered weakly:

'But you didn't see the second half of my show,' he said, laughing at Lennon's fall from grace the night before.

'I know, I know. But I heard all about it, Elvis. It said in *Rolling Stone* that you got that fuckin' church choir goin' "Blue, Blue, Blue Suede Shoes" all the way through yer version of "Blue Suede Shoes" I mean, Elvis, *Jesus!*'

'Hey, boy. What're you? The Guardian Angel of Rock 'n' Roll or somethin?'

'No. God, you can see what a fool I can be. I'm as much a clown as the next guy. But I say what I see, and what I see, Elvis, is you making a balls-up of your work, y'know?'

Elvis exhaled a short stab of breath through his nostrils.

There was a silence.

'Look, why don't we *do* some Rock 'n' Roll together?!' Lennon exclaimed.

'Well, like what?'

'I dunno, original stuff – some a your old hits – Gene's, Little Richard's, Buddy's, Chuck Berry – you know, do a proper Rock 'n' Roll record together. It'd be such a pokin' *high*, Elvis!!'

'Lemme think about it.'

A handful of weeks passed as John Lennon set the project up around Elvis. The dreamer behind this grand scheme knew what people he wanted for the sessions and, with himself and Elvis as the bait, didn't find it difficult to persuade any of them to participate.

Finally on December 14, 1973, rehearsals began in a legendary studio in Los Angeles, with one living legend behind the mixing desk and two more going through Rock 'n' Roll's hall of fame on the other side of the window. The Black Shadow, as he had dubbed himself, was feisty behind his enormous sunglasses, hunched over his crossed legs and nodding his head to the beat of the band he had been hired to produce. It had taken a name as big as Dylan to lure Ron Homburger out of his first retirement, but not even the promise of Elvis had been sufficient to entice him out of his second retirement. No, Homburger had only capitulated when Lennon assured him that he would have a soda fountain installed in the studio for his benefit, that, yes, he could use tambourines (Lennon had been against this at first), and that he could direct the operation wearing riding boots, jodhpurs and a pith helmet.

Ron Homburger had produced *Motorcycle Aquarium* for Dylan in 1969, then the single 'Feel Like Hieronymus Bosch', and 'My Self Mine' for Lennon, as well as George Harrison's enormously successful first solo outing 'God On An Enormous Amount of Money', which came with an expliqué of supertax for the deeply religious. Presumably all of this, together with the genius for record production he had shown through his masterpieces of the early and mid '60s – his work with the Shangri-las, the Raspberries, the Everly Brothers, his stint as house producer at Motown and his masterpiece *Memphis Greece* – prepared him for working with two of the great egos of Rock 'n' Roll.

Looking out at the band Lennon and Presley were rehearsing, in Shadow Studios, Homburger could feel confident of their ability in a recording studio. The rhythm section at work in there was Doug Clifford and Stu Cook, who had performed that role in Creedence Clearwater Revival, the enormously successful late '60s, early '70s band which had gone to the work of the original rockers for its inspiration. Lennon himself did the rhythm guitar, and James Burton was booked for lead guitar work but wasn't due in until the following day, as was Jerry Lee Lewis, contracted, as might be imagined, to pump his piano, and Jim Keltner to drum (Homburger wanted to have two drummers pounding it out simultaneously).

Rehearsals that first day went well and were filled with enthusiasm and joy. The only blot on the landscape was Homburger. The band were moulding into a working unit that day and there was really no need for Homburger to be there at all. As the afternoon wore on there came more and more interruptions over the mixing desk mike.

The band were busking through Chuck Berry's 'Promised Land'. When the last chords were still echoing through the studio speakers Homburger's voice came bursting through:

'Ah d' you guys wanna do it like that? At that speed? I mean I think it'd be a mistake, y'know. I don't see that it's worth doing it just like the original over again. I – '

'Ah Ron,' John Lennon cut in, 'we're only warming up y'know. It's just getting the *feel*... '

'Yeah, yeah, but I think really y'know if this is just gonna be a collection of retreads, y'know, we'll all just be wastin'–'

'Ron, will ya listen? This is just a goddam practice, mate. We're only goin' through stuff to see how we all play together.'

'Ah John, I have this concept of "Promised Land" done at half that pace with a string section and –'

'Ron, we probably won't even be *doin'* soddin' "Promised Land". It's just a *rehearsal*, okay?'

'Okay.'

For the time being.

But later:

'Elvis? What's with this vibrato shit? You doin' it for a joke?' Homburg demanded.

Elvis looked at John Lennon in disbelief. The recent star of Las Vegas was dumbstruck.

'I mean, y'know, far be it from me to criticise your good self, Elvis, but, like, you *are* just messin' around with that vibrato shit, aren't you?'

Presley stepped over to Lennon and mumbled, 'Is he for real?'

'Whassat? Whassat?' shrieked Homburger.

'Ron,' said Lennon, 'will you just *shut up*?'

'Oh, don't mind me. Don't bother about me, boys. What the hell do I know about making records? I'm merely the world's only bona pokin' fide genius producer. What would I know about a piece a Rock 'n' Roll? Hey, y'know, I mean, just *ignore* me.'

'Look, Ron,' said a still patient Lennon, 'we're not *making* a record at the moment. We're rehearsing a band. When we re making the record we'll be looking to your genius, y'know. So why don't you just piss off until tomorrow, huh?'

'You watch your ass, Lennon!' the little man screamed. 'Anyone else but you come out with a remark like that 'n I'd blow them away. I gotta gun right here, you English sonofabitch! You're lucky you know me, you bastard. Otherwise I'd a put you down for good, Lennon.'

'Okay Ron, that's jolly nice of you to say so. We'll see you tomorrow, right?'

There was no reply. Homburger had gone.

Tension-releasing laughter fluttered through the band.

'Come back Colonel Parker,' said Elvis, 'all is forgiven. Ron gets a little, ah, overwrought.'

The sessions lasted a fortnight. The album they yielded – *Rock 'n' Roll* – like *Another Place*, was jointly released by BRA and EMI and credited simply to The Backbeats.[2] Naturally it was a commercial success, but aesthetically it isn't by any means flawless. Any project that sounds so good on paper has to have its drawbacks in practice. The major short-comings of *Rock 'n' Roll* are to do with two central factors. In the first place three domineering personalities such as those who worked together here are bound to run into conflict. Basically, Lennon wanted a rough-sounding, exhilarating rock 'n' roll album that recaptured the spirit of the rocker era without slavishly plagiarising the original versions of the songs. Homburger wanted to infuse the material with the production effects that hadn't been possible in the late '50s and give it the panoramic breadth which he believed it should always have had. Presley, catalysed by Lennon's energy, wanted to sing hard and well with what he soon realised was the kind of band he should always have had. As always, he knew what he wanted to do with each song. He generally didn't like interference and specifically didn't like that 'little New York maggot tellin' me what to do'.

In the second place Elvis Presley was now heading on for forty, John Lennon was in his mid thirties and Ron Homburger was out to lunch on a semi-professional basis. In other words, in an idiom where the creative fuel is youth, all of them were a good way past their peak.

Still, *Rock 'n' Roll* is an exciting record. It isn't the raw Rock 'n' Roll that Lennon had hoped for, nor is it the big production exercise that Homburger wanted. Elvis does get to sing hard and well, the band is excellent and Lennon is on good form vocally. The structure of the album is neatly conceived too: Elvis takes the lead vocal on all but the last song on Side A, while Lennon does the equivalent on Side B. On the last song on each side the vocal is shared.

The duet on Side A appeared when John Fogerty, the songwriter in Creedence Clearwater Revival, called in at the invitation of his former partners, to check out the sessions. On a buzz from seeing Elvis put the vocal on a fulsome new version of Little Richard's 'Tutti Frutti', Fogerty went home, wrote 'Rockin' All Over The World'[3] and returned to Shadow Studios the following day to make a present of it to Elvis. It was, as we know, a Number One single around the world for The Backbeats, the following year.

The no-holds-barred finale for the album was a rocker, which Lennon had written during the recording, called 'Show Me'. The chorus:

'No promise is enough
What are you thinkin' of?
You better show me,'

[2] There was so much media fuss at the release of *Rock 'n' Roll* in 1974 that no sentient being west of Prague was in any doubt as to the real identity of the Backbeats.

[3] Which he was later to record for his 1975 album, *John Fogerty*.

was, Lennon explained,[4] about how, after a decade and a half of trying to make or actually making a living from rock 'n' roll, he had come to trust absolutely no one.

'Everybody lets you down,' he said. 'Especially yourself.'

Rock 'n' Roll's strongest tracks were, by general consensus, Elvis on Eddie Cochran's 'Something Else' and Fats Domino's 'Blue Monday' and John Lennon on Chuck Berry's 'Rock 'n' Roll Music' and Ben E King's 'Stand By Me'. Only one track was a genuine disappointment: Elvis singing Sam Cooke's 'Another Saturday Night', of which one had every right to expect greatness. When Elvis sang 'I'm in an awful way', you just had to agree.

To celebrate the release of the album, Lennon and Presley went to the Whiskey a Go-go to see Gram Parsons, whom James Burton had recommended to them, play.

Elvis Presley, the man who fused country music with rhythm 'n' blues to make Rock 'n' Roll. Gram Parsons, the man who went back to retrieve the soul of Hank Williams and filter it through a late '60s American rock sound. The meeting of two mighty, mighty men – surely an occasion of epic dimensions?

Elvis and Lennon talked and joked through most of Parsons' set, and decided at the end that the band had been 'okay'.

'You getta lotta bands like that down at home,' said Elvis. 'Mostly in bars.'

!

[4] In an interview given to *Melody Maker*, April, 1974.

Chapter 29

Down in the Barn

Nobody knows for sure who first suggested taking The Backbeats on the road; it may have been Lennon or Presley. Perhaps it was someone else. However, the notion was soon turned into a tentative and then a definite plan. While rehearsals got under way in a barn on Elvis's Memphis chicken farm, Barney Lovell, the legendary American rock promoter and baby-products millionaire whom they had hired to set up a large tour for the Backbeats, was spending long hours on the end of a telephone.

The Backbeats – same line-up as the studio band save that Rolling Stones session man Ian Stewart had been called in to dep for Jerry Lee who had commitments of his own – rehearsed for a couple of hours each day during the month of April and by the fourth week of the month Barney Lovell had finalised the tour which they would be undertaking. The show would open in San Francisco on May 10th and meander from there through Los Angeles, Dallas, San Antonio, Kansas City and Chicago to a pair of Madison Square Garden performances in New York on May 25th and 26th.

From there the entourage would shift to Paris, France, for its three sole gigs on the European mainland: June 1st, 2nd and 3rd in the Opéra in Paris. After that, it was over to London for a fourteen day engagement at Earls Court, the prospect of which Lennon was relishing with a vengeance. Europe 'done', the Backbeats would fly back to the US to tour through Philadelphia, Washington and Nashville before climaxing in a Memphis homecoming at the auditorium.

At a press conference given by Lovell to publicise the forthcoming Backbeats tour, the great promoter had this to say:

'Rock 'n' Roll began with Elvis and was refined by the great bands of the '60s, notably The Beatles. Elvis is without doubt the most successful American entertainer of all time and few would deny that John Lennon, as well as being half of the greatest song-writing team in the history of popular music, is also Rock 'n' Roll's most influential and eloquent spokesmen. The combination of these two monumental talents is, as The Backbeats' *Rock 'n' Roll* album has shown, unquestionably the most significant event in rock since Elvis's first recordings for

Sun Records. It goes without saying that neither this partnership nor this tour are motivated by financial gain – and anyone who suggests that it's two washed-up old farts scrapin' their collective barrels can just poke off.'[1]

Meanwhile, down on the chicken farm outside Memphis, life in the barn had its ups and downs. It seemed natural that The Backbeats should perform some of John Lennon's solo and Beatle hits. However, when it came to the selection of these hits, Elvis insisted on having a say and not only that, wanted to sing on them all.

'*What*?' said Lennon.

'Well, I ain't gon' stand round looking like a turkey in December while you do all your goddam songs.'

'Listen Elvis, you're a great singer n' everything, but I'm not gonna have you screwin' up 'Day In The Life'. It's a different ball-game, y'know.'

'Shit, man, I'm the King of Rock 'n' Roll. I can sing *any* song and elevate it in the singin'. You got a durn'd cheek, yuh lil turd.'

'Hey boys, cool it now,' James Burton interrupted. 'Let's not git all het up.'

'Piss off, James,' said Lennon dismissively. 'Look Elvis, I'm not tryin' to put you down, but your kinda singin' is for *American* music and my songs aren't American. I wrote 'em and I'm English, d'you see?'

'Okay, man. Tell you what, whyncha just have me open for you, huh?' I'll come on, do "Blue Suede Shoes" an' "Jailhouse Rock" an' then when the audience is all warmed up for yuh, y'kin come on an' sing yer whole 30 sonovabitchin' million-sellers.'

'Don't take it out on me that you never wrote a soddin' note in your life, buster.'

With that, Elvis jumped into a Bruce Lee squat, rotating his legs and arms around him and lining up the edges of his hands at Lennon.

'I'm gon' break ever' bone in your body, Lennon. I'm a killer! I kin kill you with muh bare hands! Don't nobody stop me! Ain't nobody gon' stop me!'

Which, of course, prompted somebody to stop him.

'You're a lucky-sonofabitch, Lennon. I'm like to 've put you in hospital for a *year*.'

The English star left the barn and was driven into Memphis by his assistant Adrian de Kamp. Parting from Adrian at the airport, Lennon said, 'Tell Elvis I'll be back alter the weekend, Ade. I can't stand this southern shit any more. I'm going to New York for a break. I *need* it.'

---

[1] Quoted verbatim from *My Headaches With The Rock 'n' Roll Greats – The True Story Of A Promoter*, by Barney Lovell (Tireless Publications, 1976).

When Lennon came back, refreshed from his weekend break in the Big Apple, rehearsals and his relationship with his co-star got under way again. It was settled that one third of the set would feature Elvis singing some of his hits with The Backbeats, ditto Lennon and the final third would be given over to material from the *Rock 'n' Roll* album. This was the most suitable arrangement for all parties concerned.

The last few days of rehearsal, energy was bubbling down in the barn.

'We're gonna knock'em *dead*, Elvis,' Lennon enthused.

'What you mean "we", limey? *Ah'm* gone knock'em dead. You gone be there for the ride.'

They laughed. Their ego-battle had become an in-joke.

A surprise visitor turned up on the eve of the departure for San Francisco. Last-minute packing of equipment was going on when a long white Lincoln Continental glided to a halt outside the barn. Five or six blacks emerged from the limousine and walked towards the barn doors.

One of them spoke.

'Ah'm lookin' for that honky clown who calls himself King. This here is the King speaking. I AM KING! Elvis, you pretender, you faker, the true King is here. Ah'm makin' a Royal visit to your chicken farm so show your pale white face.'

Elvis was in the farmhouse with the Guys. John Lennon had already flown to San Francisco. The road crew who were packing equipment into U-haul trailers to take to the airport informed the black dude that he could find Elvis up at the farmhouse and pointed the way. They had recognised his rather celebrated face.

Knocking at the farmhouse door a few moments later, the black man started all over again:

'Ah'm the KING! You in there Elvis Presley? Come out here an' meet the real ruler. Yuh hear?'

Orville Orifice opened the door and squared up to the black entourage.

'Whassamatter,' he said, 'you boys had too much to drink?'

The big one with the big mouth breezed past him to find Elvis, busy over a cheeseburger, in the kitchen. With him were two young girls to whom he had been reading Kahlil Gibran the night before.

'Elvis Presley!' shouted the big Black.

'Cassius Clay!' Elvis retorted, stunned.

'You watch yer lip, honky. M' name's Muhammad *Ali*. Where you been this last decade? Y'must know that. Yuh can call me Ali.'

'Poke a pig,' Elvis muttered, not really knowing what to say.

'Don't use profane language around me; Ah walk in the ways of Allah an' Allah don't want to hear none of your honky sewer talk.'

Undaunted by Ali's aggressive manner and a little in awe of his physical presence, Elvis caught on and managed to find his tongue: 'What y'all doin' down here in Tennessee, man? I read it in the sports pages that you was training in Pittsburgh or someplace?'

'Ah got m'own training camp in the Pennsylvania mountains and it makes this little itty bitty chicken farm look mighty thin ah can tell you.'

'Say, man, y'all come all this way just to *insult* me?' said Elvis chuckling.

'Ah'm just joshing you along, Elvis. I was in the area an' I thought I'd stop by. I heard on the TV that you're doin' a big tour for the first time in an aeon.'

'Yeah, I am. Gotta go out there an' remind those folks who's King Of Rock 'n' Roll.'

'That's the way, son. Course there ain't the same competition in your business as there is in mine. I could've been Rock 'n' Roll King if I'd a mind to, but I wanted to tackle something more ambitious.'

'I wanna tell yuh somethin' 'fore y'all say anything y'might regret, Ali. I'm a karate Black Belt. I could break ever' bone in yer body 'f I'd a mind to.'

Ali held up the palms of two huge hands.

'Whoa! Y'got me scared, white boy. I'm like to wet ma pants!'

Elvis laughed good-naturedly.

'Y'all wanna coffee or something, man?' he asked his guest.

'Well I guess Bundini an' the boys here will take a coffee, but I can't have no toxic fluids in m'body. I'm gone take Foreman in October an' I gotta be in best shape for my public. Gotta look good for those folks payin' for the tickets an' all.'

'Yeah, I read about Foreman. Y'all gone kayo him, huh?' Elvis asked.

'Ah'm gone knock that boy clean right out of his spleen!'

'I seen his picture, Ali. He's a *mean* lookin' mother, I tell you.'

'Listen, Elvis. I'll explain something to you. Foreman's a mighty fighting animal but he can't think. I can think *and* I'm a mighty fightin' animal. Plus I can write poetry. D'you ever see the like a me? Powerful, intelligent, and creative. And on top a all a that I'm beautiful. Sometimes I'm embarrassed to be so *great*, I tell you.'

'Well I sure hope you win, Ali, cause you're a – well – you're a entertaining guy, for sure.'

'Win? There ain't no question. I'm gonna float like a butterfly 'n sting like a bee. His hands can't hit what his eyes can't see. Whoa!'

The girls appeared with coffee for all except Ali, who now requested a glass of cold water.

'So what are you doin' down here, man?' said Elvis.

'As you know, Elvis, I believe in Allah and in Elijah Muhammad, the greatest black man who ever walked this earth. Well I visited

Elijah Muhammad in Chicago after I beat Frazier and he introduced me to Amiri Baraka the Black poet. Well, we gotta long fine and now we're talking about doin' a record together, so I came down here to talk to a guy called Willie Mitchell at Hi records. You know him?'

'Uh-uh.'

'Well he produced a cat named Al Green, you know him?'

'Uh-uh.'

'What you do down here? Stick your head in the sand? Anyway, I been talkin' to Mitchell about Amiri an' me making a record.[2] I'm gone show Frazier how it's *done*! Whoa!'

'I sure hope it goes well for you, Ali. I sure do,' said Elvis.

'You too, Elvis. I hope you have a great tour. I might just check it out back east, huh?'

'Yeah, you do that. Just ask for me an' I'll see y'all get good seats. No problem.'

'I could come read some a m'poetry at one of your gigs,' Ali enthused.

'You could doodly squat, man. I ain't gon' do no karate demonstrations when you go out there to Africa, man.'

They both laughed again.

When Ali was getting into his limousine, he offered a parting shot. 'An' don't forget who's King, Elvis.'

'No I won't. I been livin' with him for nigh on forty years now.'

'You honkies got your nerve. Bye now.'

'So long, Ali.'

And the big Lincoln swept up the dirt path and away towards the airport.

---

[2] This is a complete lie.

Chapter 30

Playing Out

The opening night of The Backbeats' tour was, implicitly, a major event. All the big noises in San Francisco had had their tickets for the show arranged weeks in advance. Amongst the crowds swarming around Winterland in the hour before the show was scheduled to start, you could've spotted poets Laurence Ferlinghetti, Gregory Corso and Allen Ginsberg; writers Ken Kesey, Richard Brautigan and Tom Robbins; Governor Brown with Linda Ronstadt; Jerry Garcia, Paul Kautner and Grace Slick; the Band; Francis Coppola, George Lucas and ladies; the Mayor of San Francisco, who was later to present Elvis and John Lennon with scale models of the Golden Gate Bridge; Warren Beatty and Michelle Philips; Jack Nicholson and Angelica Huston; and most of the big showbiz guns from the American media together with a sizeable contingent from Europe, Japan and Australia.

God alone knows what these gathered rich, famous and/or talented made of the tour's support act. Elvis's choice was, to say the least, eccentric. A support on a tour of this ilk could go a long way towards breaking an up-and-coming act, so the list of hopefuls who coveted the support would have been endless. Instead of raw new talent Elvis went for – well, something else. And Lennon fully approved it.

The lights went down completely. All that the capacity crowd could see was an array of tiny red neon pilot lights such as might be grouped on the control panel of Concorde: all the amps were ready. The sound-checking had been done hours since. Anticipation was at a peak. The support had been billed simply '+Special Guests'.

Ticket holders near the front were the first to see a group of shadows gathering before the pilot lights.

Somebody on stage tripped and a not terribly muffled expletive sent a laugh shimmering through the audience.

Then from the darkness came a throaty, manic voice screaming that his girl was 'reeed hot' and a collection of voices replied that anybody else's girl wasn't 'Doodly Squat.'

The lights were on, the band was there and the song was 'Red Hot' immortalised by Billy Lee Riley on a post-Elvis Sun release. Some members of the audience remembered this '50s chestnut. Most of them wondered what the hell the noise was.

His song finished, the singer spoke to the throng who had come to see Elvis and John Lennon, and not himself.

'Howdy, y'all. M'name's Billy Lee Riley an' I'm here to show y'all some Rock 'n' Roll. This here band – ' he indicated his buckskin-jacketed crew – 'is The Little Green Men and this song tells how the word was brought.'

Billy Lee Riley and the Little Green Men coursed through the Gospel According to Billy Lee, 'Flyin' Saucers Rock 'n' Roll'.

At the end of his fifth number, Billy Briggs' 'Chew Tobacco Rag', Billy Lee made the following important announcement:

'I gotta tell y'all. I'm from Mars.'

The audience laughed.

"T'ain't no joke. I'm a million miles from home. How'd *you* like to be that far from yer kinfolk? Huh? Well, don't mock the afflicted.'

After a set lasting twenty minutes, Billy Lee announced his closing piece, Roy Orbison's 'Ooby Dooby'. When he and the Little Green Men had shot through it in their by now apparent quirky style, Billy Lee had yet more to tell his audience.

'Well, that's all I got. You folk sure are on the tame side a things. This here's boogying music from outer space. I guess you boys 'n' girls are all doped up to the eyeballs. Y'all wanna stay off that stuff. So long, now.'

The audience began to applaud distractedly, but before they had really begun the man from Mars was back at the mic stand.

'He-ell, I done changed m'mind. Y'all need a kick in the ass out there. This here's 'Red Hot' again.'

When they had really finished, the audience's appreciation was much more positive. Then, like a demented toad, a squat bald figure with a beard and glasses had leapt up from the auditorium and seized a microphone.

'I just wanna say,' said Allen Ginsberg, 'that that little man is a genius of the spirit. Not many of you here today will see his like again.'

At which point Orville Orifice seized Ginsberg by the scruff of his neck, said 'Get off the pokin' stage!' and booted him straight into the front aisle.

'Sonofabitch,' the tall Tennessean muttered.

How much people enjoyed The Backbeats' show is subjective. A cross-section of press critiques of the Winterland gig gives some notion of the consensus of opinion.

'What precisely is Lennon doing on a stage with this gonzo? Making an undignified spectacle of himself is the answer.' – *San Francisco Free Press*.

'Rock 'n' Roll heaven. It *couldn't* be as good as it should be, but it was!' - *Time*.

'Whoa!' – *Ebony*.

'Presley and Lennon return to the Promised Land.' – *Rolling Stone*.

'Elvis appears to produce superlative work every six years. The Sun and early BRA material in '56, Elvis is Back in '62, Soul Heaven in '68 and now his work this year with Lennon. Here's hoping he makes one more before 1980' – *NME*.

'High on big names, low on big thrills.' – *Creem*.

And then there was the *Variety* headline:

'ELVIS, BEATLE, ROLL STONE AWAY.'

Different people had differing points of view.

Barney Lovell, the promoter: 'It was great. I'll be rocking rather than laughing all the way to the bank.'

Doug Clifford, the drummer: 'One audience looks pretty much like another 'fy' ask me.'

Irving Forbush, road manager: 'Them bins weighs a ton, man.'

Gloria Honeydew, groupie: 'Elvis is, uh, a little weird, you know what I mean?'

While in San Francisco, Elvis and Lennon were invited to do an interview with *Rolling Stone* editor and publisher, Jann Wenner. The interview took place, at Lennon s request, in the café of the de Young Museum in Golden Gate Park.

WENNER: Why did you want to have the interview here, guys?

ELVIS: Nothin' t'do with me, man. Ask him.

LENNON: I'm an artist, y'see.

WENNER: Ah, of course, of course.

The interview transcripts show a slow start, in which both Lennon and Presley are on the wrong side of reticent. Wenner tries to get the show going by asking them how they get on.

ELVIS: Like a house on fire.

LENNON: He means it's a domestic catastrophe. (Laughs)

Later Wenner asks Lennon what it was like working with his hero.

LENNON: Well, y'know, Jann, he had fallen from grace. It's like being employed to do major restoration work.

ELVIS (Ominous): What y'mean?

At this point Wenner rushes in and takes the conversation off on a different tack, but later more hostility flares up when Wenner asks Presley what he thinks of Lennon's radical stance?

ELVIS: What radical stance?

WENNER: Well, John has been one of the most vociferous anti-war spokesmen to emerge from Rock 'n' Roll. He has come to speak for a whole generation of pacifist young Americans.

ELVIS: Ain't nobody told me 'bout this.

WENNER: Well, what's your response, Elvis?

ELVIS: Sounds like a load of liberal horseshit t'me. That right what he says, Big Nose?

LENNON: I thought you knew all this.

ELVIS: The hell I did. I ain't gettin' on a stage with no communist agitator.

LENNON: You wouldn't know a communist if one sat on your lap, ya fat cheeseburger.

ELVIS: Poke a p–

And here, apparently, the tape recorder was switched off. Naturally, the interview, such as it was, never saw the light of day, and Wenner promised Barney Lovell faithfully that he would keep this little altercation to himself: bad publicity for the tour if it got out. Wenner kept his promise, but reporter Carl Bernstein, in San Francisco for a well-earned rest alter the publication of his and Bob Woodward's *All The President's Men*, just happened to be in the de Young Museum café that morning.[1] He had come to see the Matisse canvases, which were in fact in the San Francisco Palace of the Legion of Honour, not here. Disappointed, he was sipping a cup of java when he noticed a fight break out between two familiar faces. Gee, that's – ah – the name's on the tip of my tongue – um… It's Elvis Presley and John Lennon!! Jeez!! Next morning, Woodward's story was all across page three of the *Washington Post*, and by the following morning, it had been syndicated around the world.

Despite this disagreement, the tour went ahead, minting money and winning new converts to proper Rock 'n' Roll, even some Elvis fans among them.

The tour was not uneventful.

In Los Angeles, John Lennon had to have his stomach pumped alter a reunion with his old pal Keith Moon.

In San Antonio, Doug Sahm came on stage and he and Elvis duetted on 'Faded Love'.

In New Orleans, Elvis ate so many beignets, the local delicacy, that he couldn't get into the black leather jump-suit which he'd had specially made for the tour.

In New York, due to exceptional ticket demand, a further show at Madison Square Garden was added. Afterwards, Bob Dylan told Lennon how much he had enjoyed the Lennon/Ono short experimental films of the late '60s.

'I'm gonna make a half-hour documentary about a fly trapped in a room,' said Dylan.

'A fly in a room?' Lennon queried.

[1] This is a load of bollocks.

'Uh not just *any* fly.'

'No no.'

'A blue-bottle,' Dylan affirmed.

'You takin' the piss, Bobby?'

'Uh-uh. It'll be a plea for individuality in a mechanised ethos, y' see.'

'Y'wanna give up the pills, Bobby.'

'Pills?' asked Dylan.

'Lager,' said Lennon.

'You're weird, man,' said Dylan.

'Now we know,' said Lennon. 'Why don't y' get a proper producer?'

'Wanna keep it soundin' rough.'

'It sounds rough alright. Very rough.'

'Fuck you, big nose,' said Dylan.

'You're the second livin' legend to call me that this month. Anyway you got no room to talk.'

'"Genius is pain",' taunted Dylan.

'I lived to tell the tale.'

In New York also, a message came from Andy Warhol requesting a joint interview for his paper, *Andy Warhol's Interview*. Remembering San Francisco, the Lennon and Presley heads shook dolefully. Warhol also wanted to do a portrait of Presley.

'I ain't gone pose for no faggot,' cried Elvis.

'Andy's not a faggot,' said Lennon.

'Well he's fulla shit.'

'Andy's okay, y'know. He's a funny guy.'

'He may be, but he can blow it out his ass. I hate modern art.'

'You don't like any art much,' said Lennon.

'You know what, limey. I was just comin' around to likin' you again. Whyncha keep your razor wit for the press, huh?'

There was plenty of art in Paris. The place was usually full of it. Drawings, paintings, sculptures: everywhere you went in Paris there was art. It's always been the case.

Tickets were sold weeks in advance for the three nights at the Opéra. The Backbeats took over Europe's media during the last week of May.

The build-up to the return of Elvis Presley to Europe for the first time since 1965 was staggering. Elvis and Lennon filled magazines and newspapers, riddled the airwaves and suffused European TV screens; photos of Elvis in *Sportscar* or *Lady Lifeguards*, Elvis on stage in 1956, Elvis in the TV Special, Elvis in Vegas, Elvis on a unicycle, Elvis in *Batman*, Elvis, Elvis, Elvis swamped the consciousness of Western Europe. And where there wasn't (as well as where there was) there was John Lennon, cherubic mop-top, hairier mop-top, bespectacled psychedelic, long-haired Guru of a Generation, Mohican-cropped[2] primal scream subject, and, inevitably, from the very recent past, inebriated clown prince of Los Angeles.

Naturally the hordes of the devoted lapped up the Rock 'n' Roll goodies.

Afterwards, a party was held for some of the wealthy and the illustrious of Paris and several other European capitals. While the likes of Robbe-Grillet, Truffaut, Gore Vidal and Chagall chewed the rag with Giscard, Bardot, Gunther Grass, and James Last, Elvis ate a large *jambon*, poor substitute for a cheeseburger, and tried to talk to Gina Lollabrigida.

She wanted to discuss the possibility of photographing Elvis. He wanted to talk movie gossip.

'I tell you Alvis, you are a twentieth century icon,' the sex symbol-turned-photographer enthused.

'Zat so?' Elvis replied distractedly.

'You are one among only a handful in the country. An icon for the people. You, Monroe, Lenin, Mao… marvellous icons. *Ees extraordinary*, Alvis. Truly extraordinary.'

Elvis bit deeply into his *jambon*.

'Motorbikin'?' he gurgled.

'Pardon?' said Gina, smiling sympathetically.

'Whassa icon?'

In London the original four nights were extended to five, so great was the fervour which greeted the return of the King of Rock 'n' Roll and the Man of the '60s. For the whole of The Backbeats' week at Earls Court, pilgrims flocked to the shrine, being exploited by London's ticket touts and souvenir hawkers hired by Barney Lovell to flog programmes, badges and T-shirts – but nothing as tasteless as what the Colonel might have laid on.

The British rock press had mixed reactions to the concerts: 'The manifestations of nostalgia are distasteful in the extreme'– *NME*.

Record Mirror gave the gig it reviewed four stars (****) and didn't tax the intellect of its readers with anything more than the comment that 'Good ol' Rock 'n' Roll never goes out of style.'

Melody Maker enjoyed the show, but found The Backbeats' work 'staid in comparison to the pioneering work of the groups in the vanguard of contemporary music; groups such as Yes, Emerson Lake and Palmer and Genesis.'

As in every major city, the turn-out was star-studded. Almost every night it seemed as if half the cast of the western world's press gossip columns were coming to pay their respects to Elvis and Lennon.

[2] Really! Why not?

One night Elton John insisted on playing piano on 'Heartbreak Hotel', to which Elvis did not take kindly.

'If I wanted Liberace on stage with me I coulda' had it fixed back in Vegas.'

Similarly an attempt to unite Elvis, Lennon and Mick Jagger on stage for a song one of the nights was vetoed by the ex-Beatle, for reasons unspecified. However it seems probable that Lennon considered two giant egos on one stage all the potential trouble the show needed.

The oddest event in London came about when Princess Margaret attended the show with her then husband, Lord Snowdon. During the interval, word came through to the stars' dressing room that the Royal Couple were in the audience. Elvis practically went bananas.

'Poke a pig! Princess Margaret! Does she know the Queen?' he cried.

'She's the Queen's sister, you dork!' said Lennon.

'The Queen's *sister*. Gawdamighty! The Queen's SISTER!! Holy Shit, Big Nose, Holy Shit!'

'What's the big deal?' Lennon taunted. 'They're just ordinary people with costume jewellery that's in fact real. That's all.'

'That's *all*? She's a *Princess*, man. We don't have Princesses back home. Durnit t'hell, I'm fair thrilled, Big Nose.'

'Lay off the big-nose bit, will you?'

'The Queen's sister! D'you think the Queen might be there too?'

'I don't think she's too into Rock 'n' Roll, Elvis,' said Lennon. 'Look, if you'd calm down enough I'm sure Princess Margaret'd come back for a chat after the show. It's a common thing.'

'Hey, man, don' pull m'leg. I'm serious 'bout th' Royal Family.'

'*I'm* serious, you stupid bugger. Course she'll come back to meet you. You're a big star. She'd like to meet you.'

'Well... I ain't sure,' Elvis equivocated. 'I wouldn't have a durn'd clue how to act with a Princess or what t'say.'

Lennon chuckled.

'It's a piece 'a' piss, El. You just duck your head when you shake hands with her an' then play it by ear. Just act natural. Y'know, plan something spontaneous... Geddit?... Oh never mind.'

In the last half of their show, Elvis said how honoured he and his band felt that Princess Margaret and her husband 'had taken the time to honour us with the honour and privilege of their presence here tonight, without whom –' which is when Lennon discreetly kicked him in the ankle. The show went on.

Afterwards Hubert Budgey, General Manager of the Earls Court complex, escorted the Royal Couple around to the dressing room area. As Princess Margaret and Lord Snowdon were shown into Elvis's room, the Hillbilly Cat shot to his feet and more or less froze to the spot.

'Hello,' said the Princess. 'It's kind of you to see us after that show. It must've been *so* exhausting.'

'Humma hummma, ma'am,' he jabbered.

'We both enjoyed your performance very much indeed,' she continued.

'Yes, indeed,' said Snowdon. 'You've been touring quite extensively, haven't you?'

'Humma hummma, suh.'

'Quite.'

Silence.

Then, from his adjacent room, Lennon appeared. The Royal Couple greeted him and handshakes were exchanged.

'How does it feel to be back?' asked Snowdon.

'Well I don't really know yet, y'know,' he replied. 'I've not had much chance to look around yet.'

'I'm not sure if London is still swinging,' said the Princess.

There was polite, inexplicable laughter, then a pause. 'I hope you've not been taking pictures out there,' said Lennon to Snowdon, 'it's not allowed, y'know.'

Everyone laughed at the Liverpudlian cheek, and then in the relaxed moment that followed Elvis spoke up.

'Scuse me, ma'am, I wonder if y'all could do me a very great favour an' tell Her Majesty the Queen how much I admire her?'

'Certainly, Mr Presley. My sister has a fondness for your religious recordings.'

His last mouthful had been an enormous statement for Elvis in the present circumstances. The news that Her Majesty listened to his records nearly finished him off.

'Humma hummma humma…'

'Yes,' Margaret went on, 'I believe she heard your recording of "How Great Thou Art" on the wireless and she spoke of it so often that Philip eventually bought the record that contains it… ah… '

'*Deep End,*' Elvis muttered.

'I beg your pardon?'

'*Repent,*' Lennon explained.

'What?'

'*Repent,*' the ex-Beatle repeated.

'I?'

'No. The album's called *Repent*, ma'am.

'Oh, I see.'

Laughter.

'Being pricked by your conscience, dear?' Snowdon joked. His wife laughed, followed by everyone else.

'Well, we must be off,' said Snowdon.

'Yes, well I expect so. It's been a most enjoyable evening, gentlemen. Please feel free to call in for a cup of tea if you're passing our place at all – don't stand on ceremony.'

'Aw mahumna ahmm…' said Elvis.

'Kensington Palace. Ask anyone if you're in the vicinity.'

During the course of their European jaunt a very special gig had been arranged for The Backbeats to coincide with their return to the States. At the request of John Lennon, who had become frustrated with playing before enormous crowds, a unique date was to take place at the 500-capacity Lone Star café on their return. In addition to initiating this radical move, Lennon insisted that the gig was to be for honest-to-God punters. No tickets were to be set aside for journalists, record company A&R men, celebrities or friends of the management. Five hundred $5 tickets would be available to the first 500 postal applicants. And this indeed was the case.

And on the night – well; you can imagine it…

After the gig, a memorable reunion took place between John and Yoko. Yoko had bought her ticket through the post like everyone else and John nearly fell off the floor when he caught sight of her in the bar after The Backbeats' set. The couple spent a long time talking that night and twenty-four hours later, when the entourage was due to move on to Philadelphia, it had been decided that, come the end of the tour, John should return to live in the Dakota Building.

Chapter 31

Bye Bye Johnny B Goode, Hello King Burger

John Lennon had nearly learned to tolerate being called Big Nose and Elvis, on stage, had cut out practically all the karate movements that so incensed Lennon. However, no matter how much joy the tour had brought to a few hundred thousand people around the world, no matter what kind of a buzz it had been for them both to perform again regularly, neither star much felt the need to go on touring. In their respective youths it had been a source of energy to move on relentlessly and, as it were, conquer new territories. The road was a magnet of possibility. Now, it seemed, all of that possibility had been fulfilled tenfold. Neither of them said anything, but, individually, the notion was tugging their consciousness that Memphis was *really* the end of the road.

In Memphis, there was a carnival laid on by the Mayor to welcome back the world's most famous Memphian. Bandwagons and elephants, majorettes and jugglers paraded the streets in the heart of the city. Elvis and John Lennon hadn't been given much choice about joining in. They sat in the back of a large and bulletproof limousine and waved nonchalantly at the hordes who had gathered to sneak a peek at these great stars.

'This is pokin' ludicrous,' said Lennon. 'How did I let you talk me into this schlock?'

But there was no reply from Elvis, who was miles away in his head, thinking of the circus days with the Colonel. This parade was just the sort of jamboree the Colonel would have staged. Elvis reminisced about the unicycle, those goddam movies and the Colonel's shark-faced grin. The ol' buzzard! Elvis didn't regret shooting him one little bit.

Everyone was at the Auditorium that night: it was the event of the decade in Memphis. Sam Phillips and Fay Vest were seated up front, And there, too, were Rita Mae Watermelon, who, a successful model-agency proprietor now, had flown in from New York to visit her family and see the show; Sal from the Diner, who had been the first one to market Elvis's great brainchild, the cheeseburger; the other three ex-

Beatles, there at John's request; Adam West, in full *Batman* costume;[1] Jerry Lee Lewis, sporting Churchillian cigar and Miss Tennessee Steak-Houses of 1973; Irving Feldman the meal merchant, Howard Howerd and Lamar Pike, both formerly of the city dog pound; Steve Cropper and Booker T from the MG's; Luther Bostock; producer Owen Bradley; ex-manager Rob Robb; Johnston 'Porky' Prime the lecturer in Chicken Farming, now author of a strange text on combustion – *The Chickenshit Rotary Pump Engine*; Scotty Moore and DJ Fontana, both successful session men now; Destry Gumby, recently released after doing three years of a one-to-five sentence for armed robbery; Dennis Chang Jr; Nancy Sinatra and Bill Bixby with 'Myopic' Trevor Pillock who had flown down from Hollywood for the occasion; and Jennie Lee Marshall and her husband who now ran a massage parlour in the Combat Zone, Boston. It goes without saying that Vernon was there; he slept through the entire set.

Throughout the tour The Backbeats had always done only one encore. The whole business of going off to come on again to go off to come on again seemed completely false to Lennon, so he had insisted that one encore of two or three numbers (depending on the performers' mood) was all an audience would get.

In the euphoric atmosphere at the Memphis Auditorium that night, however, a second encore was given. Having left the audience with their normal show-stopper, 'Rockin' All Over The World', the stars and their band returned, after a full three minutes' chanting and yearning from the audience, to an explosion of appreciation.

'Thank you,' said Elvis, when the roar had ceased. 'I wan' tell you that this tour has been the high point of m'career. I never played to such audiences –'

CHEER!!!

' – an' I don't see how I'm ever gone top tonight.'

ROAR!!!

Then Lennon chipped in:

'Yeah, Elvis an' me 've had a ball –'

YAYYYYYYYYYYYY!!!

' – we're thinkin' of goin' professional.'

As laughter mixed with the audience's adrenaline, the band, led by Lennon on, uncharacteristically, lead guitar, stumbled into a hellbent rendition of 'Johnny B Goode.' Elvis took the first verse, John the second and on the last they shared the vocal, pumping out together the words of the song that was the story of both their lives.

Before the last down stroke on the guitars had finished reverberating around the Auditorium, the band had left the stage and seconds later the lights came up and the Rock 'n' Roll, rhythm 'n' blues tape

[1] Inexplicable, really.

selection that had sandwiched The Backbeats' set through the tour flowed through the PA. An occasion that nobody present wanted to end was over.

At the party given by the city fathers afterwards, Elvis and John told each other what they had both really known when they had arrived back here in Memphis.

''S the enda the road, son,' said Elvis.

'Yeah, I know. I wanna spend some time with Yoko,' said John.

'Me, I'm gone put m'feet up now. I done all this roadwork nearly twenty years ago. Lotta water flowed since then. I'm 'bout ready for a rest.

'That was the way to go out though, El, I tell you…'

'…Yeah. Sure was. Tell y' one thing: I ain't gone play Vegas again *ever*. Not if they offer me all the money in Hollywood.'

'I want some peace and quiet. I've done me bit for Rock 'n' Roll.'

A year later, John Lennon was a housewife and a father, contentedly living a quiet family life, in New York.

Down in Memphis, Elvis and his consultant, Sal of the Diner, were going over the books of their fast-food chain. King Burger franchises were giving McDonalds a run for their money in every major US city.

The reason?

– You couldn't get a cheeseburger anywhere like the cheeseburgers they sold at King Burger.

Chapter 32

All the Way to Memphis

Not a lot was heard of Elvis after 1974, although much was written. Considerable fuss was made of his involvement in a fast-food chain when it emerged in 1975 that Elvis Presley was the sole owner of King Burger Ltd. Elvis's business colleagues put pressure on him to capitalise on his public image in order to further the growth of the burger chain. But Elvis would have none of it.

In the press rumours arose every few months: Elvis had shaved his head and gone ga-ga; Elvis had gone native in Tahiti; Elvis had been assassinated by the CIA (ironic!); Elvis had been disfigured in a horrific car accident; some even said that Elvis had developed agoraphobia and become totally incapable of leaving Graceland.

The truth, unusually, was not as strange as the fiction.

King Burger went from strength to strength, although of course it never did topple McDonalds.

What could?[1]

By 1977 the Elvis Legend was infinitely greater than it had ever been during his performing career. Despite BRA's incessant and unfailingly tasteless repackaging of his work and despite even the regular 'Nearly ELVIS' shows given by Nobby Faron, hair now dyed black, at the International Hotel, Las Vegas, Elvis's stature simply grew and grew until it seemed to fans of the medium that he had *invented* Rock 'n' Roll singlehandedly.

Well, in a way he had.

Belatedly, a third generation arrived to retrieve the mantle set down by the British Invasion of the '60s. In Britain, through 1976 and 1977 an explosion of raw power returned Rock 'n' Roll to its roots.

'Look,' said Johnny Rotten and his peers, 'any fool can do this.'

And a great many did. Rock 'n' Roll got back to what it had originally been: short, sharp stabs of adolescent frustration. Out of London

---

[1] McDonalds were always more specialised than King Burger which, in 1974, introduced two experimental burgers – the Gooseburger (self-explanatory) and one made from pork, called, for reasons best known to Elvis, the Dutchburger.

came the New Wave catalysed and led by the Sex Pistols, The Clash and The Jam, and pursued by a thousand talented and talentless bands.

Three years later The Clash, always a roots Rock 'n' Roll band, had reached a plateau of artistic maturity with their two-album set *London Calling*, which took inspiration for its sleeve design from Elvis's first album. Arrived in America to repeat The Beatles' lesson of 1964, the band cheekily sent a copy of *London Calling* to Elvis in Graceland, with a note:

'You started it and it keeps going on and off. We think we set it back on with this record. Hope you agree.

The Clash

PS We'll be playing Memphis Auditorium May the 21st!!'

Elvis chuckled at the note and set the record aside. He picked it up again to look at the pastiche of his own debut. Very clever. He set the record down again and turned to some King Burger mail. *London Calling* got tidied away and might've been forgotten. But one night in May 1980 Elvis was watching the network news on TV when who should come on but The Clash in an interview with Barbara Walters.

WALTERS: And is there somewhere in America that you're especially looking forward to playing, guys?

JOE STRUMMER: Well, we love New York so it'll be good to get back here again, but, ah, apart from that I s'pose we're looking forward to Memphis a lot,

WALTERS: Why's that exactly?

STRUMMER: Well, it's where it all started, innit. Rock 'n' Roll began in Memphis really.

JONES: Sun Records. That's where Rock 'n' Roll started.

STRUMMER: Yeah an' we sent a copy of our record to Elvis so we're hoping that he may come down and see us when we're in town. (Turning to camera) If you're listenin', Elvis, we really wanna meet you, right. So watch out for spotty Englishmen round Graceland.

Watching this, Elvis was quite amused.

'Hey, Orville, get yer durn'd ass in here.'

Later.

'Yes boss.'

'Did you see a record by a band called the Clash anyplace?'

'I din see it boss.'

'Well, look for it, you dumbbell.'

Orville found the record and Elvis listened to it. He liked it a good deal. It was Rock 'n' Roll okay. What he particularly liked was their version ,of a song he had covered on *Elvis Is Back*, 'Brand New Cadillac.

Those who read of it in *Billboard, Rolling Stone, NME, Creem, Sounds* or any one of a thousand straight dailies found it hard to believe, but it was true: Elvis had made a brief guest appearance at the Clash gig in Memphis. The *Memphis Chronicle* report, by Dermot Sluggard, a local boy, was syndicated around the world; unfortunately no photograph of Elvis onstage with The Clash exists.

Sluggard's report was disappointingly brief:

'Last night Elvis Presley, the acknowledged King of Rock 'n' Roll, emerged from a six-year retirement to sing one song with British punk rock band The Clash.

'Just why Elvis chose this occasion to make his shock and short reappearance is a mystery to everyone in Memphis, but for three thousand young fans of the British New Wave the unexpected occurred when 45-year-old Elvis appeared on stage suddenly and belted out "Brand New Cadillac" with The Clash.

'Before the number was properly over, Presley had disappeared into the wings, and there was neither hide nor hair of him after the show.

'In a brief press statement, The Clash called Elvis's appearance "a surprise" and said that the collaboration had been "gratifying".'

Back in England later that summer, Joe Strummer revealed rather more to the *NME* in a lengthy interview. Badgered on the subject of Elvis by his interviewer, Strummer remarked that 'Elvis was well into it. It was pokin' great. Why dint we do more? It's all we had time for, mate. Then when we was talking to him up at Graceland later we asked him why he didn't do a bit a singin' again, y'know? So he says – listen, cop this – so he says "Rock 'n' Roll is a burst of teenage poetry, Joe – " he called me Joe" – and it ain't for a old fool in his forties. Beyond that I don't wanna be Frank Sinatra."

'That's what he says. I think that's bloody marvellous.'

ELVIS – the Discography

It is virtually impossible to chronicle all the Elvis record releases since his retirement as different branches of his record company, BRA, have, since that time, been given licence to release their own compilations. This discography, therefore, lists all the official British and American album, single and EP releases which, with the exception of Elvis's first Sun singles, were almost identical in both countries. All releases are on BRA Records except where stated.

A. ALBUMS

01 *Elvis Presley* (US only)
Blue Suede Shoes; I'm Counting On You; I Got A Woman; One Sided Love Affair; I Love You Because; Just Because; Tutti Frutti; Trying To Get To You; I'm Gonna Sit Right Down & Cry; I'll Never Let You Go; Blue Moon; Money, Honey.

02 *Rock 'n' Roll* (UK only)
Blue Suede Shoes; Harbour Lights; I'm Left, You're Right, She's Gone; Move It On Over; Mystery Train; I'm Gonna Sit Right Down & Cry; Shake, Rattle and Roll; Trying To Get To You; State Fair (excerpts); Lawdy Miss Clawdy; That's Alright Mama.

03 *Elvis's Christmas Album*
Santa Claus Is Back In Town; White Christmas; Here Comes Santa Claus; I'll Be Home For Christmas; Blue Christmas; Santa Bring My Baby Back To Me; Santa Claus Is Too Fat (To Get Through The Central Heating Pipes); O Little Town Of Bethlehem; Merry Christmas Baby; Silent Night.

04 *Elvis and That Hard-Headed Woman*
Hard-Headed Woman; Hot Dog; Trouble; King Creole; Got A Lot Of Livin' To Do; Mean Woman Blues; Dixieland Rock; My Baby Left Me; Jailhouse Rock; Party; Blueberry Hill; Have I Told You Lately That I Love You?

05 *A Date With Elvis*
Blue Moon Of Kentucky; Milk Cow Blues; Baby Let's Play House; I Don't Care If The Sun Don't Shine; Tutti Frutti; I'm Gonna Sit Bight Down & Cry; Is It So Strange?; Paralysed; Down The Line; I Got A Woman; Heartbreak Hotel; Don't Be Cruel; Hound Dog; Harbour Lights.

06   *100,000,000 Elvis Fans Can't Be Wrong*
A Fool Such As I; I Need Your Love Tonight; Wear My Ring
Around Your Neck; Doncha Think It's Time; I Beg Of You; Big
Hunk O' Love; Don't; My Wish Came True; One Night; I Got
Stung; Treat Me Nice; Jailhouse Rock.

07   *706,Union Avenue*
Blue Ridge Mountain Blues; Hey Good Lookin'; Why Don't You
Love Me; Rave On; I'm Walkin'; Summertime Blues; Johnny B
Goode; Kansas City; Don't Be Cruel (slow version); Good Golly
Miss Molly.

08   *Elvis Is Back*
Fever; The Girl Next Door Went A' Walking; Soldier Boy; Make
Me Know It; I Will Be Home Again; Reconsider Baby; It Feels So
Right; Like A Baby; Brand New Cadillac; Girl Of My Best Friend:
The Thrill of Your Love; Such A Night; Dirty Dirty Feeling;
Rockin's Set The World On Fire. (NB: Reissued, 1977, without
'Brand New Cadillac' & 'Rockin's Set The World on Fire')

09   *Driving A Sportscar Down To A Beach In Hawaii* (soundtrack)
Sittin' In The Sand (Looking For My Hand); Do The Frug As You
Twist About With Your Hula Hoop Spinnin' Round Your Short-
tops; I Got Sand In My Eye; Fell For You (Stood On A Jellyfish);
Sheree, Ernie, You're Both Wonderful People; Blow Up My
Tyres; I Only Need One Armband; No Hand Signals; That
Darned Shark; What We Gonna Do About Ernie?; Hawaii, It's
A Really Nice Place.

010   *Little Girls Grow Up Fast And Grope Me* (soundtrack)
Take Your Little-girl Eyes Off-a My Thighs; Don't Get Bored,
Look At The Board; Let Me Lick The Chalkdust From Your Nose;
Little Girls Grow Up Fast And Grope Me; It's 1961, We're Havin'
Lotsa Fun; That Little Turtle's In The Soup; Why Am I Eating This
Pineapple (When There's Lotsa Girls Out There)?; Who Stole My
Chalk?; Algebra; It's Christmas In The Schoolroom; Dance On
Your Desks; Throw Down Your Satchels (Let's Do The Frug).

011   *Lotsa Lady Lifeguards, Acapulco* (soundtrack)
Why Rock When You Can Make (Bad Movies); Join Me, I'm
Falling Apart; On My Inflatable Dolphin; Diving Off A Very
High Cliff; C'mon Kids, Let's Do The Twist; Blue Sky, Blue Sea,
Blue Me; Tropical Fruits (In My Hat); Here Come Dirk And
Mary; What We Gonna Do About Dirk?; Drink Tequila, Do The
Crawl; All-American Lifeguard; Look Out They're Bringing In
An Octopus; We Just saved Dirk In Time; Look out Below, I Got
No Parachute.

012   *Sun Of Elvis*
That's Alright Mama; Blue Moon Of Kentucky; I Don't Care If
The Sun Don't Shine; Good Rockin' Tonight; Milk Cow Blues;

Blue Moon Of Kentucky (alternative blues version); Blue, Moon; You're A Heartbreaker; Baby, Let's Play House; Mystery Train; I Forgot To Remember To Forget; Just A Little Talk With Jesus; Old Shep; Just Because; Harbour Lights; Volare; I'll Never Let You Go; Bear Cat; Malted Milk Boogie.

013 *The Best Of Elvis's Movie Songs plus Three Other Great Hits*
We Just Saved Dirk In Time; Hawaii, It's A Really Nice Place; Why Am I Eating This Pineapple (When There's Lotsa Girls Out There)?; On My Inflatable Dolphin; That Little Turtle's In the Soup; Too Much; Lotsa Lady Lifeguards, Acapulco; Hard-Headed Woman; Sheree, Ernie, You're Both Wonderful People; Teddy Bear; Algebra; Such A Night (live version from circus tour).

014 *First Person Elvis*
I Love You Because; Baby I Don't Care; I Got Stung; I Wanna Be Free; I Don't Care If The Sun Don't Shine; I'm Walkin'; I Got Sand (In My Eye); Look Out Below, I Got No Parachute; I Want You, I Need You, I Love You; Join Me, I'm Falling Apart.

015 *Elvis Sings/Elvis On The Telephone*
(Of all the weird BRA releases this has to be the strangest. One of the first double albums ever released outside the classical field it features one record of used and unused songs from the beach movie sessions and one album of taped phone conversations of dubious and unknown origin between Elvis and various others. The second album was quickly removed from the racks and the set reissued in its present single-album form.)
Record One: I Beat My Bongos On The Beach; Pump Up My Armbands; Who Stole My Board Rubber; Typhoon!; Hot Summer Nights, Cold Steel Guitar; Where's The Little Girl Who Helps Me Put On My Arm?; That Darned Shark (alternative take with sound effects); Plastic Sandals, Wooden Heart; It's Now Or Later; Obscenie Bikini; Out In A Boat Havin' Fun; 35 Kids All Singing At Once.
Record Two: Elvis in conversation with: a) His Grocer (about his tomatoes); b) His Grocer (about the price of meat); c) His Local Garage (about removing chickenshit from his tyre treads); d) Colonel Parker (about the pungent odour of the Colonel's cigars); e) Frank Sinatra (a wrong number); f) Dean Martin (about his vocal inflections on 'That's Amore').

016 *Western Bop & Country Boogie*
Lonely Weekends; Walking After Midnight; How's The World Treating You?' Waiting For A Train' His Latest Flame; Boogie Woogie Country Man; Lend Me Your Comb; My Happiness; Move It On Over; I'm So Lonesome I Could Cry; I'll Remember You; Gotta Get You Near Me Blues; Opportunity.

212

017 *Elvis On Tour* (soundtrack)
Great Balls Of Fire; Lonely Weekends; His Latest Flame; I Need
Your Love Tonight; Tiger Man/Mystery Train; Such A Night;
Brand New Cadillac; Boogie Woogie Country Man; Brown Eyed
Handsome Man; Hound Dog/Bear Cat; My Wish Came True.

018 *Elvis Downhome*
Yellow Rose Of Texas; Old MacDonald; On Top Of Old Smoky;
Workin' On A Building; Swing Down Sweet Chariot; Goin' To
The River; Oh Susannah; Blue-Tail Fly; Jambalaya/A Mess Of
Beans; Sea Of Heartbreak; Just Out Of Reach (Of My Two Empty
Arms).

019 *Elvis Presents A Showcase Of His Golden Records, Vol 1*
Take Your Little-girl Eyes (Off-a My Thighs); It's Your Hand On
The Joystick; Heartbreak Hotel; Don't Get Bored, Look At The
Board; Too Much; Reconsider Baby; I'm Coming Home; Little
Sister; I Gotta Know; Blue Suede Shoes; Too Much Monkey
Business.

020 *Elvis's Golden Records Vol 2 and Some Hits from His Movies*
Sittin In The Sand (Looking For My Hand); A Life Without
Helicopters; Waiting For A Train; When My Blue Moon Turns
To Gold Again; Peace In The Valley; My Baby Left Me; All Shook
Up; That Darned Shark (take 26); 35 Kids All Singing At Once;
Typhoon!; What A Big Wind That Was.

021 *Some More Hits From The Movies and Elvis Recorded Talking In His
Sleep At Graceland*
That Darned Shark (take 14); I Found A Bone (That Was Once My
Left Thumb); Diving Off A Very High Cliff; Teddy Bear…/Elvis
Talks In His Sleep.

022 *Elvis Wishes You All A Merry Christmas*
See pages 116-117

023 *Elvis Rockin'*
Too Much; So Glad You're Mine; Mystery Train; Paralysed;
Wear My Ring; Interview with Elvis, 1956; Rockin's Set The
World On Fire; Long Tall Sally; Love Me; Don't Be Cruel (origi-
nal version); Be Bop A Lula.

024 *Elvis Rockin' Again*
Blue Suede Shoes; Great Balls Of Fire; All Shook Up; Brand New
Cadillac; That's Alright; Tomorrow Night; Your Cheating Heart;
Good Rocking Tonight; Money Honey; Shake, Rattle & Roll.

025 *The NBC Special*
That's All Right/Heartbreak Hotel; Love Me; Baby What You
Want Me To Do?; Dialogue/Lawdy Miss Clawdy; Blue Suede
Shoes; One Night/Baby What You Want Me To Do?; When My
Blue Moon Turns To Gold Again; Dialogue/Where Could I Go/
Up Above My Head/Saved; Nothingville; Big Boss Man/

Guitar Man/Little Egypt/Guitar Man; Memories; If I Can Dream.

026 *Memphis*
That's How Strong My Love Is; Hold On, I'm Coming; Down In The Valley; Ain't Got No Home; Rocky Road Blues; When A Man Loves A Woman; Hit The Road Jack; Flip, Flop & Fly; In The Ghetto; Memphis Beat; Memphis; Show Me.

027 *PPP TV Special* (soundtrack)
Little Drummer Boy/O Little Town Of Bethlehem (with Bing Crosby); Volare (with Dean Martin); Memories Are Made Of This/That's Amore/O Sole Mio/Hound Dog (with Dean Martin); Santa Claus Is Back In Town; We Three Kings (Elvis, Dean & Bing); Hold On I'm Coming; In The Ghetto; Blue River/Blue Christmas.

028 *The 2nd PPP Special. Elvis & His Fans*
Interviews with Fans; Blue Suede Shoes (live in studio); Don't Get Bored (alternate film take); Fever; The Twelve Elvis Impersonators Sing Elvis (twelve hits covered by various clones); More Interviews; Behind The Scenes Waiting To Go On Stage; The Engine Sounds Of Skyburger I (from the European Tour); It's Your Hand On The Joystick.

029 *The Elvis Presley Rock 'n' Roll Correspondence Course* (double album with accompanying booklet and a piece of Elvis's clothing). Illustrated Hints By Elvis On: Constructing That Quiff; Loosening Up Your Knees; Mauling A Microphone; Caressing A Microphone; The Perfect Cheeseburger; Talking To Fans; Basic Italian; When to Hiccup Whilst Singing; Choosing That Manager.

030 *The Worldwide Telecast* (soundtrack)
False Start; Such A Night; In The Ghetto; Suspicious Minds; Stranger In My Home Town; Long Black Limousine; Memphis; Little Sister; Guitar Man/US Male/All American Lifeguard; Sea Of Heartbreak; Bang Bang, My Baby Shot Me Down (abridged).

031 *Repent! – Elvis Sings For His Soul With Herbie Lee Delmont* featuring The God Squad
Oh God, I'm Sorry; Why Did The Lord Give Me Such A Good Aim?; The Fat Man Fell Heavy Upon My Heart; Shucks, I Didn't Mean It; I Smell The Gunsmoke; Repent; His Last Cigar (Burnt My Foot); Throw Up Your Hands & Cast Down Your Arms; Oh My, What An Awful Incident; Life Goes On, But Not For Him; How Great Thou Art.

032 *A Night With Elvis At The Opera*
(NB: This album comprises Elvis singing selections from his favourite operas, these selections often proving unidentifiable to listener and backing musicians alike; thus the track listings are

given as follows:
Selections from Great Moments In The Works Of: Rossini; Verdi;
Mario Lanza; Mozart; Dean Martin.
033   *Rock 'n' Roll* (with John Lennon)
Tutti Frutti*; Somethin' Else*; Blue Monday*; Another Saturday
Night*; Rockin' All Over The World**; Rock 'n' Roll Music;
Slippin' & Slidin'; Stand By Me; Tight As; Show Me**.
* – Elvis solo vocal; ** – Elvis & Lennon vocal; no stars – Lennon
solo vocal.
NB: This album credited to 'The Backbeats' until 1978.
034   *Elvis Is Gone*
The Day I Met Marie; Gentle On My Mind; My Babe; Fools Rush
In; Promised Land; It's Midnight And I Miss You; Got My Mojo
Working; Proud Mary; This Is The Story; Tomorrow Is A Long
Time; Inherit The Wind; American Trilogy.

B. SINGLES

01   That's Alright/Blue Moon Of Kentucky
02   Good Rockin' Tonight/I Don't Care If The Sun Don't Shine
03   You're A Heartbreaker/Milk Cow Blues Boogie
04   Baby Let's Play House/I'm Left, You're Right, She's Gone
05   Mystery Train/I Forgot To Remember To Forget
      (All the above were released in the USA only on the Sun label.
      After this point all of Elvis's Sun recordings were repackaged in
      various forms under the auspices of BRA Records.)
06   I Forgot To Remember To Forget/Mystery Train
07   Heartbreak Hotel/I Was The One
08   That's Alright/Blue Moon Of Kentucky
09   Good Rockin' Tonight/I Don't Care If The Sun Don't Shine
010   Milk Cow Blues Boogie/You're A Heartbreaker
011   Baby Let's Play House/I'm Left, You're Right, She's Gone
012   I Want You, I Need You, I Love You/My Baby Left Me
013   Hound Dog/Don't Be Cruel
014   Blue Suede Shoes/Tutti Frutti
015   I Got A Woman/I'm Counting On You
016   I'll Never Let You Go/I'm Gonna Sit Right Down & Cry
017   Lawdy Miss Clawdy/Shake, Rattle & Roll
018   Too Much/Playing For Keeps
019   Paralysed/Is It So Strange?
020   All Shook Up/Harbour Lights
021   Teddy Bear/That's When Your Heartaches Begin
022   Jailhouse Rock/Blueberry Hill
023   Baby I Don't Care/Santa Claus is Too Fat

024 Treat Me Nice/All Shook Up
025 Don't Leave Me Now/Love Me
026 Don't/I Beg Of You
027 Wear My Ring/Doncha Think It's Time?
028 Hard Headed Woman/King Creole
029 Lonely Blue Boy/Danny
030 One Night/I Got Stung
031 Fool Such As I/Need Your Love Tonight
032 Big Hunk Of Love/My Wish Came True
033 Why Don't You Love Me?/Don't Be Cruel (slow version)
034 Such A Night/I Gotta Know
035 Girl Of My Best Friend/A Mess Of Blues
036 His Latest Flame/Little Sister
037 I Feel So Bad/Girl Next Door Went A-Walkin'
038 Sheree, Ernie, You're Both Wonderful People/Blue Moon Of
     Kentucky (alt.)
039 Hawaii, It's A Really Nice Place/That Darned Shark
040 Little Girls Grow Up Fast & Grope Me/Algebra
041 On My Inflatable Dolphin/That Little Turtle's In The Soup
042 All American Lifeguard/35 Kids All Singing At Once
043 That's Alright Mama/We Just Saved Dirk In Time
044 I'm Walkin'/ Wanna Be Free
045 Typhoon/Pump Up My Armbands
046 Plastic Sandals, Wooden Heart/It's Now Or Later
047 Walking After Midnight/Lonely Weekends
048 Brown Eyed Handsome Man/Diving Off A Very High Cliff
049 Old Macdonald/Sea Of Heartbreak
050 Don't Get Bored, Look At The Board/Too Much Monkey
     Business
051 What A Big Wind That Was/A Life Without Helicopters
052 Too Much/Paralysed
053 Brand New Cadillac/That Darned Shark
054 When My Blue Moon Turns To Gold Again/Memories
055 If I Can Dream/Blue Christmas
056 Rocky Road Blues/I'm Coming Home
057 Fever/When A Man Loves A Woman
058 When A Man Loves A Woman/It's Your Hand On The Joystick
059 In The Ghetto/Long Black Limousine
060 Suspicious Minds/Memphis
061 Repent/Life Goes On, But Not For Him
062 Why Did The Lord Give Me Such A Good Aim?/Shucks, I Didn't
     Mean It
063 Waiting For A Train/Just A Little Talk With Jesus
064 His Latest Flame/Blue Moon
065 Tomorrow Is A Long Time/Here Come Dirk And Mary

066 Show Me/Rockin' All Over The World (with John Lennon)
067 Shoppin' Around/Frankfurt Special
068 How Great Thou Art/Down In The Valley
069 Hound Dog/Bear Cat
070 Excerpt from 'William Tell'/Excerpt from 'The Magic Flute'
071 Burning Love/She Thinks I Still Care
072 Just Can't Help Believing/My Babe
073 Got My Mojo Working/The Day I Met Marie
074 Merry Christmas Baby/I'm Movin' On
075 The Elvis Farewell Single: I'm Leavin'/Separate Ways. (The Elvis/Beatles single, for copyright reasons, was attributed to 'The Beatles?' in an unnecessarily dramatic move by EMI Capitol, The Beatles' label. The later re-issue of 'I'm Gone/For A Laugh' was attributed to 'The Beatles Featuring Elvis Presley', this being obvious from the start.)

C. EXTENDED PLAYS

01 *Elvis Presley*: Blue Suede Shoes; Tutti Frutti/Just Because; I Got A Woman
02 *Hard Headed Elvis*: Hard Headed Woman; King Creole/That's Alright; Paralysed
03 *Old Shep*: Old Shep; So Glad You're Mine/Ready Teddy; Any Place Is Paradise
04 *Peace In The Valley*: Peace In The Valley; It Is No Secret/I Believe; Take My Hand Precious Lord
05 *Jailhouse Rock*: Jailhouse Rock; Young & Beautiful; I Wanna Be Free/Don't Leave Me Now; Baby I Don't Care
06 *Elvis At Christmas*: White Christmas; Blue Christmas/Santa Claus Is Too Fat; Message To Fans
07 *A Fool Such As Elvis*: A Fool Such As I; Too Much/All Shook Up; One Night
08 *Hey… Elvis*: Hey Good Lookin'; Kansas City/I'm Walkin'; Rave On
09 *Elvis In Hawaii*: Hawaii, It's A Really Nice Place; Fever/Fell For You; Like A Baby
010 *Elvis In Acapulco*: Tropical Fruits (In My Hat); Take Your Little-girl Eyes (Off-a My Thighs)/Dance On Your Desks; *Lotsa Lady Lifeguards, Acapulco*
011 *Elvis Sings Four Old Christmas Songs Just In Time For The Festive Season*: Santa Claus Is Back in Town; Santa Claus Is Coming To Town/Here Comes Santa Claus; Santa Claus Is Too Fat
012 Accident-Prone Elvis: Sitting In The Sand (Looking For My Hand); I Got Sand (In My Eye)/I Found A Bone (That Was Once My Left Thumb); Look Out Below, I Got No Parachute

013 *Colonel Parker Greets Elvis Fans & Introduces Songs By His Boy*: The Colonel Says 'Howdy'; Pump Up My Armbands / Hard Headed Woman; Join Me, I'm Falling Apart; The Colonel's Closing Remarks. (DJ issue only)

ELVIS – the Filmography

1. *Jailhouse Rock* (1957)
(Gargantuan Pictures)
Director: Richard Thorpe
Starring: Elvis Presley; Judy Tyler; Jennifer Holden; Mickey Shaughnessy
Elvis is Vince Everett, mean, moody truck-driver, imprisoned for killing a man in a bar brawl. Whilst in prison he appears on a TV special broadcast from the prison and becomes famous overnight but doesn't realise this as his cellmate Hunk (Shaughnessy) suppresses the fan mail that arrives after Everett's TV appearance whilst he cooks up a deal to cash in on the new felonious singer's fame. Everett is released, meets promoter Judy Tyler and, after a host of clichéd soap-opera situations have been played out, everybody lives happily ever after, with Vince successful commercially and romantically. In this film Elvis, despite the frequent tacky moments, showed a real aptitude for playing the concrete-skinned yet soft-hearted rebel. The title song sequence choreographed by Elvis himself ranks with 'Singin' in the Rain' and 'Puttin' On The Ritz' as a seminal moment in the history of cinematic terpsichore.

2. *Driving A Sportscar Down To A Beach In Hawaii* (1960)
(Gargantuan Pictures)
Director: Trevor Pillock
Starring: Elvis Presley; Nancy Sinatra; Bill Bixby
After the undoubted promise shown by Elvis in his first movie feature, *Driving A Sportscar...* was an unqualified disappointment for Presley fans the world over, more so because it came hot on the heels of what many consider to be the star's best recorded work, *Elvis Is Back*. A fuller synopsis of the 'plot' can be found at the beginning of Chapter 12, but basically, it's the song titles that give the film away as a serious work. 'I Got Sand In My Eye' and 'That Darned Shark' were unsatisfactory follow-ups to the likes of 'Such A Night' and 'Paralysed', a fact that even the most diehard Elvis fan could not dispute (though there were, of course, those who tried).

3. *Little Girls Grow Up Fast and Grope Me* (1960)
(Gargantuan Pictures)

Director: Trevor Pillock/Ernie Brimful
Starring: Elvis Presley; Carole Lavell; Dirk McGuire
The seemingly shared direction occurs because this film utilises a lot of unused footage from the first beach movie shot by Pillock. In normal circumstances this might lead to some crudity in the finished product, but in a film this bad continuity of style and action was of negligible consideration anyway. Here Elvis is a schoolteacher in Hawaii (or somewhere similar – it's hard to be precise), spending his time avoiding the jailbait advances of his unreasonably and unrealistically luscious convent schoolgirls (a convent on Hawaii!?!). Meanwhile, of course, he's working nights in a club trying to regain his voice and confidence before he returns to his real profession as a singing superstar who's had bad luck of some ill-defined sort. Especially unconvincing are the classroom scenes where Elvis, seemingly exasperated by the demands of the 2x table, exhorts his young followers to 'Throw Down Your Satchels (Let's Do The Frug)'. A mess.

4. *Lotsa Lady Lifeguards, Acapulco* (1961)
(Gargantuan Pictures)
Director: Len Smith
Starring: Elvis Presley; Lynette Calder; Bill Phillips; Ron T Ellis
The third successive film from Gargantuan. Once again the ole Colonel raked in megabucks at the artistic expense of his protégé. This time Elvis is a non-swimming lifeguard in Acapulco who keeps having to enlist the aid of available female colleagues to help him through emergencies. It turns out that not only can Elvis swim, but he's an OLYMPIC CHAMPION who – you guessed it has lost his nerve after a bad accident. The real bad accident, of course, was that this film was ever made. Its only saving grace is in its co-stars, none of whom worked again after being seen in this. A real pity…

5. *Elvis On Tour* (1964)
(Broken Dream Films.)
Director: DA Pennebaker
The one and only star of this film is Elvis Presley whose excitement and vitality as he approaches his first tour in over three years is superbly conveyed in this penetrating study of the Artist At Work and Play.

Four years later, after another lull, Elvis's *NBC TV Special* was to again prove that he was still the King. It is by these two films and the early TV footage that we can glimpse the genesis of a cultural force unparalleled before or since. As John Lennon once said, 'The Beatles always wanted to be bigger than Elvis and one day we were, but we never got to be better than he was in *Elvis On Tour*.'
Elvis On Tour was Elvis's final film for cinema release. Three TV

Specials, one superb, the others exploitation quickies in the vein of the beach movies (though decidedly superior in that they offered at least two or three great moments each of Elvis in action) and the infamous 'Death Of Parker' telecast followed.

There is no doubt that Elvis had much to offer the film medium, and vice-versa, but he was never given the chance. We should at least be grateful that he managed to step out of the awful beach movie syndrome before it sucked him up and spat him out completely. As it is we have a small but irreplaceable legacy of two or three superb performances that conclusively prove that Elvis Presley was, indeed, the King of Rock 'n' Roll.

Elvis – the Bibliography

Elvis And The Hamlet Complex, Dixie Locke (The Arden Presley, 1963).
Ten Minutes With Elvis On A Fifty Minute Show, Steve Allen (Krypton Books, 1964).
My Life Before I Met Elvis Once, Charles Minns (Dulldouanier Books, 1976).
Elvis And The B Movie – His Part In Its Downfall, Mitchell de Graft (Cashcow Ltd, 1967).
Elvis Back When He Was Just Plain Elvis Presley, Veronica Placid (Irregular Titles, 1968).
The Anita Ekberg Bumper Brassiere Book, Anita Ekberg (with Lucinda Hanfle) (Bazooka Publications, 1969).
What Elvis Likes To Eat, Dennis Chang Jr (with Johnny Carson) (Gourmet Books, 1973).
The Chickenshit Rotary Pump Engine, Johnston 'Porky' Prime (Pelican, 1973)
Elvis – I Sharpened His Pencils, Merle Barnett (Terrible Incoherent Books, 1975).
Elvis – My Part In His Exploitation, Ron Schnozzle (Schlep, Schmuck & Schlemiel, 1976).
My Headaches With The Rock 'n' Roll Greats – The True Story Of A Promoter, Barney Lovell (Tireless Publications, 1976).
Elvis & Black American Consciousness, Christo Bigglesworth (Scathing Books, 1977)
Good Clean Fun With Elvis And The Memphis Mafia, Bill Orifice (Faber & Faber, 1977).
Karate Time With Elvis, Dennis Chang Jr (with Johnny Carson) (Bimbo Books, 1978).
Feminism In The South, Ernie P Skyhook (Sacred Cow, 1978).
My Son, Elvis, The Great Entertainer and Humanitarian, But, Above All, Golden Goose, Vernon Presley (with Ricardo Elastoplast) (Viking, 1978).
Grated Not Melted – Elvis, Me And The Cheeseburger, Wilma Mae Armpit (Dislexyc Press, 1979).
Some Bullshit About Elvis, Curtis Limp (Verging Books, 1979).
The Killer Never Stops Rockin', You Mothers, Jerry Lee Lewis (Harvard University Press, 1979).

Elvis's Secret And His Enormous Dangler, Jennie Lee Marshall (Verging Books, 1980).

Elvis – The Way It Might Have Been or Let's Piss On A Hillbilly, Filbert Grossman, (Scurrilous Press, 1981).

Elvis, Me, Three Orange-Utangs & Seven Different Adhesives, Fay Vest (Restless Urges, 1981).

The Official Elvis Biography (Parker Pulps, 1981).

Elvis's Pelvis (And What It Got Up To), Fritz Klutz (Invective Dan Kamikaze Press, 1982).

Pamphlet

'Rock's Demeaning Role: Why This Contagion Must Be Expunged', Dolores Lillycrap (Alfred E Goebbels & Son Ltd, 1957).

Articles

Bruce Forsyth in a *Rolling Stone* interview, 1971.

'The Night The Stars Went Down In Vegas', Chester J Banjax, *Time Magazine*, 1973.

Joe Strummer Interview, *New Musical Express*, 6 July, 1980.

Roger Ringo talks to Richard Straight – 'I Was The One Who Taught Colonel Tom Parker All He Knows About Being A Conman, *Playboy*, 1976.

Outstanding Paperback Originals from The Do-Not Press:

It's Not A Runner Bean
by Mark Steel
"I've never liked Mark Steel and I thoroughly resent the
high quality of this book."
    – Jack Dee
The life of a Slightly Successful Comedian can include a night spent on
bare floorboards next to a pyromaniac squatter in Newcastle, followed by
a day in Chichester with someone so aristocratic, they speak without ever
moving their lips.
From his standpoint behind the microphone, Mark Steel is in the perfect
position to view all human existence. Which is why this book – like his act,
broadcasts and series' – is opinionated, passionate, and extremely funny.
It even gets around to explaining the line (screamed at him by an eighties
yuppy): "It's not a runner bean…" – which is another story.
"Hugely funny…" – *Time Out*
'A terrific book. I have never read any other book about comedy written
by someone with a sense of humour.'
    – Jeremy Hardy, *Socialist Review*
ISBN 1 899344 12 8– £5.99

The Users
by Brian Case
The welcome return of Brian Case's brilliantly original '60s cult classic.
"A remarkable debut" –Anthony Burgess
"Why Case's spiky first novel from 1968 should have languished for
nearly thirty years without a reprint must be one of the enigmas of modern publishing. Mercilessly funny and swaggeringly self-conscious, it
could almost be a template for an early Martin Amis."
    – *Sunday Times*
ISBN 1 899344 05 5– £5.99

Shrouded by Carol Anne Davis BLOODLINES
Douglas likes women — quiet women; the kind he deals with at the mor-
tuary where he works.
Douglas meets Marjorie, unemployed, gaining weight and losing confidence. She talks and laughs a lot to cover up her shyness, but what
Douglas really needs is a lover who'll stay still — deadly still.
Driven by lust and fear, Douglas finds a way to make girls remain excit-
ingly silent and inert. But then he is forced to blank out the details of their
unplanned deaths.
Perhaps only Marjorie can fulfil his growing sexual hunger. If he could
just get her into a state of limbo. Douglas studies his textbooks to find a
way…
Shrouded is a powerful and accomplished début, tautly-plotted, dangerously erotic and vibrating with tension and suspense. It deserves to
propel Carol Anne Davis to the forefront of young British writers.
ISBN 1 899344 17 9— £7

The Do-Not Press
Fiercely Independent Publishing

Keep in touch with what's happening at the cutting edge of independent British publishing.

Join The Do-Not Press Information Service and receive advance information of all our new titles, as well as news of events and launches in your area, and the occasional free gift and special offer.

Simply send your name and address to:
The Do-Not Press (Dept. Elvo)
PO Box 4215
London
SE23 2QD

There is no obligation to purchase and no salesman will call.